A HUSBAND'S PREROGATIVE

Moonlight poured through the open window and spilled onto the bed. Allegra lay with her eyes closed when she heard the door latch click. She gasped, her eyes flying open as she pulled herself to a sitting position.

"Nigel!" she exclaimed as he stepped through the door. "Whatever—where—"

"Our rooms adjoin. Did you not know?" he asked smoothly. He wore a velvet-trimmed dressing gown. It gaped open at the top, affording her a glimpse of his bare chest as he came toward her.

She swallowed hard. "No, I—that is—I hadn't thought on't."

"No?" He quirked an eyebrow "You surprise me, Allegra." His eyes swept over her with an expression she could not fathom. "What—what do you want, Nigel?" she asked, despising the hesitancy in her voice.

He did not smile as he sauntered to the bed. He sat down next to her then he put his finger to her mouth and slowly traced the outline of her lips. "I should think that would be very obvious, Allegra," he said silkily. Then he bent his head to cover his mouth with hers.

THE ROMANCE OF LORDS AND LADIES
IN JANIS LADEN'S REGENCIES

BEWITCHING MINX   (2532, $3.95)

From her first encounter with the Marquis of Pender-leigh when he had mistaken her for a common trollop, Penelope had been incensed with the darkly handsome lord. Miss Penelope Larchmont was undoubtedly the most outspoken young lady Penderleigh had ever known, and the most tempting.

A NOBLE MISTRESS   (2169, $3.95)

Moriah Landon had always been a singularly practical young lady. So when her father lost the family estate over a game of picquet, she paid the winner, the notorious Vis-count Roane, a visit. And when he suggested the means of payment—that she become Roane's mistress—she agreed without a blink of her eyes.

SAPPHIRE TEMPTATION   (3054, $3.95)

Lady Serena was commonly held to be an unusual young girl—outspoken when she should have been reticent, lively when she should have been demure. But there was one tra-dition she had not been allowed to break: a Wexley must marry a Gower. Richard Gower intended to teach his wife her duties—in every way.

SCOTTISH ROSE   (2750, $3.95)

The Duke of Milburne returned to Milburne Hall trust-ing that the new governess, Miss Rose Beacham, had in-stilled the fear of God into his harum-scarum brood of siblings. But she romped with the children, refused to be cowed by his stern admonitions, and was so pretty that he had the devil of a time keeping his hands off her.

Moonlight Veil

Janis Laden

ZEBRA BOOKS
KENSINGTON PUBLISHING CORP.

ZEBRA BOOKS

are published by

Kensington Publishing Corp.
475 Park Avenue South
New York, NY 10016

First printing: August, 1991

Printed in the United States of America

"Her valiant courage and undaunted spirit,
More than in women commonly . . ."

1 Henry VI
William Shakespeare

'Twas beneath a veil of moonlight
That I saw her that first night,
And I knew I'd got to have her,
Though for all I'd not the right.

But when reason came with daybreak,
Still my lust I'd yet to slake;
Oh, I knew I'd got to have her
Though it be a great mistake.

Once again the veil of moonlight
Hid all others from my sight;
Then she beckoned me—"Come hither!"
Whilst my sanity took flight.

But 'twas when I took my pleasure
That I found therein a treasure,
For the joy in having had her
Was e'er more than I could measure.

Thus, 'twas 'neath the veil of moonlight
That we said our vows last night,
And I know I'll always have her—
Yea, for now I have the right.

                                        Sir Isaac Mariner

Chapter One

"I'll met by moonlight, proud Titania."

A Midsummer Night's Dream
William Shakespeare

Nigel Hayves, Earl of Debenham, tugged on the reins and drew his stallion to a halt. The full moon lit the landscape as his eyes followed the gently rolling hills and settled on the manor house, just over the next rise. Caulfield Manor. Its lights were ablaze, despite the lateness of the hour, for he was expected. He'd sent word to his host that, the hour being far advanced, he'd stop the night at the Crow and Feather and make his appearance in the morning.

But Lord Caulfield would have none of it. The Crow and Feather, he'd replied by messenger, was naught but a flea-bitten alehouse. Of course the Caulfields would wait upon the earl's arrival. There would be a game of cards and a cold collation awaiting his lordship's pleasure. Nigel sighed. His pleasure at the moment was most definitely *not* a game of cards and a cold collation. Not at Caulfield Manor, at all events. But there was no help for it.

His stallion whinnied and perked up his ears but Nigel heard nothing to mar the silence of the sultry August night. He soothed Mercutio with promises of a meal and a bath in

7

the Caulfield stables and wished he could be as sanguine about his own fate.

He reminded himself that he was doing what must be done, fulfilling the promise he'd made to his late father and to himself. And so he urged his horse once more down the path that led to Caulfield Manor. And Margaret Caulfield. Her miniature rested even now in his coat pocket. She was beautiful and blond. She was his betrothed wife. And she was a woman he'd never met.

Mercutio whinnied again and kept trying to veer to the left. The earl reined in and this time he heard it. The lapping of a stream and an occasional splash. South Devon was full of streams and tributaries, but every one he'd passed today had been completely still in the unrelenting heat. Again a splash, and then suddenly he heard the unmistakable sound of a giggle. A very feminine giggle. Intrigued, he allowed Mercutio's unerring ears to lead him to the stream.

It was a pond, really, set behind a screen of trees and sunk deeply into the meadow. He'd never have found it without his horse. He saw her hand first, as it swept up in an arc, bringing a graceful arm with it until it slid once more into the water. The droplets that fell in its wake glistened like diamonds in the moonlight. Nigel sat upon his now silent stallion, some ten feet from the water's edge, and watched the sleek movements of this nocturnal mermaid as she swam the length and breadth of the pond. She flipped over onto her back, and began to float, affording him a clear view of her profile as the water pillowed her head. Her nose and chin looked delicate and pointed and the tips of her full breasts, encased in some flimsy fabric, peaked up and out of the water. An errant servant girl, no doubt, who'd slipped away from the stifling kitchens of the manor house. He smiled into the night at the thought of distracting her a bit.

Nigel caught himself up short and shook his head rue-

8

fully. There would be no dalliance for Rake Debenham this night, nor for some weeks to come. Not whilst he visited his betrothed and stayed to hear the banns read! Sometime after the wedding, when he'd installed his bride at Deben Court, his seat in Suffolk, he might return to the voluptuous charms of the lovely, widowed Barbara Lacey, or take a new mistress in Town. But for now he must be a pattern card of rectitude.

But a man could hardly be faulted for feasting his eyes when the banquet was laid out so temptingly before him, now could he? And just as he was debating whether or not to move on before the mermaid discovered his presence, she submerged herself and swam to shore.

Nigel stood immobile as first her head, framed by a short, impudent crop of curling dark hair, and then her upper torso rose from the water. A wet chemise clung to her shapely form, outlining her breasts, her small waist, and the flare of her hips. But she was no mermaid, her legs clearly outlined as she stepped from the pond.

Nigel felt his mouth go dry as she raised her arms to smooth the moisture from her eyes and then ran her fingers through her hair. Her breasts rose with the movement, straining against the wet fabric. He took a deep breath and let his eyes look their fill.

She moved to her right and only then did he notice the pile of clothing at the water's edge. She bent to retrieve her dress and Mercutio chose that moment to sneeze. The girl jerked upright, clutching the dress to her breast.

"Whatever—oh! Good Heavens! I did not—why, no one *ever* comes here!"

"No?" Nigel asked, eyes gleaming. "Now that, I must say, is a great pity!"

"Sir!" she exclaimed in a huff. "You forget your—oh, you are quizzing me!" She paused, her eyes sparkling, yet still she clutched the dress to her chest. "But, sir, if you were any kind of gentleman you would . . . would turn about so I might dress."

He arched his brow, bemused. No demure miss, she. Embarrassed, perhaps, at being caught out, but certainly not about to have the vapors. And the voice was more cultured than he'd expected. His interest piqued, he vaulted from his mount. "At your service, my dear," he drawled, and bowed with an exaggerated sweep of his arm before slowly turning his back.

Oh dear, Allegra thought as she slithered into her dress. It was not at all the thing for him to be here. Or for *you* to be here! a little voice at the back of her head reminded her. Oh, stuff and nonsense! she told the voice. She'd been coming here for years; this was her home, after all.

But he's seen you with nary—the voice began, but she silenced it. 'Tis water over the dam, she told the voice. There was naught she could do about it now, except dress as quickly as possible. She tugged the dress over her wet chemise with no small difficulty. It was not at all pleasant to be obliged to do so without having a chance to dry off a bit in the warm night air. But she did not suppose the man would have left had she asked him to. He was obviously not a gentleman, for all his manner of speech and dress would have proclaimed him so.

The fact that his cravat was loose, his coat thrown over the back of his mount and his shirtsleeves rolled up she attributed to the heat, not a lack of breeding. Even in the moonlight she could see that his shirt was of the finest lawn, and that the shirt as well as his riding breeches fit him perfectly. Too well, she thought, recalling his muscular thighs and the breadth of his shoulders. He was a very large man, she observed now as she stared at his back, and struggled with the buttons at her own back. She was, she realized, quite alone and isolated with him. Yet she did not fear him. Perhaps that was because she had never in all her eighteen years had cause to fear any man, not even her father at his most blustery. Or perhaps it was because of that certain

10

glint in his eyes that bespoke a keen sense of humor.

Well, she was not about to be the object of his amusement, she vowed indignantly, sitting down to pull on her stockings and shoes. And just who *was* he? He must have lost his way, for he was far from the main road. Certainly he was not bound for Caulfield; the only one expected this night was the Earl of Debenham, and he would undoubtedly arrive with an entourage of servants and carriages. For his stay was, unfortunately, to be a long one . . .

And this trespasser was no poacher. His clothes were too expensive and his manner too forthcoming. Besides, it was rather late at night for poaching.

Well, some traveler then, she thought, and rather rag-mannered, however well-born he might be. Any proper young lady would give him a set down on the evils of trespassing, turn her back and walk away. No, she amended, a proper young lady would have fallen into a fit of hysterics at first sight of the man, have grabbed her clothes and high-tailed it for the nearest bush. But no, she amended anew with brutal honesty, a proper young lady would never have been here at first stop, swimming in such a shocking state of undress. Allegra sighed, for the truth of it was that she was *not* a proper young lady, and probably never would be. And she supposed that this was another of what Papa would refer to as her "scrapes."

But it wasn't really a scrape if no one knew of it, was it? she asked herself. Besides, the damage, in a manner of speaking, was already done. It wouldn't be *so* terrible if she stayed a moment to find out who he was, would it? Who could blame her for not wanting to go home straight away, what with the tension and frayed nerves that prevailed at the house just now. And she was so very curious. One of your besetting sins, that irksome little voice reminded her, but she chose to ignore it.

Her shoes fastened, she stood up and reached back to do up the remaining few buttons of her dress. It was then that the trespasser, without awaiting an invitation, turned round. His eyes, crinkling in amusement, met hers.

"Shall I help you?" he asked, taking several steps forward.

Insufferable man! Allegra thought, and was furious with herself for blushing. Could he see that telltale redness in the moonlight? "No, thank you," she snapped.

Nigel grinned, and watched her finish her task and slide her hands into her pockets. Her eyes swept his length and he actually found himself a bit discomfited by her scrutiny. He returned it with a bold gaze of his own. She was clad in a simple but pretty evening dress of some pale-colored silk. The dress was a little too fine and pretty for a servant girl. Perhaps it was a cast off from a lady of the house. Her throat and arms were bare and her skin gleamed white in the moonlight.

The water from her chemise had already begun to seep through the dress, darkening it in several suggestive places. "You'll take a chill in your damp clothes," he said mockingly.

"In this heat? I shouldn't think so," she said ingenuously.

He forced his eyes to her face, and moving closer, took a good look at her for the first time. Her dark hair was cropped short, in a style that he supposed was all the crack in London, more was the pity, but whatever was it doing on a serving girl in this Devon backwater? He did have to admit that the dark curls framed her face rather engagingly, however. And her face, while not precisely beautiful, had a certain gaminlike quality that was most attractive. Her cheekbones were high, her eyes slanted and of a color as dark as her hair. Her little pointed nose and determined chin bespoke trouble, though, if he did not mistake the matter, as did the fire in those dark eyes. It was just as well he was not able to dally just now. He'd had all he'd needed of fiery females in his life a long time ago.

He let his eyes linger for one moment on her lips. The bottom was full and sensual, and the top had no dip to it, but seemed to go straight across. Never had he kissed such a lip and he could not help wondering . . .

Allegra looked closely at the man's face. She supposed it would be handsome except for that faintly mocking air. He had a very nice mouth, actually, his lips full and well formed. His cheekbones were broad, his nose strong and chiseled. She could not tell the color of his eyes, but they looked light, perhaps green or blue. His hair was dark, perhaps black, a bit long at the nape. He had impossibly long, dark lashes and very full brows that arched into two inverted "V's" when he grinned. They gave him a devilish look that she imagined might have frightened or seduced any number of ladies, depending upon their dispositions. Allegra, however, was made of sterner stuff.

"Finished your chores, have you?" His deep voice interrupted her scrutiny.

"Chores? At this hour? I should hope so. That is, I did as much today as was possible, what with the house at sixes and sevens because of the earl's visit."

The earl did not miss the downward turn of her mouth as she said this last. "You do not seem particularly eager for this visit," he said dryly.

"Oh, it is not *I* so much as poor Meg. And who can blame her, betrothed to the earl when she has not even met—" Her eyes widened as if she'd just realized she'd said too much.

"Does she not *want* to wed the earl?" He could not keep the note of incredulity from his voice. He was, after all, considered quite a catch by those who concerned themselves with such matters.

"No, for you see she—but, that has nothing to say to the matter. You were asking me about chores. Let me see. worked on the linen inventory, and I helped with the menus, although I own they are not my forte. And I finished with the lessons some hours ago. So I daresay my time is my own now."

"Is it now?" the earl said, advancing to her. She intrigued

13

him more and more. She was not acting at all as he expected. She had not shrieked and run because he'd caught her out with nary a stitch on, but neither did she simper and flutter her eyelashes, nor touch him in that way a wench has of indicating her willingness. And she did not sound anything like—

"Sir, what—what are *you* doing here? You *are* trespassing you know." She took two steps back and he grinned. Trespassing was he? Not nearly as much as he'd like to.

He moved to her and placed his hands on her slender shoulders, then pulled her closer and slid his hands up and down her arms. He felt a warmth that had naught to do with the sultry night. "I hardly think that need concern you, my dear," he said softly.

He ran his index finger over her lips. Amazing. There *was* no indentation in the upper lip. He leaned forward. "Now, tell me about those lessons you take. Perhaps there are some lessons that I could give you as well."

His mouth was only inches from hers. He was going to kiss her and Allegra knew she mustn't allow it. But his hands—such large hands, with strong, well-tapered fingers—held her firmly and enveloped her in a warmth she'd never felt before. She supposed she was not a proper young lady at all, for she was most curious as to what his kiss would feel like. She instinctively knew it would be nothing like that insipid kiss her piano teacher had given her just before Papa turned him off.

Thoughts of Papa made her draw back just a little and recall the trespasser's words. "I—ah—do not take lessons, sir. I give them."

He lifted his head. "You *give* them! Lessons in what?"

"Why, reading, of course."

"Reading lessons! To whom?"

"To the servants, of course."

"To the—" Suddenly Nigel dropped his hands and eyed her suspiciously and with a growing sense of unease. "Just

14

who *are* you, ma'am?" he demanded.

Something in his tone sent alarm bells ringing in Allegra's head. She stepped back from him: "I am Allegra Caulfield," she said with dignity. "Daughter of the Baron Caulfield."

At that the trespasser cursed softly but eloquently, and Allegra's eyes narrowed. "Who—who are you?"

"I am Nigel Hayves, Earl of Debenham," he snapped.

"But you can't be!" she exclaimed.

"Oh? May I ask why not?" he queried, torn between pique and amusement.

"Well, because you are alone, of course, along a back road. I expected the earl to come with several carriages, a groom, valet, and—"

"They are stopping the night at the Crow and Feather. One of the horses threw a shoe, and the hour being so advanced, I thought it more expedient. Do not concern yourself, ma'am. I shan't disgrace myself by trying to tie my own cravats. And *what,* pray tell, is a lady of the house doing out here in the middle of the night, barely clothed, frolicking like—"

"I was *not* frolicking. And pray tell me what a man, about to meet his betrothed, is doing dallying with—"

"Dallying? That was hardly dallying, my dear," he said suavely.

"Call it what you may, my dear sir, but you were about to *kiss* me, and well you know it!"

"Was I? Ah, but you would have let me, and well *you* know it!" he countered, beginning to enjoy himself.

"I did *not* want you to kiss me!"

"No?" he retorted, eyes gleaming. "Well, then, you did a damn good imitation of wanting just that! Your eyes wide, your lips parted just so. Where the devil did you learn such a—"

"I haven't the foggiest notion what you're talking about, my lord. I was merely curious."

15

"Curious?"

"Yes. About whether your—er—kiss would be anything like Mr. Peterson's."

"Mr. Peterson?"

She nodded. "He was my piano teacher, until Papa turned him off."

"After he kissed you, I presume," the earl muttered.

Allegra sighed. "Yes. Papa caught us, you see."

"Mr. Peterson has my sympathy," he said dryly.

"Yes, well, it was hardly a compromising kiss, I shouldn't think. It was most insipid, and brief, and his hands remained fixed on the piano bench and—"

"You, young lady, are a shocking flirt!"

"No, I'm not! I'm merely curious, and I—well—I do like men, you see. They are such fascinating creatures, so different from my sex."

"Oh, Lord, you need a keeper!" the earl groaned, running his fingers through his dark hair. "Just how old are you?"

"I am eighteen, my lord, not that it is at all your concern. And I take leave to tell you that you will make a wretched husband for my poor sister!"

"I beg your pardon," he said icily.

"Being high in the instep does not change the fact that you cannot contrive to keep your hands off the first woman you see."

"I hardly had them on—"

"No?" she asked incredulously.

He felt himself flush. "Ma'am, it must be obvious to you that I had no idea who you were. And you, my dear young lady, were inviting all manner of improper advances."

"I am not your dear young lady, and my identity does not alter the fact that you were quite willing to dally here in the grass while poor Meg is awaiting you at—"

"Ah yes, about Meg. I want to talk about 'poor Meg.' Just why is it always 'poor' Meg, and why does she not wish to wed me?"

Allegra bit her lip in consternation. She'd been hoping he'd forgotten that dreadful slip she'd made a few minutes ago. Whatever had possessed her to speak so freely to a stranger? She drew herself up, prepared to brazen it out. "I own I do not know *what* you are talking about, my lord."

"Cut line, Allegra Caulfield," the earl said inelegantly, and grabbed her arm. "Now, tell me what the devil is going on here."

Allegra was very well aware that his hand held her in a firm grip, but it was not at all painful. Quite the opposite, in fact. And she was very aware that his forearm, uncovered by his shirt, was hard and well muscled, its dark hairs curling in a most intriguing way. Never mind that, she admonished herself. He was an odious man and somehow she had got to see an end to this sham of a betrothal. She'd known that before she'd met him, but now she was even more determined. Heaven knew Meg would not do aught, though it was her future that hung in the balance. And why *not* tell him, Allegra thought. Papa would flay her alive did he find out, and Meg would be horrified, but if they would not put a stop to this, then perhaps the earl would.

But she simply could not converse with him while he held her arm thus. His fingers had gentled and her skin tingled. She looked pointedly down at where those strong fingers gripped her slender arm and then she met his gaze. His eyes glittered dangerously and he dropped her arm as if scalded.

"If I tell you, my lord, you must promise me not to let on that I have done so. I am in the suds often enough as it is," she said candidly.

"That I can well imagine," Nigel murmured. "You have my word."

"Very well." Allegra wondered why she trusted him, but somehow, in the matter of his word, she did. She was not quite certain how to say this, and so she began, "In the very

17

short time of our acquaintance, my lord, I have come to the conclusion that you and Meg simply will not suit." He looked thunderous and she hurried on. "But truth to tell, I have known it ever since Papa first told us about the betrothal."

He crossed his arms over his chest but said nothing and so, having started, Allegra plunged ahead. "It is not only because you are an acknowledged rakehell—"

"What??" Nigel exploded, torn between mirth and fury.

"Oh, do not trouble to deny it, my lord. I've had ample evidence of that tonight and—"

"Where—ah"—Nigel struggled to compose himself, for mirth was winning out—"wherever did you hear such a thing? And do not use words whose meaning you cannot possibly comprehend."

She lifted a brow in disdain. "I may be young, my lord, but I am hardly a fool. And I heard it in the stables. That is, I overheard it and—"

"Eavesdropping, were you?"

"Certainly not!" she exclaimed indignantly. "I was playing cards with Clem in the loft when—"

"Playing cards? In the stables? Oh, Lord. I need to sit down," he groaned. "Join me, won't you, ma'am?" He swept his hand toward the grass and after a moment she sank down onto the ground. He followed, keeping a good two feet between them. "Now, then," he went on, "who is Clem?"

"One of the stable boys, you must know. Actually, we were teaching little Marcus the game of piquet. He has a very quick mind and—"

"Marcus?"

"Oh, he's the climbing boy I rescued from—"

"Whoa! Halt! Never mind! I find I do not want to know! Just—just tell me about Meg. Why have you been so certain we should not suit?"

Allegra sighed. There really was no wrapping it up in clean linen. "Because Meg is in love with John, and has been for years."

"And just who is John?" the earl asked ominously.

Allegra met his gaze. "John is the vicar."

"The vicar?"

"Yes. It's all rather a dreadful coil, for of course the vicar cannot very well fly off to Gretna Green, which is what I advised them to do, but—"

"Gretna Green? Are you mad?"

"Yes, well, I realize it will not answer, but you see Papa will not hear of Meg crying off, for he considers it a point of honor, especially as your father and he were such fast friends at school. Besides, the settlement is quite generous and Caulfield is much in need of funds. And so I—I said that I would marry you instead." Allegra shuddered now at the thought and the earl's eyes widened in mounting wrath. "Oh, pray do not have the apoplexy, my lord," she said, perversely miffed that the idea seemed so odious to him, "for Papa would not hear of it. 'The eldest must wed the earl,' he said, and he would not countenance a match between Meg and John at all events."

"And why is that?"

"Papa doesn't believe in love matches."

"Ah. A man of sense."

Allegra glared at him and went on. "But, of course, if *you* were to cry off, then Papa *might* allow Meg and John to marry. As it is, Meg will not disobey Papa, and John, who has already asked for her hand and been refused, will not pursue the matter, he being the vicar of course. So, you see, *you* are our only hope." Her dark eyes gazed at him earnestly, and for a moment he found himself bemused by her candor. But then he remembered just what she was being candid about. The damned impertinence—

"I regret to inform you, ma'am, that I am in accord with your papa," he said loftily. "I do not believe in love matches."

"Oh, but surely—"

"And furthermore, Miss Allegra Caulfield, this is between Margaret and me, and I'll not have you meddling!"

"I am not meddling!" Allegra jumped up, causing the earl to do the same. "I am merely trying to save Meg from having her heart—"

"I will deal with Margaret, is that clear, Allegra?" he said sternly.

"Surely you cannot mean to go through with this! Why, you cannot possibly be happy with a woman who loves another man!"

"Concerned for my well-being, are you? How very gratifying, to be sure," he drawled. "Now, I thank you for telling me all this, but at the risk of repeating myself, I tell you that I want you well out of it!"

"Oh! You are insufferable!" She stamped her foot. "Papa should have left you to the tender mercies of Mrs. Grimshaw at that flea-bitten alehouse! I bid you good night, my lord!" With that she gathered up her skirts and flounced away.

But he caught her at the elbow and swung her round, pulling her toward him with enough force that she stumbled and fell against his chest. She quickly righted herself, certain that her accelerated heartbeat was the result of her near fall.

"And just what would you know about the Crow and Feather?" he asked smoothly.

"I—ah—stayed there once." Why was she troubling to answer him?

"Really? So close to home?"

She lifted her chin. "Yes. I had run away, you see," she said quickly.

"Ah. And do you run away often, Miss Allegra Caulfield?" His voice had grown soft and his eyes compelled her to answer.

"No, my lord. Only—only when necessary."

It was an odd thing to say, and Nigel would remember those words many weeks later. But by then it would be too late.

Oh! The man was impossible, Allegra fumed, not for the first time, as she climbed into bed some two hours later. Minutes later she climbed back out and began to pace the carpet, fists clenched at her sides, her white nightgown billowing about her. Really, she did not understand why it was necessary for proper young ladies to wear such voluminous garments to bed, especially in this heat. Surely a simple chemise would be more the thing. Were men required to sleep in such overly abundant garments? Did the earl—

Goodness! Where had such a wayward thought come from? She forced herself to think of the earl as he'd been tonight, in the drawing room. He'd straightened his cravat and his black coat had stretched across his broad shoulders with nary a crease. The moment he'd appeared at the threshold, nearly filling the doorway, she'd known he was the sort of man who dominated any room he entered.

She had arrived at the manor a full quarter hour before he had and, to give the devil his due, he kept his counsel. He was politeness itself during all the introductions and acted as if he'd never met her before. For that, she was most grateful, considering that Papa assumed she'd merely gone out to take a turn about the garden. But there her gratitude ended.

She pictured Meg as she'd sat tonight, on the edge of the embroidered settee in the Green Salon, her hands shaking as she poured the earl a cup of coffee. The earl was seated in the wing chair across from Meg, with Papa and Allegra nearby. Lord Debenham had partaken indifferently of the cold collation set out in the dining room, and now he sipped his black coffee in desultory fashion as he studied Meg beneath half-closed lids. Allegra could sense poor Meg squirming under his scrutiny.

Papa tried several conversational gambits, to which the

earl responded perfunctorily. And then quite abruptly he turned to Meg. "Have you ever been to Suffolk, Miss Caulfield? My principal seat is there, you must know."

"No, my lord, I have never been there." Meg's voice was a mere whisper. Lord Debenham waited for her to say more and when she did not, his jaw seemed to tighten.

Well then, say something else! Allegra wanted to snap at him. Make her feel more at her ease. Allegra opened her mouth, having no idea what *she* would say, but Papa spoke first.

"Beautiful country, Suffolk. Remember it from when I was a boy. Used to visit your father on holidays, don't you know."

He engaged the earl upon that topic for several minutes, and Allegra watched Meg sink back into the settee as if by so doing she could" make herself invisible.

"Meg and I have never been outside of Devon," Allegra interjected, wishing to draw Lord Debenham's attention back to her sister.

"Well, I daresay Meg will travel aplenty once she's wed," Papa said with great good humor and Allegra bit her lip to keep from screaming.

"Indeed we will," the earl responded. "Should you like to see London, Miss Caulfield?"

"Yes, of course," Meg murmured demurely.

A strained silence ensued and some imp inside her pushed Allegra into the breach. "Indeed, Meg has heard all about London from John Dalton. He's the vicar, you must know," she said ingenuously, ignoring the clatter of Papa's coffee cup.

Meg quickly lowered her eyes and a blush rose to her cheek. Forgive me, Allegra silently pleaded with her. But someone had to do *something!* They could not go on as if John did not *exist!*

The earl was looking dagger points at her and Papa set his coffee cup down and cleared his throat. "To be sure, the vicar enjoys extolling the architectural wonders of St. Paul's Cathedral and Westminster Abbey to *all* his parishioners," he said pointedly.

"Oh, but there is so much more!" Allegra chimed in. "Why, Meg said John spoke of the Elgin Marbles and the Tower, Bond Street and the shops. I *do* hope I may come and visit you there once you and Meg are wed, my lord. Why John said—"

"Pass the earl some of those strawberry tarts, why don't you, Allegra," Papa cut in ruthlessly, and Allegra decided she'd said enough.

The earl made no further attempts to draw Meg out. Instead, he and Papa fell to conversing about his own father and their exploits at school. And then the earl began discussing the posting of the banns and a wedding date, quite as if Allegra had never uttered a word to him on the bank of that pond! And all this while it was perfectly obvious to anyone of the merest intelligence that Meg was looking more miserable by the second. John aside, she seemed terrified of the earl. Allegra had rather suspected she would be, for Meg was sweet and compliant and no match at all for a man of the Earl of Debenham's stamp.

Allegra paced the carpet with increased agitation now as she recalled seeing Meg several times wipe away a surreptitious tear. Allegra had wanted to scream and stamp her foot and shake them all. Could they not see how idiotish they were being, creating such misery in the name of honor? Could Lord Debenham and Papa not see how cruel it was to separate Meg and John?

But no, Papa could not see. He had already told them about himself and Mama. It had been a love match, but by the time of Mama's death just over a year ago they had not been happy, had not been, in fact, for quite some time. And all for lack of funds, Papa would have them believe. Mama had not been able to abide their increasingly straightened circumstances. And so Meg must marry a fortune.

Which, Allegra believed, was all so much moonshine. Mama and Papa had argued about many things, lack of funds only one of them. And Meg and John were two gentle souls, very different from the fiery natures of Papa and Mama.

As to the earl, he certainly could not or would not see how dreadful it was for Meg. How could he, really, when he made but a halfhearted attempt to draw her out? And he had pointedly ignored Allegra when Papa began speaking of the banns. She wondered if he would broach the subject of John privately with Meg at all.

Perhaps if he would stumble upon Meg and John in the garden one day, as Allegra had done just last week, he might think differently. Of course, it wasn't as if they'd been doing anything improper, but the look in their eyes told its own story.

However, now that the Earl of Debenham had come, Allegra doubted that John would meet Meg in the garden again. John Dalton always did the proper thing. It was one of the things Meg loved about him, and it nearly drove Allegra to distraction. Nigel Hayves, she imagined, did the proper thing only when it suited him. And as to Allegra, she admitted ruefully, propriety was simply never her foremost consideration.

She sighed and leaned her head against the large window that overlooked the rear gardens. It was open but the hot, stuffy night air begrudged even the slightest breeze.

Somehow, despite all the romantical novels she had read—and there had been many—she had never realized how wretched a true life situation could make one feel. She and Meg, who was two years her senior, had always been close. This despite the great disparities in their personalities, or perhaps because of them. Allegra had been the one who made Meg laugh and led her into scrapes, and Meg was always the calm one, full of wisdom beyond her years. And then there had been John, handsome and kind and blond-haired John, who'd come to the parish as a young curate four years ago, when Meg was sixteen and Allegra a child of fourteen. They'd allowed Allegra to trail along after them until Meg was eighteen, and then suddenly they wanted to be alone. Which, for one of Allegra's romantical nature, was just as it should be. She could not help wondering, though, if they ever did more than talk about the uplifting literature John was always giving Meg to read. Meg would do well to read an occasional Minerva Press or Nora Tillington novel, Allegra thought now. Then perhaps she would not be so resigned to her fate. Perhaps she would *do* something!

Allegra remembered Meg's face the day, four months ago, when Papa had told her of the long-standing betrothal. She'd been ashen, and she'd gone to her room to cry. It had been left to Allegra to rail at her father. But this was one time she'd been unable to sway him. Allegra knew full well it was up to the father to choose his daughters' husbands, he'd railed right back. Then why, she'd wanted to know, had he not told Meg years ago, before her attachment to John Dalton had grown so?

At that Papa's eyes had bulged. What attachment? If the vicar had been carrying on with his eldest daughter he'd see him defrocked! Allegra had tried to reason with him, then stared at him in despair. Could he really have been so oblivious to what was going forth? And then she realized that he might very well have considered John's visits in the nature of pastoral calls. Besides, Papa had been most preoccupied with trying to keep Caulfield afloat, and with Mama's long illness and then her death.

It was then that John had asked for Meg's hand, even though the year of mourning was not over. But Papa had not softened and now the year *was* up. And so the earl had come.

And the worst of it was that even had it not been for John, it was plain as pikestaff that Meg and Nigel Hayves

25

would not suit. Why, he'd eat her alive! And he'd break her heart with his numerous peccadilloes — Allegra was certain he had at the least one mistress in keeping and had no intention of mending his ways! Poor, sweet, innocent Meg, who'd never hurt a soul, she thought.

But when Allegra finally fell asleep it was not of Meg that she was thinking, but of the Earl of Debenham. His eyes were green, she'd noted when she finally saw him in the candlelight, and his hair a very dark chocolate brown. And his most expressive features were his devilish brows. She had never quite seen their like.

All things considered, Nigel decided some two hours later as he prepared for bed, matters could not have been worse. Oh, his bride-to-be was as beautiful as her miniature had promised, her demeanor as biddable as a man could want. Her carriage was all that was excellent in a future countess, her face as composed as befit her station.

She was nothing at all like her sister.

Margaret Caulfield had been perfectly polite and charming when they were introduced. She had poured the tea graciously, had spoken only when spoken to, had sat with her hands folded demurely in her lap.

She was nothing like her sister.

Margaret was everything that Nigel wanted in a wife, had wanted these many years since that debacle with the fiery, raven-haired Gina.

That was why he was going to marry Meg. Exquisite, blond, proper, quiescent Meg. Why then, did his eyes keep wandering to her fiery, dark-haired sister?

He cursed into his pillow and pounded it before turning over to find a more comfortable position in the bed. How the devil was he to know why he kept looking at Allegra? Damned meddlesome child! No, he amended. Not a child. No child looked like she did in a dripping wet chemise.

Hellfire! He was avoiding the real issue and he knew it. For even had Allegra not spoken as she had, Nigel would have known something was wrong. He was not a fool, and though Margaret's reticence might be put down to maidenly reserve, her surreptitious tears could not. Nor could the fact that her knuckles were white as she gripped the teapot. Unlike her sister, who would undoubtedly not balk at making a scene, Meg Caulfield was a lady.

Nigel sighed heavily and rose from the bed. He padded to a sidetable where his host had thoughtfully provided a decanter of brandy. He poured himself a glass and sipped at it. He would have to take the bull by the horns and speak to Meg, without, of course, letting on that he knew anything he oughtn't.

He and Meg must clear the air if they were ever to have a comfortable life together. And a life together they would have, of that he was certain. Meg seemed a sensible woman, not given to the fits and starts of her sister. She knew the advantages that would accrue to her, indeed to her entire family, as the Countess of Debenham. And undoubtedly she knew, from her father's instruction, that love matches should be consigned to romantical novels.

Nigel had learned *that* from bitter experience. He sat now in a wing chair by the empty grate and swirled his brandy in the snifter, remembering. He'd been only two and twenty, had already sold out of his regiment and gone traveling on the Continent. And he'd tumbled head over heels in love with Gina, a stunning, dark-eyed Italian actress. They'd had a wildly passionate affair and he'd determined to marry her. Of course, one could not consider marrying an English actress, but as she was foreign he'd hoped they might contrive to pull it off. She declared she couldn't bear to be apart from him, and so he'd taken her home to break the news to his father.

His father, with whom he'd heretofore shared an affectionate relationship, had flown into a rage and threatened to disown him. And Gina, who only hours ago had sworn her undying love for him, had flown into the night. She'd left a brief note saying only that she really was not cut out for a life of poverty.

Nigel had been crushed, and worse, humiliated almost beyond bearing. After that he'd stayed far away from dark, tempestuous sirens, and had entertained no further thoughts of marriage. And, after all, there had been no hurry; he was the second son.

But Charles, his elder brother, had not had Nigel's experience to guide him. Charles had adored his beautiful raven-haired wife, had loved her beyond all bounds of reason. He had been fiercely jealous and Lucinda had given him cause. And now they were both dead.

Nigel recalled that horrible time four years ago all too vividly, and he pushed the memories away. His father had never fully recovered from the death of his heir, and of course he'd partially blamed Nigel, who'd disappointed him once before. And so when, two years ago, his father lay on his death bed and asked that Nigel agree to wed the eldest daughter of his old school friend, Nigel had not refused him.

Nor had he wanted to. Margaret Caulfield would make an unexceptionable countess and an exemplary mother for the heir he now very much needed. Margaret Caulfield, he had thought then, was precisely what he wanted in a wife.

He snapped the brandy down onto a table and stalked to the bed. She still was exactly what he wanted! The evening had not changed his mind one whit! If Meg was willing to abide by their betrothal, then he would take her to wife. They would have a comfortable, sane, pleasant existence. No great heights of passion, no foolish declarations of love, no depths of despair. Passion, after all, belonged in the boudoir with one's mistress, and love was merely a figment in the imagination of fools.

And Nigel Hayves, betrothed husband of Margaret Caulfield, was not a fool.

Yet as the earl climbed once more into bed, it was the image of Meg's sister, oh-so-innocently dropping the name of that vicar into the conversation, that danced in his mind. What a troublemaker, he thought drowsily. An irksome child.

But his last thought as he finally drifted off to sleep was that Allegra Caulfield was not a child at all.

Chapter Two

"The chariest maid is prodigal enough
If she unmask her beauty to the moon."

Hamlet
William Shakespeare

Allegra was up early, as was her wont, and rode out on Leda, her chestnut mare. Flushed from her exertions, she headed for the breakfast parlor, hoping that Papa would still be there. She must try once more to make him see reason. Meg's room was next to hers and Allegra had heard her crying late into the night. She could not bear to see her sister suffer so.

But it was not her father who sat at the breakfast table reading the *Gazette* and eating eggs Benedict. It was the Earl of Debenham. And he did not smile at her entrance as one might expect a gentleman to do. He frowned. And then he belatedly rose and held a chair for her.

"You are up rather early, are you not?" he queried once they were seated and a footman had served her and resumed his place beside the sideboard. The earl sounded none too pleased.

She spread marmalade on a piece of toast with great care. "Oh, I am always up at this hour, my lord. I do so enjoy an early ride," she said cheerfully. "Where is Papa?"

"He just left. And Margaret? Does she also break her

30

fast so early?" he asked, his green eyes narrowed.

"Meg prefers to stay abed in the mornings. She takes her chocolate and toast in bed."

"Most admirable behavior in a lady"—he paused—"and a wife. Of a certain Margaret understands that a husband prefers a solitary breakfast table." He refilled his coffee cup and peered at her coolly across the table. "Contrary to your belief, ma'am, I am persuaded that Margaret and I will suit very well," he said smoothly.

Oh, drat!! Allegra fumed. Was he baiting her or did he actually believe his own words? "You must be clairvoyant, my lord, for I vow you do not know Meg well enough to make such a statement," she snapped. "Of a certain you made little effort to draw her out last night."

His eyes blazed and she thought she'd gone too far. But she would not back down.

"I told you before, ma'am, that I will brook no interference in what is none of your affair." She noted that his brows arched into those twin "V's" when he was angry, just as when he grinned. "This matter is heretofore closed between you and me. Is that clear?"

He stabbed at his eggs for emphasis and Allegra nibbled at her toast, cudgeling her brain for a suitable reply. She knew a retreat of sorts was in order, however temporary. Her next step was Papa. She would get no further with the earl just now. "You have made your feelings in the matter most clear, my lord," she said equably, and his expression relaxed. He picked up his coffee cup. "Would you mind sharing part of the newspaper, my lord?" she asked.

His set his cup onto his saucer a trifle shortly and rather abruptly separated and folded the paper. He handed it across the table to her in silence.

And thus they ate their meal, the silence broken only by the sounds of forks and knives scraping against the china. Allegra could not concentrate on the article on the Corn Laws which she was attempting to read and instead her eyes kept drifting to the earl. Her gaze swept over the strong planes of his face, set now in anger, over his broad, muscular chest, encased in a coat of brown superfine. Her eyes came to rest on his hands, one of which clutched the newspaper he seemed to be reading with great interest. With the other hand he brought his coffee cup to his lips.

One could tell a great deal about a man by his hands, she thought. The earl's hands were very large, well formed and strong. They were hands that bespoke power, temper, even passion. They were unlike Mr. Peterson's hands, which she remembered as thin and delicate, rather, she realized now, like his kiss had been. John Dalton's hands were long and slender but with a deceptively quiet strength. His hands would suit Meg quite well, Allegra mused, while the earl's would suit — would suit his many mistresses!

Allegra found her father in his study, poring over the account books. But today he looked more relaxed than usual, and Allegra knew very well the reason. No doubt he and the earl would discuss the settlements today; she was not a moment too soon.

But having met the earl, Papa was no more willing to listen to her pleas about the unsuitability of this match than he'd been before. Even less so. He sat back comfortably in his tufted leather chair and gazed at Allegra. His silver hair was meticulously combed. His navy blue coat, while several years old, still fit him perfectly. He was a good deal shorter than Nigel Hayves, and just a bit stocky, and were it not for the lines of worry etched into his face, he would be a handsome man still.

"My dear Allegra," he began, "the earl is a fine figure of a man. A man of breeding, grace, and reason, a man not given to excess. He will treat Meg with all the dignity and respect she deserves."

"There is more to marriage than dignity and respect,

32

Papa," she said quietly.

"Do not go spouting platitudes about romantical love, Allegra. I am much too old and wise for that. You are but eighteen years of age, with no knowledge of the world. You simply must trust that I know better."

"Could you not see how frightened Meg was of him? Do you not believe that she cries for John every night?"

"That is quite enough, Allegra!" Her father rose abruptly from his chair and stormed to where Allegra sat in front of the desk. "We have discussed all of this before. This is none of your affair, my girl! And if you jeopardize this betrothal by filling the earl's ears with fustian about Meg and that vicar, I'll—I'll—" Papa stopped, clenched his fists, and began pacing before her. "I have put up with a great deal from you, Allegra. I've put up with your rescuing that climbing boy—"

"Oh, but you *do* like him, Papa, don't you? Marcus is such a dear boy. And when I think of all those wretched burns he had on his little body—"

"Yes, well, he *is* a good boy. I've grown rather fond of him myself. He's taken to the horses rather well. I mean to make him my tiger one day."

"Thank you, Papa."

"But that is neither here nor there. You are always championing some stray or other. Besides Marcus there were those two maid servants in interesting conditions of which a young girl should have no knowledge. And I allowed you to take one in and find a place for the other. And I turn my back when you sneak off to the stables to play cards—oh, yes, my girl, I am well aware of your nefarious activities— but, here, today, I draw the line." He leaned down and put both hands on the arms of her chair, pinioning her with his gaze. "Meg will marry Nigel Hayves, no matter what you say or do. Regardless of what attachment she thinks she has formed, in the long run it will be best for her. It is certainly best for this family and, according to what I know of Nigel

33

from his late father, it will be best for him as well."

"But Papa—"

"No! There are no 'buts,' Allegra. And you might just as well scotch any nonsensical schemes you may be hatching in that devious little mind of yours. I will not be gainsaid in this matter!" Papa straightened up and glowered at her.

Allegra knew this was not the moment to attempt to shout him down. Instead she said softly, "You are not the one who will have to live with a man you cannot love, nor to leave one who—"

"Love! Oh, for pitysakes, Allegra, 'tis time you grew up!" He began to pace again, running his hands through his hair. "Perhaps it is my fault. All those damned Nora Tillington novels you read. I have been too lenient with you, that is certain, but I assure you, your husband will not be. And husband you shall have as soon as Meg is settled and can bring you out. And make no mistake, Allegra"—here he leaned toward her again and lowered his voice—"though I shall have your best interests at heart, you shall have no more choice of husband than she did. You, my girl, do not know the first thing about marriage!"

Her father stepped back and Allegra rose, facing him with her back ramrod straight. Her voice quavered as she said, "You are a most unfeeling man, Papa. I had not thought it of you."

She walked slowly from the room, the only thing preventing her tears the knowledge that they would do Meg no good at all. But oh, how she ached to cry. Not only was she about to lose her sister to a hardened rake, but she felt as if she'd already lost her Papa. For if he indeed forced this marriage, things would never be the same between them again.

Nigel had been putting off his interview with Meg, trying, he supposed, to decide exactly what to say to her. He strolled out to the gardens, thinking to clear his head.

Luncheon had been a rather strained affair, with Meg subdued and Allegra surreptitiously glaring at her father and then at him. Nigel surmised she had tried once more to persuade Caulfield to nullify the betrothal. Of course, the baron had refused. Nigel had met with him in his study just before luncheon. They had discussed the settlements, a fairly simple matter, of which the solicitors could handle most. But though he admittedly needed the funds Meg's marriage would bring, the baron had been most concerned about what manner of man Nigel was.

Caulfield had not attempted to intimidate Nigel—indeed, he would never have succeeded—but neither had he minced words.

"I have heard much of you, Nigel," the baron had begun, "from your late father, from others. Much that is good. You are a man of honor, I make no doubt. I believe you will treat my daughter kindly. But I also know you to be a rake of the first order. My daughter is a very gentle soul, unschooled in the ways of the world."

"I am aware of that, Caulfield." Nigel had paused, framing his words carefully. It would not do to be less than truthful with the baron, who was no one's fool. "I can assure you that I shall always treat Meg with courtesy, respect and in time, affection. I can be a man of discretion, you must know, despite my reputation. Your daughter will always be able to hold her head up in society."

The baron stared at him for several long moments, and then nodded. Nigel breathed an inward sigh of relief. They were both men of the world, and they understood each other. The baron had not asked for marital fidelity, nor had Nigel promised such. They were both realists, after all. Meg would have a good life as the Countess of Debenham, and the baron knew it. Else he would not consent to the marriage.

Nigel ambled now through the rose garden and then further back, through a series of arbors. Dimly he was aware that the gardens had become slightly overgrown. He tried to think of Meg and was vexed when it was the image of her irksome younger sister that rose in his mind's eye. And then he stopped thinking, as voices drifted toward him from behind a hedge. Meg and a man, no doubt the vicar. With only a twinge of conscience, Nigel moved toward the voices. It really was best that he see for himself just how the wind lay in that quarter.

He could just barely see the two figures through the thick hedge. They sat on a stone bench facing each other, close but not touching. John looked to be a medium-sized man, reasonably good looking with blond hair to match Meg's.

"This is the last time I can see you alone. You know that, don't you, Meg?" John said.

"Yes," Meg replied softly. "Oh, John, I do not know how I shall bear it!" She covered her face with her hands.

The vicar took a deep breath and cupped her chin with his palm, forcing her to drop her hands and look up at him. "Oh, Meg. My dear Meg. I would it were otherwise. But we have been through this before. There is no help for it."

"No," Meg cried, covering his hand with hers. "There must be—"

"Meg, we are given many crosses to bear in this life. We must—we must make the best of them." The vicar's voice had grown husky with emotion.

Nigel clenched his fists. So, he was a cross to bear, was he?

The vicar rose and walked several paces away, turning his back. He seemed to be trying to compose himself.

Meg, eyes moist, rose and went to him. She did not touch him but stood just behind him.

"John," she said so softly that Nigel had to strain to hear her. "I—I have not slept well of late. And the earl . . . frightens me. He is so large and dark and—and not at all like you." She seemed to shudder, with fear or distaste, Nigel did not know. But it was hardly flattering. And then unbidden there rose in his mind the thought of Allegra. She certainly wasn't frightened of him, and he'd wager she did not think him too large or dark. All of which, he reminded himself, did not signify in the least; it was Meg he was marrying and not her sister!

"Oh, God, Meg!" the vicar cried out, and turned and gathered her in his arms. He pressed her blond head into his shoulder. "If I think too much about you and him, I shall go mad."

Nigel closed his eyes and wondered what sort of cad he was to stay and witness such a private moment. And yet he *had* to stay.

When he opened his eyes Dalton was gently pushing Meg from him. "Meg, my dear, you—you must be brave. And I am certain the earl is—is a pleasing enough man. Perhaps—perhaps your father does know best. You are above my touch, Meg."

"Oh, John, how can you—"

"Meg, I could not afford the dress you are wearing now."

Meg smiled sadly. " 'Tis two years old. I could not afford it now either."

"Meg, I do not think you understand. I will always be poor by the standards to which you, even in your somewhat straitened circumstances, are accustomed. Indeed, I have known these many years past that I had no right to aspire to your hand. I should look to the daughter of a local squire or solicitor, or—"

"I do not care a whit for such things, John, as you know full well. Mama did, but I do not. If you were not the vicar, I would fly off to Gretna Green with you in a trice!"

The vicar strolled to the hedge behind which Nigel stood. Nigel held his breath, but John went back to Meg a minute later. "Meg, attend me. This is a calling for me, not something I do for lack of aught else."

"I know that, John. I did not mean—why, your devotion to duty is one of the reasons I love—"

37

"Meg," the vicar interrupted, taking her hands, "From this time forth we share only the affection of good friends. You must see that it is the only way."

Meg nodded slowly, her eyes brimming. The vicar kissed her brow and then stepped back. "Your sister invited me to tea, but I do not think that would be a good idea," he said, somewhat unsteadily.

"Oh, but—"

"No, Meg. I—I do not wish to meet the earl just yet. And you must tell your dear but meddlesome little sister to cease her machinations. They will not work."

Meg laughed. "Trying to stop Allegra is like trying to stop a tidal wave. I believe we have become another of her causes. But she means well. She knows that I—I do not sleep at night and—"

"Meg! I do not sleep either. But it doesn't signify. Even were there a way, I could not in good conscience take you away from the life for which you were born. Tell your sister of our conversation, and that she, too, must accept the inevitable."

The vicar's voice was firm and Nigel knew that, despite the tendre he obviously had for Meg, he meant every word he said. He was a sensible man who understood what was most important in marriage. In time, Meg would understand as well. And as to Allegra, Nigel would deal with her as the need arose.

He beat a hasty retreat, and resolved to give Meg time to compose herself before seeking her out. Now he had a much clearer idea of what to say to her.

Their interview took place in the morning room just before tea time. She was standing with her back to the big picture window overlooking the front of the house. Her lemon yellow gown became her, Nigel thought, but she was too pale, and her eyes held a hint of redness.

His eyes swept the room, which was done in a rather fussy manner in varying shades of pink and blue. Nigel disliked it on sight. He wondered if the late baroness had decorated it, and if Meg shared her taste. He suspected that Allegra would hate the flounces on every chair skirt and the lacy pillows strewn about everywhere.

He kept his stride light as he approached Meg. "Why don't you come sit down, Meg? I think we should talk," he said in a gentle voice and was pleased to see her relax a trifle.

He led her to the pink chintz sofa and, sensing that she would prefer it, seated himself in an adjacent chair rather than next to her. She had not yet said a word and so he began, "Now, Meg, I have spoken with your father. I know his feelings in the matter of our betrothal, and I know mine. I do not know yours."

"I—I do not understand, my lord."

"We have not had a traditional courtship, as you know. I have not paid my addresses to you. Our betrothal is a fait accompli. I wish to marry you, Meg. In short, I am asking whether you wish to marry me."

She kept her eyes lowered, her hands in her lap. "Of course I do, my lord," she said, too quickly. "I am most sensible of the great honor you do me. I shall contrive to be a good wife to you."

Nigel bit back a sigh. "Meg, look at me, please." When she complied, he went on. "Honor aside, do you *wish* to wed me?"

"I—I hardly know you, my lord. But my father thinks highly of you and, of course, I want to comply with his wishes."

Well, she was honest enough, but still it was not the answer he wanted. He tried again. "I have not had my—er—hopes in any other quarter disappointed. But you are a very beautiful young woman. Despite your isolation here in the country you must have had several suitors. Have you perhaps formed a tendre for any one of them?"

It was the best he could do without revealing prior knowledge, but it was enough. She looked down again and twisted her hands. "John Dalton—he is the vicar, you must know—he and I," she paused, her voice merely a whisper. "He and I are particular friends, but Papa has made me see that a match between us is impossible. John—John says the same thing. I do not say this to overset you, my lord, but only because you asked, and you have a right to know. But you mustn't think I shall be any less of a wife to you because of it. In time I—I shall forget and I shall always endeavor to make you comfortable."

She smiled that sad little smile of hers and he knew that she would indeed make him comfortable. And he would endeavor to do the same for her. She was brave and she was honest, and he admired her greatly.

He moved to sit next to her on the sofa. "Thank you for telling me this, Meg. You are a most sensible woman. I think we shall deal very well together." He took her hands and lightly kissed each one. And he told himself that the shudder that rippled through her was due to maidenly modesty, something her sister knew nothing about.

Allegra was restless. The air was hot and very humid. Clouds had overtaken the blue skies and a hot wind was rising. A summer storm was in the making, and she felt as if one were churning inside of her. She needed some distraction and headed for the stables. The laughter of Marcus and Clem and the others was just what she needed.

She heard Marcus's young voice when she was still in the stableyard. "Cor, Jamie, you'll not have tuppence left, playin' like that!" he exclaimed. He was obviously enjoying himself, but who, she wondered, was Jamie?

"Why 'tis fleeced I'm bein', and ye little more than a wee bairnie at that!" came the good-humored reply. Jamie, it seemed, was a Scot.

Slowly Allegra pushed open the door of the first set of

stalls. Clem was polishing a saddle, off in a corner. Marcus sat before an overturned barrel, his eyes intent on the cards before him. Across from him sat a huge bear of a man with bright red hair and a beard to match.

"Oh! Miss Allegra!" Marcus, just noticing her, jumped up and scampered over to take her hand and drag her forward. Marcus had been at Caulfield for three months. Every day his eight-year-old body seemed to heal a bit more. His frame was filling out and the burn marks on his back and legs were becoming less prominent. "I'm about teachin' Jamie how to play piquet!" he said excitedly. Lately Marcus always seemed excited and eager about something, as if suddenly he'd discovered that the world was a marvelous place, which indeed he had.

The huge Scot had risen from his bench and his blue eyes twinkled down at Allegra. "The laddie's a true Captain Sharp, I vow. Takin' advantage of the fact that I dinna ken the game," he said, then wagged a finger at Marcus. "But I'm warnin' ye, laddie, I'll soon come aboot."

Marcus did not look the least intimidated, and something about Jamie's tone told Allegra he was an old hand at the game of piquet. She liked the large Scot immediately.

"Jamie's my new friend, Miss Allegra," Marcus piped up. "He's the earl's head groom and majordome."

"That's major*domo*, Marcus," Allegra corrected gently, and then to Jamie said, "I'm pleased to meet you."

He bowed slightly. "I am Jamie MacIntyre, Miss Allegra. I feel as if I already ken ye well frae Marcus's chatter. And then—" here he lowered his voice and his gold-tipped lashes—"of course, the earl has told me a wee bit as well."

She could not help the flash in her eyes. "Noo, lassie, dinna be gettin' yer dander up." He excused them both to Marcus and led her outside the stable door. The sky had darkened and a hot breeze whipped tendrils of her hair loose. "I ken ye mean well, lassie, but there is naught ye can do. There are things ye dinna ken aboot his lordship. Dinna fash yersel'. He'll make a fine husband for yer bonny sister."

Jamie's words and the firm look in his eyes told Allegra two things. One was that he cared deeply for the earl, that his loyalty was absolute. And the other was that, whether he called himself groom or majordomo or aught else, he was much more than a servant. Jamie MacIntyre might be anywhere from thirty to fifty years old. It was impossible to tell, for though there were fine lines etched around his eyes, half his face was covered by his full beard.

She cocked her head. "You are his friend, aren't you, Jamie?"

"Aye, miss," he said simply.

She wondered at the connection between them, instinctively knowing it was deep and strong. She also knew that she must leave no stone uncovered, even if it meant speaking out of turn. "Then surely you must wish for his happiness," she said ingenuously.

"Aye, miss," he agreed, but there was a suspicious gleam in his eyes.

"Well, then, Jamie, if you knew my sister at all, you would see how impossible this match is. Why—"

"Nae, lass, dinna be wastin' yer breath. His lordship is set on this marriage, and yer sister has accepted him." At Allegra's raised brow, he added, "Aye, this afternoon. 'Tis no for either of us to gainsay them or the baron. Ye must wish them happy, lass."

Allegra's eyes narrowed. Had the earl put him up to this? "Do you believe they'll be happy, Jamie?"

Jamie did not meet her eyes. "They are no different from many anither betrothed couple, Miss Allegra. 'Tis best."

She sensed pain behind his words, whether for himself, the earl or both she could not say. And she could not ask. She knew that, for now at the least, no answers would be forthcoming. Nor would any help from this quarter. She was on her own. She squared her shoulders.

"I see. Well, I'd best be getting back." Her tone sounded

too stiff and she gentled it. "Thank you, Jamie, for befriending Marcus."

" 'Tis my pleasure. What ye did for him, lassie, well, 'tis something few would have done. Ye are a brave lass, savin' him from the sweep. Marcus told me how the brute was proddin' him up the chimney with the hot iron, and ye heard his greetin' and went after the sweep with a broomstick. Aye, 'twere a sight I wish I'd seen." His eyes crinkled in amusement and then a moment later sobered. "But, lassie, yer sister is a different kettle of fish entirely. She doesna need savin', ye ken? Leave be, lassie."

Allegra closed her eyes and sighed. "There's a storm coming up, Jamie. We'd all best take cover." His brow lifted as he pondered her double entendre, but then she added, "Would you please see that Marcus stays out of the rain? I still do not know if he's strong enough to fight off a chill."

Jamie seemed relieved and they parted amicably. But Allegra was most perturbed as she walked back to the house. For her options were dwindling rapidly.

The storm had finally broken at dinner time, straining everyone's already taut nerves. Allegra, however, had always found the advent of a storm a great relief. It was the anticipation that was unnerving.

She stood now before the open window of her chamber, watching the storm. The wind caused her ivory lawn nightgown to flutter pleasantly about her. The house was abed and the noise of the rain and occasional crackle of thunder had prevented her from hearing Meg's nightly sobbing. But still she could not sleep.

Allegra never slept during thunderstorms. Not, of course, because she feared them, but because she enjoyed them excessively. They were wild and primitive and terribly exciting! When, that is, one was comfortably ensconced within some sturdy structure. She was not so hen-witted as to wish

43

to be abroad on such a night. But to be inside looking out, or better still, to be in her favorite place—the small covered terrace outside Papa's smoking room—ah, that was lovely!

She donned her slippers and a light cotton wrapper and, pausing only to snatch a taper from her bedside table, made her way to the smoking room. It was a relatively small corner room on the first floor of the house, not far from Papa's study. The terrace had been built by her great-grandfather, and its roof formed the floor of an upper terrace leading out from some guest room or other. A spiral stairway connected the two.

Leaving her taper on a side table, she unlocked the French doors of the smoking room and stepped outside. The wind rifled her nightclothes but the air was so warm that she felt as if it were enveloping her. She let her wrapper fall to one of the two wicker chairs set against the wall and walked to the waist-high stone parapet at the edge of the terrace. Droplets of wind-carried rain sprayed her face; she reveled in the sensation. In the moonlight she could see the garden below, the lush, slightly overgrown greenery bending and rippling under the force of the rain. And then the heavens let loose a bolt of lightning and for one moment the garden was as bright as daylight. The crackle of thunder followed and Allegra remembered comforting a frightened Meg oftimes during such storms when they were children.

But they were not children any longer, and what frightened Meg now could not be soothed away so easily.

"Oh, Meg! There has got to be a way!" she said aloud, her face turned up to the moon and the trees.

Blast her! Would she never give up? Nigel cursed inwardly from the shadows of the terrace. And whatever was she doing here in the middle of the night? The peace he had sought out here had fled the moment he'd watched her shrug off her wrapper and walk toward the moonlight. He moved forward; she gasped and whirled about, leaning her lower back against the parapet.

"Allegra, do you have any idea what time it is?" the voice queried, and Allegra expelled a sigh of relief. For a moment she had not been certain who it was.

But her relief was short-lived, for as the earl stepped out of the shadows, his eyes raked over her in a most disconcerting manner. Oh, why had she not kept her wrapper on?

"I—ah—do not know precisely, my lord. I suppose 'tis well past two of the clock," she answered hesitantly, forcing herself to meet his gaze.

"Long past time you were abed, is it not?" he demanded, moving inexorably closer to her. His hair was sprinkled with raindrops and he smelled of rain, masculine soap, and brandy. The combination was heady.

"I—ah—could not sleep," she managed to reply, and then made the mistake of letting her eyes sweep over him. "You—you are not dressed. That is, you are wearing your dressing gown!"

His lips twitched. "Most astute of you. It *is* two of the clock, as you say. My room is just above here."

"I did not realize—"

"Obviously," he said dryly.

She cocked her head and stared at him in that ingenuous way of hers. It usually heralded trouble. "I—I have never before seen a man in his—"

"Allegra! You really must not say such things!"

"Oh. Ought I to politely ignore your deshabille, then?" she asked in all seriousness.

Oh, Lord, he thought, not for the first time, she *did* need a keeper. "Er—yes, something like that." He prudently refrained from commenting on *her* deshabille. Her gown was ivory, and much too sheer, and he wondered if she wore anything at all under it, and why the deuce she had removed her wrapper.

"Why could you not sleep, Allegra?" he asked, needing to shift the subject. But somehow, his voice sounded softer than he'd intended and he found himself moving closer to

45

her, until only a few feet separated them.

She wished he would not come so close; his nearness was most unnerving. But there was no place to retreat to, for the parapet was at her back. "I expect it was the storm," she replied in a voice that sounded strangely weak.

"Frightened, are you?" His mocking tone snapped her back to herself.

"Certainly not! I love thunderstorms! They are so wild and free . . ." She pivoted around and waved her arms toward the furious skies. She turned back to him but kept her hands behind her. "It seems a shame to sleep through them. Is that what kept you awake as well?"

"No," he replied curtly, refusing to be drawn in by that rather engaging look in her brown eyes, determining to ignore the way the fabric of her gown stretched across her breasts. He did not know what had kept him awake, except some unaccountable restlessness which he had no intention of discussing. As to Allegra, he'd warrant the storm was not all that had kept her from sleeping. She enjoyed creating a few storms of her own.

"But that has naught to say to the matter. The point is that I heard what you said. I thought I'd made it clear I would brook no more of your meddling, Allegra," he said sternly.

"But, my lord, you seem to have forgotten that you have no hold over me," she pointed out with her gaminlike face tilted up at him. "You are not betrothed to *me*, after all."

"Thank heaven for that!" he murmured under his breath and saw her brown eyes flash.

"My sentiments exactly!" she retorted.

He closed the remaining steps to the parapet but kept a foot's distance between them. Damn her for wearing only that flimsy nightgown! Though its high neck and long sleeves were modest enough, the wind caused it to ripple against her body, outlining her breasts and hips almost as clearly as that blasted wet chemise last night.

46

"I will have you know that I overheard Meg and the vicar in the garden today," he told her.

"Eavesdropping, my lord?"

His lips twitched but he refused to be drawn. "Be that as it may," he went on, "the vicar was giving Meg some very sound and reasonable advice about marrying me. And Meg herself, when I had a private interview with her, was most amenable."

Allegra's hands flew to her hips. "Good God! You cannot be that blind or—or muttonheaded. Of course she—"

"At this point, Miss Allegra Caulfield, the only one unduly overset about this betrothal is you! Oh, I grant you she may shed a few tears after the wedding, but by the time she presents me with an heir she will have forgotten all about John the Vicar."

"Oh!" Allegra's fists clenched at her sides and she stamped her slipper-clad foot. "You are the most insufferable, conceited, overbearing, unfeeling brute I have ever encountered!" Her eyes were wild with fury. Her short curly hair blew in the wind, and her gown billowed about her. She looked completely unruly, at one with the storm that raged behind her. She looked glorious, a voice at the back of his head whispered, but he stifled it ruthlessly.

"And you, my girl," he said grimly, "are an ill-bred, interfering child who doesn't know what's best for her own family!"

"Ooh!" she shrieked and swung her right hand up and straight at his face.

He grabbed her hand and dragged it down, pinioning both arms to her sides. She squirmed but he tightened his hold, his strong arms enveloping her, clamping her tightly against his full length. Only his dressing gown, gaping open at the chest, and her thin lawn nightgown separated them. The top of her head came to his chin; her hair brushed his chest. As his right hand slid down to her hip, a wave of desire pulsed through him, shocking him in its strength.

47

She tilted her face up and his eyes locked with hers. They were wide, a deep luminous brown, the fury in them turned to something else entirely. Was it curiosity, desire, anticipation? All three, perhaps. He remembered how she'd looked last night, just before she'd discovered his identity. She had wanted . . .

He lowered his gaze to her pointed nose, to the intriguing pink lips with no indentation in the top. Her full breasts were pressed against him. She was wearing no more now than she had last night.

"Damn you, Allegra," he cursed, but his words came out in a whisper. "Can you not contrive to keep your clothes on once the moon is up?"

She parted her lips as if to speak and that was when, inevitably, he lowered his mouth.

Only a touch, only a taste, he told himself with his last remaining particle of rational thinking. Just enough to satisfy his curiosity about that mystifying upper lip. And then he'd never touch her again.

I cannot abide this man, Allegra thought. He was insufferable, and yet his strong hands, especially the one at her hip, brought a certain delicious tingling sensation to her body. And she was rather curious about what his full, beautifully shaped lips would feel like on hers . . .

Nigel brushed his lips over hers. They were warm and soft. Just a taste, he told himself again, and ran his tongue over that upper lip. Desire curled through him. He tried to bank it. But then she tasted back. He hadn't expected it. She nipped at his upper lip, and then the lower. Her tongue darted between her teeth. He was not sure which one of them groaned, but suddenly his mouth was open, full and hard and demanding on hers. He forgot who he was, who she was. Her lips and teeth parted for him and his hands began to move.

He was plundering her, Allegra thought, his tongue pillaging the inside of her mouth, his hands almost frenzied as they kneaded, massaged, caressed her body. This, she knew instinctively, was what a kiss should be. She could not think, could hardly breathe, could only feel her body sway and mold to his. She gave him her tongue; she felt hot all over. Somewhere in the back of her head she knew it was wrong; she wanted it never to end.

But it did. Suddenly the warmth stopped. His hands had left her; he lifted his head. She stumbled. He caught her, steadied her, then let her go. She felt bereft, ashamed, furious that he had done this to her.

Nigel struggled to catch his breath. "I'm sorry," he rasped. "This should never have happened, Allegra, and we both would do best to forget it."

" 'Tis not so simple, Nigel, and you know it."

They glared at each other. Allegra could feel the tension in the hot, steamy air as a palpable thing.

Very well, he thought. So he was "Nigel" now. Hellfire, what a pass she'd brought him to, parading about with next to nothing on.

"We'll do it anyway, Allegra," he growled in an undertone. "Because in a few weeks' time we'll be brother and sister!"

Utter rage filled her eyes, but before she could frame a suitable retort he turned and strode from the terrace.

Allegra watched him go. Never had she thought she could hate anyone quite so much.

Chapter Three

"Chanting faint hymns to the cold, fruitless moon."
> *A Midsummer Night's Dream*
> William Shakespeare

Nigel rose even earlier than usual, in part because he hadn't slept well, in part because he wanted to avoid Allegra. He had resolved, somewhere in the depths of the long night, to avoid her as much as possible before the wedding. Afterward, he and Meg would help the baron marry her off very soon. Such was, he'd decided, the only way.

As to that ill-advised kiss, of that he would not think at all. He would not remember her warmth, her passion, nor his own explosive reaction to her touch. He would only remember the explosive nature of their every conversation.

Jamie was brushing an already immaculate Mercutio when Nigel entered the stables. No matter how early Nigel arose, Jamie was always there before him.

"Och, ye're up early, yer lordship. Too early. What ails ye, lad?" Jamie asked.

Nigel shook his head ruefully. Jamie knew him too well. Their friendship had become very strong and very important to him in the four years since they'd met, not long after

Charles's death.

"Let us just say that I thought it the better part of valor to—ah—begin my day a bit earlier," Nigel said cryptically.

But Jamie was no fool. His brow rose knowingly. "I met her yesterday, laddie."

"I see." Nigel sighed. "She is a complication I hadn't expected, I must own."

"Aye, the lass is a wee bit tenacious, is she no?"

"She spoke to you about—about my impending marriage?"

"Aye. Tried to enlist my aid, she did."

"Good God! I hope you didn't encourage her!"

"Are ye daft? I agree with ye, Nigel. Ye and Miss Caulfield will do verra well together."

"Thank you for that, Jamie. I shall be glad when the banns are read. Better still when the knot is tied. Allegra is a most irksome child; one never knows what she'll do next."

"A *child*, my lord? I dinna think so."

"A *bairn* then?" Nigel asked with a grin. Jamie shook his head. "Well, you will own that she's trouble."

"Aye, but engagin' for all that."

Nigel's face sobered. " 'Tis the engaging ones who are the most trouble, Jamie," he said pointedly.

A wave of pain washed over Jamie's eyes. Nigel had seen it before but had never learned its true source, despite all they'd been through together. "As ye say, my friend, 'tis the engagin' ones who are the most . . . difficult."

Jamie's face was remote as he saddled up Mercutio, and Nigel was pensive as he rode out.

The first time he'd seen Jamie he'd had only a fleeting glimpse of a large man with a red beard and piercing blue eyes. Had they never met again, Nigel would not have recalled that first encounter. But Jamie had, and months later would recount the story to Nigel. Nigel's carriage had incurred some difficulty and he and a friend were walking through a rather unsavory section of London's East End, intent on hailing a hackney coach. A ragged urchin had come barreling out of an alleyway, bumped into Nigel and neatly lifted his purse from his pocket. The child had run and Nigel's companion had yelled "thief!" and the two had set off in pursuit. A moment later they'd cornered the boy and Nigel's friend had been all for calling Bow Street. But Nigel had taken one look at the frightened boy, his clothes inadequate to the cool autumn weather, his small frame much too bony, and he'd bent down to the boy and asked what he meant to do with the money.

"Buy some medicine for me mum, Gov'nor," the child said between sobs, "and some food for the little ones. They ain't 'ad more than a bit o' gruel for three days."

And Nigel had emptied half the contents of his purse into the child's hand and did not bother admonishing him not to steal again. For, of course, he would, and soon.

Nigel's friend had been appalled; they'd rarely seen each other since.

A moment later Nigel had looked up and seen the large red-headed man staring at him from some ramshackle doorway. They had no communication, and did not meet again until that spring.

It had been a lonely road, a moonlit night, when Nigel's carriage was abruptly halted by the proverbial command, "Stand and deliver!" There were two highwaymen; his coachman opened fire. He'd reached for his own pistol and opened the coach door. Suddenly there was a smoking pistol at his head. He saw his coachman on the ground, blood oozing from him. The man holding the pistol to his temple whispered that he was next; Nigel heard the gun cock. And then suddenly the other man, still on horseback, called for his cohort to lower the gun. A shouting match ensued; the pistol swung toward the masked man on horseback. A shot rang out, whizzing by inches from Nigel's head, singeing his captor on the shoulder and lodging in the coach door. The gun was dropped from his temple and Nigel turned with new respect to the man now dismounting. He was a crack shot, and all that was visible beyond the mask were a shock of red hair and a red beard. Nigel felt the faint stirrings of memory but said not a word as his strange benefactor took his purse, counted out a hefty sum of gold coins to the villain cursing his bloody shoulder, and sent him on his way.

Next they saw to the coachman. He would survive, his attacker not nearly as good a shot as the red-headed man.

And then Nigel turned to that man and spoke one word. "Why?"

That was when Jamie smiled and removed his mask. "I'm never forgettin' a face," he said, and recounted the incident in the East End.

They introduced themselves and Nigel, amazed and grateful, had offered Jamie honest employment, which Jamie refused. But they had parted amicably, Nigel telling Jamie to call on him should he ever be in need of assistance.

Somehow Nigel was not surprised at the missive which arrived months later from Newgate prison. Jamie had been hauled in for killing a Bow Street runner.

"I've done some verra bad things, I dinna deny it, my lord," he said, "but murderin's no one of them."

Nigel believed him. He spoke for Jamie and the charges were dropped. This time Jamie MacIntyre accepted a position as groom in the Debenham stables. But Nigel soon found out that he had acquired more than a groom. For while Jamie was a genius with horses, he was also a genius with numbers, and he had a great talent for managing and arranging things. And though he would not leave the stables and become a steward, for he was a man made for the outdoors, he began to assume more and more responsibility. It was Jamie who apportioned rooms for guests, who made all of Nigel's travel arrangements, who oversaw purchases of new farming equipment. He also insisted on acting as bodyguard whenever Nigel left Debenham Court.

Nigel's brother had been dead less than a year. His father

had retreated further and further into himself, leaving the running of the estate to Nigel. And so Nigel and Jamie had been much in each other's company. Jamie was just four years Nigel's senior, and Nigel had discovered that they had a good deal in common. They shared a sense of humor and the pain of loss in their pasts. For Nigel it was the debacle with Gina, of which he spoke only briefly, and the fresh horror of Charles and Lucinda's deaths, about which he confided completely. For Jamie it was the loss of his family, scattered, murdered and starved in the wake of the evil clearances. Jamie spoke only sporadically of what was happening to his beloved Highlands, but over the years Nigel had once understood the tragedy. The clan chiefs, who had since fought to the death to protect their land and clansmen, were now evicting masses of those very tenants to make way for more profitable sheep.

Jamie's father had been a tacksman and cousin to the chieftain, but he'd been forced off the land right along with his subtenants. He did not go without a fight, and he was shot by a factor; his mother died of the cold that first homeless winter. Cousins had been forced onto the emigrant ships. Jamie rarely spoke of his family, and only once had he alluded to a wife. But Nigel knew that she, too, was gone.

And so he and Jamie had become friends, at a time when both had needed one. They had saved each other's life and felt responsible for one another. Jamie knew full well why Nigel meant to marry Meg, and he would support him. Nigel was done with pain and passion. Within the month he would be wed to Meg Caulfield, and Allegra could do naught to stop him.

Allegra had slept nary a wink all night. The storm outside had subsided, but her body had raged with unnamed emotions and her mind had churned.

She could not forget that kiss; she never would. Nigel's touch had made her blood pound throughout her body. His mouth had made her feel hot and weak all over. She hardly knew *what* had happened between them, but she recognized it as passion. And she knew instinctively that there was something wild and extraordinary about it; such was not always the way between men and women. And all of Nigel's attempts to deny it, and his hateful parting words last night, could not change that fact.

And then she thought of Meg. She did not feel guilty for having kissed Meg's betrothed. After all, she had not initiated the kiss. But she felt more strongly than ever that this marriage must not go forth. It was not just because of John Dalton. It was because of Nigel Hayves, and what Allegra had learned about him this night. He would terrify Meg, devour her with his passion. Meg's passion, Allegra was certain, was quiet, sweet in a way that Nigel would never appreciate. He would be bored within a month and go off to his mistresses. And Meg would be devastated.

Allegra simply could not allow it.

She found Meg at the morning room escritoire sometime after breakfast. Meg quickly covered the letter she was writing and Allegra smiled. She knew it was a letter to John. She suggested they stroll through the garden and Meg agreed, pocketing the missive as they left the room arm-in-arm.

In the sunlight Allegra could clearly see the dark circles under Meg's eyes, yet her sister reiterated her resolution to proceed with the wedding.

Her voice, however, was not so steady as it had been a few days ago. Allegra pressed her, and as they ambled toward the rose garden Meg finally confided, "It is only — oh, Allegra, I do so want to do the right thing. But as the days pass and Sunday approaches and I know the banns will be read, I — I get a sick feeling in the pit of my stomach. And I think of never seeing John again, and I remember the look on his face when he left me yesterday—oh, dear God, Allegra, I do not know if I have the strength!"

Meg somehow held her tears in check, but Allegra heard the desperation in her sister's voice, and her resolve strengthened. Somehow she must stop this marriage.

Kingston, Nigel's valet, was divesting him of his riding clothes when Jamie entered his chambers bearing a missive. Kingston sniffed. He resented the intrusion, just as he resented the presence of "that Highlander" in the earl's life. But Kingston was as much a genius with cravats and boots and superfine coats as Jamie was with everything else, and so Kingston was kept on.

The missive, Nigel learned when he was properly attired and both men had retired, was from the Viscount Creeve. What the devil did Creeve want? Nigel frowned. He did not at all care for the man, would prefer to have naught to do with him.

Nigel read the letter quickly, frowning more deeply. It concerned the one unfortunate, tenuous connection which he and the viscount had. Creeve's family seat was in Dorset, not far from Cliff House. Cliff House belonged to Nigel, had been his family's summer home for all the years of his childhood. He'd not been there in years and knew the house and surrounding land had fallen into disrepair. The house, perched on a cliff overlooking the English Channel, had once been beautiful and someday Nigel meant to restore it.

Creeve asked that Nigel grant permission for the Revenue Officers to patrol the beach at Cliff House if they deemed it necessary in the fight against smugglers. It seemed a simple enough request, especially after the embarrassment Creeve had suffered some months before when it was discovered that a large smuggling ring was using the beach of Creeve Hall as its base of operation. Creeve, enraged, had become zealous in his attempts to help catch the smugglers.

And yet, something did not seem quite right. There had always been an aura of unpleasantness, even evil, about the man. And Nigel could not quite comprehend why Creeve spent so much time in London if he were really so interested in catching Dorset smugglers.

And then, of course, there was the matter of Roger, Nigel's childhood friend. Thoughts of smuggling, and Creeve, invariably brought his mind round to Roger.

Nigel rose abruptly to pour himself a glass of brandy, then sank down into a wing chair. Roger, the son of an upstairs maid and a father unnamed, had been part of Nigel's summers at Cliff House as far back as he could remember. It was only once they'd reached manhood that Roger's more than fleeting resemblance to Creeve had become noticeable, but as Roger had been rather elusive these last few years, it had not been much remarked upon. Roger himself had never identified his father, but had once, while in his cups, vowed vengeance upon the man who'd hurt his mother. The last time Nigel had seen Roger was two years ago, just after his own father's death. Nigel had run Roger to ground in a ramshackle Dorset alehouse known to be a smuggling lair. As usual, Roger had refused all offers of assistance, been evasive about his life, and they had parted amicably.

Since then Nigel had heard rumors that he'd gone to America, and nothing more. But now Creeve had written about the Revenue and Nigel wondered once again, where was Roger?

With a great deal of reluctance, Nigel answered Creeve in the affirmative. He really had little choice. Whatever his feelings about smuggling, Creeve, or Roger, he could not very well deny the Revenue access to his land. And yet he did not like it.

By dinner time the earl had still not franked the letter to Creeve. He could not shake the niggling feeling that he had ought to attempt to communicate with Roger as well. Exactly how to do this eluded him, however. Instead his mind kept wandering back to the prickly problem of the Caulfield sisters, in particular the prickly sister. Though he could not resolve what to do about Roger, he *did* resolve to avoid Allegra by the light of the moon. It seemed the most prudent course.

As such he retired straightaway after dinner and spent a most unrestful night. He fell asleep near dawn and arose late enough to encounter Allegra in the breakfast parlor. The baron was there as well, apparently having just come in from riding.

Allegra's simple blue-gray dress made her look absurdly young on the one hand, yet hugged her figure in a manner all too mature on the other. She did not look as if she'd slept any better than Nigel, and that fact made him most uneasy. For he did not suppose that she had tossed and turned restlessly in her bed, but rather that she had paced the floors, trying to dream up ways to thwart him.

Well, she would not succeed. All of her efforts to enlist aid thus far had failed, and she was running out of time. It was, thankfully, already Thursday. Once the banns were read on Sunday, once the betrothal was made public, even Allegra Caulfield would have to admit defeat. He would do well, Nigel decided, to begin treating her like the little sister she would become.

After the initial greetings he filled his plate from the sideboard and took a seat next to the baron, across from Allegra.

"I trust you slept well, Allegra," the earl said in a condescending tone that would have set Allegra's teeth on edge had she not seen the dark circles under his eyes. Somehow that dissipated all her pique.

"Alas, I cannot say that I did, Nigel." She began buttering a blueberry muffin. "And I am persuaded neither did you. There is no use pretending otherwise." She caught a flash of temper in his eyes and heard Papa cough.

But whatever turn the conversation may have taken was abruptly halted in the next moment.

"Morning, Caulfield. Are you there?" called the husky female voice from outside in the garden. Mrs. Bridgebane, Allegra realized, and her eyes flew to Papa's.

"It's that Bridgebane woman. Come to plague me again. While we're at table, as usual," Papa grumbled. "She's probably here to have a look at you, Nigel." One of Nigel's devilish brows lifted. "Damned meddlesome tattlemonger," Papa muttered.

"Now, Papa," Allegra put in, "she is not all that bad. I am persuaded she is merely lonely, not at all malicious and—"

"The fact remains," Papa interrupted, addressing himself to Nigel, "that the parish is in no need of a newspaper with that woman around. Spreads news faster than any town crier. Trompin' about the countryside with that mongrel of hers, Wellington, she calls him, as if he were chaperon enough—"

"I daresay she hardly needs a chaperon to come here, Papa. You have two grown daughters, after all, and 'tis not as though she's just out of the schoolroom."

As if to underscore Allegra's words, Nigel saw a solidly built woman of indeterminate years, wearing a nondescript tweed dress, come trudging up to the half-open French doors. A large, long-haired dog of indeterminate parentage panted at her heels. The woman's tousled gray and brown hair was the same color as the dog's coat, Nigel noted in some amusement. She could never have been called beautiful, with her hawklike nose and dark ferret eyes, but she was rather handsome looking in the way that only older women could be.

"Come in, Mrs. Bridgebane," the baron said rather grudgingly, and quite unnecessarily, for the lady was already stepping over the threshold.

"Good morning to you, Caulfield, Allegra," she said,

making a feeble attempt to pat her wiry hair into place. The mongrel had the good manners to remain out-of-doors. Nigel and the baron rose and a footman held out a chair for the lady. "Oh, you have company!" Mrs. Bridgebane exclaimed as she took her seat. She looked at Nigel for all the world as if she were genuinely surprised.

Caulfield made the introductions. Mrs. Bridgebane regarded Nigel with her dark eyes alive with interest. "And what brings you to South Devon?" she asked in her deep, husky voice.

The baron snorted. Nigel's eyes met Allegra's and found them dancing with amusement. He could not help returning the look.

"Debenham is Meg's betrothed, Mrs. Bridgebane, as you well know," the baron drawled.

"Oh, how lovely! Well, then, allow me to wish you happy, Lord Debenham," she responded, then frowned. "Oh, but I thought Meg and Joh—well, that is nothing to the point. I daresay I must be mistaken."

The baron, Nigel noted, turned several shades of red and purple. He himself wanted to strangle the woman, but Allegra seemed to be stifling a giggle.

"Yes, you are mistaken," Nigel said icily to Mrs. Bridgebane, but his eyes looked daggers at Allegra.

She attempted a look of bland innocence but could not suppress the imp in her eyes. He felt his annoyance grow and a glance at Mrs. Bridgebane told him she was well aware of all the undercurrents. Damn the woman!

"Have some coffee, Mrs. Bridgebane," Caulfield offered. It was more a command than a suggestion, but the lady graciously accepted.

She added cream and two lumps of sugar to her cup and all was blessedly silent as she sipped. She broke the silence moments later.

"And when is the wedding?" she asked politely. Those dark ferret eyes betrayed more than polite interest, however.

60

"The banns will be read Sunday," Nigel began, "and then in a couple of—"

"Four weeks after the ba—" Allegra put in.

"Two," Nigel interrupted ruthlessly. Allegra glared at him. The Bridgebane woman barely contained her glee. She drained her cup.

"Excellent coffee, Caulfield," she remarked. "I always say so. I do wish your cook would impart the secret to mine. Oh, but that reminds me of my errand. I've come to invite you to luncheon. All of you, and Meg as well, of course. My cook is busy whipping up his best syllabub. We'll be a small number at table. Just us, you must know. Oh, and the vicar will be there. I'm persuaded we'll all be able to have such a comfortable cose!" she gushed ingenuously, but her sharp eyes gave her away. Nigel had the unpleasant sense of a spider spinning her web.

The baron, thank God, was of like mind. "Mrs. Bridgebane, I really don't think—"

"Oh, but we'd love to come," Allegra interjected. "After all, we have no plans for luncheon, Papa. And you know how you simply adore syllabub!"

Nigel contemplated Allegra's very dainty neck and what it would be like to put his hands on it. And squeeze.

Quite satisfied, Mrs. Bridgebane named a time and bid a polite good day to the table in general. But instead of taking her leave, having done sufficient damage, she turned to the baron. "Care to continue our game?"

"Oh, I suppose so," Caulfield replied gruffly, and rather to Nigel's amazement he escorted her from the room. Wellington gave a single bark and trotted off, presumably following his mistress.

"Game?" Nigel could not help inquiring, tabling his annoyance for the moment.

"Chess," Allegra responded.

"Chess? That woman plays chess?"

"Oh, yes. I daresay it suits her very well." Allegra

sounded too damned smug but a moment's reflection told him she might be right. Chess required intricate plotting and the laying of traps. It was obvious the Bridgebane woman was good at both.

"Perhaps," he conceded. "But your father cannot abide the woman."

Allegra's lips twitched. Nigel was uncomfortably reminded of that intriguing upper lip with no indentation. "So he says. But I've always suspected part of that was merely bluster. Besides, she's the only one in the entire parish who can give him a decent game."

"Ah, I see. You do not play chess, Allegra?"

"Oh, no. I haven't patience for it. And I'm far too impulsive."

That, he was very much afraid, was all too true.

Meg sat very tensely beside Allegra as they rode in the carriage to Oak Knoll Cottage, Mrs. Bridgebane's two-story, timber-framed residence. Meg, she knew, was ambivalent about the prospect of luncheon with John. Papa looked annoyed and Nigel's face was rigid and shuttered.

John, when they had arrived and been ushered inside, looked decidedly uncomfortable. Allegra had the feeling he'd been informed of their inclusion in this luncheon party but moments ago. He and Nigel shook hands with cautious civility as they were introduced for the first time. Mrs. Bridgebane wasted little time with preliminaries and shortly ushered them into the dining room.

She sat Papa at the foot of the table, across from her. To her right she placed Nigel, with Meg next to him. "One would never sit a married couple together, of course," Mrs. Bridgebane prattled, "but with a betrothed pair 'tis quite different, is it not? Always smelling of springtime and flowers, are they not?"

Complete silence greeted this pronouncement as everyone

dutifully took his seat. Allegra was placed to Papa's left, with the vicar to her right. Mrs. Bridgebane's seating arrangement meant that Meg and John sat diagonally across from each other, with Allegra and Nigel forming the opposite ends of an imaginary "X." The vicar said little and tried to concentrate on his food as the first course of fish soup a la russe and boiled salmon was served. But his eyes kept straying, inevitably, to Meg. Allegra thought her sister looked a perfect confection in a mint green dress with a white lace underskirt. There was hunger in John's eyes as he regarded her.

Allegra was pleased to note that Nigel was well aware of that fact. He did not have the luxury of attending to his soup or fish in silence, however, for Mrs. Bridgebane addressed herself to him, asking when he'd arrived, where he'd come from, and what his principal seat looked like. He answered each query as politely and perfunctorily as possible. And then the second remove of braised calves liver and roast chicken garnished with fresh vegetables and truffles was served. Mrs. Bridgebane leaned forward, elbows on the table, her eyes narrowing. Allegra had seen that look before. Nigel was not going to be best pleased.

"I had no idea you and the vicar had not yet met. I feel honored to have been the one to introduce you," she said effusively. "And you are performing the marriage ceremony, are you not, Mr. Dalton?"

"Yes," John answered tightly. Allegra saw his hand clench his wine goblet. She sincerely hoped Mrs. Bridgebane knew what she was doing.

"My, my, and only two weeks after the banns are read. How eager you are, Lord Debenham!" the lady exclaimed. Nigel nearly choked on his calves liver. " 'Tis a great joy, is it not, Caulfield, to see young people enter the wedded state with such alacrity!"

Nigel carefully chewed his mouthful of liver. The baron's fork hit his plate with a clatter.

"Chicken's dry, Mrs. Bridgebane," the baron declared. "But the calves liver is nice enough. I wouldn't mind a bit more."

Mrs. Bridgebane signaled a footman to serve the baron and then silently dismissed him. Unfortunately, she was not to be diverted. "And have you purchased your bride clothes yet, Meg?" she asked.

"No, not yet," Meg said in a small voice.

"I mean to take Meg to London soon after we are wed and refurbish her wardrobe there," Nigel interjected smoothly.

Mrs. Bridgebane smiled slyly. It was not a pretty smile. "How nice for you, Meg. I am persuaded you will simply *adore* London. All the bustle, the crowds, the excitement!"

Meg tried to smile. Nigel had a feeling she would not care for London at all. And if their hostess knew that as well, why was she being deliberately cruel? He glanced about the table. The baron was glowering at Mrs. Bridgebane, Dalton had barely eaten and Allegra . . . Allegra was gazing with a speculative, almost bemused look at their hostess. Blast the chit; she was enjoying herself! The look in her brown eyes told him her brain was churning. If he did not know the train of her thoughts, he would have said she looked most engaging, a small smile playing about her intriguing lips, her violet crepe round dress with its high waist emphasizing her very feminine charms. The dress was simple but quite pretty, albeit not in the first stare of fashion. It presented quite a contrast to Meg's frothy lace-trimmed dress. Their hair, too, was a study in contrasts. Meg's blond locks were pulled into a neat topknot, while Allegra's short hair framed her face in a riot of curls. He wondered if she'd even taken a brush to it. Impatient, she'd called herself; he could not imagine her sitting overlong at her toilette.

In that moment, as if she'd just become aware of his scrutiny, her gaze met his. But she did not blush, as might be expected of a proper young lady who discovers herself the object of a gentleman's gaze. Instead her lips curled and those brown eyes sparkled with challenge.

"Oh, but Meg much prefers the quiet of the country. Is that not so, Meg?" Allegra inquired solicitously.

Meg took a moment before replying. "Well, in truth, I *have* always enjoyed my country life. But I have never been to London, after all. Perhaps I shall enjoy it when my lord takes me there."

Dalton looked decidedly grim. Nigel felt sorry for the fellow, but there was naught to be done. They were all, for the moment, caught in the Bridgebane woman's web.

"I am persuaded you shall have a splendid time, Meg," Nigel said. "And if you do not, well, we needn't stay long. I have several other residences, after all. And I do spend a great deal of time at my principal seat in Suffolk. I am much intrigued with new agricultural techniques, you must know." There, Nigel thought, casting a subtly smug look toward Allegra, he'd routed her quite thoroughly.

Leonora Bridgebane resolutely repressed a chuckle and gave the signal for the syllabub to be served. She was enjoying herself hugely. From her vantage point at the head of the table she could see all manner of interesting cross currents, many more, in fact, than she'd imagined when she'd planned her seating arrangement. Dear Meg and the vicar were trying very hard to be discreet about the looks they cast each other. Of course they failed miserably.

Leonora had been appalled to hear from her cook, whose niece was upstairs maid at Caulfield Manor, that Meg was to marry the Earl of Debenham. Leonora had been aware for some time of the attachment between Meg and John Dalton; she'd come upon them in the gardens often enough. Truth to tell, there were few secrets in this part of Devon of which Leonora was not aware. But contrary to common belief, she was not an incessant gossip. She collected information but passed it on only when she wished to, because it amused her to do so. She had kept silent about Meg and the vicar, waiting upon events. But now, she'd decided days ago, was not the time to remain silent. She could not approach the baron directly, of course. It was not at all her place. And besides, he was as bullheaded as any man and had to be handled carefully.

Hence this little luncheon party, an attempt to shake things up a bit. But even for Leonora the afternoon held a few surprises. Oh, she'd had an inkling this morning, and still it was purely speculation, but how perfectly delicious to sit here and watch the silent, rather intense communication between Allegra and the earl. He was looking quite pleased with himself just now, and Allegra's brown eyes glittered dangerously. And just moments ago it was Debenham looking at daggers drawn. Such fire across Leonora's very luncheon table! It did set one to wondering . . .

And what was wrong with Caulfield, to allow his eldest daughter to be so mismatched? Oh, she supposed he needed the funds such an alliance would bring, but money, after all, was not everything. Leonora had little enough herself, from her late husband, but still she contrived to amuse herself.

Meg's voice interrupted her reverie. "I am persuaded that must be very interesting, my lord," she said dutifully. Poor dear. She did not sound at all convinced.

"Yes, I am certain it must be," put in the vicar bracingly. "Have you been experimenting with new farming methods, my lord?"

"Yes, I've been gradually converting from rye to wheat production, as Coke has been doing in Norfolk. And I've been working on improving breeding techniques for my cattle and sheep."

"Breeding techniques! How fascinating, my lord," Allegra exclaimed. "I own you must be quite an expert by now."

Debenham's eyes bulged with fury. Caulfield spluttered into his wineglass. Heavens! The child could not realize what she was saying! Leonora deftly shifted the subject.

It had been a long day. Luncheon had been a debacle, and later on Nigel had engaged in a rather strained conversation with Meg. Her fear of him was becoming increasingly obvious.

In the afternoon he had retired to the sitting room adjoining his chamber to ponder the problem of Roger. In the end he wrote to Mrs. Crowley, the ancient housekeeper still at Cliff House, asking her to forward the enclosed letter to Roger if she possibly could. It was a slim chance, but he had to take it. Occasionally in the past Roger had communicated with her. The letter to Roger took some time, for it had to be carefully worded. Nigel had no idea what Roger was up to, if anything, but he could not let his friend fall into a trap, if such it was.

The missive he finally composed began with warm greetings and then relayed news of Deben Court. Nigel did not mention his impending nuptials, for reasons he did not care to think about.

Only at the end did he casually mention Creeve's request. "I am loathe to have the Revenue overrun my land, but I cannot very well refuse. I fail to apprehend what Creeve thinks to find at Cliff House, but then I cannot begin to fathom the motives of a man of his stamp."

And that was all. If the subtle warning applied to Roger, he would heed it and understand the spirit in which it was given. If it did not apply, then the letter was simply a gesture of friendship. Of course, if Mrs. Crowley could not pass the missive on . . . He cursed softly, but knew that for the present, at the least, he had done what he could.

Now, in the dark of night, Nigel told himself that it was thoughts of Roger, and no one else, keeping him awake. He shrugged into his dressing gown and went out onto his terrace. He needed the air. But the moonlight poured over him and he could not help but think of Allegra and their encounter two nights ago. Well, there would be no repeat of

67

that. She would not dare come to the lower terrace again, and even if she did, he would not be down there. She might be naive or foolish, or even—what was her word—curious. But he was none of those things; he had seen too much.

Allegra had found herself restless all afternoon and was no less so now that the household had settled itself down to sleep. Suddenly she felt the overwhelming urge to be away from the house. Recalling her other nocturnal encounters with Nigel, she decided to shed her nightgown and to dress.

She tiptoed out of the house and wandered aimlessly to the first of the rear gardens, the one closest to the house. She inhaled the fragrance of roses and fuchsias and tilted her head up to the moon. She'd always loved the gardens, especially at night, and had always thought the moon hid delightful mysteries. But tonight she took no pleasure in her surroundings. The garden merely seemed overgrown, and the moon cold. It held no answers for her.

She sighed and let her eyes drift over the house. And that was when she saw him, standing on his terrace. She could see him clearly, his hands in the pockets of his dressing gown, his naked, well-matted chest visible between its folds. Warmth coursed over her at the memory of his kiss. But then she remembered his odious parting words that night, and she suddenly felt cold.

And then her eyes met his, across the expanse of greenery, and despair washed over her. His expression was stony, his eyes cold and calculating. So must he be in his very soul, she thought, cold and devoid of emotion. But no, she had seen moments of warmth. She supposed they must be few and far between. Else how could he contemplate this marriage? And how could he kiss her as he had and then act as if it had never happened?

She lowered her eyes and turned away from him, wrapping her arms about herself. And then, without once looking back at the terrace, she slowly returned to the house.

Nigel watched Allegra walk silently back. He ran his hand jaggedly through his hair and sighed inwardly. And then he found himself staring out at the moon. It stood alone in a cloudy sky devoid of stars. It looked bleak and cold, the way Nigel felt.

Chapter Four

"It were an easy leap, to pluck bright honour from the pale-faced moon."

I Henry IV
William Shakespeare

It was Friday morning. The reading of the banns was only two days away and still Allegra had no notion of how to prevent it. Mrs. Bridgebane's luncheon yesterday seemed to have done nothing more than put everyone on edge. Nigel avoided Allegra, which, she told herself, was all to the good. When they met at luncheon he said little to her, but his eyes eloquently bespoke his anger.

She supposed she had expected as much, after yesterday. But still, she was finding it increasingly uncomfortable to be the object of that harsh look in Nigel's eyes.

Damn and blast it all! Nigel cursed as he ruined yet another pristine white cravat. How the devil had that Bridgebane woman contrived to invite herself to dinner? At least, that was how the baron had explained it to Nigel.

Mrs. Bridgebane was already in the Green Salon sipping sherry when Nigel made his appearance one half hour before the appointed dinner hour. She wore a satin gown of a garish peacock blue that somehow did not look as ghastly on her solid frame as it ought to have done. She and Caulfield had their heads together and suddenly the baron threw back his head and laughed. Nigel blinked in astonishment. If she had indeed invited herself, the baron seemed not at all averse to her company.

Bemused, he turned his gaze to Allegra. She smiled conspiratorially, and he decided she looked like some elf of the forest in a dark green gown, her nut-brown locks framing her gamin face. The gown, he decided, was too low cut, revealing as it did a tantalizing glimpse of bosom. He supposed Meg's gown of last night had been no different, but somehow on Allegra it looked much more improper.

He greeted everyone briefly and as Caulfield and Mrs. Bridgebane seemed inclined to resume their discourse, he strolled to Allegra. He forced himself to keep his eyes on her face, despite their inclination to sweep lower.

A footman handed him a glass of sherry. "Good evening, Allegra," he said evenly. "Your father is a gracious host."

The conspiratorial smile deepened. "Oh, they've been sparring and amusing each other for years. She is not a bad sort, really, just—"

"Just inclined to meddle where she doesn't belong?" he taunted.

Her little chin jutted out defiantly. "I do not believe she ever means anyone a harm."

He regarded her in patent disbelief but forbore to respond to that, instead asking abruptly, "Where is your sister?"

Allegra met his eyes over the rim of her glass. "She has the headache, Nigel. Poor dear, she hasn't been at all the thing of late."

Nigel raised a brow. "She seemed right enough this afternoon. She was out visiting several tenants, I believe."

"Yes, she does so enjoy that. She and John often—well,

that doesn't signify." Allegra took a sip of her sherry, her brown eyes too damned wide and innocent looking. "I daresay she felt the headache coming on and thought dinner, and the . . . company, might prove too—ah—strenuous for her."

Somehow Meg did not seem the sort to be afflicted overmuch with headaches, and he could not squelch the notion that her absence tonight was rather cowardly. Unbidden there rose the thought that Allegra would never—

"Does she often have the headache?" he asked.

Those oh-so-innocent eyes grew round as she shook her head in denial. "Oh, no, Nigel. Only lately."

"I wonder why?" Mrs. Bridgebane's voice intruded. Nigel's brows snapped together. He had not realized that she and Caulfield had been ambling toward them. "Caulfield, perhaps you'd better have the doctor for her," the lady continued, and then tilted her slightly disheveled head of wiry gray and brown hair. "On second thought, perhaps it is an affliction of a different sort, some trouble of the spirit. She may have need of wise counsel, Caulfield. In such a case it is a man of the cloth who can best provide surcease. Yes, that will answer," she went on brightly. "Do have John Dalton call upon her. I am persuaded his presence will be a great comfort to her."

The baron looked apoplectic. Thankfully, the butler arrived in that moment to announce dinner. Allegra, Nigel noted, was having a difficult time suppressing a giggle, and collapsed into a paroxysm of coughing to hide it.

As he took her arm to lead her into dinner, he resisted the urge to squeeze the lovely, bare, slender white arm a bit too hard. And squelched the thought that said arm felt altogether too warm and soft and silky under his hand.

Meg was crying. Allegra could hear her clearly from the next room. The rest of the house was silent. When Allegra and Nigel had bid their separate good nights to the company, Papa and Mrs. Bridgebane had been just settling down to a continuation of their eternal chess game. By now Allegra supposed Mrs. Bridgebane had long since departed. Even the last of the servants had gone to bed, for the house had that feeling of having settled down for the night.

As usual of late, Allegra was restless. She went to the open window and peered out. It was another hot, still, moonlit night. She found herself longing for another storm; it, at the least, would mirror her feelings.

There was movement in the rose garden. It took a moment to realize that it was Nigel, his buff waistcoat with its gold buttons clearly reflected in the moonlight. He was still wearing his dinner clothes, although he had discarded his cravat. She remembered how he had looked tonight at dinner, his black coat stretched to perfection across his broad shoulders, his dark silky hair gleaming in the candlelight. And his eyes, green and deep and too often regarding her with an intensity that made her squirm inwardly. She recalled, too, the wave of heat that had coursed over her when he'd taken her arm. It had not been at all unpleasant, nor had the strange flutter in her stomach been each time his eyes swept over her person. No, not at all unpleasant, and yet she knew such feelings must be highly improper, especially engendered by the man who was determined to become her brother!

She could not see his face, for he had turned away, but there was tension in his stance. She thought it all to the good that he appeared perturbed. But he was a stubborn man and she knew it would take something drastic to shake him from his course, especially when he deemed it an honorable one.

It was then that the idea came to her. She would make it a matter of honor! She let the plan take shape in her mind. That little voice at the back of her head warned her that it was a shocking notion, a most drastic measure. But she silenced the voice, for this seemed the only hope. It was an impulse, like so many others she'd had, and she determined to see it though.

And just as she'd rushed headlong to little Marcus's rescue, so she donned her wrapper and slippers and rushed headlong, albeit silently, down the stairs. It was not a child nor a servant girl she was going to rescue this time, but her sister. And, she told herself, Nigel as well. For of a certain he would be no more happy than Meg in such a misalliance.

She knew very little of the business of seduction, Allegra thought frantically as she rounded the outer corner of the house and proceeded to the rear gardens. Her instincts told her, from their previous nocturnal encounters, that Nigel desired her. Still he thought he could keep away from her, from any woman, in the name of honor. Somehow, she must show him, once and for all, that he could not. Then surely as a man of honor he would break the betrothal!

He had wandered a little away from the rose garden, and stood now with one hand against the sturdy trunk of an old oak, his foot propped on a low, fat branch that almost ran parallel to the ground. She was yards away from him, hidden from his view. He had, she realized, removed his coat and slung it across the tree trunk. His shirtsleeves were rolled to his elbows. She took a deep breath, noting the play of moonlight across his broad shoulders, noting the strength of his forearms. Just so had she seen him that first night. Perhaps she oughtn't—no! This was her only hope.

She came upon him from the side. He turned his head abruptly when she was but ten feet away. "Allegra! What the devil are you doing here?" he demanded, his eyes flashing.

"Oh, the same thing as you, I should imagine," she replied with a great deal more nonchalance than she felt. "I could not sleep."

He lowered his foot to the ground and turned to face her. "I see. And in all the vast expanse of gardens here, this was

74

the only place you could think to come," he drawled mockingly. She saw him start to take a step forward, then check himself. "And for pity sakes, Allegra, you are not even dressed! Have we not been through this before?"

She came slowly toward him. "Yes, Nigel, but I was already abed, you see," she said softly, determined to remain calm. She stood just two feet from him now. His body seemed even more rigid than before. Only his head moved, following his eyes as they made a very slow, unnerving tour of her. She had left her wrapper open and she felt as if his gaze would bore right through the thin ecru lawn of her nightdress.

Well, she told herself staunchly, this was what she wanted, was it not? At the least, it seemed a beginning. But now that she was here she hadn't the foggiest notion how to go on. He had kissed her once before, on the terrace, but she could not now remember how it had started. And that kiss had not been enough to dissuade him from marrying her sister. Perhaps it had not gone on long enough, or perhaps they had ought to do something else besides. Oh, dear! She really was most inconveniently ignorant of such matters.

He put his hands to his hips. The movement stretched his waistcoat tautly across his chest. And then her eyes fell lower, to where his gray evening britches fit so tightly, accentuating every ripple in his strong, hard thighs. She swallowed hard and forced her eyes upward. Without his cravat his shirt fell open, revealing a triangular matte of dark hair. She had occasionally seen one of the stableboys, or the blacksmith, working without a shirt, but none had chests quite so broad, nor hair so dark. And never before had she felt the urge to reach up and touch . . . She nibbled on her lip and gazed up at Nigel speculatively.

It was that elfin look, he decided, more than her very presence here, more than the way she looked in that flimsy nightdress, that was his undoing. He ought to turn away and leave, but he couldn't. He ought to order *her* to leave, but she wouldn't. "What the deuce are you thinking, Allegra?" he demanded suspiciously.

When she spoke her voice was suddenly hoarse. "A man is so different from a woman, Nigel," she said in wonder, her eyes sweeping over his torso in such a way as to make him feel positively naked. "And you are very different from most men, I think."

Hellfire! It wasn't fair. He hadn't even touched her and already his body was betraying him. Her hand came slowly up toward his chest. What the devil was she about? If he didn't know better he'd have thought she'd come out here deliberately, to seduce him. As it was, he surmised she simply meant to provoke him.

And damn her, she was succeeding! Standing here before him in nothing but moonlight and scant deshabille, her gamin face tilted up just so, her perfectly rounded breasts protruding enticingly from under the single layer of thin lawn. Blast it all! He was growing more heated by the minute.

And now she was going to touch him! He could not at this moment answer for the consequences if she did. Already the mere thought of her little hand on him was doing things to his body that he hoped to God she would not notice.

"No, Allegra," he growled, and caught the small hand midair. He pushed it down but the maneuver brought her stumbling into his chest. They stared at each other and he realized they were both breathing erratically. He felt the heat of her through the fabric of their clothes. He felt enveloped by her scent, the sweet, fresh scent of flowers in springtime. Her lips were slightly parted, her dark eyes round. God help him, but he wanted her! She was an irksome chit, nowhere near as beautiful as her sister, but he wanted her.

He could not have her. No matter how much—damn her

for putting him through this! How dare she come out here to entice him so, however unwittingly!

"Damn you!" he exploded, his hands sliding to her shoulders, grasping them tightly. "Have I not told you not to go about in such a state? Have I not?" He began shaking her, his fury, fueled by his frustration, mounting with each word. "Why the devil can you not stay abed where you belong?"

"N-Nigel," she stammered, her head fairly snapping back and forth, "I—"

"Why, Allegra? Tell me why, dammit!" he raged, unable to stop himself.

"Y-You are hurting me, Nigel," she whimpered. It was the tears in her eyes, rather than her words, that brought him up short.

"Oh, God," he groaned, relaxing his grip, the harsh pressure of his hands becoming a caress. Whatever was wrong with him, to hurt her so?

She stared at him out of big, bewildered brown eyes, moist with unshed tears. Hellfire! He did not even know himself anymore.

"Damn you, Allegra," he cursed hoarsely. "What have you done to me?"

She opened her mouth to speak and he ground his mouth down onto hers. With one hand he cupped her nape; the other held her fast around her back. She stiffened and pressed her lips closed.

Fury and pent-up desire merged within him. She had come here and he had got to taste her. There was no room for rational thought. He thrust his tongue between her lips and forced her mouth open. His hand began to move up and down her back. He lost all sense of time, only knew that at some point her body softened, her mouth opened willingly. He tasted her sweetness and thought he would go mad with wanting all of her. He could not get enough, not this way, standing up. The low, horizontal branch of the old oak was just behind him, and with no thought at all he sat down, pulling her onto his lap and bracing himself against the trunk. His mouth devoured hers. Her hand crept up to his chest. His skin was on fire. His body throbbed. His hand caressed her back and moved to her hips.

Allegra knew she had lost control of the situation long since. She did not know who was seducing whom, only that she did not want him to stop. He was taking from her mouth everything she had to give, and she wanted to give more. His large hand stroked her hips and down her leg. She wriggled to accommodate him. There was no thought left in her, only the most intense explosions of pleasure and some elusive sense that she was exactly where she belonged.

Nigel heard a heavy, panting sound and could not tell if it came from himself or Allegra. It was not until moments later, when it was much too late, that he realized it was neither of them. It was Wellington, that mangy mongrel of Mrs. Bridgebane's.

At first the voices, still far away, barely penetrated his consciousness. He was aware only of Allegra's leg, pressing against him, her mouth warm and wet under his.

"I do not know, Caulfield, but surely he heard *something*. Wellington would not set up a riot and a rumpus for naught."

"Mrs. Bridgebane, that mongrel wouldn't know a hedgehog from a poacher if it—"

"Now, Caulfield, you—oh! Oh, my heavens! 'Tis his lordship and—one of the maids! I—oh, dear God! Caulfield!" Mrs. Bridgebane cried out. " 'Tis not a maid with Debenham, 'tis *Allegra!*"

And *that* was when Nigel finally came to his senses. For only in that last, fateful moment had that voice, and the words, become clear to him. He yanked his mouth from Allegra's and in one lithe move twisted and slid to his feet, taking Allegra with him. He held on to her to keep her from falling, but she stumbled against him anyway, her hand going to his chest, and the picture they must have presented sent Mrs. Bridgebane wailing anew. The baron came up from behind her, his face mottled with fury.

"Debenham! Allegra!!" he exploded and seemed too shocked to say more. Wellington was barking and jumping and wagging his tail furiously. He'd found his quarry and was obviously proud of himself.

Nigel righted Allegra and separated himself from her, grabbing hastily for his coat. But he knew that it was a futile gesture at best. He realized with chagrin that several buttons of his shirt were undone, as was the drawstring lace at Allegra's throat. Good God, when had all that happened? And what would have transpired had they not been interrupted? Hellfire! How had he let this happen?

Mrs. Bridgebane and Caulfield had taken in every detail of their appearance. Allegra belatedly sashed her dressing gown, not that it helped a whit. Caulfield looked ready to draw swords and Mrs. Bridgebane clutched a hand to her breast. "Such—such goings on I never thought to see!" she exclaimed.

"That's enough, Mrs. Bridgebane!" the baron finally barked. Amazingly, the Bridgebane woman closed her mouth.

Caulfield looked thunderous, a vein throbbing at his silver temple. Allegra seemed to be shrinking behind Nigel, trying to make herself invisible. Nevertheless, the baron raked them both with merciless eyes. Mrs. Bridgebane remained silent. Nigel knew he had got to say something, but for the life of him he could not think what.

Resolutely, he stepped forward. "Caulfield, I—"

"I should call you out for this, Debenham," Caulfield growled in an undertone, his fists clenched at his sides. He was visibly trying to control himself. "I will see you in my study in one half hour," he commanded after a moment. "And you, Allegra, are to go to your chambers *and stay there! Now!*" And then with a last baleful look at Nigel and his daughter, the baron led Mrs. Bridgebane and her mongrel away.

The baron clearly expected Nigel and Allegra to follow straightaway, but neither of them moved.

"Bloody hell," Nigel muttered as soon as the others were out of earshot. He whirled around to look at Allegra, but she refused to meet his eyes. And it was only then, as he stared at her bent head, that understanding dawned. And with it came a rapidly mounting fury. She had planned it, every bit of it; there was no other explanation. The dressing gown flapping open, the little hand fluttering up to his chest . . . Oh, yes, she'd planned it, knowing that Mrs. Bridgebane, the county crier, was here.

"Look at me, Allegra," he demanded.

Allegra gulped but could not raise her eyes. She did not know if her heart was pounding so from the shock of being discovered or from the extraordinary sensations that she'd felt just minutes ago. Wondrous, hot, pulsing sensations! Who had ever thought that a man's lips, his hands, were capable of such magic?

He was so strong, she thought, so different from a woman. But now he was furious, and whatever magic warmth he had created moments ago had been replaced by the icy chill of his disfavor.

"Look at me, dammit! 'Tis a little late to play the demure maiden," he snapped, and slowly, she met his eyes.

Somehow she was not prepared for what she saw there. His eyes were narrowed to thin shards of green glass. She had expected his anger, but not the pure hatred with which his eyes impaled her.

"Why?" he demanded. She swallowed but could not speak.

"Why?" he repeated from between clenched teeth as he towered over her.

When she found her voice it was weak; she could not seem to speak above a whisper. "You must believe that I did not mean for this to happen. I did not know that Mrs. Bridgebane—"

"Spare me the Banbury tale, Allegra," he cut in bitterly. "You came out here clad in the flimsiest of nightclothes, knowing I was here, knowing full well—"

"I—I meant it all for the best, Nigel. I did not expect to be discovered. I only wanted to—to prove to you that you and Meg would not suit, that with another woman you—"

"I am not wed yet, Allegra, and I am a man. A man will take what he is offered," he retorted, his eyes raking her contemptuously. She felt a flush creep up her cheeks. "But that was not your real purpose and we both know it. You knew perfectly well that the Bridgebane woman was here, with that mongrel of hers." His brows were drawn together ominously, his body rigid with anger. "Tell me, was she in on it, too, or—"

"No, of course not. Nor did I—"

"You will not gammon me, Allegra. Do not even try," he spat, and took a menacing step toward her. "Do you realize the enormity of what you've done with your self-indulgent, interfering little scheme?"

At that Allegra felt a spurt of answering anger, and with it came her full voice strength. She nudged her chin up. "Perhaps I've saved Meg from a lifetime of heartbreak and you from marriage to a woman in love with another man. And as for me, well, I hadn't planned—that is to say, I suppose I will be in disgrace for a time. And then—"

"In disgrace for a time?" he repeated with mocking incredulity. "You disappoint me, Allegra. I had taken you for a meddler, but never for a fool."

Allegra narrowed her eyes in puzzlement. "Whatever do you—" She stopped midsentence and her mouth fell open. Resolutely, she shut it. It could not be. Papa wouldn't . . . She looked into Nigel's cold eyes and felt a wave of despair. Papa might well force them, and, dear God, how wretched it would be!

"Just so," Nigel said, his lips twisted sardonically.

Allegra could not utter another word, merely stared at him miserably. The anger—even hatred—that emanated from him was palpable.

"Nigel, you must believe me that I had no notion—"

"Oh, you had every notion, Allegra. The only thing of which you were not aware was that you could not control what you'd started. And you couldn't, could you?" he drawled derisively.

Allegra felt a deep flush suffuse her cheeks. " 'Tis a little late for that schoolgirl blush, wouldn't you say?" he mocked. "Shall I tell you what would have happened here had Wellington's senses been a little less acute?" He reached out and grasped her chin between his thumb and forefinger. "That you are yet innocent does not redound to the credit of either of us. It is a matter of that mongrel's timing. Even *you* could not have planned that." She tried desperately to turn her head away but he would not allow it. "But it matters not, Allegra, for in the eyes of the world, you are already ruined, unless I marry you." He released her chin none too gently and stepped back from her as if he could not bear the closeness.

"No! You do not have to m—"

"Go back to the house, Allegra. Leave me in peace," he said with such bitter coldness that she backed away and ran from the garden without another word.

She did not stop until she reached her bedchamber. She shut the door and leaned against it, trying to calm her breathing and the tumult of emotions she felt. First there had been the fire of Nigel's kiss, then the shock of being discovered. And then finally, Nigel's anger, his . . . his hatred. She remembered clearly the look in his eyes and knew that he would never believe that Mrs. Bridgebane had not been part of her plans. And she did not know if he would ever forgive her for going out there at first stop.

He would be with Papa soon. What would happen?

Surely Papa could not force them to wed! She alternately paced the floor and sat on the bed. She could not bear to gaze out at the garden. Sleep was impossible. When would Papa send for her?

"Caulfield, do calm down," Mrs. Bridgebane said as they entered the rear salon in which sat the chessboard, still set up. "You're like to have the apoplexy!" She went to the sideboard and poured a small amount of brandy into a snifter.

"And 'tis no wonder!" The baron paced the floor agitatedly. "God's blood! Meg's betrothed and my *other* daughter! And—and then *you,* madam, screaming loud enough to wake all the dead in Hades!"

Mrs. Bridgebane came forward and handed him the brandy. He stopped pacing and downed it in one gulp. She faced him squarely, but he saw that she was wringing her hands. "Caulfield, you must know that I am truly sorry for that. I can only plead the shock of the moment."

There was a note of sincerity in her husky voice that he could not doubt. "Be that as it may, Mrs. Bridgebane, it doesn't signify now," he said gruffly, setting aside his glass. "Allegra has been compromised." He sighed deeply and ran a hand through his silver hair. "The betrothal of Meg and Debenham cannot go forth. It is Allegra, now, who needs must—"

"Caulfield," she interrupted him, putting a hand to his sleeve, "the betrothal need not be nullified. That is, Allegra's reputation need not be compromised."

The baron arched a brow in patent disbelief. If he weren't so angry he could have laughed. The greatest gossip monger in Devon actually dared—

"Caulfield," she began again, dropping her hand from his sleeve. He noted irrelevantly that the hand was very delicate, almost at odds with her stout and sturdy form. "I know I am accounted a—a tattle monger. And I cannot truly deny it. But I do know how to keep a still tongue in my head when need be."

He threw her a skeptical glance. She went to the French doors and peered out into the night. He did not speak, merely watched her. Abruptly, she turned to face him. "Caulfield, I shall take the events of this night as a secret to my grave. If you wish the marriage to go forth as planned, then so be it. I've no wish to see Allegra ruined, nor to see her, nor *anyone,* forced into a marriage that is abhorrent to any of the concerned parties."

He stared piercingly at her for a long time, taking the measure of her shrewd, dark eyes. At length he breathed an almost imperceptible sigh of relief. He believed her.

"Thank you, Leonora," he said quietly. "I do not yet know what the end of all this will be, but at all events, I shall be grateful not to have my daughter's name bandied about."

She nodded in acknowledgment, the hint of a smile on her lips. And he decided that the strong, rather handsome features of her face bespoke a strength of character he had not heretofore imagined.

"Come," he said after a moment. "I shall rouse your coachman and see you safely on your way." And then, he thought with renewed rage, he would deal with Debenham.

Nigel entered the baron's study to find Caulfield sunk deeply into a worn leather chair, a glass of brandy in his hands.

The baron stood at his entrance, his gray eyes glittering with fury. His hand gripped the brandy snifter tightly.

"What have you done to my daughter?" he demanded, his voice thick with anger, and anguish.

Nigel banked his own anger, trying to imagine himself in Caulfield's place. Murder would seem too good . . .

"Caulfield, I realize that I have—have compromised Allegra, and I shall do everything in my power to make amends, but I did not—that is, her virtue is still intact."

The baron's eyes narrowed and he stared at Nigel for what seemed an interminable length of time before he breathed a small sigh of relief. His entire body seemed to relax a trifle, and the fire in his eyes was replaced by a great weariness. "So, we appeared in time," he said guardedly.

"No! I mean, yes!" Nigel's hand rifled through his hair. "That is, I never intended—"

"This was Allegra's doing, wasn't it, Nigel?" the baron interrupted, his eyes suddenly wide with comprehension.

Allegra Caulfield might have acted like brazen Haymarket ware, but Nigel Hayves was still a gentleman. And a gentleman always protected a lady, even a fallen one.

"No, Caulfield. 'Tis entirely my fault. I brought her—"

"Nigel, please." The baron smiled mirthlessly and put up a hand to halt him. "You may save your breath. It was Allegra's doing. We both know it." The baron sat back down in his chair and rubbed his eyes. He sighed deeply this time and his whole body seemed to deflate. Without opening his eyes, he motioned Nigel to an adjacent chair.

"I suppose I should have known it from the first, but when I saw . . ." His voice trailed off and he took a swig of brandy. "She's always been prone to mischief, and she's gotten up to some queer starts, but *this!*" He looked Nigel in the eye. "Damnation, but I never thought her capable of *this!*"

Nigel leaned forward, his expression grim. "I will, of course, marry her straightaway."

Caulfield peered at him intently. "I will not force you to wed her, Nigel," he said quietly. "Mrs. Bridgebane has given me her word that she will remain silent about what transpired this night."

"And you believe her?" Nigel asked incredulously.

Caulfield did not evince so much as the hint of a smile. "Yes," he replied soberly, "I believe her."

Nigel considered this for a moment. "Very well, but of a

certain she was not silent out there in the garden. Any number of servants might have heard her," he pointed out.

"Perhaps, but I have not heard any stirrings about the house, nor the stables. Even Mrs. Bridgebane's coachman had to be roused from slumber. But that's as may be, Nigel. I know Allegra's role in this and I will not force you to wed her. It is your decision."

Nigel's eyes took the measure of the man sitting before him and then he rose and went to the window. He wanted Allegra Caulfield; there could be no denying that now. But he most assuredly did not want to wed her.

Yet whatever Allegra's role, he had been equally as culpable. Besides that, he was not so sanguine as the baron about Mrs. Bridgebane's promised silence. And even if she never uttered a word, Nigel knew that he had compromised a lady of quality. There was only one way that a gentleman could erase that stain upon his honor. He really had no choice at all. Meg, he knew, would understand, and, he admitted to himself, would likely be relieved. And as for Allegra, she had no say in the matter.

Nigel walked slowly back to his chair and sank down onto the cushion. "I will wed her, my lord," he said with quiet determination. "I am, after all, a gentleman."

He thought Caulfield sighed again with relief and went on, "I only thank God that my betrothal to Meg was not made public. I would not wish her to suffer any humiliation because of this."

"Oh, Lord, Meg," the baron said dejectedly, and took another sip of his drink. "The betrothal might not have been announced, but I am persuaded it was known to some. And then if there *are* any murmurings about this night—damnation! 'Tis all grist for the gossip mills, that is certain."

Nigel swallowed, wishing for a healthy swig of brandy himself. He forced himself to speak. "If I may be so bold as to suggest, my lord, that I wed Allegra as soon as may be, by special license. That will stop any scandalbroth before it even has a chance to simmer. Weddings have a way of doing that," he added dryly.

"And how to explain the haste of such a marriage, Nigel, not to mention the change in brides?"

Nigel thought for a moment, tapping his fingers on the arm of his chair. "You may explain our haste by putting it about that I must soon travel abroad or some such and wish to have my wife with me. As she and I will retire to Suffolk straightaway, it will not signify. As to the other, I am persuaded that a few discreet words in the right ears will convince the tattle mongers that, of course, it was Allegra all along to whom I was betrothed, that they must have got the sisters confused. Perhaps Mrs. — ah — Bridgebane might help you on that head?"

Caulfield merely frowned, looking pensive, and Nigel forged ahead. "As to Meg, you might perhaps, er, have a word with the vicar, and have the banns posted for Meg and Dalton."

Caulfield's eyes widened. "So, you know about that, do you?" Nigel nodded. "And you would have wed her anyway?"

"Yes. We were betrothed, after all. And at all events, I thought it best, for both of us."

"So did I, dammit! But it seems it is out of our hands now. It is obvious you cannot marry Meg." He looked pointedly at Nigel and Nigel felt himself color. The baron drained his glass. "Of a certain you must have enough connections to obtain a special license staightaway, come morning. I've no wish to tempt Fate, lest this night's work become the ondit throughout half of Devon. God's blood, what a coil this is!" Caulfield rose agitatedly and went to refill his brandy snifter. He hesitated, then poured one for Nigel before resuming his seat and continuing, "I shall speak to the vicar about performing the ceremony tomorrow evening. You are right. It is the only answer.

"And I — I suppose I *shall* have a word with John about

Meg." Caulfield abruptly pounded his fist on the arm of his chair. "Damn that girl! I am going to wring Allegra's neck."

"No! Leave her to me," Nigel retorted forcefully. "I shall see her when I return on the morrow."

The baron lifted a brow. After a long moment he said, "Very well. She will remain in her room all day, seeing no one. After your interview with her, bring her to me."

Nigel agreed and downed his drink, hoping it would ease some of the tension coiled within him.

Caulfield rose and prowled restlessly about the room. Even in his fury, Nigel felt empathy for the man. "Caulfield, I know that an apology is woefully inadequate, but truly if I could undo . . . that is, I—damnation! I should never have touched her, no matter what the provoc—ah—" Nigel fumbled over the word and saw that the baron was regarding him with an odd, speculative look.

Then he nodded. "Just so, Nigel. I know that you are an honorable man. I shall, when I have calmed down, be proud to have you as a son-in-law."

"Even if I am marrying the wrong daughter?" Nigel asked bitterly, before he could stop himself.

The baron frowned and walked to the window. He stared out, hands behind his back. "I had not thought to see her wed so soon." His voice was gruff now. "She is so very young. And she does mean well, Nigel; you must know that." Nigel made a sound that could best be described as a snort. "Oh, I will own that she is rather—well—unconventional," the baron added.

"She has been allowed a great deal of freedom," Nigel ventured. It had to be said.

"I know," the baron said wearily. "And that is my fault. But she is so free-spirited. I could not bring myself to break her. And do not mistake me." He turned now to face Nigel. "She is charming and good-hearted and most delightful. But, alas, she is also impulsive and quick-tempered and headstrong. I am afraid"—the baron sighed—"Well, I fear she will not make you a comfortable wife."

For the first time Nigel permitted himself to smile. "No. 'Comfortable' is not a word I would use to describe Allegra."

The baron returned to his seat and fixed Nigel with a steady gray gaze. "Take care of her, Nigel," he said softly.

"Have no fear, my lord," Nigel replied. "You may be certain I will take care of her." He knew that the steel in his voice gave his words a meaning the baron did not intend, but that could not be helped. Nigel was furious; he would not pretend otherwise.

"So be it," the baron said at length.

For a few minutes, they discussed the settlements, which would remain basically the same, and then parted, in guarded charity with each other.

But when the earl had gone, the Baron Caulfield put his head in his hands. "Oh, my little girl, whatever have you done?"

Allegra watched the dawn come up and still there was no summons. Breakfast was brought to her on a tray and soon after came a soft knock at the door. It was not her summons, however, but Meg.

"Oh, Allegra, Papa forbade me to come here, but I had to see you. What—what happened? Papa is in a rare taking, Lord Debenham is closeted in his rooms, and the servants are in a fever of speculation. You've been in one of your scrapes, have you not? And I have the most dreadful feeling it concerns my betrothal. Oh, dear, I shall never forgive myself if you—"

"Now, Meg," Allegra said soothingly, putting her arm about her sister. "I merely went out to the garden last night, you must know. Nigel was there, you see, and I—well—I wanted to—to try to persuade him that you two should not suit. 'Twas rather late at night and I—ah—did not know that Papa and Mrs. Bridgebane were about. But they were and—well, I fear I am in disgrace now," Allegra said with what she was coming to realize was great understatement. "But perhaps it will all come out right in the end," she added bracingly. "Perhaps now you shall marry John and—"

"No, Allegra, Papa will never let me marry John. But that has nothing to say to the matter. Why should—Allegra, what exactly happened last night?" Meg asked, eyes narrowed with concern.

"Meg, you are not to trouble about me. I shall come about. And perhaps—" She stopped, hearing one of the maids down the corridor. "You'd better go back. Do not become blue-devilled on my account, Meg. All will be well, you'll see," she added and wished she could believe her own words.

"Oh, Allegra, I love you," Meg said softly, and hugged Allegra tightly before darting surreptitiously from the room.

Allegra's eyes were moist. The die was cast, and now she must await the consequences.

Jamie said nothing as he saddled Nigel's horse. No one else was about, but Nigel wondered if hints of last night's escapade had indeed drifted about belowstairs. Jamie was clearly waiting for the earl to offer some explanation for this sudden and solitary departure.

"Well, Jamie? Pray do not play the taciturn Scot with me. Have there been no whispers about last night's debacle?" Nigel demanded.

Jamie gave him an odd look. "Aye, there's talk, laddie. But only aboot the baron bein' in the devil's own takin', and Miss Allegra nowhere to be seen. And now here ye are, settin' oot w' yer saddlebags full. Well, and 'tis no to be a simple mornin' ride for ye, I'll vow."

Nigel sighed, relieved that, at least thus far, there'd been no gossip. Or was it simply that Jamie, a stranger among the Caulfield servants, wasn't privy to it? "No, it isn't, Jamie." Nigel put one hand on the saddle, prepared to mount. Jamie merely gazed at him expectantly. Jamie would never ask, and Nigel was under no obligation to tell him aught. Jamie was his servant, after all.

Jamie was his friend; he needed to talk to *someone*. He let his hand slide from the saddle. "Last night," Nigel began, his face going rigid with anger at the thought, "I was in the garden, and Allegra came—" Nigel paused, remembering that he was a gentleman. "That is—we found ourselves together in the garden. I . . . kissed her. Lord knows, I did not mean to, but . . . Oh, hellfire! It just . . . happened."

He thought Jamie's lips twitched slightly, though it was hard to tell because of the full red beard. Dammit, there was nothing the least bit amusing about any of this!

"Aye, such things do happen, laddie," Jamie said with a twinkle in his eye. "'Tis no the end of the world."

"Caulfield and Mrs. Bridgebane came upon us," Nigel said curtly. The twinkle fled his friend's eye. Jamie cursed in Gaelic under his breath.

"Just so. I will not bore you with the sordid details," Nigel went on bitterly, "but 'tis the devil's own coil. Even if word never gets out—"

"And perhaps it willna, laddie, if it hasna started yet, ye ken."

Nigel shrugged, his shoulders tense. "In truth, it doesn't signify now at all events."

Jamie lifted a brow. "Well, an' where might ye be goin' the noo? Yer no runnin' away, I'll wager."

Nigel's lips curled in a travesty of a smile. "Hardly, old friend. There is no running away now. I'm off in pursuit of a special license, blast it all!" He balled his hands into fists and his voice was hard. "The parson's mousetrap closes tonight, you see."

Jamie's eyes widened and he put a hand to the earl's shoulder. "Ah," he said in quiet commiseration. "And need I ask which sister ye'll be weddin'?"

"No, Jamie. You needn't ask." He did not mention to Jamie that he'd just come from a brief interview with Meg. She had managed with endearing effort not to sound too relieved when he'd told her of the necessity to terminate their betrothal. Nor had she asked the obvious question about herself and John Dalton. She was the consummate lady, and Nigel wished her well. "Matters do not always come about the way we wish, do they?" he said at length, calmer now.

"Nay. But ofttimes they do come aboot for the best, ye ken. And Miss Allegra—well, noo, she *is* verra engagin'. Her sister is the bonnier, some would say, but *she* has all the fire."

"I don't want fire, dammit!" he snapped, and then mentally shook himself. "Forgive me, Jamie. I—"

"Never ye mind. A man's allowed a bit of temper on his weddin' day."

Nigel glowered at his friend as he rode off.

Chapter Five

"Cupid's fiery shaft quenched in the chaste beams of the watery moon."

Love's Labors Lost
William Shakespeare

It was after luncheon and still no one had come for Allegra. She knew it was deliberate, knew that her father wanted her isolated until he was good and ready to mete out her punishment. She wondered what had transpired between her father and the earl. Surely Papa hadn't really called him out! But, dear Lord, if Papa actually forced a marriage . . . Her stomach was in knots and yet it rumbled with hunger, for she had barely touched the two trays Betsy had left for her.

The hours ticked by with agonizing slowness. She alternately paced, tried to read, took up some needlework at which she was hopelessly inept, and paced again.

There was a curious tapping at her window just before teatime. She whirled round toward the sound, then gasped as she saw Marcus perched on the branch of an oak tree, trying to gain entrance. She swung back the casement and pulled him in, chiding him gently for risking life and limb. "Oh, 'tweren't nothin', climbin' up here. I thought you might like a spot of company. And look, I nipped some biscuits quicklike when Cook turned her back!" he exclaimed, proudly pulling from inside his shirt a rolled up serviette full of biscuits and cheese.

She hugged him and for his sake forced herself to eat. Marcus munched with her as he spoke.

"Yer in the suds, right 'nough, Miss Allegra. The baron don't want no one comin' here. And the earl's gone hightailin' it off for somewhere, but Jamie's keepin' mum."

Allegra's eyes widened and she stopped chewing for a moment. Where had the earl gone, and why? "Did you — did you hear anything else, Marcus?"

Marcus, sitting on the bed next to her, shook his head. "Everyone's busy whisperin' belowstairs like as if they know somethin's amiss but ain't no one tellin' 'em what. And, any gates, they shut their mummers soon as I come 'round. Miss Allegra —" here his voice became troubled — "you ain't gonna leave or nothin', are you?"

Allegra did not even have the heart to correct his grammar. "I — I don't know, Marcus," she replied quietly, and saw his face pucker up with anxiety.

"Can I go with you ifn you leave Caulfield?" he asked in a small voice.

She put aside her bundle of biscuits and drew him close to her, hugging his little body fiercely. "I do not think so, Marcus. But I will come back, or at the least, to visit" — if Papa ever speaks to me again, she added silently — "and the baron will take good care of you. Why, he told me you're a right one with the horses, and he means to make you his tiger someday!"

Marcus was somewhat cheered by that news, and departed the way he'd come several minutes later. Allegra, however, was more agitated than ever.

It was early evening when the summons finally came. She was to dress for dinner and meet the earl in the Green Salon in one-half hour. The earl, not Papa? She wondered at that, certain that it did not bode well. But relieved finally to have something to do, she dashed to the armoire in her small dressing room. She chose to wear a pale aqua silk round dress which parted in the middle to reveal an ivory satin slip. It was a beautiful evening dress, fairly new, and one that Nigel had never seen before.

But, of course, she admitted ruefully as Betsy came in to help her dress, that didn't signify. For he would not look upon her with favor this night no matter what she wore.

In truth, Allegra had never attempted to use her looks to advantage, had never been overly concerned with her dress or toilette. She'd not had the patience, and besides, she had always accepted that Meg was the beauty in the family and that she herself was well enough looking, no more. It had never seemed to signify. Did it now? No, for why should she wish him to admire her? she demanded of herself as Betsy did up the last few buttons and straightened her petticoats. The maid murmured words of encouragement and Allegra tried to smile. She slipped on a pair of ivory satin evening shoes and let Betsy brush her hair. She liked the way the short curls framed her face, though no doubt Nigel considered her cropped hair slightly scandalous.

She took one final glance at herself in the looking glass and pinched her pale cheeks for color. And then, squaring her shoulders, she exited her chamber.

The Green Salon was a beautiful room with forest green damask sofas and draperies, and accent chairs in lemon yellow. The family ofttimes took coffee here after dinner and Allegra had spent many a pleasant hour here.

But there was nothing pleasant about Nigel's facial expression as he stood before the empty grate and motioned her inside. She prudently shut the door behind her and walked across the Oriental carpet to the earl. He stood erect, just three feet from her, his hands clasped behind his back, his countenance angry, his green eyes cold and remote. Yet for all that he still looked most handsome. His heavy brows and long dark lashes framed his eyes beautifully. His broad cheekbones and strong nose bespoke a man of power. Strangely, that power did not frighten her, even now. And his lips . . . She felt a tingle run up her spine as she recalled what his full, well formed lips were capable of.

She forced her eyes downward. His muscular torso was encased in an impeccably tailored black coat and crisp white shirt and cravat. Her wayward mind conjured the image of him without his coat, with his shirt open . . . She looked up at his face again and the full impact of his coldness hit her. He was looking her up and down, his eyes registering not a flicker of emotion.

He did not suggest they be seated before he began, "Your father and I have decided that the only way to scotch any potential scandal is for us to be wed as soon as possible. To that end I have procured a special license from the bishop in North Devon. The vicar will be here after dinner to perform the ceremony."

Allegra sucked in her breath. Marriage! It was to be marriage! "T—Tonight?" she managed, clutching a chair for support.

"Tonight, Allegra," he said grimly, his jaw stiff. She had gone pale and looked about to fall over, but he steeled himself not to reach for her. "If the notion was so unpalatable, you should have thought twice before enacting your little charade last night," he said scathingly.

Allegra bit her lip, stifling the angry denial. He would not believe her, and besides, this was not his doing, after all. This was Papa's, and she had to admit, hers. Oh, he had kissed her, but *she* was the one who had gone to him . . . And it was Papa, undoubtedly, who was insisting on marriage.

"You do not have to wed me, Nigel," she said quietly.

His mouth twisted. "I do not think you comprehend the extent of what would be your disgrace, Allegra, should even a hint of last night's little . . . rendezvous be bandied about. You would be ruined. You could never marry, and the doors to polite society would be forever closed to you."

"That is hardly your problem, Nigel. It is *my* disgrace. I meant to free Meg, not to shackle *you*. I am fully prepared to accept the consequences of my actions."

By God, but she had pluck, he mused, and quickly chased the thought away. But he could not keep his eyes from wandering her length again, and this time it was harder to keep his expression blank. The aqua gown looked beautiful on her, soft and feminine, hugging her body in places that only last night . . . No, dammit! He would not think of that.

He forced his eyes upward. Her hair curled saucily about her face, her brown eyes were dark with a curious mixture of spirit and contrition, and her mouth, with its straight upper lip, tempted.

Very deliberately he narrowed his eyes and hardened his voice. "And did you not think of *my* disgrace when you hatched your little scheme, Allegra? Not to mention that of your family. What you did was selfish in the extreme."

"Selfish!" Her hands flew to her hips. "You call *me* selfish!! Hah! *You* were the one ready to marry Meg to suit yourself, despite her unhappiness." She saw his brows arch into those ominous "V's" and knew she'd hit home.

"Allegra, you will curb your tongue."

"And as to your disgrace, Nigel," she went on, quite ignoring his warning, "even had I done all you accuse me of, I own I would not have thought of it. You are, after all, Rake Debenham. I do not suppose that one more—"

"Damn you, Allegra, I do not go about debauching innocents!"

"Well, you didn't debauch me either, so I am persuaded that the uproar will all eventually die down. Let us simply shred your special license and—"

"Allegra, you are a naive child," he interrupted.

She cocked her head at him. "If I were a child we would not be in this situation."

"No, we would not. We will be wed this evening, Allegra.

There is no gainsaying me, or your father."

She folded her hands at her waist. "Very well, Nigel. I will wed you, but I wish to speak to Papa, for I have one condition."

"You are hardly in a position to make conditions, Allegra."

She tilted her pointed chin upwards. "Nevertheless, I *will* see Papa before I agree."

He thought he knew what the condition was and could afford to be magnanimous. He nodded and without a word escorted her to the baron's study.

Papa did not seem at all surprised to see her as Nigel ushered her inside the study and left them alone. The baron's face was as bleak as Nigel's but at the least he asked her to be seated.

He said nothing, forcing her to begin. "I am sorry, Papa. I did not mean, that is, I did not know anyone else was about last night. I wanted only to—to persuade Nigel that—"

"None of that signifies, Allegra. You were there," Papa said coldly. "That is enough."

"But do you not see, I—I had to do *something*. Meg is my sister, my dearest friend in the world. I—"

"You will wed the earl this night, Allegra," he interrupted, clearly unmoved.

She looked down at her hands and up again. "I—I have one condition, Papa." He quirked a brow and she went on. "I will marry Lord Debenham if—if you will consent to the marriage of Meg and John Dalton."

The baron's gray gaze was steady, hard, and unrelenting. At length he said wearily, "You leave me no choice, do you, Allegra?"

"Papa, please," she entreated, reaching a hand out across the table that separated them.

But the baron stood up and towered over her. "I have a condition of my own, Allegra," he said sternly. "You will be a good and obedient wife to Lord Debenham. You will not disgrace the Caulfield name further." She looked up at him and despaired. There was no warmth in his eyes. She was not to be forgiven. At least not yet. Perhaps, if she *was* a good wife . . .

"Yes, Papa," she said quietly, and allowed him to take her into dinner.

Allegra could only be thankful when dinner came to a close. She had been unable to eat, and the tension at the table had been palpable. The earl and Papa had spoken quietly to each other and occasionally to Meg. Papa had addressed Allegra once, Nigel not at all. In truth, he had all the while either glowered at her or stared at her as if she weren't there. Meg had squeezed Allegra's hand beneath the table; she seemed bereft of words.

Allegra hoped to have a word alone with Meg when the gentlemen took their port. But such was not to be, for the men declined port and escorted them straightaway to the Green Salon for coffee. John Dalton arrived as soon as the coffee did, and the only one who looked pleased to see him was Meg. The baron looked grim and Nigel's eyes were narrowed to dagger points.

The baron drew John to a corner of the salon to speak with him and Meg excused herself and left the room. Allegra and the earl stared at each other across the width of the carpet. Then he turned and sauntered out to the terrace. The coffee sat untouched and forgotten on the sofa table. After a brief debate with herself, Allegra followed Nigel outside. She put a hand lightly to his arm. "Nigel," she said softly, "can we not cry pax? A truce, at the least. We are to be wed and—"

"I will do what must be done, Allegra. Do not expect me to be pleased as punch about it." He stared down at her hand as if it were some manner of insect. She removed it, feeling her hackles rise.

"Nigel, I—I do not understand you," she said in an angry undertone. "You wanted marriage to a woman befitting your station, to a woman bred to fulfill the position of countess, to, in fact, a Caulfield. You wanted a marriage unencumbered by protestations of love, unhampered by emotions you consider of no relevance to the married state. Well, that is precisely what you are getting! Why should it signify who the bride is?"

For a moment she saw a flash of anger in his eyes. But then it was gone and his lips curled menacingly. "You're quite right; it doesn't signify. I intended to take to wife a quiet, biddable lady who knows her place—and that, my dear girl, is exactly what you shall be."

Those were the last words he spoke to her before John Dalton performed the marriage ceremony.

Allegra stood at the window in her nightdress. The moon was dim; her chamber was in darkness. She had spoken her marriage vows just two hours before, but she did not feel very much like a bride. She closed her eyes and pictured the scene of her very brief wedding. Her father had been somber; John had been nervous and Nigel had seethed. Meg had smiled at her tremulously throughout. Allegra had almost burst into tears when Meg had come back into the Green Salon, moments before the ceremony, carrying a garland for her hair. Meg had spent the afternoon weaving the roses and lilies together; it was the only kindness shown her this evening. She supposed she deserved no more, but still, she would forever be grateful to Meg for helping her feel just a little bit like a bride.

When it was over Papa had woodenly toasted the bride and groom, and then departed for his study. John had taken Meg out onto the terrace and Nigel had simply told Allegra to go up to bed. They were to leave at first light, he'd said.

So she'd come back to her bedchamber to find Betsy busily packing her clothes into several portmanteaux. Betsy had apologized profusely, saying she was following the baron's orders, and Allegra had silently helped her to finish, glad of something to do. And then Betsy had assisted her to undress and had long since gone. But Allegra had been too restless to read, or even attempt to sleep.

She sighed wearily and wondered what it would have been like to have made a love match. Perhaps there might have been a wedding trip, and surely her new husband would have come to her on their wedding night . . . Her wayward mind conjured up images of Nigel and herself, last night in the garden . . . She felt herself flush, whether at the brazenness of her behavior or at the memory of Nigel's touch, his kiss, she did not know.

But he was so angry at her now; there was hatred in his every look. Dear God, what sort of marriage were they to have?

At length she climbed into bed. For the first time in weeks she heard silence; there was no sobbing coming from Meg's room. Meg's nightmare had ended at last. But Allegra very much feared, as she eventually drifted off to sleep, that her own had just begun.

They said their good-byes in the eerie light of dawn. There were no golden rays of sun illuminating the horizon; it was going to be a cloudy day. Meg cried as she promised to write and whispered her thanks to Allegra for bringing her and John together. Marcus clung to her until the last possible moment. Her father was stiff with her until she turned to mount the earl's traveling carriage. And then he called her name and she turned back. His eyes were suspiciously bright and he touched her cheek. "Be a good wife, Allegra," he said, and then added in a thick voice, "I—I wish you happy."

"Th—thank you, Papa," she whispered, and kissed his cheek. He didn't hug her; he had not forgiven her, but he did not totally repudiate her either. There was hope.

She began to wonder, as the day wore on, if there was hope for her and Nigel, however. He rode Mercutio in the morning and so there was no opportunity for discourse. Her own mare, she had noted when they were still at Caulfield, was not traveling with them. Her heart had sunk at that, but she did not think it prudent to ask for favors just now. Perhaps Leda could be sent for later.

And so, she rode alone in one carriage, the earl's valet and all the luggage in the second. Jamie was driving her carriage and when they stopped for a brief luncheon and change of horses, he alone had a smile for Allegra.

The rain began just after luncheon and the earl joined her in the coach as it lumbered eastward. He sat across from her, either gazing out the window or staring stonily ahead. He seemed so tense; his jaw was clenched. Every so often, she thought he stole a glance at her when she seemed not to be looking at him. And those surreptitious glances surprised her, for in those moments he did not seem cold at all. On the contrary, his eyes burned into her. All of her attempts at polite conversation, however, he met with curt, cool monosyllables.

"What is Deben Court like, Nigel?" she asked, determined to draw him out. "What do you do there?"

"It is very large. I farm." His eyes did not leave the rain-splattered window.

She prattled for a few minutes about the farms at Caulfield, but when this merely drew a bored frown from him she shifted the subject. "Have you any other estates?"

This time his lips curled in disdain. "Counting my money, are you, Allegra?"

"No!" she retorted. "You know full well I am merely making polite conversation."

He arched a brow. "I have never known you to be exces-

102

sively polite. But very well. I will oblige you," he said, then went on in bored tones, "I own a house in London, several minor estates in the north country, and one in Scotland. Oh, and Cliff House."

"Cliff House?"

He nodded. 'Tis in Dorset, on the coast. We used to spend summers there. But it has long since fallen into disrepair and is no longer habitable." He folded his arms across his chest and frowned, as if annoyed that he'd spoken at all.

She smiled dreamily. "Summers at the beach must have been lovely," she ventured.

"Yes. It was all a very long time ago," he said dismissively. "And now, Allegra, I find that I do not care to conduct polite conversation any longer."

He did not utter another word to her until they stopped for the night, somewhere north of Southampton. And then he merely instructed her to go to her chamber and change for dinner. She struggled to unpack the necessary clothing for the evening and to see to her own toilette. It seemed that neither her father nor Nigel had considered it necessary for her to have a maid along. Of course, she'd often done without one at home, having to share Betsy with Meg and the cleaning of numerous upstairs chambers. But the fact that her husband, especially, had not considered it rankled. Her husband, she thought, repeating the word to herself. It sounded strange. She did not feel at all like a wife. Not yet . . .

Dinner seemed interminable. Neither she nor Nigel seemed to have much appetite. If Nigel approved her pink coral evening gown he gave no notice. Indeed, Allegra strove not to keep stealing glances at him, for he looked quite dashing in a forest green coat and buff pantaloons.

The silence stretched on between them. Allegra considered making polite conversation, but, remembering his reaction to such in the carriage, she thought better of it.

Instead, in between bites of buttered peas, she simply

said what was uppermost in her mind. "Nigel, I own I do not feel at all like a wife yet."

Nigel paused in the act of raising his wine goblet to his lips. Now, just what did she mean by that? He was not in the mood for conversation and would have preferred silence. He would have preferred, in fact, to pretend she was not here at all. Lord knew he was trying to keep his eyes off the way she looked in that gown. He wanted her, and yet he did not want even to be near her. The fury was still seething inside him. He schooled his voice and his expression to practiced ennui. "I am persuaded you will feel more like the Countess of Debenham once you are mistress of Deben Court."

He sipped his Madeira, watching her eyes narrow in puzzlement. "No. That is not what I mean. Oh, of a certain I shall endeavor to administer Deben Court properly, but that is not, I am persuaded, the essence of being a wife." She leaned forward, resting her breasts on the white tablecloth, and propped her chin on her hands, pondering. He forced his eyes to her face and drank more wine. What the deuce was she thinking?

In truth Allegra did not know quite *what* she meant, only that this was a most inauspicious beginning to a marriage. She'd always imagined marrying a man with whom she felt mutual respect, friendship and love. Nigel and she shared none of those feelings. Why, they positively disliked each other!

Of course, there was one other element to their relationship, and that was what happened between them every time he kissed her. She did not dislike that at all, and neither, she knew, did Nigel. Even now, she felt the warmth course over her at the memories. And she suspected that such . . . passion was a very important part of marriage.

But Nigel was so furious at her now that she knew he would not—would not come near her. His anger might last for days, even weeks . . . And then another thought struck her, a rather disturbing one, and before she could stop herself, the words tumbled from her mouth. "Nigel, I know that you are angry at me, and I own you—you have some justification, but do you—ah—do you mean this to be a marriage in name only?"

Nigel choked on his Madeira. When his spluttering ceased, he set his goblet down carefully. Only Allegra would ask such a thing. He stared piercingly at her. She did not look as if the prospect of such a marriage appealed to her. She licked her lips nervously and he followed the movement of her tongue. Innocent siren, he thought, and then remembered another siren, albeit not an innocent one. With the memory of Gina came the reminder of just how furious he was with Allegra, and why.

Allegra watched shutters come down over the green eyes that for just a moment had shone with a certain warmth. Now there was only coldness. "The answer is no, Allegra," he said in clipped tones. "I am in need of an heir. Now, if you have finished, you may retire. I shall stay and take my port."

Nigel had watched her leave the small dining parlor of the inn, determined not to dwell overlong on the way her hips swiveled beneath the flimsy silk of her gown, nor on the creaminess of her breasts as they rose above her low neckline. No, it would not be a marriage in name only. When he was good and ready, he would make her his wife in fact. After all, she had done everything in her power to achieve that position; now she would do her duty. And that was all it would be for him as well. Duty. Nothing more.

A moment later he rose from his chair and began to pace the room. You lie, Debenham, he admonished himself. He cursed inwardly. For it would *not* be duty on his part and he knew it. Oh, he needed and wanted an heir; that much was true. But he also wanted Allegra, and had from the moment he'd seen her emerge from that pond.

Yes, by God, he wanted her and he would take her! Why should he deny himself when he'd paid the ultimate price for the privilege? And why the devil should he wait?

Nigel poured himself some of the innkeeper's best port and sank back into his chair as he sipped. There *was* no reason to wait. It would simply be a matter of the fulfillment of duty and the assuagement of physical desire. Nothing more. He would keep his distance from this wife he had so precipitously acquired. He would take her to Deben Court and after a suitable time he would go his own way. He would go to visit one of his other estates, or to see Coke in Norfolk to discuss the new steam pumps. Or perhaps he would visit one of his bachelor friends, although come to think on it, their numbers seemed to be dwindling rapidly. Penderleigh in Lancashire had recently taken a marchioness, and Charles Ainsley was even now awaiting the birth of his heir. Well, perhaps he would go to Yorkshire to see Adam Damerest, Duke of Marchmaine. Adam, if he was not off somewhere carousing, would no doubt be holed up in his ancient family seat, pouring over architectural designs for its improvement.

As to Allegra, if she was so bent on rescuing poor unfortunates—climbing boys and serving girls and heartbroken sisters—she could just as well do that at Deben. As long as she did not interfere with the efficient running of his home, he amended. *That* he would not tolerate!

Oh, no, Allegra, he reaffirmed, this would not be a marriage in name only. But it would be one in which *he* defined the terms.

He rose, quite satisfied with his ruminations, and made his way abovestairs.

The night air was warm and still. Moonlight poured through the open window and spilled onto the bed. Allegra lay with her eyes closed, listening to the rhythmic hooting of a nearby owl. If it failed to lull her to sleep, at the least it allowed her mind to drift and cease its cogitations for a time.

And so it was that the click of a door latch came as something of a shock. She gasped, her eyes flying open as she pulled herself to a sitting position and stared at the corridor door. But it was not that door which opened in the next moment; it was the smaller one next to the wardrobe.

"Nigel!" she exclaimed as he stepped through. "Whatever—where—ah—"

"Our rooms adjoin. Did you not know?" he asked smoothly. He wore a dark brown dressing gown, trimmed in velvet. It gaped open at the top, affording her a glimpse of his bare chest as he came toward her.

She swallowed hard. "No, I—that is—I hadn't thought on't."

"No?" He quirked an eyebrow. "You surprise me, Allegra." There was a faintly mocking tone to his words which made her decidedly uncomfortable.

His eyes swept over her with an expression she could not fathom. She resisted the urge to tug the blanket up to her chin; she would not allow herself to become missish with Nigel at this late date. "What—what do you want, Nigel?" she asked, despising the hesitancy in her voice.

He did not smile as he sauntered to the bed. He sat down next to her with a very determined air. "I should think that would be very obvious, Allegra," he said silkily, one hand gently but inexorably pushing her back against the pillows.

Allegra's eyes widened. She hadn't realized, when he'd answered her earlier question in the dining parlor, that he'd meant *tonight!* He put his index finger to her mouth and slowly traced the outline of her lips. The touch of his finger made her shiver, even though her lips burned. She wanted to speak out but could not. She wanted to move but dared not.

107

Then he let his hand fall, grazing her chin, her throat, and finally cupping one of her breasts through the thin fabric of her nightdress. She suddenly felt warm all over, but she frowned as she looked into his eyes. They seemed . . . cool, devoid of emotion. How could he touch her so intimately and yet—

"Nigel," she rasped, "I—I do not understand you. If you are still angry with me, how—how can you—"

"One thing has naught to do with the other, Allegra," he said coldly, and bent his head.

She tried to turn away; he grasped her shoulders and held her firmly. "Nigel, I—" she began, but his mouth clamped down onto hers.

Neither of his previous kisses could have prepared her for this one. It was hard, bruising, his tongue and teeth ravaging her mouth. He was punishing her, she realized in a flash, and pushed at him, but he merely shifted his weight, pressing her into the bed. She twisted, attempting to free her mouth, but his tongue found hers and she felt a flood of hot, unaccustomed sensations.

His hands began caressing her sides, her breasts. There was nothing gentle about his touch, yet he did not hurt her. She tried to deny the heat that pulsed through her in the wake of his hands, tried not to return the pressure of his lips on hers. But her body was treacherous. She heard someone moan and realized it was she. No, she thought. She would not let him take her in anger! But of their own volition her hands wrapped themselves about his shoulders.

She felt an urgency in him that made her blood pound. She knew it was futile to fight him. He was too strong and—and—Suddenly she realized that she did not *want* to fight him! Whatever else was between them, here in this moonlit chamber there was only this extraordinary, flaming passion. She would not deny herself, or him. She was, after all, his wife.

Nigel had been expecting her to fight him; he was prepared. He would drag a response from her, even as he rigorously controlled his own. He would take what he wanted and when it was over he would get up and calmly take himself off to bed.

But then she moaned, and her small hands clasped his shoulders. Her lips became soft and pliant; her tongue tentatively met his. Instinctively, he gentled the pressure of his mouth, his tongue dancing with hers. His hands moved to her hips. He felt her quiver and cursed the barrier of her long, prim, nightdress.

His movements became jagged, his breathing erratic as he somehow divested them both of their garments. His eyes devoured her; he thought he would explode with need. And then she extended her arms up to him, offering herself in all her innocent, giving passion.

Oh God, Allegra, don't do this, he groaned inwardly. It wasn't supposed to happen this way. But he could not stop himself.

He was kissing her again. Allegra realized that they were both naked. He was half on top of her; every part of him seemed huge and strong. She ran her hands over his shoulders, his back. She loved the feel of him, his body hard and muscular and sprinkled with hair.

Her own body burned everywhere he touched her. She wanted more and more of something she could not quite fathom.

Nigel was drowning in her. He knew he ought to take her slowly; he was afraid to hurt her. But he realized that she didn't want that; she wanted all of his strength. He thrust into her and she gave a small cry of pain. Cursing himself, he soothed her with soft murmurings, with gentle hands, holding himself still until she smiled tentatively at him. He began to move and she arched her hips, the heat building in her again. Her hands grasped his nape; her mouth sought his. He kissed her deeply, and as he took her with all his masculine power, her cries mingled with his own.

And then it was over. He collapsed atop her and listened to the sound of her ragged breathing, and his own. Finally he raised his head and looked down at her. She smiled at him. He kissed her eyes. Neither of them spoke. He rolled to the side and took her with him, pulling her back into the curve of his body. His hand wrapped itself around her; he buried his face in her hair. With his free hand he pulled the comforter up to cover them. A heavy languorous contentment settled over him. Vaguely he remembered that he was supposed to get up; he couldn't move if his life depended on it.

Allegra snuggled against him, her body still humming with delicious sensations. Never had she imagined it would be like this. Men, she mused, were wonderful creatures. And *this* man was especially wonderful. He'd been gentle and not-so gentle at all the right times, and he'd kissed her eyes. And now he held her tightly, and she never wanted to move.

She felt his breathing even into sleep, but her own body would not relax. She felt a curious kind of tension in her body; she could not imagine what it was.

She wondered, as she finally drifted off to sleep, if she could ask Nigel about it.

Allegra awoke to the sound of the nightingale; it was still deep in the night. Nigel's hand was still clamped firmly about her middle. She stirred and shifted her legs slightly.

The movement must have awakened him. He pulled her even closer and murmured, "Go back to sleep. 'Tis still full night."

"Mmmm," she replied dreamily. "Good night, Nigel."

He nuzzled the back of her neck and she shivered. "Cold?" he asked, and wondered why he had. He ought not to talk to her; indeed, he should have left her bed hours since. But he was much too warm and comfortable to con-

110

sider moving, his mind still too drugged from sleep. Instinctively he pulled her closer.

"No. Not cold at all." She twisted her hips a bit to get more comfortable.

"Don't do that," he commanded gruffly, "or I shan't answer for the consequences."

"Oh." She drew the lone syllable out as comprehension dawned. After a moment's deliberation she wriggled again.

"Allegra!" His voice was very low. "I do not want to hurt you."

At that she turned in his arms to face him. She put her hands to his chest and looked up at him. "Nigel, what we did — ah — earlier was quite . . . wonderful, you must know, but I have the oddest feeling that — that somehow it was not complete. I do not know —"

"Oh, Lord," he groaned aloud, and silenced her with a hard, fast kiss that caused his senses to reel. *She* might not know, but *he* did, and he felt a tumult of emotions assail him. He felt amazement at her candor; would he ever become accustomed to it? He also felt decided pique at himself for even being here, still, in her bed. But most of all he could not repress a small bubble of masculine delight. No one had ever called what went on in his bed "quite wonderful." And no one had ever, now that he remembered fully just what *had* transpired hours before, been quite so warm, and willing, and . . .

This is a mistake, Debenham, he told himself. If you were fully awake you would bolt even now. But he was not proof against the innocent invitation in those dark eyes, nor the feel of her soft, pliant body, subtly pressing his. Nor the thought that she felt "incomplete." Slowly, he bent his head.

It was the second kiss that did it. The first had been merely a prelude, but the second was long and deep and so thorough that it left her trembling, her very insides melting. How could he do that to her so quickly? she wondered, even as his hands were caressing her body, heating it, stirring her

111

blood to some urgency she still didn't understand. She clutched at him, certain she would explode. She did not know what was happening to her, only that she needed . . . Nigel. Instinctively she moaned his name and pulled him closer, and he answered her need, bringing them together in one swift, hard thrust. There was no momentary pain, as she'd felt the first time, only the wondrous heated feel of his body enmeshed with hers. He began to move and she arched to meet him, as the exquisite, frenzied sensations built. She felt as if she were flying, as if she were going to die!

"No, you won't, sweeting," Nigel rasped. Had she spoken aloud? His hands held fiercely to the sides of her head. "Stay with me, Allegra! Oh, God, Allegra. Oh . . ."

Her cries matched his as suddenly her body stiffened and convulsed in violent, pulsing shudders. And then Nigel was shuddering with her, flying off some precipice with her, until they came gliding, gliding down.

She could not catch her breath. Nigel took his weight from her, but kept her wrapped in his arms. " 'Tis all right," he whispered, and kissed her gently. She could see his eyes gazing into hers and smiled tremulously.

Finally catching his own breath, he tucked her into the curve of his shoulder and covered them once again. Never, never had he felt so replete. Never, even with Gina, had he felt what he had moments before.

His hand stilled in its light stroking of her hair. What the hell was he doing here, still, in her bed? Why had he made love to her again? For that is what he had done, he admitted now to himself. The cold possession he had planned on had turned into passionate lovemaking. Twice, for pity sakes! What was wrong with him?

Damnation! He had meant to take her, coldly. But instead, she had taken some part of him. And he knew that somehow he would never be quite the same again.

She murmured something unintelligible and he looked

down to see that she had fallen asleep. A soft, secret smile played about her sensuous lips. No! He did not want to see that smile. And he *would* be the same again, he assured himself, come the morrow. Whatever sensual spell she had cast would be broken, come daylight, and he would be his sane, eminently rational self. The self that would not be lost to any woman, ever again.

Tomorrow, he reminded himself sleepily. For now, he would stay just a few minutes and then take himself off to his own bed, where he belonged. Her small hand was entangled in his chest hair, her smooth leg entwined with his. In just a few minutes . . .

The Earl of Debenham fell instantly, deeply asleep.

Chapter Six

"You may as well forbid the sea to obey the moon."
A Winter's Tale
William Shakespeare

Allegra came slowly awake, the sound of the lark sweet background to her thoughts. She lay on her side, remembering every delicious minute of the night before. The marriage bed, she decided, was going to be one of the nicest parts of marriage. As to the rest, surely after last night . . .

She snuggled back against Nigel, only to encounter the feel of empty sheets. She stretched her foot back. Still no Nigel. She turned round, then sat up in bed. The bed, and the room, were empty.

Quelling a stab of disappointment, she told herself that perhaps he wanted to see to the preparations for their departure so that they might leave early. He was probably conferring with Jamie and would no doubt send word for her to join him in the breakfast parlor. Well, she would not wait. She would hurry about her toilette and join him straightaway.

She threw back the bedclothes and gasped. There was blood on the sheet! Not a great deal, but two very distinctive spots of dried blood. She looked down at herself but could see no injury nor sign of blood on her person. Certainly it was not time for her monthly flux—that was weeks away.

It must be Nigel, then. Perhaps he'd cut himself. But how could that have happened in bed? Rather puzzled, she could only hope, from the size of the stain, that it was not a severe injury. Oh, dear, why had he not wakened her, so that she might tend to him? She supposed he'd gone straightaway to Kingston. He was, after all, not accustomed to having a wife.

She bounded from the bed, determined to waste no time before seeking Nigel out in the breakfast parlor.

She was fastening the last few buttons of her mint green traveling dress when there came a knock at the door. A moment later, a rosy-cheeked maid entered, carrying a tray upon which appeared to be a light breakfast.

"Oh, you be up and about, your ladyship. An' 'tis a good thing, I'm thinkin', cause his lordship be in a powerful hurry."

"Is his lordship all right?" Allegra could not help asking.

The maid nodded. "I reckon so, your ladyship. Just impatient to be off, I'd say."

Allegra breathed an inward sigh of relief. "Well, then, thank you for the tray, but I mean to join his lordship in the breakfast parlor. You may tell him I shall be down in a trice."

"Oh, but my lady, 'tis finished he be, and outside with the horses. Said as how you was to eat and come down straightaway."

Allegra tried not to let the maid see the disappointment in her face as she thanked and dismissed her. And she told herself there was nothing untoward about what Nigel had done. After all, it was understandable that he would be in a hurry. No doubt he wished to reach Debenham before nightfall tomorrow. And she knew he liked a solitary breakfast. Still, after last night, she would have thought . . .

Allegra ate her breakfast hurriedly, tasting nothing.

When she arrived at the inn yard a short time later, it was to find Nigel in conversation with Jamie, while Kingston supervised the strapping of their portmanteaux into the second carriage.

Nigel's broad shoulders were encased in a coat of dark brown superfine and Allegra was forcefully reminded of the way he'd looked in his dressing gown of the same color. She walked purposefully forward.

"Good morning, Nigel, Jamie," she said, searching Nigel's face for signs that he might have injured himself.

Jamie returned her greeting and then with a glance at Nigel, stepped back to the horses. Nigel said nothing for a moment, merely looked her up and down, his face expressionless.

"Good morning, Allegra," he said with cool civility. "Now that you are here we can be on our way."

His rather formal demeanor took her aback. Nevertheless she asked, "Nigel, are you all right?"

"Am I—" he paused, and seemed to be stifling some bit of amusement. "Yes, of course I am all right, Allegra." He took her arm and led her off to the side, stopping at the rather ramshackle fence that surrounded the inn yard. He dropped her arm and stepped back two feet.

So much, he thought, for his efforts to maintain his distance. He sighed, knowing full well he had ought to have asked the question of *her*.

"Are *you* all right, Allegra?" he asked in an undertone.

"Yes, of course," she said dismissively. "But the blood, Nigel. Did you cut yourself? Why did you not tell me? Why—"

"Whoa, Allegra. Halt!" Nigel did his very best to keep his expression grave. "Of just what—er—blood are we speaking?"

116

"Why, the blood on the bed, of course. Not such a great deal, you must know, but enough for me to—"

"Allegra, please! Lower your voice," he said urgently, moving close to her. This was a damnable place for such a discussion!

"Allegra," he began evenly, "the blood is—well—er—brides often bleed er—the first time. Not always, and I did not think you had, as you evinced no discomfort, and so I—"

"That was—was *my* blood, Nigel?" He watched a flush suffuse her face and resisted the urge to smooth it away.

"Yes, Allegra," he said gently. "Are you certain you feel right?" Devil take it! He did not want to talk with her, did not want to hear the unaccustomed softness in his own voice, did not want to feel concern for her. And yet how could he not? "Do you have any lingering—er—discomfort?"

"No. I—well," she smiled conspiratorially, "I *am* a bit sore perhaps, but nothing to signify. 'Tis just that I had no idea—I mean to say—"

"Allegra, we are in the courtyard of an inn. Hardly the place for such a discussion, you will own. Now, my dear, if you are indeed well, I should like to continue our journey."

She cocked her head at him and an impish gleam lit her eyes. Blast it all! He did not want to see that look on her gamin face. He did not want to be this close to her, to inhale that elusive scent of wildflowers that seemed to emanate from her.

"You are quite right, Nigel," she agreed genially. "This is hardly the place. The place, I daresay, is the bedchamber. But as you saw fit to steal out of my chamber in the wee hours, I could not very well—"

"Allegra," he interrupted, forcing himself to harden his voice. He would not be disarmed by her shocking candor. He would not be lured by the gleam in her dark eyes.

Perhaps he had lost himself last night, but she must not be allowed to think that it changed aught between them.

"I am your husband," he continued. "You must accustom yourself to my coming and going to and from your chamber as I wish." His voice grew colder as his resolve strengthened. "You will not question me, Allegra. Do I make myself clear?"

Allegra put her small hand onto his forearm. "Nigel," she said softly, "I only meant that I missed you this morning and—"

"This conversation is not seemly, Allegra. We leave straightaway," he said icily. "Now, if you please, go to the carriage."

"B-But Nigel, I—"

"Do not make a scene, Allegra," he interrupted. His eyes, that had shone with a fleeting warmth just moments ago when he had seemed concerned, were cold and remote. He looked pointedly, almost contemptuously, down at her hand, which still lay upon his forearm. Swallowing convulsively, Allegra withdrew it; he strode away without a backward glance.

Allegra stood stock-still, letting the waves of hurt and confusion wash over her. Something was dreadfully wrong. Why was Nigel acting like this? Oh, she was not so naive as to believe that what happened last night would have dissipated *all* of his anger. But she *had* expected some . . . softening. And there had been, if only for a brief time.

Her eyes, of their own accord, followed Nigel to where he now stood with Jamie. Jamie was glaring at him. She hoped Jamie hadn't heard any of her exchange with Nigel, especially not the last part. Somehow it would make her humiliation that much worse. She must move herself, get into the carriage before Nigel turned her way again. But her body actually trembled as Nigel's frigid voice sounded in her head.

How could it be that the tender, passionate lover of the

night before and this cold, aloof man were one and the same? And yet they were. It was obvious that last night notwithstanding, Nigel was still furious with her. He was as odious as ever. Nothing had changed.

She willed her body to stop trembling and slowly moved to the carriage. It was a gray, cloudy day and the warm humid air hung heavily, oppressively, about her. It matched her mood. She climbed onto the plush leather seat of Nigel's luxurious traveling coach. An ostler closed the door behind her with a resounding click. It had a finality to it that made Allegra's spirits sink even lower. Then she chided herself. What did she expect, after all? Nigel would ride his stallion. He would not ride with her. He did not want to be near her.

Nothing had changed.

The carriage lurched and began lumbering out of the inn yard. Allegra leaned back in her seat and pressed her fingers to her eyelids. She *would* not cry! She remembered everything about last night in perfect, poignant clarity. The heat of the first time, the sweet languor of falling asleep in her husband's arms. And then the sound of the nightingale, waking her to moonlight, even as Nigel awakened her that second time to that extraordinary fire within her.

Nigel cantered past the window of the coach, his eyes fixed straight ahead, the strong planes of his face set like granite. She'd seen that look before, when he'd stood on the terrace and looked down at her in the garden. She'd thought then that the coldness on his face must reflect the coldness in his soul.

Nothing had changed.

No! That was not true! Something *had* changed. A great deal had changed. She was not the same person she'd been yesterday. And, she realized with a start, neither was he. He couldn't be.

Allegra was inexperienced in the ways of men and

119

women, but she had strong instincts, and she trusted them. And instinct told her that some elemental connection had been forged between them last night. Theirs had been no cold or casual coupling. He had called to her in a way that had naught to do with words, and she had answered.

But as surely as she knew that, she also knew that Nigel, were he even aware of it, would never admit it. There were two more things that Allegra realized that gray and brooding morning. One was that she did not, could not, hate Nigel Hayves, if indeed she ever had. And the other was that, Nigel, having touched something deep and elemental within her, now had the power to hurt her. Very badly, indeed.

Luncheon was a strained affair, not at all helped by the ever darkening sky and the mediocre fare of the second-rate inn which they favored with their custom. Every one of Allegra's conversational gambits was met with icy civility and eventually she lapsed into the silence Nigel obviously preferred. After the meal she climbed into the carriage; Nigel headed for Mercutio, his stallion. She sighed deeply, wondering how she was ever going to breach those icy walls her husband had erected about himself. The carriage had not begun moving yet as she leaned her head back against the squabs and tried to think of ways to divert her thoughts. It was then that she espied, in the corner of the carriage, the odd-looking, blanket-covered mound where before there had been only several folded blankets.

A hamper, perhaps? she wondered, but decided it was too bumpy. She scooted over, leaned down and pulled up a corner of the dark blanket. And then she gasped, for two large, terror-filled, amber-flecked eyes peered at her through a thin curtain of disheveled honey-blond hair.

And that was when the shouting started. "Well, an' I mean to search everyone o' these here carriages, Innkeeper. Damned slut's got to be here somewhere!" bellowed a harsh voice.

It was the owner of the amber eyes who gasped this time and instinctively Allegra covered her with the blanket.

Her eyes flew to the window, from where she could see the innkeeper and a rotund, most unpleasant-looking man marching about the inn yard, flinging open empty carriage doors. And then they started for the Debenham carriages and Allegra sat up straight, prepared to do battle. But when the door opened, it was her husband's green eyes that peered sharply inside. They darted from her to the seats to the floor and came to rest unerringly on the huddled mound. His eyes, narrowed now to icy slits, flew back to her, and she returned his gaze with one of unabashed pleading.

He slammed the door shut and she held her breath, trying to keep hidden as she peeked out the window.

"Out 'o my way, man!" shouted the rotund man.

"That be the earl's carriage, Hurley, an' you can't go in there!" squeaked the innkeeper as they approached the luggage coach.

"That's as maybe, but still and all—"

"Well, noo, is there some sort of problem, Mr. Weems?" Jamie asked the innkeeper. It was Hurley who answered.

"Might be. I'll just have me a look inside this carriage here."

"And just what might ye be lookin' for?" Jamie demanded, and Allegra saw him exchange a glance with Nigel, who stood just outside her own coach.

Hurley sucked in his belly and pulled himself up to his full height. His mouth twisted viciously. "I got me orders, see, to take this little fancy piece to a certain nib cove what lives up north a ways, an' I mean to do it. All paid

121

for right and tight, she is. Like as not she's hidin' somewhere hereabouts, with no one the wiser."

Jamie shot a questioning glance to Nigel, who nodded briefly. "Well, 'tis only luggage ye'll be findin,' but here ye are," Jamie replied, throwing open the door.

Hurley leaned his bulk into the carriage and reemerged a minute later, snarling. He turned immediately to her own carriage.

"Beggin' yer lordship's pardon," Hurley said grudgingly, "but I—"

"Mr. Weems, if the horses are ready, I mean to be off straightaway," Nigel interrupted in a moderate tone. Allegra heard the steel beneath it. "As for you, Hurley, I regret that you have—er—misplaced your charge, but I fear I cannot be of help to you."

"Hold now," Hurley responded belligerently, taking a step toward the carriage. "I'll just be checkin'—"

"Hurley, my *wife*, the Countess of Debenham, is in this carriage. Surely you are not suggesting that I would harbor a lightskirt in such proximity to my *wife!*" Nigel proclaimed with commendable imperiousness. Allegra breathed a sigh of relief.

Hurley seemed to deflate just a little. "Now, yer lordship, I wasn't meanin' to suggest—"

"Good. If you'll excuse me, then," Nigel blithely interrupted and called to Jamie, who shouted orders for the entourage to depart.

Hurley, his ruddy face made even more unpleasant looking in his frustration, had no choice but to step back. The carriages moved out.

They had been traveling for a full half hour, Allegra checking behind them for Hurley on horseback, before she deemed it safe for her stowaway to throw off her blanket and climb onto the seat beside her.

"Now," she said to the trembling, too-thin, young girl, "pray, tell me your story."

Nigel was furious with himself. Why had he let the expression in those ingenuous brown eyes sway him from his good judgment? He would rue this day . . . No! He would have it out with Allegra as soon as may be. He would drag the truth from her and then proceed with objective, logical reasoning to do the proper thing. Rescuing climbing boys was one thing, but this! More than likely the bit of muslin she was harboring really did not want rescuing at all. Perhaps she'd merely been playing at some game. Blast his damned, interfering wife for involving him in such business!

Her name was Katie. She was sixteen years of age, the daughter of an impoverished parson. About a year ago she had been drugged and kidnapped from an inn where she was staying with her father. She would not tell Allegra her family name, nor from whence she came. Allegra did not press her. But very delicately she explained to the girl that if she was to help her she must know something of what she had just run away from.

The carriage jolted over ill-paved roads but Allegra was oblivious as she listened to Katie's soft, tremulous voice. She'd been taken to a discreet lodging in London that she later learned was called the *Le Petite Maison*. The proprietor, the abbess she was called, was Mrs. Graves; Katie shuddered as she said the name.

But then, instead of the telling becoming more difficult, the narrative began to flow from Katie's lips. Allegra saw that her eyes were dilated. She hardly seemed aware of her audience, but was looking inward, remembering. And Allegra had the distinct feeling that it was a great relief for the girl to tell someone, finally.

Katie came to realize that Mrs. Graves's house catered

to men who liked very young girls. At fifteen, Katie was by no means the youngest. Almost all were there against their will; there were no means of escape. Hurley and several others guarded it as if it were Newgate Prison.

Katie was raped on her second night in residence by a titled "gentleman" whose name she didn't know. He was, she later learned, a great frequenter of the establishment. The flat remoteness with which she related this part of the tale told Allegra more than words could have. After that night Katie fell ill with fever and when she recovered, she vowed to kill herself before allowing herself to be violated again.

Mrs. Graves had surveyed Katie with a dispassionate, calculating eye and had called one of the older girls to instruct Katie in how to "service" her most discriminating customers. At this point Katie hesitated, not willing to meet Allegra's eyes, and would only say that she would be on her knees and the "gent" might sit in a chair.

"Twasn't as bad as the other, but 'twere bad enough, my lady," she said in a low, thick voice.

Allegra could not envision what she was speaking about and forbore to ask. Perhaps one day she would ask Nigel. For now the important thing was that Katie, two years younger than she herself, had been made to live a life of degradation such that Allegra could not begin to fathom.

Several times she halted Katie, assuring her it was not necessary to go on, but Katie insisted. Once having started, she seemed to need to finish. The same man who'd raped her was ever her nemesis, requesting her special services whenever he was about. Sometimes it made her so sick that she could not eat for days. And then she would be beaten till she did.

Katie ended her narrative with having been requested by some nobleman whose seat was somewhere north of London—she had not been told his name nor place of residence—and having been consigned to the none-too-gentle ministrations of Hurley for the journey. She had seen Allegra alight from her carriage, and when Hurley was busy downing Blue Ruin in the tap room, Katie had seized her chance.

"I'll do anything, my lady," she pleaded. "I'll work in the scullery, the laundry, the fields . . . anything but go back to that place." Katie's voice broke at last, and Allegra gathered her into her arms and let her sob her heart out.

When she subsided, Allegra gently asked whether Katie wished to be returned to her family. At that Katie's eyes widened in great distress. "Oh, no, my lady. I could not—not after . . . My father is a very devout man, you see, and very stern, and . . . and it is . . . better that they think me . . . dead." The girl's voice trailed off into a whisper, and Allegra nodded, understanding, though she hoped that someday Katie would feel differently.

She assured Katie that there would be a place for her at Debenham and the girl went into a fresh spate of sobbing interspersed with wet and mumbled expressions of gratitude.

Katie had gone through two of Allegra's handkerchiefs when the carriage ground to a halt. They seemed to be in the middle of nowhere but Allegra knew very well why they'd stopped. She'd been half expecting it but had hoped Nigel would wait until they could be completely private. That, however, was not to be.

She just had time to whisper reassuring words to Katie before the door flew open and Nigel's fierce visage appeared.

"Out!" he snapped at Allegra. Katie visibly shrank in her seat.

" 'Tis all right Katie. Do not fear. I shall return straightaway," she murmured and followed Nigel out.

He led her to the side of the road, out of earshot behind a clump of bushes.

"Now, Allegra. What the *deuce* do you think you are doing?" he demanded, whirling round to face her.

Allegra lifted her chin. "She was in the carriage when I got there, Nigel. She's younger than I, and so frightened and I—"

"Dammit, Allegra!" Nigel raked a hand through his hair. "This is the outside of enough! I knew about your penchant for rescuing chimney boys and maids in the family way, but *this!* Hellfire! You do not understand what she is, what—"

"She was kidnapped, Nigel, when she was *fifteen,*" she interrupted, trying to keep her voice low so that they would not be overheard. Nigel narrowed his eyes; at last he seemed ready to listen.

And so Allegra related, as briefly as possible, Katie's story. Nigel punctuated her narrative with numerous pungent expletives even worse than those she'd overheard in the Caulfield stables. He seemed as sickened by the tale as Allegra had been, and relieved that Allegra did not understand certain parts. He did not seek to enlighten her but on the contrary was most distressed that she'd heard any of it.

"I understand why you felt compelled to aid her, Allegra, but you should not have listened to such a tale. It is not fit for your ears. You are a virtual innocent and—"

"If memory serves, Nigel, I am hardly an innocent," she declared. He had the grace to flush and she pressed her advantage. "Surely you must see that my sensibilities cannot signify—why, we are speaking of this girl's very *life,* her body and soul!"

Nigel sighed. She thought she caught a gleam of admiration in his eyes but it was gone in a flash. "Very well, Allegra. We shall keep her with us. I suppose I can find a tenant at Debenham willing to take her on. Though when this story gets about, as it—"

"No, Nigel," she said flatly.

His brows arched. "No? What do you mean, 'no'?"

"The girl is terrified. I cannot send her to strangers," she said resolutely. "And—and the farmer might have a roving eye, or an older son. No, I want to keep her with me. She can be my companion or—or my maid!. I *am* in need of one, you must know."

"Your *maid?* Are you mad? You are the Countess of Debenham, and she's a—a—" Nigel ground to a halt and glared at her. "Such a thing is unheard of, Allegra," he said stiffly.

"But kidnapping and raping virtual children are not, is that it?" she shot back, her hands flying to her hips.

He followed the motion of her hands, then met her gaze again. "I do not condone such things, Allegra. But one thing has naught to do with another. It is not proper for her to be your maid."

Her eyes lit with that impish expression that somehow always spelled trouble. "I own you are in the right of it, Nigel, for she is of gentle birth. But I am not really in need of a companion, you must know, and she is a bit young for that office. Besides, I daresay Katie would prefer to be well occupied and—"

"Dammit, Allegra! You know perfectly well that such was not my concern. And aside from the proprieties, it will never serve. As the Countess of Debenham, you will need an experienced dresser."

"I shall teach her, Nigel. It need not be all that difficult. I have no wish to cut a dash, at all events. I had much rather see that terrified look leave her eyes."

Nigel stared at her for a long time. "Very well, Allegra," he finally said quietly.

And as he turned back to his horse, he reflected that his wife was a truly amazing woman. He could not imagine another woman of his acquaintance saying such a thing, let alone doing what Allegra had. But then he reminded himself that he did not wish to be wed to an amazing woman. He wanted a quiet, pliable, simple woman. Allegra was none of those things. She was fiery, and complex, as passionate in her defense of the girl as she'd been . . . Damnation! He did not want her passion! Not *in* bed or *out* of it! He did not want *her!*

Tonight, he vowed, he would stay away from her. So resolved, he vaulted onto Mercutio and took off at a gallop, leaving a gaping Jamie to follow as he might.

It rained that night, a hard, driving rain that pounded the windows of the little inn mercilessly.

Nigel did not come to her. Allegra lay awake, listening to the rain and aching for him. He had said nary a civil word to her all the day, had rebuffed her attempts to thank him for not sending Katie away, had ignored her whenever possible. And yet she ached for him with every bone, every muscle of her body, ached in a way she'd never known she could.

It was dusk the next day when they finally arrived at Debenham, for the previous night's rain had caused the roads to be awash in mud, much delaying their arrival.

It had been a difficult day at all events. Nigel had spoken very little to Allegra, joining her in the carriage only during a brief downpour. Katie had become tense and frightened at the sight of him and had prepared to go and join Nigel's valet in the second carriage. Nigel had forestalled her, saying in the most soothing of tones that she would be drenched the minute she put foot to ground and might just as well stay here. Katie had stammered gratefully, relaxing a very little bit, and Allegra had stared at her husband in amazement. Never had he addressed *her* in such a gentle tone. She did not know if he ever would, but for now, it was almost enough to know he was capable of it. Almost.

Once the rain had let up, Nigel again mounted his stallion. Katie had been astonished and grateful yesterday when Allegra suggested that, at least temporarily, she become Allegra's maid. Now Katie seemed very quiet, lost in her own tortured world. Allegra tried to engage her in discussion about what her responsibilities as lady's maid would be. Katie listened and nodded but remained subdued. Wishing to distract her from unpleasant thoughts, Allegra tried to interest her in the passing scenery.

The Suffolk terrain was soft and undulating farmland at its best. Dairy cows were everywhere in evidence, as were windmills and timber and plaster houses. The latter were colored with light rose, cream and green washes, giving the countryside a soft, peaceful air. Allegra wanted to ask Nigel about the houses, about the streams and rivers they crossed, about the water mills and fine wooden churches they passed. But he was not there, and Katie's interest was merely polite.

And so she was more than grateful to alight before the magnificent Palladian mansion that was Deben Court. A sweeping double-sided staircase led to a front portico flanked by classical columns. The entire house was faced with stone, which she knew was rather unusual for Suffolk. As she peered up in the rapidly fading light, she could see that the corner towers of the house were crowned with domes and cupolas. They gave Deben Court an almost fairytale aspect and Allegra fell in love with it straightaway.

They were met in the entry lobby by a very tall, very thin, and exceedingly proper-looking butler named Manners, and by the housekeeper, Mrs. Helmsley. She was nearly as tall as Manners and equally thin, but whereas Manners greeted "the new countess" with a genuine, albeit subdued smile, Mrs. Helmsley could barely mask her shock.

Oh dear, Allegra wondered, had she seen the miniature

of Meg? Did she realize the wrong sister had become countess? If so, there would be no stopping the gossip and speculation belowstairs. Well, there was no help for it. She forced her chin up, reminding herself that the Countess of Debenham must not be intimidated by the servants. Mrs. Helmsley was now subjecting Katie, hovering behind Allegra, to a most thorough scrutiny. Lord, Allegra thought, wait until Katie's story got about! For it undoubtedly would—every outrider who'd accompanied them had heard the scuffle in the inn yard.

Allegra smiled engagingly at Mrs. Helmsley and received a subdued response before the woman proceeded to tell "his lordship" how happy everyone was to see him home again. And Allegra feared that with very little effort on her part she and the housekeeper would be at loggerheads.

She sighed inwardly and heard Nigel request dinner, which had been held for them, in the family dining room in a half hour. He also ordered that all the staff be assembled after breakfast on the morrow for formal presentation to her ladyship. Allegra could feel unseen eyes peering at her from behind pillars and doors, and she was more than happy to wait until the morrow. Today had been quite eventful enough.

In what seemed like a very short time, Nigel had disappeared and Mrs. Helmsley was leading Allegra up the great horseshoe staircase and through a maze of corridors to the master apartments. The countess's suite had a large, beautifully furnished sitting room, a bedchamber dominated by a carved four-poster bed hung with gold brocade draperies, and a dressing room nearly the size of the sitting room. It was to the dressing room that she and Katie repaired as soon as Mrs. Helmsley left them. The footmen, carrying the luggage, had preceded them by just a few minutes and Allegra set to washing off her travel dirt. She suggested Katie do the same but instead Katie began unpacking the first of Allegra's portmanteaux.

Allegra selected a simple dinner dress of spruce green and was pleased at Katie's dexterity in helping to make the creased garment presentable.

Her toilette completed, Allegra gave Katie instructions for the unpacking and organization of her wardrobe. It seemed strange to Allegra that this was not another inn, nor a country house visit. She was here to stay. She supposed that by and by it would all begin to feel like home.

Katie said she would see to everything and bravely added that she would see to her own accommodation as well. But that was something Allegra wanted to do herself; she would see about it on the morrow. And she would also speak to Manners and Jamie regarding the male staff and Katie. Just before she went to join her husband for dinner, Allegra turned to Katie.

"You have nothing to fear in this house, Katie. No one will trouble you," she said pointedly.

Katie merely bobbed her thanks, but her eyes were suddenly brimming.

Nigel was not in the best of humors as he made his way to the family drawing room before dinner. The days of travel had been exhausting and today had been the worst of all. Mostly because he was furious with Allegra—harboring a female of ill-repute was the outside of enough! It was completely unacceptable by all standards of the polite world. And he was furious with himself for acquiescing. He poured himself a glass of sherry and sat down next to the empty grate. Damn that troublesome chit he'd married! She'd left him no choice; he could not turn this Katie out. For all she'd been through, she was little more than a child, and she'd been living in that ill-famed house against her will.

The thought of Mrs. Graves's *Le Petite Maison* sickened

Nigel. He knew of the place, of course. It was not at all a "little house," as the name implied; it was only the girls living inside who were little. He would have loved to have the evidence to close the place down. But the peers who frequented it were exceedingly discreet, especially whichever nobleman it was who was rumored to be Mrs. Graves's silent partner. Certainly the word of one pitiful victim such as Katie would not weigh very much.

But for Allegra actually to take the girl on as her maid! Lord, what was his household going to think? And word would get about, of that he had no doubt. Just as there would be speculation about the haste of his marriage, not to mention the fact that the new countess was called Allegra and not Margaret. The look Mrs. Helmsley had given Allegra had told him that, blast it all!

Nigel sipped at his sherry, hardly tasting it. His own fury at Allegra about their marriage he wished to keep private. Publicly, he would treat her with all due civility. And he would not countenance any of the staff treating the Countess of Debenham with anything less than respect; he would set the tone for such on the morrow.

Still and all, he knew it was Allegra herself who would have to earn their respect. And something told him that his household would be at sixes and sevens before that ever happened.

Having taken on Katie, he suspected, would not endear Allegra to his rather proper senior staff. Damn her! Why could she not be sensible and bundle Katie off to one of the outlying farms? Nigel took another sip of his sherry. He did not suppose Allegra would be sensible too often. She would act from her heart, not her head. And this time — hellfire! He knew she was right, not only in hiding Katie but in keeping her here in the house. Katie *did* need protection of the kind only Allegra could give her now.

Nigel swore profusely under his breath and got up to

pour himself more sherry. He resumed his seat and stared at the grate. He'd only been married for three days and his life was already inordinately complicated. And as for the nights . . . He did not want to think about what had transpired between them two nights previously, but he had been hard put to keep the images from his head these two days past. Somehow, he had steeled himself to stay away from her last night, but she had disturbed his restless dreams, and several times he'd awoken in a state most uncomfortable for a man with no relief in sight. But he had forced himself to stay away.

As he would again tonight. And he *had* to, lest he drown in her warmth. The images came now, and he could not keep them away. Allegra naked beneath him, her arms around him, her mouth pliant and giving. And those soft, desperate, delicious cries . . .

Damnation! Nigel's body tightened and he had all he could do not to dash his glass into the empty fireplace. Instead he stood abruptly and began to pace.

This was his *wife*, for pity sakes! A man shouldn't have such thoughts about his wife! It simply wasn't proper! But more than that, he would not allow himself to become besotted with her, as — as he'd been with Gina.

Nigel stopped pacing and set his glass down, running his fingers through his hair. Actually Gina and Allegra, other than their similarities in coloring, were quite different. Gina had been sensual, but her passion had been demanding in a way Allegra's hadn't. She'd had, he realized now, none of Allegra's innocence, her openness. Gina's passion had been calculating. And that, he told himself, was neither here nor there. They were *not* different. They were both passionate, devious women. As Lucinda, Charles's wife had been. And he wanted none of their kind — not in the marriage bed at all events.

He heard the rustle of her skirts and turned to the doorway, his face set in stern, resolute lines. And then she appeared, and he took a deep breath to steel himself. She wore a simple, form-fitting gown of spruce green silk. It was cut fairly modestly across the bosom, and yet the effect was devastating. His hands itched to span her small waist, to stroke her . . .

She greeted him cheerfully and he responded with subdued civility. After they had shared a glass of sherry he escorted her to the family dining room.

Conversation was curtailed through the first three removes because of the hovering footmen. Nigel was glad of their presence; he did not wish to make conversation. But when the braised goose with calf's sweetbreads and glazed root vegetables had been served, the footmen and Manners withdrew.

"You have an excellent cook," she ventured.

"Yes. You'll meet him, and the entire staff, on the morrow. Allegra," he said, putting his fork down, "you have, I assume, been schooled in how to run a large household such as this."

"Ah, of course, Nigel," she said lowering her eyes to her glazed root vegetables.

Something about her tone of voice made him decidedly uneasy. She sounded much too uncertain.

"Allegra?" he queried. She was seated immediately to his left, and without thinking he put his hand over hers. "Look at me, please."

She complied, and he wished that her rich brown eyes would not shine so in the candlelight, that the deep green of her dress would not make her skin look quite so soft and vulnerable. He cleared his throat and went on.

"Are you or are you not capable of administering this household, Allegra?"

Her pointed chin rose fractionally. "Of course, I've been schooled in how to run such an establishment, Nigel. Caulfield is not exactly a thatched roof hut, you must know."

134

"I am aware of that, Allegra," he countered, suppressing a grin, "and you have answered my first question, but not my second. Are you *capable* of—"

"Naturally, I—" He raised a brow and she sighed, propping her chin on her hand. "The truth is that when Mama took ill, Meg tried to teach me. And I *tried*, I really did, but I haven't her patience, you see. I am rather good at certain things—special . . . projects, you must know. 'Tis the daily tasks that—"

"Special projects?" he echoed. "Such as saving climbing boys?"

She sat up straight again. "Well, yes, and replacing worn draperies, and settling contretemps in the kitchens and—"

"I get the picture, Allegra," he said dryly. "All very meretorious, no doubt, but you must realize that a great deal more will be expected of you as the Countess of Debenham."

Her chin came up again. "I realize that, Nigel. I shall not disgrace you."

He could not help the smile that came to his lips. "Good. Tomorrow I shall present the staff to you. Mrs. Helmsley will review the routine with you and she is always here to help you. But I caution—you must establish at the outset that you are, indeed, mistress here."

Allegra's brow lifted fractionally. "Do not trouble about it, Nigel. I have every intention of doing just that."

His lips twitched. "Excellent. And, Allegra, you will oblige me by making no major changes in the routine here at Deben Court."

Her eyes became very round, as if to say, "I'd never think of such a thing." And then she tilted her head. "Are there any *minor* changes that you might wish me to make?"

A footman came in then, to serve an orange trifle. He lingered as they ate, so it was not until they had adjourned to the drawing room for coffee that they continued their conversation.

Allegra strolled into the room ahead of him, her skirts swaying enticingly, the faint scent of wildflowers lingering behind her. Nigel had ignored his port in order to join her and wondered now whatever had possessed him. He did not want to be here with her, did not want to be alone with her. And besides, it was setting a deuced poor precedent.

Allegra poured the coffee and settled herself on the dark blue damask sofa. Nigel sat in an adjacent wing chair. She gazed at him expectantly, not saying a word. At length he said, "I cannot think of any changes at present, but I am persuaded your feminine eye will note things. *Small* things," he emphasized. "And of a certain you will wish to do a complete inventory. Linens, crockery and the like. I own it hasn't been done in years."

"Not since your mother's time?" Allegra asked.

He frowned and shook his head. "My mother died many years ago. The inventories were done, for better or for worse, by Lucinda." As soon as he'd spoken he cursed inwardly. Whatever had possessed him to mention Lucinda?

Allegra heard the sneer in his voice as he said the name. "Lucinda?" she asked, her curiosity piqued.

His face went rigid. "She was my brother's wife."

Allegra blinked. "Your brother's wife?" She hadn't known anything of a brother, nor his wife. "Did you say *was?*"

Nigel set his cup down and rose, needing to move. He went to the window and stared out at the darkness. "She is dead. They both are," he said curtly.

He heard her come up behind him. She stood very close but did not touch him. "How did they die?" she whispered.

"A carriage accident," he said woodenly.

136

He felt her hand on his shoulder. He wanted to push it off but didn't. "I am sorry, Nigel," she said quietly. "When did—"

"Allegra," he interrupted, his voice harsh, "I do not wish to discuss it further."

The hand slipped away. He heard her take a step back. He tried to ignore the fact that he suddenly felt cold. Slowly, almost against his will, he found himself turning around.

It was a mistake.

She was much too close. He could smell her elusive fragrance. He could see the pulse that beat delicately at her throat. He could so easily reach out and touch her. But he didn't. Instead he found himself staring into deep brown eyes that regarded him with a mixture of curiosity, hurt, and something else he could not name.

"Nigel, please," she breathed, "will you not talk to me? I am your wife. Not by your choice, I know, but, nonetheless, we are wed."

"I am aware of that, Allegra," he replied, but somehow his voice had lost its angry edge. "And now I think it time you retired." It was safest that way. He did *not* want to talk to her. They had talked far too much already.

"Very well, Nigel." She took several steps back and started to turn but then checked herself. He thought she took a deep breath before she asked, "Are you—are you going to come to me tonight?"

"Allegra!" He closed the space between them. "I've told you before that you must not—Allegra, a lady simply does not speak—"

"I am merely supposed to wait, is that it, Nigel? To wait and wonder?"

"Damnation, Allegra!" Nigel whirled away and ran a hand through his hair. Had she really waited and wondered? No, he did not want to think about that. "A lady simply retires for the night. She—she doesn't ask questions!"

"I see." She sashayed to him. He wished she'd stay away. "Well then, how often, in general, does a husband usually visit his wife?" she asked with that disturbing naivete of hers.

He could not believe this! She was incorrigible! He wanted to shake her. He also wanted to kiss her. His eyes went to her mouth, to the intriguingly straight upper lip and the full, sensuous lower one. No! He very deliberately put his hands behind his back and said coolly, "That entirely depends, Allegra, and it is not a fit topic for conversation. Now, I suggest, once more, that you go up to bed."

She did not leave, however. She cocked her head at him. He knew that look. "Nigel, that night when—when we were together, did I—did I do something to displease you? You—you were so angry the next day and—"

"No!" he blurted, unwittingly putting his hands to her shoulders. However angry he was, he could not let her think such a thing. Displease him! Lord, if she only knew . . . His body grew taut at the memory, and the feel of her slender shoulders beneath his hands did not help. Yet he did not remove them. Instead he gentled them and let them slide over her arms. "No, you—you did not displease me, Allegra," he rasped, his voice suddenly hoarse. "Do not ever think such a thing."

Allegra smiled tremulously. It was all she could do not to sway toward him. His hands were so firm and large and strong. "I am glad. I did not truly think so, but I—I wanted to be sure. And Nigel?"

"What, Allegra?" Nigel asked cautiously.

"You did not displease me either."

He groaned inwardly and started to pull her close. But he checked himself and resolutely stepped back from her. This was *not* what he wanted. "Go to bed, Allegra," he growled.

"Very well, Nigel." Allegra quelled the stab of disappointment but not her curiosity. "Just one more question."

He sighed. "Yes?"

"Is it—could it be that—that a man does not wish for—well—for what we did, as much as a woman?"

He gasped. "Damn and blast it all, Allegra! I refuse to answer such a question!" Lord, he could not believe he was having this conversation. "Now go to bed!" he roared.

His raised voice did not seem to discommode her in the least. She peered at him out of unwavering deep brown eyes. "Good night, Nigel," she said at length, and then to his amazement stood on tiptoe and kissed him, ever so briefly, ever so softly on the lips.

And then she was gone, leaving Nigel to curse volubly after her. For the absurd conversation, and the kiss, had done their damage. He wondered for a moment if she had planned it and knew she had not. She was merely naturally candid, and sensual. And she was driving him mad.

He mounted the stairs only a few minutes after she did, hating himself, hating her, all the while, and knowing that for tonight at least, he would not be able to resist her.

Chapter Seven

"It is the error of the moon; She comes more nearer
earth than she is wont
And makes men mad."

Othello
William Shakespeare

Allegra was sitting at her dressing table in her nightrail
and wrapper, Katie brushing her hair, when Nigel came in
through the connecting door. Katie gasped softly and her
hand stopped midstroke. Allegra was no less surprised. She
had not expected him. He was wearing a burgundy dressing
gown this time. Allegra swallowed hard.

"Leave us," he said curtly to Katie, who fled.

Allegra remained seated and Nigel came to her. She could
see his face reflected by candlelight in the looking glass.
"The girl is terrified," he observed, one hand going to the
back of her chair. He did not touch her. Her nape tingled.
"What does she think—"

"She has had a terrible time of it, Nigel. 'Tis only natural
that she consider . . . being with a man the worst sort of
nightmare." She shivered. "I cannot conceive—"

"You must put what happened to Katie out of your mind,
Allegra." His hands went to her soft nape. He did not want
to say the next words, but knew he must. "You are my wife,
Allegra. There is no similarity at all between what transpires

140

in our marriage bed and what happened to Katie. You know that, do you not?"

He prayed she would not ask for detailed explanations; he did not think he was up to that.

She surprised him, for in answer she merely smiled softly into the mirror and clasped his hand over her shoulder. They stood this way for a long moment, the silence stretching peacefully, the warmth of her seeping into him. He did not like this silent communication. He did not want it with Allegra. Yet he could not leave, nor did he wish to simply pull her to the bed. Somehow, it did not seem right, not now.

Slowly he withdrew his hand and picked up the hairbrush. He began to brush her short thick brown curls and felt her body relax against the back of her chair. He imagined her body melting against him; his blood began to pound at the thought.

He forced himself to calm down and continued the rhythmic motion with the hairbrush. Tonight he wanted to take his time. He did not understand why. Of a certain, talk in the bedchamber was dangerous, could lead to feelings best left unfelt.

"Why did you cut it?" he heard himself ask, and set the brush down.

She turned in her chair to face him and smiled impishly. "I wanted to see what it looked like."

Amazing, he thought. As simple as that. Only Allegra . . .

Gently he drew her to her feet. He placed one hand on her shoulder and ran the other through the feathery curls. He felt a shudder go through her and knew it was not one of fear.

"Do you mind it?" she whispered.

He smiled. He did not want to but he smiled. "No. It suits you. Yet I should love to see it long. It would be magnificent."

Her luminous brown eyes searched his. "I will grow it for you." No, he thought desperately. He did not want her to do such a thing for him.

He must tell her so, but instead he said, "I would like that," in a tone he hardly recognized.

Allegra moved closer to him. His hand slid to her cheek and down her throat. Her body felt over warm. Her breasts, though he had not touched them, began to ache. She longed for him to kiss her. And at the same time she wanted to ask him about yesterday, and today. Why had he been so cold to her after their night together? Would he do so again on the morrow?

But she knew she could not ask. He would not answer and, indeed, the growing fire she saw in his green eyes might turn once more to cold shards. She could not bear that. No, she would take what warmth he wished to give tonight and deal with the morrow as it came. Tonight it was enough that he was here.

"Allegra," he was saying in a low voice. He slowly unbelted her wrapper and slipped it from her shoulders. It fell in a pool at her feet. Not for the first time she wished for any other nightgown but the billowing white one she wore. It seemed to trouble Nigel not a whit, however, as he deftly unfastened every button from throat to breasts. Her breathing became shallow. If he did not kiss her, or really touch her, soon, she was like to scream! She leaned toward him. With one hand he traced the line of her lips, and with the other he began lightly stroking her breast.

"Nigel," she moaned, swaying to him. He caught her close and silenced her with his lips. He kissed her softly, tantalizingly, until she opened her mouth for him and wrapped her arms around his neck. And then he deepened the kiss and she felt his hunger and answered it, her body growing heated, her limbs weak.

Without realizing it she reached for the sash of his dressing gown. He groaned and swung her into his arms and carried her into the bedchamber. He lay her gently on the bed and shrugged out of his dressing gown. There was no candlelight here, only moonlight, but it was enough to see him as he stood over her, naked, large, utterly male.

"You're beautiful," she whispered, and held her arms out to him.

Was it her words or that innocent yet passionate gesture that moved him so deeply? Something shifted inside of him; he did not know what. Very gently he removed her nightgown and when he gazed down at her beauty his breath stopped in his throat. "Oh, God, Allegra," he rasped as he gathered her close. And he knew, as he bent to claim her willing lips again, that he was going to drown in her, as he had two nights before. But he would surface again, of a certain, and eventually he would get her out of his system. Allegra Caulfield would *not* be his undoing!

Allegra *Hayves,* he corrected himself, and lowered his mouth.

Nigel was gone, once more, when Allegra awoke just after daybreak. But the bed was still warm from him, and she sensed he'd not been gone long. She took hope from that. That and the memories of Nigel's heat and tenderness, his urgency tempered by gentleness, buoyed her spirits as Katie helped her with her toilette.

She met Nigel in the breakfast parlor. He was polite but uncommunicative, silently handing her a part of the newspaper. She accepted that this was his morning humor. She would not let it discommode her. And perhaps she was invading a masculine domain. Ladies, she knew, were expected to breakfast much later, in bed.

But apparently Nigel had anticipated her early appearance, for when they left the breakfast parlor it was to find the entire staff ranged about the huge entry lobby and on the great horseshoe staircase. Manners, looking tall and dapper and twisting his white mustache, presented the male staff first. There were, as she'd expected, innumerable liveried footmen, then stable boys, grooms, gardeners, undergardeners, two undercooks and, of course, Monsieur Andre, the most excellent Deben Court cook. And then Mrs. Helmsley, though rather less graciously, introduced the range of chambermaids, housemaids, laundry and scullery maids.

It might have been a bewildering array, but Allegra was good with faces and tried to memorize as many names as possible. And she found herself wondering how many of them could read and write.

Kingston and Katie were not in evidence, but Jamie was there. Although he hung back in the shadows, Allegra had the distinct impression, from strategic looks cast his way, that the staff held him in the highest regard. And furthermore, she would have known without being told that despite his official position as head groom, his bailiwick at Deben was far and wide.

Mrs. Helmsley stepped aside and it was Allegra's turn to make the bride's speech to her staff. She kept this short and brief, stating that she was certain everyone was doing a fine job and hoped they would continue to do so. She would perhaps be making some minor changes in the routine in the coming weeks and knew she would have everyone's cooperation. And then she quite shocked Manners, Mrs. Helmsley and several others by concluding that she looked forward to getting to know as many of the staff as possible as she settled into her new home.

Her little speech was greeted by applause and more than one smile. Mrs. Helmsley looked formidable, Jamie grinned, and though Nigel's face remained impassive, she thought she saw a flicker of admiration in his eyes. It was gone by the time the staff had dispersed and he informed her that Mrs. Helmsley would now conduct her on a tour of the house. She might spend the day settling in. Nigel would be meeting with his steward for the better part of the day. Tomorrow he would take Allegra out over the estate.

He spoke to her in the polite tone one would use with a houseguest with whom one enjoyed a passing acquaintance. She wanted to shout at him, to pound on his chest and jar him out of his impassivity, to say "This is Allegra! The woman whose name you cried in your passion last night, the woman you held through most of the night. Talk to me, Nigel! Look at me as if I am really here!"

But his eyes, if not his tone, were remote, and she knew that last night withstanding, he did not want her here. Besides, Mrs. Helmsley hovered in the background.

Allegra squared her shoulders, bid her husband a formal good day, and turned to the housekeeper. It was time to begin her tenure as Countess of Debenham.

The house was everything Allegra had expected. There were elegantly appointed salons, a lavish ballroom, innumerable bedchambers, a conservatory, a music room, several dining rooms—in short, a room for every conceivable pastime. And though some of the rooms were in need of new draperies or upholstery, most of it looked beautiful.

Mrs. Helmsley softened a bit under Allegra's sincere praise for the house, but was not best pleased by Allegra's request to go belowstairs and see the nether regions of the house. Among the maze of rooms, there were the wet and dry laundries, the servants' hall, butler's pantry, still room, numerous storerooms and the housekeeper's room. Other service rooms, Allegra knew, were housed in outbuildings.

In one of the two kitchens, Monsieur Andre, who looked shocked to see her, was furiously stirring eggs as he screamed in French at one of the undercooks. The kitchens were well equipped and the meals she'd had thus far had been excellent. She supposed she'd have to deal with menus, but otherwise she would not interfere in this realm.

When they were once more ambling about the first floor, Allegra asked a few questions about the daily routine, which Mrs. Helmsley answered guardedly, as if she were imparting state secrets. Allegra assured the housekeeper again that she would make no major changes and she meant it. For the truth was that Deben Court seemed to run quite efficiently, and Allegra, though she was loathe to admit it, found the whole place rather daunting. It was much bigger and more complex than Caulfield. And besides, she had never paid quite enough attention to what Mama and then Meg had tried to teach her about managing such a household. She was, as she'd told Nigel, better at "special projects." Well, there was no help for it. She would simply have to learn as she went along. It would be pleasant to have some help from the staff.

But Mrs. Helmsley, her shoulders rigid and her thin lips pursed, did not look exactly helpful. At best she looked non-committal, as if she was reserving judgment about the new mistress of Deben Court. But judgment there would be, of that Allegra was certain.

Exactly what she had to do to receive a favorable judgment escaped her for the moment. However, she sensed that it was important, not only because it would make life more pleasant here but because of Nigel. Mrs. Helmsley had made it known to Allegra that she'd been at Deben since "his lordship were in short coats." Nigel obviously would have loyalties to the housekeeper and would not be best pleased to find his bride at odds with her. And Allegra very much wanted to please her husband.

"Will that be all, your ladyship?" Mrs. Helmsley's voice jarred Allegra from her reverie.

"Yes—ah—no! That is—oh, dear." Allegra did not really know what to say next. She remembered Nigel's cautionary words about establishing herself as mistress of the house and knew that she did not want to dismiss the housekeeper just yet.

Mrs. Helmsley's brow was raised in question, and Allegra did what she always did when in doubt; she told the truth. "Mrs. Helmsley, I am afraid I need your help. Deben Court is rather more grand than Caulfield Manor, you see, and — well, I do not quite know where to begin." As soon as she'd spoken, Allegra was sure she'd made a mistake. Nigel wanted her to assert her authority, not —

Mrs. Helmsley's eyes widened and her lips cracked into a smile. "Well, now, my lady, I will be pleased to help you, I will. 'Tis no wonder 'tis all a bit dauntin' for you, you bein' such a young bride and all. Why, there aren't many houses like Deben and that's a fact. Well, now, shall we discuss the menus, my lady?" Mrs. Helmsley paused in her monologue, awaiting some reply.

Allegra, amazed that somehow she seemed to have struck the right chord, smiled. "Yes, the menus. They are done once a week, are they not?"

"Yes, my lady, unless there's to be a dinner party."

"On what day did the late countess do the menus, Mrs. Helmsley?" Allegra asked and was surprised to see the housekeeper's face twist into a scowl.

"If you be meanin' *that one*," she said, "she did 'em whenever it suited her fancy, and that weren't none too often, I can tell you."

"Mrs. Helmsley, of whom are you speaking?"

The tall, thin woman squared her shoulders. "Why, *that one*. The last countess. Lord Charles's wife," she said with ill-concealed contempt.

"I see. Well, I was speaking of the earl's mother. I know it was a long time ago, but perhaps you would remember."

Mrs. Helmsley smiled again, and this time there was a warmth that had been lacking before. She nodded. "I remember, my lady. 'Twere every Monday we did the menus."

"Very well, then. I will do the menus with you every Monday."

After that there ensued a rather pleasant discussion of the

147

linen inventory, the state of the crockery, visits to sick tenants, and various other duties, once carried out by Nigel's mother. They would now be Allegra's responsibility; by tacit agreement neither of them spoke of Lucinda. Allegra very determinedly banked her growing curiosity about the last countess; there would be time enough later for that.

They had reached the morning room. Allegra gazed about her, at the small escritoire and several yellow and green damask sofas.

"The late countess did all her correspondence and accounts here," Mrs. Helmsley was saying.

It was a very pretty room, but Allegra knew instinctively that she would not be able to work here. She debated the wisdom of telling the housekeeper so now, when they seemed to have reached some understanding. But then she recalled Nigel's words, telling her she needs must establish herself as mistress straightaway, and knew what she must do.

She began by commenting on the beauty of the room. But her courage deserted her momentarily, and she heard herself instead speaking about something else entirely. She had noted this morning that some of the servants' livery seemed worn, certain maids' uniforms rather the worse for wear. She requested that these be replaced straightaway. Mrs. Helmsley's eyes flickered in surprise, but Allegra could tell she was pleased.

Emboldened, Allegra broached the topic of her own apartments. The sitting room and bedchamber were very beautiful, she assured Mrs. Helmsley. Ascertaining that Nigel's mother, and not the infamous Lucinda had done the decoration, she decided to leave the rooms as they were. Mrs. Helmsley's face relaxed even more and her smile did not falter when Allegra qualified that pronouncement. She wished the heavy gold draperies surrounding the bed removed. The canopy, she felt, was quite enough. She wanted as much sun or moonlight touching her bed as possible.

Mrs. Helmsley's tacit approval gave her the impetus to go

on. She seated herself at the Hepplewhite chair behind the small escritoire and bade the housekeeper take an adjacent chair.

Allegra took a deep breath and began. "Mrs. Helmsley, this *is* a charming room, and I am certain the late countess, er—Lord Debenham's mother, enjoyed working here very well."

"Yes, your ladyship, and the Dowager Countess before her," the housekeeper assured her. She sat straight in her chair, hands folded in her lap.

"Yes, of course. But you see, I do not think I will be able to work here. This room has a western aspect, and I prefer to do my desk work before nuncheon, with the morning sun streaming in. Besides, the morning room is used to receive visitors, is it not?"

Mrs. Helmsley's smile had turned down into a flat line. She nodded.

"I really prefer a room that is more private." Allegra paused, thinking, "I seem to recall a small pink sitting room, not far from his lordship's study. Is it in use?"

"Well, no, my lady." The housekeeper's eyes narrowed suspiciously.

"Splendid. I should like to take it over for my own use. Of course, it needs must be redone—all that pink chintz is a bit much, is it not? I should prefer blues and greens, I think."

"But, my lady, 'tis called the Pink Room! Why, it's always been pink!"

"I daresay it has, Mrs. Helmsley. But after all, an unused Pink Room does not make nearly as much sense as a much-used blue and green room, does it? And I shall need a desk there. Is there one in the attics, do you suppose?"

"B-but, my lady, the countesses have always used the morning room!"

Mrs. Helmsley looked genuinely distressed, and Allegra felt a sudden pang of sympathy for her. It was never easy to have one's little world overset in any way. But even so, Allegra would not change her mind. Nigel had told her to establish herself as mistress, and that is what she was doing. She wondered for a moment, belatedly, if she had ought to ask Nigel's permission in the matter of the Pink Room, but dismissed the notion. He *had,* after all, said she might make minor changes, and surely this was one such. Besides, Mama had always taught her that decoration was a woman's province; she needn't consult her husband except in matters of exorbitant expense or the displacement of family heirlooms. Allegra did not think yards of faded pink chintz constituted family heirlooms.

No, she was not doing anything untoward. Still, she did not want the housekeeper unduly perturbed. She smiled warmly. "Dear Mrs. Helmsley, I fear I have overset you. Indeed, that was not my intention. But you see, the Pink Room has an eastern aspect, and a terrace as well. 'Tis just the place for me to work in the mornings! And I hope you will come there, and sit with me, and help me with the accounts. You have so much more experience than I. Do say you'll help me!" Allegra cocked her head, awaiting a reply.

A bevy of emotions paraded across the housekeeper's angular face until finally she smiled and said of course she would help her ladyship. And so they went back to the Pink Room to decide exactly what needed to be done. Mrs. Helmsley promised to have the necessary tradespeople— painters, linen drapers, upholsterers, present themselves in two days' time.

And then they made their way to the third floor, where Allegra approved the room, just off the nursery, that had been given to Katie, and blushed when Mrs. Helmsley expressed her wish that the nursery be filled again sometime soon.

And so they were much in charity with each other, and would have remained so, had not Allegra, in the next few moments, let her wayward tongue run away with her. Oh, why, she lamented later, could she not have held her peace, just for a little while? She had made so much progress this morning . . .

She and Mrs. Helmsley had started down the great stairwell again, when through an open door Allegra espied a maidservant sweeping the hearth of a great stone fireplace. That was when the question popped into her head and onto her tongue before she thought to stop it.

"Do you have one of Mr. Smart's new chimney-sweeping machines?"

Mrs. Helmsley stopped short. "One of those new—why I should say not! All those newfangled machines are for vulgar mushrooms and such! No proper country family would own such a tricky device and that's a fact! Deben chimneys are cleaned right well and good by the master sweep himself, your ladyship. No need to trouble yourself about it, not at all," Mrs. Helmsley finished proudly, her hands clasped at her gaunt chest.

They stood on the first landing, facing each other. "And does the master sweep himself ascend the smoking chimneys, Mrs. Helmsley?" Allegra asked, only vaguely aware that this was far too public a place for this conversation.

The housekeeper fairly gaped at her. "Why of course not, your ladyship! That is the job of the climbing boy," she replied in the patient tone of one instructing a veritable slowtop.

"I see." Allegra felt her hackles rise and with it her confidence. This was one area of household management she knew well. And surely Nigel would agree with her on this matter, especially having met little Marcus. "Please attend me, Mrs. Helmsley. I'm afraid there can be no more use of climbing boys at Deben Court from this time forth. We shall instead make use of Mr. Smart's rather ingenious new machine."

Mrs. Helmsley's gray eyes widened in astonishment. She took several quick, agitated breaths. "Well! I'm sure it's not for *me* to say how the chimneys are cleaned!" she huffed in a tone that implied it wasn't for Allegra to say either. " 'Tis somethin' for Manners or—"

"Speak to whomever you must, Mrs. Helmsley. Manners or the steward or—or Jamie MacIntyre. Yes, do speak with Mr. MacIntyre. But do see that it is done. When are the chimneys next due to be cleaned?

" 'Tis summer, so in a fortnight, I should say."

"Very well, then. Let us see if we can obtain Mr. Smart's machine within the fortnight," Allegra said brightly, then thanked Mrs. Helmsley most graciously for the tour. But Mrs. Helmsley did not respond in kind. Her reply was in the nature of a grumble, and as Allegra glided down the stairs she felt distressed that she and the housekeeper had not, after all, parted in charity with each other. But what choice had she? There was not much time before the sweep was due.

She thought she heard a chuckle from somewhere below the stairwell and thought of Jamie. Had he overheard the conversation? Surely he would understand. But he did not seem to be about and so she sought out Manners instead. She spoke to him briefly about Katie and the need for distance on the part of the male staff.

Manners twirled his mustache and did not meet her eyes as he assured her he would see to it. Then he surprised her by stating that his lordship had already spoken to him about this very matter. Her husband, Allegra mused, was rather a puzzle.

He was not a puzzle one hour later, however, when he stormed into the sitting room of her suite.

"What the *devil* do you think you're doing, Allegra?" he demanded without preamble, causing her to jump up from the pretty but insubstantial escritoire at which she sat.

"Oh, Nigel! Do come in and close the door," she said breathlessly, and assured herself she was not afraid.

Nigel slammed the door and strode to her. "Do not seek to turn me up sweet, Allegra. You have been here less than

152

twenty-four hours and already you've contrived to set the house at sixes and sevens. Painters, upholsterers—not to mention that chimney-sweeping machine! Just what do you think you're about?"

"Nigel," she began, staring at the buttons of his silver-gray waistcoat, "you did say that I was to establish myself as mistress straightaway, did you not?"

"Yes, dammit, but that does not mean to say you needs must overset long-established routines, redecorate the house and set up a riot and a rumpus amongst the staff. Why, you sent Mrs. Helmsley hightailing it off to Manners, who went to Jamie. Only Higgins, my steward, was left out. Hellfire, Allegra, this is the outside of enough!"

Allegra forced her eyes upward. Nigel's brows were knotted into those ominous "V's." He towered over her, and yet she found that, indeed, she was *not* afraid. Instead she had to resist the urge to let her hands creep up onto his broad shoulders. She did not suppose he would appreciate that at all.

"I am truly sorry if you are distressed, Nigel, but I do assure you, I am not oversetting any routine," she said equably. "I have made no changes in the menus, nor in which days the washing and polishing and the like are done. Nor am I redecorating the house—not but what several salons need new draperies and upholstery. But I decided those could wait, for I expressly did *not* wish to set the house at sixes and sevens." Nigel twisted his mouth and she went doggedly on. "I am merely making a few minor changes in my rooms and—"

"And what of the Pink Room?" he demanded. "That is hardly a minor change."

She gazed at him pensively. "No, I suppose not," she said quietly. She did not wish to be at loggerheads with him. "But it *is* unused, you must know, and I thought—" she stopped, seeing no softening of his expression. "Oh dear, was it very presumptuous of me, then? 'Tis merely that the house has so

153

very *many* rooms, you see, that I did not think my use of just this one would discommode anyone. Perhaps I misjudged. I shall make do here in my sitting room, if you wish."

She sighed and added, "I am afraid I *am* rather impulsive, Nigel, and not very—well—self-effacing. If that is what you wish in a wife, I-I suppose I can try. Perhaps if you would but explain precisely what you *do* wish me to do as mistress of the house . . . I had thought all these things in my purview, but perhaps I was wrong. Certainly they were in Mama's at Caulfield. I know you wish me to do the inventories since you mentioned that yesterday. Is there aught else? I did give orders for the replacement of worn livery. Shall I rescind them?"

Nigel stared down at her through narrowed eyes, trying to catch any sarcasm in her tone. But he could find none. Unwittingly, his eyes traveled her length. She wore a navy blue muslin round dress that was too thin for decency, and he realized he was standing too close to her. He took a step back. She continued regarding him with wide, innocent eyes. She could not be that guileless, he thought. She did not truly mean what she was saying. She would rescind no orders. She was merely baiting him, with a sarcasm so subtle as to be nigh undetectable. She was a typical, manipulative female. Hadn't he seen evidence enough of her machinations? He would trip her up on the chimney issue.

"And then there is the matter of the chimney-sweeping machine. Of a certain you can see how *that* will overset an age-old routine here at Deben."

At that she drew herself up, and suddenly there was fire in those deep brown eyes. "No, Nigel," she said firmly. "I am willing to concede the Pink Room, even the livery and almost anything else. But I can not condone the use of climbing boys! Why, you've met Marucs. Surely you—"

"Allegra, I understand and, indeed, applaud your concern for the climbing boys," Nigel interrupted. "But these new machines are not always practical. They do not work on all chimneys, you must know."

"I am sensible of that, Nigel. At Caulfield we had to rebuild two of the chimneys so that the sweeping machine would work."

"You had to—and you expect to blithely order the rebuilding of chimneys here as well, is that it?" he nearly shouted. "Do you realize the disorder and disruption involved, not to mention the cost—"

"Oh dear. I own, I hadn't thought of that." She looked genuinely stricken. "Are you pressed for funds, then?"

"No, blast it all, I am *not* pressed for funds!" He strode away from her and then back again. "That is much beside the point, which is that I cannot have you coming in here and after one day riding roughshod over—"

"Oh, Nigel, truly I did not mean to do any such thing. 'Tis only—oh, if you had seen little Marcus's burned and bruised body! Why, I—I had rather try to climb the chimneys myself than allow one of those poor little boys to do so!" she cried passionately.

Nigel whirled away from her. He was vanquished and he knew it. She had meant every word she'd said, about rescinding her orders, about the Pink Room, even, he suspected, about climbing the chimneys herself. She was being forthright, not manipulative. And she had a kind heart that could not bear the sight of suffering. When it came close to her, she needs must rectify it. Lord knew what would happen if she ever saw the seamy side of London. For her own sake, as well as his, he must prevent that.

For now, he had several choices. He could, of course, countermand her orders, establishing quite clearly in her eyes and those of the staff that *he* was master here and would brook no nonsense. Or he could allow her that sweeping machine but no other of her proposed changes.

Nigel ran a hand through his hair, ignoring Allegra, who stood several feet behind him, waiting. If he did either of those things, Allegra would be humiliated before the staff.

She would never be able to issue an order in this house without having Manners or Mrs. Helmsley run to Jamie and ultimately, to him. She would never have the respect of the staff and her situation here would be untenable.

His third option, of course, was to let Allegra's orders stand. And now he thought on it, they were not especially exceptionable. All except the chimney business, but how could he deny her that? He admittedly had never thought much on *how* the chimneys were cleaned, but once she'd thrust the matter before him, he could not in good conscience cavil. As to the rest, she certainly had a right to refurbish her own rooms, some of the livery *was* badly frayed, and the Pink Room—Damnation! The truth was that he hadn't been inside the room in years. It certainly would not discommode him, or anyone else, come to think on it, if she took it over. Nor would his allowing it cause the staff to question who was master in this house. He was the ultimate authority at Deben and everyone, including Allegra, knew it.

No, he admitted to himself, she had not truly planned to set the house on its ears. Nor had he been truly overset by any of her proposed changes, or that the staff had been in something of a taking. No, what really had raised his hackles was the realization that there was now another person living in his house. Someone *entitled* to give orders, to make changes. And not a pliant, proper, peaceful someone, like Meg, but an incorrigible, intrepid, impassioned someone who would cut up his peace at every turn. A woman—Lord, had he ever really thought her a child?—a woman to be reckoned with. Allegra. He did not want her here.

She was his wife.

She had not moved, was waiting for an answer. "Your orders will stand," he said curtly, and then strode from the room without so much as glancing at her.

Chapter Eight

"I do wander every where, swifter than the moon's sphere."

> *A Midsummer Night's Dream*
> William Shakespeare

Nigel did not appear for luncheon. Allegra had known he would not. She felt decidedly blue-deviled. For even though she was pleased that she had won in the matter of the chimney-sweeping machine, she was not pleased that she had won out over Nigel. She did not wish any more stumbling blocks between them. She became aware, as she silently ate her meal, that the footmen were regarding her with something akin to awe. And when Mrs. Helmsley acknowledged her with the minimum of civility in the corridor a short time later, she realized that Nigel's ruling had become known. Peace at Deben, she knew, was a long way off.

In the early afternoon she went to find Jamie. Manners oversaw the indoor staff, but the stable boys and perhaps the gardeners as well were under Jamie's eye. She must speak to him about Katie.

After wandering among various outbuildings for a while, she was directed to a medium-size room attached to the side of the stables. At her knock, Jamie bade her enter and she saw that it was not, as she had surmised, a tack room, but a well-appointed office with a cheerful fireplace and a massive oak desk.

Jamie sat behind it, and he and the other occupant of the room stood as she entered. The second man was short, balding, and quite loquacious as he greeted her in response to Jamie's introduction. He was Mr. Wiggins, estate steward, and he deferred to both Jamie and Allegra before taking his leave.

Jamie seated her in a padded armchair by the side of the desk before resuming his own seat. Now she was here, she did not quite know what to say to him. He was a servant yet he and Nigel were friends. She glanced about the office, with its bank of wooden file cabinets. It was clear that he and Nigel ran Deben Court. Just how much did Jamie know about her and Nigel? Would he be cold to her as well?

It was Jamie who began. "Ye've had an eventful day, have ye no, lass?" he asked, his blue eyes crinkled up in amusement.

Allegra expelled a breath and felt her body relax. "Yes, Jamie, I suppose I have. I fear it will be quite a day when the sweeping machine arrives as well. My goodness me, what a time we had at Caulfield, teaching the footmen how to use it, for of course, the maids were too frightened to go near it. Oh dear, I do hope—"

"Dinna fash yersel', my lady. No one here will be givin' ye any trouble," he said determinedly, and she believed him. "But I'm thinkin' ye didna come here to discuss yer newfangled machine," he added.

"No, Jamie. I came about Katie. Did the earl tell you about her?"

"A bit," he replied briefly.

"Well, she has had a very bad time of it, and I came to ask if you would have a word with the stable boys and—"

"Och, lass, ye've no need to fash yersel' aboot that either. 'Tis all taken care of. His lordship and Manners and I spoke on't this mornin', ye ken. Katie is safe here, my lady."

"Th—thank you, Jamie." She was very moved by the quiet determination in his voice and was loathe to leave just yet. There was something comforting about Jamie's presence. She supposed some would say it was not proper to stay and converse with a servant, but she did not think Nigel would be of their number.

As she searched for a new topic of discourse, Jamie surprised her by saying, "His lordship said she was kidnapped."

Jamie watched the lassie's face. He did not want to distress her unduly, but he had to know. Nigel had ventured no details, and Jamie could not ask him, lest his friend wonder at Jamie's sudden curiosity.

"Yes," Allegra said with a bite in her voice. "And taken to a place called the *Le Petite Maison*. Good Lord, Jamie, how could such a place exist in this country?"

Jamie fought to still the pounding of his heart and to keep the feeling of horror from his face. *Le Petite Maison!* God's teeth, was it possible? He'd been afraid it was, given Katie's age. And now, knowing Katie had been held there unwillingly, he felt his blood go cold. Never, in all the time with Flora had it occurred to him . . . Christ, but he'd got to get Katie to talk to him. That would be difficult, for no doubt the lass was skittish around men, especially one so large as Jamie. But somehow he would win her trust. And he could not involve Lady Debenham. It would not be proper. She already knew more of that place than she ought, he'd wager.

"Jamie?" Her voice recalled him to her question.

"Och, lass," he said at length, "I'm thinkin' there is good and bad in everyone, and everything, England included." And in me, he thought in anguish. Lord, what did I do? I left her, my Flora, my wife, thinking 'twas what she wanted . . .

Allegra sighed, quelling her curiosity about the strange look on his face moments ago, "I suppose so," she said doubtfully.

"Ye must no be dwellin' on't, lass. In time Katie will come aboot," he said bracingly, trying to believe it himself. If there was hope for Katie, might there not be hope for Flora as well? But first he'd got to find her.

Jamie's eyes looked troubled and Allegra wondered what ache lay behind them. She wanted to offer him friendship, to return some of the comfort he had given her. But she did not quite know what to say, and so rose to leave. Jamie stood also and walked her to the door. They stepped out into the sunshine and on impulse she turned to him and said, "Thank you, Jamie."

Jamie's eyes crinkled again. "And what would ye be thankin' me for, lass?"

"For — for being kind."

Jamie said quietly, "Och, noo, lass, I havena done verra much, ye ken. Besides, his lordship is my friend. What I would do fer him, I do fer ye."

"I, too, could use a friend, Jamie," she said.

"An' a mon can always use anither, Lady Allegra," he responded, smiling openly now.

Allegra smiled back and wondered, when she skipped back to the house, when her husband would ever smile at her like that.

And when the lassie and her sunny smile were gone, Jamie's own smile faded. *Le Petite Maison!* The very name chilled him to the core, brought forth a rush of memories he'd thought long buried. But he could not allow them to remain buried now. Not when there was a chance . . .

Jamie went to find Katie. Perhaps she would know

about Flora. But Katie was in her ladyship's dressing room, and she jumped at his knock, fair cowered behind the wardrobe when he entered. No amount of gentle words would coax that terrified look from her face, and Jamie felt sick that he'd put it there.

"Dinna fash yersel', lassie," he finally said as he took his leave. "I only wanted to talk to ye. I'll no trouble ye noo."

Tomorrow, Jamie thought, he would try again. Perhaps the dressing room was too small; she'd felt cornered. He'd look for her tomorrow, on the first floor, or mayhap the garden. He clamped down his frustration and went about his work.

Nigel had been on his way to Jamie's office when the door opened and Jamie and Allegra stepped out into the sunshine. He was not close enough to hear them, nor could they see him. Nigel wondered fleetingly what Allegra was doing there, and took a step forward. But something stopped him in his tracks. It was the look on each of their faces, he decided. He could not say what disconcerted him so. It was only a momentary, shared smile, after all. He wanted his wife and majordomo to be in charity with each other, did he not? He was being foolish, he knew, and tried to shake off the odd feeling he had. Abruptly he turned about and went back to the house. He would see Jamie later.

By the time he did, his equanimity had returned. The strange feeling had receded, and he set his mind to business.

He worked diligently in his study all afternoon, but unwelcome images of Allegra kept intruding. Allegra last night, Allegra as she smiled at Jamie in the sunshine, Allegra in her impassioned defense of that chimney-sweeping machine. Blast! He would not let her dominate his every waking thought!

He spoke little to her at dinner, trying not to let his eyes stray to her too often. Her hair, threaded now with ribbons, framed her face with soft, silky curls that looked luxurious, eminently touchable. Her coral satin evening dress was lovely, but all he could do was imagine her without it.

No! She would not seduce him again tonight, however unwittingly. She was drawing him more and more into her web and he would not allow it!

He sent her up to bed and lingered over his port. There would be no coffee in the drawing room tonight. Nor would he think of Allegra.

He tried to distract himself with thoughts of Roger and the Viscount Creeve. It was too early to have heard from either of them, and he wondered what each was up to.

Creeve was working with the Revenue, but Nigel did not trust him. He could not shake the uncomfortable feeling that the man's sudden law-abiding fervor was really an attempt to mask nefarious activities in some other quarter. Precisely what those activities were he could not say. But somehow he knew that the letter he'd had from Creeve was not the last he'd hear from the man.

Well, that was as might be. He had granted permission for the Revenue to patrol the beach at Cliff House and now he would have to wait upon events. But he was not best pleased. In point of fact, he was rather ambivalent about smuggling. Oh, he knew it was against the law of the land, and no loyal subject of His Majesty could openly condone it. On the other hand, the economy being what it was, the running of goods provided a living for decent folk who might otherwise starve. And he believed they were decent folk, most of them, not given to violence unless provoked, nor any other criminal activities.

Perhaps his tolerance for the smuggling trade came from enjoying contraband brandy in the home of many of his friends. Or perhaps it came from his association with Roger. He sipped his port and let his earliest memories of Roger wash over him. They were near to the same age, and Nigel, Charles and Roger had spent countless summer days dodging waves, collecting sea shells and playing pirate in the caves beneath Cliff House.

Nigel poured himself another glass of port. Charles was dead now, the caves had long since collapsed, Cliff House was decrepit, and Roger . . . yes, Roger. *Where* was Roger?

Nigel sat back in his chair and tried to recall when he had first realized that he and Roger were of different "stations." Nigel had not been unduly perturbed by these "differences," which other people alluded to, but as time went on Roger was. And at some point Nigel began to realize other things, things of which Roger never spoke. Roger's mother was very young, must have been little more than a child when Roger was born.

Only once, when he'd been in his cups, had Roger spoken of his origins. He and Roger had been about seventeen and had surreptitiously dipped rather heavily into the earl's stock of brandy. Roger had volunteered the information that his mother had been housemaid in a great estate and had been cast off when her interesting condition was discovered. The earl and countess had found her and had taken her in and allowed her to stay on once Roger had come.

"I'll never forget your parents for that," Roger had said, and then for the first time Nigel asked about his father.

Nigel had only just begun to notice Roger's uncanny resemblance to the Viscount Creeve. He did not know if anyone else, including Roger himself, had.

And so Nigel, having shot the cat himself, framed his question. It was a mistake; Roger was not that drunk.

"Do you know, old boy, that you look like —" Nigel had begun, but Roger interrupted him.

"She was fourteen," he spat bitterly, and would say no more, except to vow vengeance against his still-unnamed father.

Roger's mother died that year and he went off to live on his own, refusing the earl's offer of employment at Cliff House or Debenham. When Nigel's own mother died two years later, the earl closed Cliff House. Nigel had gone back periodically, for love of the sea, but mostly to see Roger. But Roger could not always be found. He kept touch only with old Mrs. Crowley, the housekeeper who, with her ancient husband, lived on at Cliff House to this day. But even she could not always locate Roger and had once said that it was better Nigel not know "what all the lad got up to."

And what *had* he got up to, this time? Was it just coincidence that Roger had once frequented smugglers' lairs and that a smuggling ring had been operating on Creeve's land? Good Lord, Nigel certainly hoped so.

His mind whirled with thoughts, exhausting this particular topic, and returning, inevitably, to his wife. He would not go to her. He did not need her. That his body said otherwise was irrelevant. He downed his second glass of port but did not make the mistake of pouring himself a third. He knew from bitter experience that its consolation was only temporary, and he had no wish for a vile head in the morning. He rose and slowly made his way to his solitary bed.

Kingston was waiting for him, his usually impassive face looking rather agitated. After much prompting as to the cause of this, he finally said, "I do not have your brown dressing gown, my lord, as the dry laundry was occupied most of the afternoon." Kingston's nose was in the air as he held the burgundy dressing gown aloft.

"Occupied by whom?" Nigel asked, though he suspected the answer.

"By a young person, my lord." Kingston, ever high in the instep, did not trouble overmuch to hide his disdain.

Nigel sighed. "If you are referring to her ladyship's maid, her name is Katie. She is to be treated with all due courtesy as a member of the senior staff, Kingston."

"Yes, your lordship." Kingston sounded decidedly unimpressed.

Never mind, Nigel told himself. He was not about to discuss this with his valet, for pity sakes! Katie was Allegra's problem. He sashed his dressing gown and turned to dismiss Kingston for the night. Instead he heard himself say, "The girl was drugged and forcibly taken from her father's care. You have two daughters, Kingston, and a grandchild. Can you imagine if such a fate befell one of them?"

Kingston's eyes fell. "It does not bear thinking of, my lord," he mumbled.

"No. Good night, Kingston."

Kingston, rather shaken, left straightaway, and Nigel wondered what had come over him. Never had he chastised his ever loyal and competent valet! And in defense of Allegra's latest foundling at that!

He stormed into his bedchamber, threw himself down in a fireside chair, and resolutely opened a book. He did not even trouble to look at the title.

Allegra had heard what she thought was Kingston departing Nigel's dressing room. Katie had long since left hers. By now Allegra knew Nigel would not come tonight. She told herself she could sleep perfectly well without him, but she'd already tossed and turned and discarded three books. Such did not auger well.

There had been too many servants at dinner for all but the most general discourse, and when they'd departed, Nigel had lapsed into a forbidding silence. Then he had sent her to bed. He had never, she realized, given her the opportunity to thank him in the matter of Mr. Smart's new machine. Dare she go to him now to thank him?

She had never been in Nigel's rooms; indeed, she did not think she was welcome there. Certainly it had been made clear to her that in the matter of the marriage bed, it was for Nigel to come to her and not vice versa. Why that should be she did not know.

But surely Nigel could not object to her coming in simply to talk to him! Assuring herself that that was all she had in mind, Allegra drew on her wrapper and slowly walked to the connecting door.

She knocked and held her breath; he took his time about answering. When he did the breath she expelled was not at all steady. How could it be when he looked so handsome? The candlelight flickered over his dark hair and his chest, ever naked beneath the dressing gown. For the second time this day she knew the urge to rest her hands on his shoulders.

"May I come in, Nigel?" she managed, for he said nothing at all, his green eyes wide with surprise or anger or both.

Nigel blinked. What the hell was she *doing* here? Had she no regard for the proprieties? Had he not made it perfectly clear that it was up to him to decide when . . . And when he did it would be in *her* bedchamber, not his!

But she looked beautiful and uncertain and she smelled of wildflowers. He remembered her scent in bed last night. Damnation! It simply wasn't fair! He stepped aside and motioned her into the room. She glided in and turned to face him. He did not suggest she sit in one of the chairs flanking the chimney piece. At all events his bed, a very large bed now he thought on it, stood between them and those chairs.

"What is it, Allegra?" He knew his voice sounded too curt, but his manners had gone abegging. The sooner she left the better.

She took a deep breath. He could see the faint rise and fall of her breasts beneath her nightclothes. Ridiculously virginal nightclothes. He would have to see about replacing them with—No, dammit!

"I—I did not have the opportunity to thank you for—for allowing the purchase of Mr. Smart's new machine," she said at length. Was that truly the reason for this visit, or was it a pretext? "Truly, I do not mean to discommode you, Nigel. It is only that I cannot bear the thought of what happens to those poor little boys. I do not expect you to understand, but—"

"I do understand, Allegra. I am not an ogre, you must know," he heard himself say.

She cocked her head at him as if seriously considering the issue. Her face had that gaminlike expression that was all too enchanting, her pointed little chin turned up, her dark eyes narrowed pensively.

When had he stepped closer to her? Why did he not clasp his hands safely behind his back?

"No, Nigel," she replied at length, "You are not an ogre. Though I own you try very hard to be, with me at all events."

Hellfire! "Allegra, I—"

"Do you hate me, Nigel, or is it only that you are still so angry with me? For how long will you be angry?"

Her voice was soft, almost a threadlike whisper. It was she who moved closer this time. Their bodies were almost, but not quite, touching. His blood raced even as his mind cursed her. Did she have to be so damned forthright? Could she not dissemble a little, or say nothing at all? Was not a woman supposed to know the value of silence? How the devil was he to answer her? Yes, he was still angry, and would be for a long time and — and no, he did not hate her, much as he might wish he did.

He had got to get her out of his room. He could not answer her and he *would* not touch her. His hands balled into fists as he searched frantically for something to say in reply.

But perhaps she did not expect an answer, for she went on. "I know you did not want me here, at Deben, but I am. And now I — well, you barely speak to me all day and I — I do not know what you want of me." Her lower lip trembled, the tips of her breasts nearly grazed his chest, and he was lost.

"This," he rasped, putting his hands to either side of her head. "I want this."

He pulled her close and felt the warmth of her soft, sweet body against him. And he groaned, no longer knowing how to survive without her, yet knowing that with her he would not survive at all.

Allegra knew that this was all he wanted of her now. For how long could she go on telling herself that it was enough? For as long as necessary, she thought, and then his mouth was on hers. His large, strong hands were stroking her, cupping her breasts, making her body moist and warm and so weak she could barely stand. Impatiently he rid her of her wrapper and night rail. She swayed to him, trying to push off his dressing gown, pressing her lips to his bare shoulder.

She heard him groan deep in his throat and then he picked her up and carried her to bed. His bed. And then there was no more thought, only exquisite shattering sensation and a need so strong she thought she would die with the fierceness of it. But Nigel answered her need, matched it with his own, and she wondered, in the shuddering, breathless descent, how it was possible to feel so at one with another human being.

Even before she awoke she knew she would be alone. What she did not know, did not realize until she sat up in bed, was that she was not in her own chamber but in Nigel's. And then she remembered. Everything. Why could he not stay with her, just once? Especially in his own bed!

Oh, dear, what if Kingston were to find her here? It was full light out and entirely possible. Frantically she searched for her night things. They were folded neatly at the foot of the bed. She prayed it was Nigel who'd put them there. She donned them hurriedly and tiptoed to the dressing room in the vain hope that Nigel might be there. He wasn't.

She scampered to her own rooms, telling herself that some day things would change. And truly, matters stood better than she'd had reason to hope for. At the least this was not a marriage in name only. That fact was indisputable.

She rang for Katie and dressed hurriedly, hoping to catch Nigel in the breakfast parlor. He wasn't there. Nor was he in the stables when she checked a short time later. This morning Nigel was to ride with her over the estate. Perhaps he'd stopped to talk to Wiggins then, she thought. But Wiggins, his small balding head becoming rather red, said that he hadn't seen his lordship nor had any idea of his whereabouts.

Manners, when she inquired of him, twirled his mustache and looked everywhere but at her as he said that his lordship was not at home and that he did not know when he was expected.

Beginning to feel decidedly uncomfortable, she sought out Jamie, only to be told he was out riding. Her curiosity mounting even as a sense of foreboding overtook her, she ran Mrs. Helmsley to ground in the linen room. Mrs.

169

Helmsley was only too happy to enlighten her.

The tall, thin woman clasped her hands at her waist and twisted her mouth into a smile that did not reach her eyes. "Oh, did you not know? His lordship's gone to see Coke up Norfolk-way. He'll be gone some four days by my guess."

Allegra fell back against the wall to steady herself, reeling as if struck. She did not even have the wherewithal to save her pride and say something like, "Of course, I'd forgotten." Besides, dissembling was not her style.

"He and Coke visit often, don't you know," Mrs. Helmsley was saying. " 'Tis all that talk about seed drills and steam pumps and such like, I—" Mrs. Helmsley stopped short and regarded Allegra piercingly for a moment. And then her eyes softened and with them, her tone. "Now, don't be about worritin' too much, my lady. Mayhap this time he'll make the trip shorter."

Allegra mumbled something—she could not say what—and somehow got away from Mrs. Helmsley. She expected Katie might still be in her rooms and so Allegra went out to the gardens. She collapsed on a stone bench and stared unseeing at the fish pond at her feet.

He was gone. Gone to Norfolk, for several days. And everyone knew—Wiggins, Manners, no doubt every maid and footman. Only she hadn't known. He had left her to find out from the servants. Waves of hurt and humiliation washed over her with the bright morning sun. How could he have gone without telling her, without at the least leaving a note?

And how *could* he have gone at first stop, so precipitously, especially after last night? She sat for some time before the answer came to her. He had gone *because* of last night. *He* had not come to *her,* nor had he meant to. But he could not, once she had gone to him, send her away. There was some deep bond between them that went beyond the desire they obviously shared. She had known it from their first night together. It was that bond that he wanted at all costs to avoid. She did not know why. 'Twas something beyond his anger at being forced to wed her; Nigel had secrets she could not begin to fathom. And yet she instinctively knew that somehow, she must do just that. If Nigel would not tell her aught, perhaps someone else would. Someone who knew him well. Jamie.

Allegra stood up, feeling a new determination. Mrs. Helmsley might have caught her off guard, but Allegra was not about to spend the day repining on her couch or having a fit of the dismals. There was work to be done, and her first priority was to tour the estate. In the absence of her husband, who better to conduct that tour than Jamie?

He was back from his ride and she tracked him down in the tack room. "Jamie, Nigel was to have shown me over the estate today, but he is gone, and I—I wondered if you might take me. I should like to see the land and meet the tenants as soon as may be."

He straightened up from the tack he was working and gazed pensively at her. There was no twinkle in his blue eyes today. Instinctively she knew that *he* knew about Nigel's abrupt departure and her own ignorance of it.

"Aye, lass," he said at length. " 'Tis a fine notion. Shall we say after luncheon, then?"

She nodded and Jamie watched her go. Ye're a fool, Nigel Hayves, he thought, then chided himself. Who was he to judge, after all? Had he not been a fool many times over, long ago? A fool for loving Flora, so much younger than he, a fool for wedding with her when her father died in that last wretched clearance. A fool for thinking he could make her happy, he without tuppence to his name. A fool for bringing her to the land of the Sassenach, to London, trying to find work. A fool for railing back at her when she blamed him for the poverty she couldn't stand, and for storming out night after night and drinking too damned much.

And then one day she'd been gone, with only a note to say she loved him but could not go on this way. He'd scoured London for her, asking for a bonny Scots lass with hair as red as his own. And he'd tracked her down eventually to . . . to Mrs. Graves's *Le Petite Maison*.

He grimaced even now at the name; he remembered the place well. A discreet enough house, in a neighborhood of gaming hells. He'd been sick to his stomach at the thought of Flora, his young, bonny Flora, in such a place. And sicker yet that he'd brought her to this pass, whence she'd prefer such a life of shame to living with Jamie MacIntyre.

He had needed to see her, one more time, to try at the least to persuade her to come away with him. Then they'd leave London, go back north if she liked. And if she refused, why then, he'd know at the least that this was truly what she wanted. And then he would leave her in peace. What else could he do, after ruining her life so?

He thought it best to gain entry as a patron of the house, but a night's watching the door had shown him the folly of that. For every man who came and went, for all he might be in his cups same as Jamie, yet wore the look and the dress of a gentleman. And some very highborn ones at that, it seemed to him, though no passersby would tell him a single name. *Le Petite Maison,* for some reason, promised the utmost discretion, and so it was.

As Jamie had neither the speech nor the wherewithal to obtain the clothing of a Sassenach gentleman, he resolved to rely on his considerable size and sway of personality to gain him entry and an audience with his wife. Humiliating though it might be to admit that his wife was there, yet surely even in this harsh, unforgiving land there were laws about coming between a man and his wife.

172

Jamie laughed mirthlessly now at the naive, pitiful lad he had been. He'd gained entry, right enough, only to be pounced upon by two evil-looking ruffians whose size made him feel like a wee lad. They'd knocked him breathless, nearly cracked his skull, and then asked his business . . . When he'd demanded to see his wife, they'd laughed again, holding him down, and said he could not have been much of a husband if she'd come here for her satisfaction.

That was when a very elegant-looking man came into the anteroom, still buttoning his waistcoat, and demanded to know what the disturbance was about. Jamie's captors addressed him as "your lordship" and none too gladly encouraged Jamie to explain his errand. When he did, the man's cold-looking face had broken into a nasty smile.

"The little Scottish filly? Why I've just come from her. Welcomed me with open arms, you must know, and for the second night in a row. I left her purring like a little kitten, a wee kitten as she would say, and a good deal richer."

Jamie felt sick to his stomach. He was also so angry that he wanted to kill someone. But those two huge swine had him pinned down, and kept him thus as "his lordship," whose name he never learned, gave further testimony to the pleasures provided by the little Scottish whore. When he described a certain beauty spot Flora had on her right hip, Jamie nearly choked on his rage. There could be no doubt it was Flora. He fought to be free, meaning to tear up the stairs and break down every door until he found her.

Later he would remember only being caught midflight and pummeled brutally. He knew nothing more until he awoke, broken and bleeding, in some alley the next day. Twice more, accompanied by friends, who hadn't known his true purpose, he'd tried to force his way into that vile house. All he'd gained for his pains was the sickening

173

knowledge that the *Le Petite Maison* catered to a discreet, highly placed clientele with a predilection for very young girls. Flora, at sixteen, was not at all among the youngest. He'd gotten that and a broken arm, two black eyes, cracked ribs and a swollen knee which to this day still pained him on occasion.

In desperation he'd stolen what he thought was enough money to enter as a paying customer. But despite his attempts at disguise, he was too easily recognizable and too obviously not a fashionable gentleman. His money was taken and he barely escaped with his life. But before they threw him out, a very young, very scantily dressed whore came down to tell him that Flora was otherwise occupied but had sent him a message. He was embarrassing her, she said, and wished he'd go away and go on about his life while she went about hers.

Jamie had never gone back. He'd taken to the bottle and to life in the streets with vengeance, not much caring what happened to him. And then he'd met up with Nigel Hayves, and when Newgate was staring him in the face, he'd found he did not want to die after all. And so he'd come to Debenham. To a new life.

He let everyone think his wife was dead; at times he half believed it himself. It was quite possible, at all events, that disease had long since claimed her.

He had never breathed a word of the truth to another living soul, so great was his shame. Least of all would he tell his lordship. For the earl might have wanted to help, might even have had the wherewithal to pull it off, but Flora did not want to be helped. Even the life he could offer now, with a cottage on the estate, would not lure a woman used to the fripperies her whoring could buy her.

And so he'd kept his own council, not wanting even his friend to know his shame. And sometimes Jamie was able to forget for weeks at a time, and he sought solace with willing girls from the village, whom he treated as generously as he was able.

Life went on. Until Allegra Caulfield Hayves had rescued a frightened young girl who'd been forcibly taken to the *Le Petite Maison*. And drugged, if rumors belowstairs were to be believed. Oh, God, could they have drugged Flora, drugged her and forced her to—His entire body went cold now at the thought. Horrible, twisted images of what might have been her fate had tormented his dreams last night.

God's teeth, why had it never occurred to him that she might have been there against her will? Because the girls he *had* seen had looked perfectly happy, because he'd heard testimony to her willingness, because she'd left Jamie of her own free will. He still had her note to prove that. Also because Jamie had never been quite sober in those days, and because, for all his street-surviving ways, he was a Highlander unused to London and it had never occurred to him that such a thing was possible.

But now he knew it was, and it might be too late. Flora might well be dead. Katie might know. He had got to try again to talk to Katie.

A sudden urgency, born of all the horrid memories, seized him, and once more he went in search of the girl. This time he found her in the laundry garden, pulling clean linen from the line. She jumped when he softly called her name, then cowered behind a long, hanging night rail. A wave of remorse washed over him, but still he persisted. He could not back away again.

"I'll not harm ye, lass. I'm sorry I frightened ye yesterday. Indeed, I only want to talk with ye a minute, if ye'd give me the time."

She regarded him with the frightened eyes of a startled doe.

"Och, lass, I'm a friend to his lordship, and her ladyship, and I mean to stand yer friend as well."

"What do you want of me?" she rasped. Her fright twisted like a pain in his belly. Flora had been nearly her age. Had she stood thus, terrified when . . .

"I am in need of help, lass, and ye are the only one who can give it," he said in a gentle voice. He did not move, and slowly she came out from behind the night rail.

"How can I possibly help you, Mr. MacIntyre?" she asked, bewildered.

He smiled. "Ye can start by callin' me Jamie. Near everyone does, ye ken."

She smiled back hesitantly, and he invited her to be seated on a stone bench. He did not sit beside her but hunkered down in front of her, so that his large frame was on a level with hers. And then he began. "I'm needin' to ask ye a question, lass, aboot—aboot that terrible place ye come frae."

"No!" she cried, jumping up. "You cannot ask me to speak of that!"

Jamie stood as well, his face crestfallen. It was too soon for her; she needed more time. But he did not have time.

'Tis sorry I am, lass. I should no have spoken. 'Tis only that I thought . . . happen ye might have heard aught o' her."

"Of—of whom?"

Her voice was a mere whisper; his cracked as he next spoke.

"There—there was a lass. I need to find out if—if she's still there."

Slowly, Katie sat back down. "Who is she?" she asked without looking at him.

Jamie sank down onto the far end of the bench. "I maun have yer promise, lass, not to repeat aught of what I tell ye to a livin' soul, not her ladyship, nor his lordship, nor anyone."

176

At that her head came up and her eyes met his in puzzlement. " 'Tis my shame, ye ken," he said quietly. "Ye understand aboot shame, do ye no, lassie?"

She lowered her eyes and nodded. "I promise," she whispered.

"She—she'd be aboot two and twenty the noo," Jamie began, and found that he had to force the words out. Even after all this time, they burned in his throat. "Her name—her name was . . . Flora. She had flamin' red hair and green eyes."

Katie looked at him again. "Was she a Scot, like you?"

"Aye. She was kin to me, and—" Jamie's voice faltered and he looked away. But he forced himself to finish. He needed Katie's help; she had to know the truth. "And she was my wife."

Katie gasped; their eyes met and flew apart. "I havena seen her in nigh onto six years. She—she ran away, ye ken, and I tracked her to—to that place. But they wouldna let me in, though many's the time I tried. And I—God's teeth—I thought she wanted to be there." Jamie's voice was thick with emotion; he pounded the bench beside him. "And so I left—left her there. And grieved fer her. But never, until *ye* came here did I imagine that—that they might ha' been forcin' her, my Flora, all the while."

It was as well he was finished, for he could not utter another word. His eyes were wet and there was a huge lump in his throat.

He heard the sound of sniffling and looked over to see that Katie's cheeks were wet. He wanted to touch her hand, to give comfort and take, but dared not.

"A few of the girls seemed to—to like it there," Katie began in a threadbare voice. "But I think most were—were like me. Young and—and very frightened. 'Course, they didn't let me talk much to the girls."

"Did ye hear aught o' my Flora?"

"I never heard the name Flora." Jamie felt a burning, an explosion somewhere in the region of his heart. To have had hope rekindled and then dashed so fast.

"But there was someone," Katie was saying, "someone they called Emerald. I only saw her once. She was very sick, you see. One day one of the girls asked me to bring a tray to her."

Jamie sighed heavily. What had that to do with him? But Katie's next words caught his attention, and held it. "Mrs. Graves changed many of the girls' names. I was called Daisy. I think it made it harder for—for us to be found. Emerald—well, I only saw her the once, you see, but I remember her. She seemed much older than your Flora, perhaps even thirty. But she did have green eyes and—and I think her hair was red. It was partly hidden under a cap, and very matted down—she being so ill and—"

"What was wrong with her?" Jamie asked, terrified and hopeful all at once.

"I do not rightly know. Perhaps an inflammation of the lungs. But not the wasting disease, nor the pox, or Mrs. Graves would have turned her out."

Jamie tried not to let the bubble of hope in his chest grow too big. There could be countless women with green eyes. And this Emerald was too old. But then, illness did that to one . . .

"There is one more thing you should know, Jamie. When she spoke to me—"

"She spoke to ye?"

"Yes. A little. Her voice was weak and raspylike. I brought her a tray of tea and biscuits and she said, 'Thank ye, lass.' Only those three words, Jamie, but—but she sounded just like you."

Jamie's eyes were full; now it was his cheeks that were wet. Blindly he reached for Katie's hand and she let him take it. He released her after a moment and looked out at the billowing clothes on the line. "Did anyone ever speak of her, lass? Do ye ken anythin' more of her?"

"I own I was curious, Jamie. But all I ever learned was that she'd been there for a long, long time and that Mrs. Graves wanted to keep her if—if she recovered."

It was little enough to go on, but it was possible. His Flora might still be there, ill but alive. He had to go after her. He *had* to find out if Emerald was, indeed, Flora. And if she was, to get her out.

He thanked Katie profusely, asking if he might speak to her again once he'd thought up some plan.

"Yes, of course," she said, but stopped him as he rose to leave. "Jamie, pray do not do anything foolish, or rash. The house is well guarded. You will need help. Perhaps Lord Debenham—"

"No!" Jamie burst out. Telling Katie had been difficult enough, but it was, in a sense, a shared shame. Telling the earl would be impossible. Jamie would never be able to look him in the eye again. Nor could Jamie allow his friend to become embroiled in such a sordid business. And it might all be for naught. Emerald and Flora might not be one and the same.

"I understand," Katie said softly. "But—but if it means—"

"Aye," he interrupted. He did not need her to finish her sentence. If it meant Flora's life, he would swallow all this pride, he would do anything! But first he had got to be sure!

"Lady Allegra would understand," Katie ventured and he knew was true. But how could he speak of such things to a lady born and bred? "I do not think her ladyship would have the vapors, you must know, and I am persuaded that she is most resourceful."

Jamie smiled at Katie and shook his head sadly. What

179

she was suggesting was unthinkable. And yet, in truth, he did not think Lady Allegra would condemn him. Would the earl? They were friends, after all. But somehow Lord Debenham represented to Jamie all that was good and noble in this Sassenach land. He had saved Jamie and had placed utmost trust in Jamie's integrity. In a way his lordship would be more shocked than Lady Allegra. But most of all, he would be disappointed.

No, Jamie must go about this business alone. At least until he found out the truth. And if Flora *was,* indeed, in Mrs. Graves's house, then Jamie would put cap in hand and go to the earl. He would tell him the whole and beg his help. And *this* time Jamie would not give up until Flora was back with him.

Jamie took his leave of Katie and spent a very pensive morning dreaming up and discarding dozens of ideas for breaking the walls of the evil *Le Petite Maison.* He finally settled on the first problem he had got to face—how to convince the earl to let him go to London. That alone would be difficult enough. The earl knew Jamie hated London; usually it was his lordship convincing Jamie to go.

His muddled thoughts took him right through his luncheon, and then it was time for his ride with Lady Allegra.

Allegra had spent the morning familiarizing herself with the house, engaging in brief conversations with various servants, and finally settling down to begin working on the linen inventory. Mrs. Helmsley's manner had softened somewhat as they worked side by side in the cramped linen room, and Allegra had been very glad of the work. It kept her mind off Nigel.

Jamie was smiling when he met her in the stable yard after luncheon. Allegra smiled back, telling herself not to dwell on the fact that it should have been Nigel showing her the estate. Nigel was not here. He did not want to be here, or rather, did not want to be here with Allegra. Not during the daylight, at all events. He had made it very clear that all he wanted of her was what happened between them in the moonlight.

Perhaps one day his anger, and whatever other demons drove him, would abate. For now, Allegra must build a life for herself, by herself, at Deben Court. She suspected this would not be the last time he would leave her here on her own. And she supposed she could rail at him about this and let him know she would not stand for such shabby treatment in future. To be left behind was bad enough, but to be left alone straightaway after their arrival as newlyweds, and then not to be informed . . . Yes, there was plenty to fly up into the boughs about. And perhaps once she would have.

But now, somehow she did not think she would. He had still not got over his shock and anger over the circumstances of their marriage, and she bore some guilt in that. But there was more. She could never be satisfied with a marriage that consisted of only nocturnal visits whenever it pleased her husband. No matter how wonderful those visits were, Allegra wanted more of a marriage. Much more.

She did not know how she was going to get it. She knew only two things. One was that she was going to need a great deal of patience, a quality which she'd always been sorely lacking. And the second was that railing at Nigel would not avail her anything.

And so she had thrown herself into work this morning and determined to put on a cheerful face as she toured the estate with Jamie. It was not difficult. Jamie was an excellent guide. She suspected he knew the estate as well as Nigel.

He had met her in the stable yard with a beautiful dapple gray gelding named Windstar. The gelding was just frisky enough to still the pang of homesickness that swept through Allegra when she thought of her own mare, Leda. Jamie's green eyes twinkled at her when she nodded her approval of Windstar. Did he know that she missed Leda? Horses were his specialty, after all.

For a time they had ridden in silence. Allegra was enjoying the feel of a lively gallop once more. It seemed so long since she had last ridden. She did a quick mental count. Good Heavens! Was it truly less than a fortnight ago that they had left Caulfield? Oh, to be riding over the land again! She would ask Jamie if she could ride Windstar again tomorrow. Eventually she would have to get up the courage to ask Nigel to send for Leda.

After a while she forgot which horse she was riding and simply gave herself up to enjoyment of the scenery. Nigel's part of Suffolk—and it was, she gathered, a very large part—was quiet and pastoral and lush. There were gently rolling hills and woods so thick with trees she thought she would get lost for days without Jamie's expert guidance. There were half-timbered houses plastered and colored with green and rose washes. And then there were the farms, small, well-tended tenant farms and large stretches of the home farm where Jamie pointed out many of the earl's new innovations. The wheat that was rapidly replacing rye, the steam pumps, the crop rotation. Then there were tracts of fenland, with tower mills to drain them. Windmills and watermills seemed to dot the landscape, their perpetually rotating wheels a testament to the fact that there was prosperity in the land.

Jamie stopped to introduce her to several of the tenant farmers and their wives and the brief conversations she had with them confirmed what she already surmised from the land. Nigel was a very good landlord. And he was quite a farmer.

She was happy to talk to the tenants about Nigel, about the land, and she asked questions about their families. At one farmer's cottage the latter prompted an invitation to take tea with the farmer's wife. Jamie encouraged her to accept while he followed the woman's husband out to the barn. Allegra enjoyed the strong tea and scones and home-made jelly, as well as listening to Mrs. Johnston relate amusing stories about her grandchildren. Allegra told a few stories of her own, including one about Marcus, city born and bred, setting up a riot and a rumpus on his first encounter with the Caulfield chickens. Mrs. Johnston seemed very interested in little Marcus and Allegra told her briefly about how he'd come to be at Caulfield. But then she thought perhaps she oughtn't to have — Nigel might not like that particular story to be got around. However, it was too late now, and so she simply enjoyed the rest of her tea.

When she and Jamie were about to depart, she caught a brief look that Mrs. Johnston gave Jamie. It was one of approval, and something else, perhaps . . . relief.

She waited until she and Jamie were mounted and on their way again before speaking. "Jamie, why do I have the feeling that I've just passed some kind of test?"

At that Jamie threw back his head and laughed heartily. "Aye, 'tis a verra clever lass ye be," he said, then added, "Ye canna blame folk fer bein' curious aboot the earl's new bride, noo can ye, lass?"

"No, I suppose not. 'Tis just that she looked . . . relieved. What was she expecting, Jamie?" The minute she spoke the words she thought she knew the answer, or part of it. But she was not sorry she'd asked the question.

Jamie sighed heavily and a glance in his direction told her he was weighing his next words carefully. "Well, I daresay ye'll hear aboot it sooner or later. There'll be some . . . comparin' ye . . . to the late countess, wife o' Charles, the late Lord Debenham. Ye see, they—ah—didna like her verra well, ye ken."

"Why, Jamie?"

"Och, well noo, who can say—"

"Jamie," she interrupted pointedly, "please tell me the truth. I—I need to know."

He looked at her oddly, his green eyes piercing. " 'Tis no fer me to tell ye, lass."

"My husband told me that the late earl and countess died in a carriage accident. But that is all he would tell me. He—he seemed overset about it still."

"Aye. It happened right before I met his lordship. Some four years ago, it were. 'Twas a verra black time for him, ye ken, and I think he still grieves for his brother."

"And Lucinda?"

Jamie sighed. "The lady was verra bonnie, with dark hair an' dark eyes, like ye, lassie. But she dinna have yer nature, ye ken?"

"Whatever do you mean, Jamie?"

"She—she was no a good woman," he said grimly and then, as if he thought he'd said too much, he spurred his horse to a gallop.

Allegra pondered his words for hours afterward.

Chapter Nine

"Mumbling of wicked charms, conjuring the moon . . ."

King Lear
William Shakespeare

Allegra spent a restless night, tossing and turning and trying to tell herself that she did not miss a husband who did not want to be with her.

The next morning there was no sign of Nigel, nor a message from him. Allegra told herself she had expected neither one and went resolutely about her business. Having secured Jamie's permission to ride Windstar at any time, she took the gelding for an early gallop over the hills and then ate a large, if solitary, breakfast.

The tradesmen she'd requested arrived — the upholsterers, two painters and the linen draper. A carpenter arrived as well, a Mr. Applegreave, saying that as he heard there was work being done at the Court, he thought a carpenter might be needed. Mrs. Helmsley, Allegra learned later, was all for sending him away but Manners insisted on asking Lady Debenham. Allegra took one look at the lean man in his slightly threadbare clothes, and recalled that the cupboard in her dressing room needed repairing. So, now she thought on it, did the table in the linen room. And perhaps she could do with a bookcase in her soon to be blue-green sitting room.

The man's face lit with gratitude and Manners, his eyes

twinkling, silenced Mrs. Helmsley's grumbling about what the earl wouldn't like.

Allegra busied herself all that day and the next with the tradesmen. She tried to keep the disruption to the household at a minimum, tried to stay clear of Mrs. Helmsley. She did beg the housekeeper's assistance, Saturday morning, in foraging in the attics to choose a desk.

"For I own you will know the history behind each piece of furniture we happen upon, Mrs. Helmsley. If I find a desk I like, I should like to know who used it, and when. You are so much a part of Deben Court—do say you'll help me!"

And so the housekeeper had done. And by the time Allegra had chosen a substantial but graceful mahogany desk that had belonged to Nigel's grandmother, Mrs. Helmsley had gone so far as to smile at her new mistress. Allegra felt her spirits rise and was not at all prepared for the conversation she overheard a short time later.

She was rounding the corner near the butler's pantry when the voices froze her in her tracks.

" 'Tis a good thing you've done, Mrs. Helmsley, helping her ladyship to find the desk and all," Manners was saying. Allegra blinked. She did not imagine it was like Manners to be so forthcoming.

"I do hope so, Mr. Manners, and that's a fact. She has a way about her, most engagin' she is, makin' a body loathe to refuse her aught. Not but what it don't seem the earl finds her all that—I mean to say—"

"Mrs. Helmsley!" Manners blurted in shocked tones. Allegra felt sick in the pit of her stomach and was forcibly reminded of the words of some long-forgotten governess. Something to the effect of eavesdroppers never hearing well of themselves. But no power on earth could make her leave her present post.

" 'Tisn't seemly, what you're meaning to say," Manners continued. Allegra could imagine his nose in the air, hands behind his back.

"P'raps not, but 'tis truth all the same, Mr. Manners, and well you know it. I've known the earl since he were in short coats. I know when he's happy and I know when he's not. And I'll warrant his lordship ain't happy now." Mrs. Helmsley paused and lowered her voice. "He was supposed to have married the other sister, you know."

"Well, you don't say? But he did not, did he?" Manners would be twirling his long, white mustache by now, Allegra thought. "You've been listening to kitchen gossip, Mrs. Helmsley. Not at all the thing, you know."

"I do not hold with gossip, Mr. Manners!" the house-keeper declared indignantly. Allegra pictured her clasping her hand to her thin bosom. "But there be no escapin' facts. And facts say there's somethin' havey cavey 'bout all this. The wrong sister, and then tyin' the knot so hastylike, and then that maid of hers, well!"

"Mr. MacIntyre has made it clear that we are to treat Katie with all kindness," Manners said warningly. Allegra silently blessed him.

"All well and good, Mr. Manners, and a poor dear soul she is, I reckon, not puttin' herself forth nor nothin' untoward, but what sort of lady takes such a one on as maid, I'd like to know?"

"The same sort that insists on a chimney-sweeping machine, I'll warrant. And if you'd spend less time at the gossip mill, and more using your eyes, woman, you'd see that the earl married the right sister, after all." Allegra blinked. There was a warmth in his tone she'd never heard before. She could almost see him smiling. Whatever did he mean?

"Whatever do you mean?" Mrs. Helmsley echoed her thoughts. "Seems to me his lordship avoids the countess often as not."

"Maybe so, but he can't take his eyes off her all the same."

"How do you know that means aught?"

"Well now, I was wed once, I was, Mrs. Helmsley, and I know." He actually chuckled. "Yes, indeed, I do believe I know." Allegra felt herself flush slightly, and a most pleasant warmth rippled over her. Did he know? Could he be right?

Mrs. Helmsley's voice interrupted her thoughts. "I see," she said in an exceedingly odd tone. "And—er—tell me, Mr. Manners"—the housekeeper hesitated and for some reason Allegra imagined her patting her gray hair under the white mobcap—"would you be thinkin' to wed again sometime?"

Complete silence greeted this extraordinary question. Finally Manners cleared his throat. "No, I would not, Mrs. Helmsley!" he declared. "Now I believe we both have duties to attend to," he added imperiously, and strode toward the door.

Allegra, stifling a bubble of merriment, grabbed her skirts and ran for the nearest turn in the corridor.

On Saturday afternoon Allegra received the first of the expected bride's visits. Two ladies came, Mrs. Bailey, the vicar's wife, and Lady Wickens, the wife of the squire. Mrs. Bailey was a kindly woman with pink wrinkled skin and silver-blue hair. She seemed ill at ease and Allegra sensed that Mrs. Bailey thought it too soon for a bride visit. Allegra thought so as well—especially since the groom was not in residence!

She sincerely hoped the ladies were ignorant of that mortifying fact, but Lady Wickens dashed that hope straightaway. She was a tall, stout, formidable-looking woman with a strong nose and a smile that for some reason Allegra did not trust. After three minutes in her company Allegra knew that she disliked the woman heartily.

It was obvious that she had bullied the vicar's wife into this rather premature visit. While Mrs. Bailey was all flustered apology, Lady Wickens merely smiled cagily and said, "I know 'tis rather early for our visit. Why you've been wed less than a fortnight, poor dear! But when I heard that the earl had gone north to see Coke again, leaving you *all alone* in this big, strange house—well! I said to dear Mrs. Bailey that we simply must come to bear you company. I do hope you will consider us your friends, Lady Debenham."

Allegra thought she would rather befriend a viper than Lady Wickens, but she smiled as sweetly as she was able over the rim of her teacup.

She was still smiling twenty minutes later when Lady Wickens invited her and Nigel to a dinner party on Thursday night. But her smile was becoming more and more forced.

"Just a few people, you understand," Lady Wickens was saying in a voice dripping with honey, "to give you the opportunity to meet some of your new neighbors." There was something about the way she spoke that made Allegra think there was poison in the honey. She had the distinct feeling that she would not enjoy this dinner party, and that Lady Wickens had a hidden motive in organizing it. And that motive had naught to do with hospitality.

She thought of Mrs. Bridgebane and her little luncheon party with its decidedly hidden agenda. But somehow Allegra knew, had always known, that Mrs. Bridgebane meant well. Instinct told her that Lady Wickens did not.

Nevertheless, Allegra met the woman's gaze steadily. "How kind of you, Lady Wickens. I shall relay the invitation to Lord Debenham when he returns."

"Excellent. Then you *do* expect him home this week?" Lady Wickens probed.

"Yes," Allegra replied tautly. She did expect him, after all, though she had no idea of his plans.

Mrs. Bailey, Allegra noted, was looking most overset, and was probably as relieved as Allegra when Lady Wickens rose to signal the end of the visit.

Allegra decided not to go to church on Sunday. Perhaps she was being cowardly, but she did not care. She simply could not face the whispers and speculation that she was certain to encounter about Nigel's absence.

And so she spent a rather quiet morning writing to Meg—a task which took a great deal of time as she tried to avoid telling the truth of how matters stood here—and trying to fight heretofore unaccustomed pangs of loneliness. In the afternoon she busied herself with taking food baskets to several tenants who were ill. It was just before teatime that she happened to ask one of the maids to convey a certain book to her. She had left it with a pile of others by her bedside and she was on her way to the garden. The red-cheeked maidservant's name was Sally, and she stammeringly admitted to Allegra that she could not read.

And so Allegra had her first pupil at Deben Court. They would meet two afternoons each se'enight in the schoolroom. As Sally skipped away, Allegra's mood brightened perceptibly. Perhaps if she kept herself busy enough, she would shake the ever increasing and oppressive feeling of loneliness that seemed to engulf her.

Of course she would, she told herself bracingly. She only felt this way because she was far away from family and familiar faces. She would become accustomed to Deben Court and then all would be well. Of course it would. This was to be her home. She would make friends here. She already had Jamie and Katie to talk to. And perhaps there would be someone in the neighborhood, someone of her own station, near to her age, whom she might befriend.

Her loneliness, she told herself, had naught to do with her husband's absence. She did not miss him. How could she, when he said nary a civil word to her all day, when he obviously did not miss *her?* Nor did she miss him at night. The strangely sensual images that disturbed her dreams at night had nothing to do with Nigel!

Nigel Hayves was not best pleased with himself. What was he doing, cantering down the winding road toward Deben Court at dusk on this hot, dusty Sunday? Coke had invited him to stay at Holkam Hall for several more days to discuss the new strain of cattle he was breeding. Why had he not stayed? Why had he pleaded pressing demands at home?

There *were* no pressing demands at home—Deben Court ran quite well in his absence, especially when Jamie was there, and nothing had changed. Deben still ran quite well, despite—oh blast!

Everything had changed. *She* was there. But she was not, of course, the reason for his precipitous return! He had not missed her at all, had not thought of her every-time he passed some chit with nut brown hair along the roadside, nor every time he stood before one of the magnificent chimney pieces at Holkham Hall and found himself wondering how it was cleaned. Nor had he missed her in the nights, which seemed inordinately long and over-warm, the canopied feather bed at Holkham somehow too big and too hard for sleep to come easily.

No, he had not missed her, nor was he looking forward to being home. Lord knew what a disturbance his wife might have created in his absence.

And then there was the other matter. He had left abruptly, just two days after their arrival at Deben. Had left his bride of less than a se'enight and—and worse, he had left without a word to her. Not a whisper while she slept, not a note propped on the pillow. He shook his head even now with chagrin at himself. He could not remember when he had last behaved so poorly.

He had known what he was doing early Thursday morning but had been unable to help himself. All he had known from the moment he'd awakened was that he had to get out. Out of his bed, where she slept beside him, out of his chamber, out of his house. As great as his need to have her the night before, so was his need to leave her in the morning. He could not even bring himself to write a note, to communicate in any way.

He simply had to get away, before it was too late. Too late for what was something he was unable, or unwilling, to contemplate.

And now he was back. He would see her again. She would be angry. And that, he told himself as he ascended the sweeping staircase leading to the front portico, was just as well.

Manners opened the door for him. Nigel swept inside, handing the butler his hat and gloves as they exchanged greetings. And then he was bounding up the stairs, taking them two at a time. He stopped himself halfway up. What the devil was his hurry? He proceeded at a more decorous pace. Allegra, he imagined, would be dressing for dinner. He would go to his own rooms, remove his travel dirt, and await Kingston. He would see his wife at dinner.

Instead he found himself knocking at her door just a moment later.

"Come in," she called and he entered her sitting room. She was at the escritoire, writing. She looked up at his entrance and the quill dropped from her hand. Then her gamin face lit in a smile of welcome, her brown eyes shining as she jumped up and turned to him. That smile did something to him. It was a smile of pure delight, sensuous and childlike all at once. Instinctively, he held out his arms. She hurried toward him, her step light, almost prancing.

And only then did he realize what he was doing. He dropped his arms. She stopped in her tracks; the smile faded. He watched it leave with regret, but knew it was best this way. She stood now some five feet from him. She still wore an afternoon dress, a form-fitting round dress of teal blue muslin. She had undone the top two buttons, a concession, no doubt, to the heat. He felt his own heat rise as his eyes swept her length and he contemplated her soft curves. He had missed—no, blast it all, he hadn't!

"Nigel," she said evenly, "what a surprise. Welcome home."

He listened for sarcasm in her tone, looked for it in her eyes, but could find none. Her smile was tentative now, yet he knew her welcome was genuine. He was relieved and at the same time bewildered. Where was the anger?

She took an uncertain step toward him. He ought to nod curtly, tell her he would see her at dinner and depart. Instead he moved forward, slowly, inexorably.

They met somewhere in the middle. He took her hand. It was so small in his, so delicate. He brought it to his lips and felt a tremor go through her. He felt none too steady himself. "I was able to conclude my business early," he managed.

"I'm glad."

"I—I went to see Coke."

"Yes, I know." He raised a brow in question. "The servants told me."

He wished he hadn't asked. He did not need the reminder that he'd left her to find out from the servants. He searched her eyes for the reprimand he knew he would find there, but he saw only their deep, brown warmth. And then unwittingly his eyes traveled to her lips, pink and full, with no indentation on top at all. He wanted to take them with his own, and yet he wanted to maintain his distance. He knew he had ought to apologize, and yet he did not want to. He was a man; he could come and go as he pleased.

"I had to leave," he said firmly. "My business often calls me away."

She heard the challenge in his voice; he would not apologize for his abrupt departure. She had understood why he left, and she understood this, too. It was a matter of his pride. Men seemed to have an inordinate amount of it. But what of *her* pride, and the humiliation she'd felt when the servants had had to tell her he'd gone?

She cocked her head at him. He had stiffened. He was steeling himself, she realized, for her anger. Fury which would be most justified!

But she had realized days ago that railing at him would avail her nothing. She'd thought she would have to clamp down on the fiery words waiting to be spoken. Instead, it suddenly occurred to her that she did not *want* to be angry with him, to argue with him. She wanted to enjoy his company. Perhaps he might even enjoy hers.

Besides, he seemed so prepared to face down her wrath. She would surprise him.

"I know you had to leave," she said simply. That much was true. "You must be tired. Have you traveled all day?"

It took him a moment to respond. He appeared taken aback, disoriented. She wondered if he'd been spoiling for a fight, if she'd taken the wind out of his sails. She smiled inwardly at the thought.

"Yes. I—I suppose I had ought to go and remove my travel dirt. I had thought you would be dressing for dinner.

"No, I told the staff I would simply have a tray up here. Would you care to join me?" she asked impulsively, but then added, "Or shall we both dress for dinner?"

Of course they had ought to dress for dinner, Nigel told himself. It would be beyond foolishness to dine with her here, so intimately. She stood so close to him, her small hands at her waist. She smelled of wildflowers. Her pointed little chin was tilted up, her eyes expectant. Why was she not furious? What was going on in that elfin little head of hers?

"I shall dine here with you," he heard himself say, and

wondered what the devil was wrong with him.

Nigel wore a chocolate brown coat, open to reveal a deep green waistcoat and buff pantaloons. He looked achingly handsome as he sat across from her and shared a meal of cold capons, fresh bread and orange trifle. She asked about Coke and his work, and Nigel spoke easily about what Coke was doing in Norfolk.

Allegra was surprised and pleased that he was willing to talk with her about it. So often he shut her out. She did not know what had prompted his sudden garrulousness, but she meant to enjoy every minute of it. She watched his face as he answered her questions about the feasibility of implementing some of Coke's new breeding programs here at Deben. He seemed so excited, so dedicated to what he was doing.

"You are a very good landlord," she said at one point.

His lip curled in surprise. She watched him slip out of his coat and unbutton his waistcoat. The room was overwarm. "Now, how do you know that, Allegra?"

"Why, I can tell by your enthusiasm, and besides, I've seen the land, met some of the tenants . . ."

He looked curiously at her.

"Jamie took me on a tour the day — ah — the day you left."

He did not know why it bothered him that she'd gone with Jamie. He supposed he had aught to thank Jamie for relieving him of the task of taking her about himself. He could not fault Jamie, or Allegra. Nigel had promised to take her and then he'd gone off. It made sense that Jamie had taken her.

And yet, Nigel did not like it. Not at all. He didn't like to think of Jamie introducing *his* wife to the tenants, or showing her the new wheat fields, or the cattle he was breeding.

"I see," was all he said, but decided he would take her out himself in the near future. Surely Jamie could not have shown her everything.

It was while he poured her a second glass of Madeira that she told him of her first bride's visit. He cursed inwardly. He did not like Phillipa Wickens at the best of times. That she had come in his absence infuriated him. That she planned a dinner party worried him not a little! Lady Wickens was a bit too cozy with Barbara Lacey for comfort. Surely she would not invite Barbara as well . . .

Blast it all! She might do just that. Well, before Thursday night's dinner party, Nigel would call on Barbara Lacey and explain to her that their liaison was at an end. Temporarily, of course. There was no reason why he still could not keep a mistress. A gentleman need not let marriage interfere with such things, after all. But he would not resume his liaison with Barbara just now. His wife was too young and innocent. It would take her time to adjust to such notions. If indeed she ever did.

She would have to! he assured himself. But he would give her time. Besides, he wanted her to be able to hold her head up in the neighborhood. She could not do that did it become known that he was seeing Mrs. Lacey less than a fortnight after his nuptials! And, unfortunately, he knew it *would* become known. Such things always did.

"Yes, of course, you must reply in the affirmative to Lady Wickens," he said in answer to her question.

Allegra said nothing more than "Very well," but her lips were pursed and she looked decidedly uncomfortable. He sensed that she did not like Lady Wickens and could only applaud, however silently, her shrewdness in character judgment.

"I suppose I must return the bride visits," she said with a rather childlike reluctance, her full lower lip turned down in a pout.

A ghost of a smile touched his lips. "It won't be so bad,

my dear. I shall accompany you to Lady Wickens, if you like," he heard himself say. It was the least he could do, he told himself.

Her face lit with that smile again, that look of warmth and delight. Her brown eyes shone and he thought he could drown in them. But he did not want to drown.

Impulsively, she reached across the table between them and gave his hand a squeeze. "Thank you! I should like that above all things."

The feel of her hand sent a jolt through him. His hand burned, and suddenly so did his body. He did not want to burn for her.

He looked down at their clasped hands and then at her face. She blushed and withdrew her hand. He watched the movement of the teal muslin against her breasts as she straightened herself. The top two buttons of the dress were still undone.

They were alone in her rooms; dinner was concluded. He could pull her to her feet and unbutton the rest of her bodice. The tops of her breasts would spill from her chemise. He grew heated at the thought. She would sway to him with that natural warmth he'd encountered in no other woman. And he could lose himself in her.

He did not want to lose himself. He cleared his throat and forced his eyes back to her face. Her color was high, as if she'd read his thoughts.

Nigel rose and bid his wife a formal good night.

Allegra told herself that Nigel had been tired last night after traveling. That was why he hadn't come to her. And she reminded herself that they had spent a very pleasant, unprecedented evening together, that he'd been willing to sit and talk with her. She must take heart from that. Still, it was difficult for her to put on a cheerful face as she went about her morning tasks. Of those there were many, which was all to the good, for she needed to keep busy. She suspected that Nigel would not seek her company, and, indeed, he did not, but rather proved decidedly elusive.

And so Allegra sat down to do the week's menus with Mrs. Helmsley, who actually smiled as they worked. For Allegra, having paid little attention to the menus at Caulfield, allowed herself to be entirely guided by the stern-faced housekeeper. Allegra *was* a trifle bored, however, and was not at all sorry when they were interrupted once by the arrival of the painters with a host of questions for Allegra, and a few minutes later by Applegreave, the very eager carpenter.

"I'm needin' to ask yer ladyship about the bookcase in the sittin' room. The one what was pink and now they're makin' over into blue and green, you see," began Applegreave, twisting the battered brown cap he held in his hands. His gray eyes looked anxious and his lean torso kept bending forward from the waist as if to emphasize his words. "Yes, and I'm needin' to ask yer ladyship about the cupboard as well," he continued. "The one what be in yer dressin' room, yer ladyship. I thought you might be in the way of wantin' another shelf, you see. Oh, and there be a portion of the railin' on the third-floor landin', east wing, I reckon, well, it's in a fair way to crumblin', you see, and I wondered—"

"Perhaps I'd better come with you, Applegreave," Allegra interrupted, casting a rueful look toward Mrs. Helmsley, who grumbled disapprovingly.

Allegra glanced hurriedly at the remaining menus, scribbled a few changes, and decided the rest looked fine.

Mrs. Helmsley looked down at the pages before her. "But, my lady, I am not at all certain—"

"I am, Mrs. Helmsley. Thank you for your assistance," Allegra said with just a hint of imperiousness. She recalled Nigel's admonition to establish herself as mistress. "You may give the menus to Monsieur Andre now," she added as she turned to precede Applegreave out of the morning room.

The sound of Mrs. Helmsley's grumbling drifted behind them. Allegra stifled a giggle. Truly, this menu business was not all that complicated. Mrs. Helmsley was making a great deal more of it than need be.

Allegra knew that Nigel had ridden out with Jamie just after daybreak, and now in the late morning was closeted in his study. When Manners came to announce luncheon, Allegra followed him to the family dining room. Two places were set; Nigel's was empty. She filled her plate with the delicious-looking cold collation, dismissed the footman who hovered solicitously, and sat down to wait. Nigel did not come. Could he really be that busy or was he avoiding her? Last night he'd been willing enough to talk with her, until . . . until she'd taken his hand, she realized. Then he'd become distant and, of course, he had not come to her bedchamber.

Such thoughts notwithstanding, Allegra was tired of eating alone. Abruptly, without thought, she pushed her chair back and padded lightly down the corridor to Nigel's study. Perhaps he did not want to spend time with her, but he had to eat, did he not? He rose stiffly at her entrance, his green eyes remote.

No thank you, he said, he did not care to eat just now. He would have something brought to him later. He had a great deal of work to do.

His desk was strewn with papers, Allegra saw. She was curious about his work, and she wanted to talk with him, wanted some kind of contact with him. She frowned slightly, wondering at his quick changes of mood, but determined not to let his brusque tone daunt her.

Nigel cleared his throat impatiently but his wife did not take the hint. Instead she sauntered forward, the skirt of her thin violet cambric round dress outlining her legs all too clearly. She stopped in front of his desk, close enough for him to inhale that now familiar scent of wildflowers. Her brown eyes widened in curiosity.

"All these notes, Nigel! Do they have to do with your visit with Coke?" she asked ingenuously.

He peered at her sharply, wondering if her interest was genuine, forgetting entirely their conversation of last night. Instead he was remembering another time, another dark-haired siren who'd asked about the notes on his desk. It was only after the fact that he'd realized her interest, like so much else, was feigned.

"Some of them do," he replied dismissively, "but you needn't concern yourself with my work. Was there anything else?"

Allegra's head snapped up. His tone was so cold, the rebuff so clear. His green eyes were frosty, matching his voice. He did not want her here. He did not want to talk with her. Last night had been an oddity, brought on, no doubt, by the fatigue of travel. Nothing had changed. At least, not yet. But she would not be cowed.

She tilted her head saucily. "No, nothing else, Nigel. For now. I am perfectly content with my own company. I hope you like yours as well." With that, she turned and sashayed toward the door.

And Nigel, torn between amusement and a fury he did not understand, called after her, "Allegra!"

She whirled round, just a foot from the door, her chin high in the air. "I do not wish to be disturbed until the dinner hour," he said imperiously.

"I would not *dream* of it, my lord husband!" she said with dancing eyes, and stalked out without another word.

Chapter Ten

"The moon's an errant thief,
And her pale fire she snatches from the sun."
                              Timon of Athens
                              William Shakespeare

Allegra wanted to be angry with Nigel; surely that was more comfortable than feeling hurt. She ate listlessly and made her way to the schoolroom, determined to enjoy her first lesson with Sally, the upstairs maid. Mrs. Helmsley had balked at releasing Sally for two hours each week, had grumbled something about lower servants getting ideas above their stations. But Allegra had mollified her with the idea that once Sally learned to read, she might be able to help Mrs. Helmsley with the more tedious household accounting.

And now Allegra and Sally sat at the old schoolroom table, and for a while Allegra was able to forget her difficulties with Nigel. When they were finished, Sally timidly asked Allegra if her friend Mary Ellen might join them. Mary Ellen, it seemed, was one of the dairy maids. Allegra, having no idea how she would placate Mrs. Helmsley about this one, of course said yes.

She and Sally set off for the dairy to speak to Mary

Ellen. The sight that greeted them was not at all expected. Mary Ellen was indeed there, but she was not attending to any of the milk cows. Instead her braided blond head was bent over. She sat on an upturned milk bucket, her face buried in her pinafore as she wailed loud enough to wake bats in the attics. Allegra hurried forward, Sally at her heels. Mary Ellen's head flew up at their approach; she looked terror-stricken. Allegra had seen maidservants in this state twice before. She wondered if the cause was the same.

It was. After much coaxing the maid finally revealed that she'd fallen in the family way and that the young man would have naught to do with her. This last brought on a fresh spate of weeping after which she tearfully revealed his name.

"It be the butcher's boy, your ladyship. The one what delivers the meat and such. We was steppin' out on my days off and now . . . and now . . ."

More caterwauling ensued. Allegra looked up into Sally's red face. "Stay with her," she said briskly, "while I see what needs must be done. I—"

A movement caught the corner of her eye. Allegra turned and saw Mrs. Helmsley glaring from just inside the doorway. Allegra walked to her and motioned her outside. "I suppose you heard, Mrs. Helmsley."

"Yes. And beggin' your ladyship's pardon, but 'tain't fit for a lady born and bred to be privy to such goin's on."

Allegra hid a smile. "I have dealt with this before, at Caulfield, Mrs. Helmsley. You needn't trouble about me. Besides, a lady born and bred should always involve herself in the welfare of her servants. I may not know much about menus, but I *do* know that."

The housekeeper blinked and eyed her very strangely, but with what Allegra took to be a glimmer of approval. She went on to instruct Mrs. Helmsley to take care of the distraught girl while Allegra went about seeing what could be done about the butcher's boy.

This was a job for a man, as she knew from experience. But Nigel had made it very clear that he did not wish to be disturbed today. Allegra could not imagine asking Manners; despite the conversation she'd overheard, she was certain he was much too formal and proper. And Wiggins, the estate steward, would no doubt turn purple and pink did she broach such a thing with him.

That left Jamie. He, Allegra was persuaded, would know just what to do. And so she crossed the hot dusty stable yard to his office.

From the corner window of his study Nigel had a clear view of the stable yard. He saw Allegra cross the yard, a frown of concern and determination on her gamin face, her short, curly, nut-brown hair rippling gently in the slight August breeze. He frowned himself when he realized that she was headed for Jamie's office. What the deuce did she want there?

She emerged twenty minutes later with a smile on her face. Jamie was with her, his blue eyes twinkling down at her. Now whatever had put him in such a fine humor? And what had he said, or done, to erase the frown from Allegra's face? If she'd been perturbed about something why had she gone to Jamie and not . . . not whom? Nigel demanded of himself.

Certainly he did not want her running to *him*, had in fact made it very clear that he did not wish to be disturbed. Allegra was merely following his instructions.

Still, he did not like it. This was the second time he'd seen his wife smiling up at Jamie. He told himself there was nothing untoward about a mere smile.

Nonetheless, he did not like it, not at all.

There had been a letter from the Viscount Creeve awaiting Nigel on his return. It sat in the middle of the neat pile of correspondence that Manners had, as always, arranged in the top left drawer of his desk in his absence. Having cleared the desk top of estate matters, Nigel turned to his correspondence, determined to put Allegra from his mind.

The letter from Creeve was brief and to the point, thanking Nigel for his cooperation in the matter of the smugglers. It was unexceptionable in all but one respect. The letterhead said "Creeve House, Berkeley Square." Whatever was the man doing in London, in the midst of summer's heat, if he was so intent on catching Dorset smugglers? What held him in London?

Nigel could not quell the uneasy feelings those questions induced, and the letter from Mrs. Crowley at Cliff House, just arrived today, did nothing to allay his uneasiness. Her scrawl looked a good deal shakier than it had been the last time he'd corresponded with the elderly housekeeper.

"My lord," the letter read, "it be right good to hear from you again. I'm hopin' the countess and my two young scamps be well. Old Crowley, he be fine, when he ain't shot the cat, leastways. As for me, well, my bones ain't gettin' any younger and that be a fact, your lordship, what with my rheumatism and suchlike actin' up all the time. But don't you be worritin' none about Cliff House. I'm keepin' it as spankin' clean as always, just awaitin' your next visit.

"Now, you're askin' about Roger, my third scamp.

Well, 'tis fine he be, missin' the boys, but takin' care of his mama and runnin' around the beach and the caves and what all.

"You tell the boys I'll have gooseberry tarts waitin' for them when next they come.

Your obedient servant,
Mary Rose Crowley"

Confused, Nigel read the letter a second time, and then a third. And then he understood and a lump formed in his throat. Mrs. Crowley must be near to eighty by now, yet still it was shocking that her mind had deteriorated so badly. For the countess she wrote of was long dead, and so was Charles, one of her "young scamps." As for Nigel, he was thirty years old, hardly young. As to the "third scamp," whatever he was up to, it was obvious that Mrs. Crowley would be of no help. It seemed she lived in a world of her own now.

All of which left Nigel with the same questions he'd had before he'd sent off his own two letters.

He pondered the matter for some time, but remained uncertain as to what, if anything, to do about Roger. And then Jamie knocked on the door and reminded him that they were engaged to ride out to one of the tenant farms to check on the new seed drills.

That was when his thoughts shifted back to Allegra, and the smile she'd given Jamie. And the tour of the estate that he'd given her.

"How was . . . everything in my absence?" he heard himself ask as they were saddling up. They'd already spoken this morning of business matters. He told himself now, as he had this morning, that he had no intention of discussing Allegra with Jamie.

But Jamie peered at him out of deep blue eyes that seemed to see too much. He paused in the act of tightening the girth on his mount. "What exactly might ye be askin' me, laddie?"

Nigel shrugged nonchalantly and then turned to lead his stallion out into the sunshine. When they were both mounted in the stable yard he finally said, "Did my wife enjoy her tour of the estate?" He kept his voice even, his expression bland.

Jamie's eyes twinkled. "Aye, that she did. Made a conquest of Mrs. Johnston, too, I'll warrant. Aye, 'twas a verra fine afternoon, that."

Nigel should have been pleased. He knew he should. Instead his jaw was clamped rigidly shut. He flicked the reins and led his horse out of the yard. When they were on the road leading to the nearest rise, he urged Mercutio to a canter and Jamie followed suit, keeping abreast of him. The silence between them was tense.

"I would have taken her out upon my return. There was no need for you to take the time." Nigel hoped he sounded civil enough.

The twinkle in Jamie's eyes disappeared, "Aye, my lord. But the lass asked me, ye ken. She—well—'tis neither here nor there. I am sorry if I—"

"No, you did nothing wrong. 'Tis only, oh, devil take it, Jamie! Was—was she all right when I left?"

Jamie looked uncomfortable, a quite unaccustomed state for him. That told Nigel more than he needed to know. Nonetheless he eyed Jamie questioningly. "Well, noo, I'm thinkin' 'tis no for me to say," the large Scot demurred.

"Cut line, Jamie! The subservient pose does not suit you at all."

Jamie sighed. "What are ye wantin' me to say, laddie?" he asked gently. "That she wasna overset, and blue-deviled, nor surprised to find ye gone? I'll not be tellin' ye that, laddie."

"Damnation!" Nigel exploded, and inadvertently kicked Mercutio, who bolted ahead.

Jamie caught up with him moments later as Nigel was pulling back on the reins. The stallion's explosion had somehow calmed him. Now he spoke quietly, but kept his eyes on the roadway. "I knew even then, that I should . . . hellfire, Jamie, I *had* to leave, and that is an end to it."

"Aye, laddie," his friend said noncommittally. His very expressionless tone compelled Nigel to continue.

"This marriage — well, it took me by surprise. You know that, Jamie. She reminds me of — oh, never mind. 'Tis neither here nor there."

Jamie favored him with a level stare, then nodded. "She looks a bit like the late countess, does she no?" he asked conversationally. "Mrs. Johnston thought so, too, ye ken. De'il of it is, though, she doesna act at all like her late ladyship. Leastways, that is what Mrs. Johnston said."

Nigel cast his friend a wry look. "Doing it much too brown, old fellow. How could the good Mrs. Johnston know that on such a brief acquaintance? She is no fey Scot, after all."

"Aye, but she'll tell ye so, nonetheless," Jamie replied complacently. "And I'm thinkin' she's right."

Blast! Nigel did not need his majordomo making comparisons for him. He knew well that Allegra and Lucinda were different. Lucinda had been much taller, her features stronger, more beautiful, actually. Her face had not had any of the engaging, gaminlike quality of Allegra's.

But it was in their natures that they were devastatingly similar. Both were passionate, devious women. And all that was neither here nor there. For though the unfaithful Lucinda provided a lesson for any man in the deadly pitfalls of becoming besotted with one's wife, she had not been Nigel's woman.

Nigel had learned his lessons in the deceit of women, or certain kinds, from Gina. Jamie knew little of her. She, too, had had dark hair, dark eyes, her stature closer to Allegra's, her figure just a trifle more voluptuous. But she'd had none of Allegra's air of innocence, her eyes none of Allegra's sparkle. Gina's eyes, Nigel knew now, had glittered only with greed.

He acquitted Allegra of the latter. But she *was* conniving, and far too sensual for Nigel's peace of mind.

"It is not merely Lucinda," Nigel said at length. He could feel himself hold the reins too tightly, and forced his hands to relax. He kept his eyes fixed ahead. "There was a woman. Gina. I believe I told you about her. We met in Italy. We were betrothed. It was all a very long time ago."

Jamie glanced surreptitiously at his lordship, waiting for him to say something more, beyond what Jamie already knew of this Gina.

But the earl's jaw was clenched, face flushed. He still felt the pain when he spoke of this woman. And shame too, Jamie thought. It was in his lordship's eyes, and on his face. Jamie knew because he felt the same. He thought that if the earl would speak of Gina, Jamie might then speak of his Flora. But the earl said no more, and so neither did he. And perhaps it was just as well. A man had to work out his *own* problems, after all.

And then the path turned onto the rolling green hills and they took off at a gallop. Jamie kept his eyes on the ground ahead and let his mind drift to the problem of London. He'd already written to a friend he hoped would still be there, telling him of his imminent journey and need for help. But what was he to be telling his lordship about needing to go there, and just what was he to be doing once he got there?

Jamie having assured her that he would take care of the butcher's boy and the dairy maid in an interesting condition, Allegra spent the remainder of the afternoon working on her correspondence. Once the work on her new sitting room and the repairs in the rest of the house were completed, Allegra would settle into a routine. Correspondence was something she preferred to do in the morning. For now, she had neither the time nor place to work as she wished. But in truth, she was glad of the distractions. They gave her less time to dwell on unpleasant thoughts.

She penned a message to Lady Wickens, accepting her dinner invitation for Thursday night. And then she reread the letter just arrived today from Meg. Dear Meg, obviously not having received Allegra's first missive, was full of anxious questions. How had the journey been? Was Deben Court excessively grand? Were the servants kind or wretchedly high in the instep? How was Lord Debenham?

And then there were all the questions Meg did not ask, but were there between the lines nonetheless. The questions about whether Allegra was happy, and whether the earl was still angry. They were the difficult ones, and the reason Allegra had been so remiss as to write only once before this, and that letter rather brief. She tried to think of a reply as she read the remainder of Meg's letter, the news from home.

"Papa is rather blue-deviled, and does not speak of you unless I mention you first. I fear he has not yet reconciled himself to your marriage, but do not despair, my dear, for I feel certain he will come round. It is most odd, but only Mrs. Bridgebane seems to be able to bring Papa out of the sullens. Whenever she is about he grumbles a good deal, but laughs occasionally as well.

"And, dear Allegra, she is about quite a bit more often than before. They have begun a new chess game, which seems to occupy them every morning and most evenings as well. I truly had no idea chess could be so all-consuming! I do not know what they will do when I have wed—of a certain Mrs. Bridgebane cannot run tame at Caulfield when no other female is about!

"Which brings me, dearest sister, to my wonderful news! Papa has agreed that John and I may be wed in a fortnight's time, on Saturday, 1 September. I am sorry it will be too soon for you to make the return journey, and I know you will wish to be settling in as mistress of Debenham. (You are so brave, Allegra! I could never manage such a grand household. Nor could I possibly contrive conversation of sufficient wit to hold the earl's interest. You, I am persuaded, will have no problem on either head.)

"At all events, Allegra, I shall miss you excessively when I say my vows, the more so because if not for you I should not be wedding my dear John at all."

The letter went on a bit more in that vein before closing. Allegra realized her eyes had misted over. She missed Caulfield and Meg and Papa. And she could read between the lines. Meg was being tactful in the matter of her wedding. Allegra was not invited. Papa did not want her there. Perhaps, she thought, it was just as well, with things so unsettled between Nigel and herself. Papa would only become more overset did he see how matters truly stood. Perhaps, in time, they might visit . . .

She answered Meg as best she could, describing the house and the staff, avoiding the unwritten questions that had no answers. She penned a missive to Papa as well, trying to sound happy and contrite all at once.

It was not easy, for she felt neither. She was not sorry

she'd married Nigel Hayves, but she was a long way from being happy. She would not give up, however. Everyday was a new day, every night a new night.

With that thought lingering in her head, Allegra went in to dress for dinner.

The candles cast a muted glow over the gleaming mahogany table. Nigel thought the family dining room seemed smaller, more intimate, than usual. Too much so. Allegra sat to his left, wearing a deep rose silk gown with tiny puffed sleeves that looked as if they might come sliding down with the slightest movement of her bare shoulders. The fact that the gown was cut very low, its bodice high-waisted and all too brief, did not help any. She was so close, too close, and those sleeves tantalized.

And why, he wondered, had her place been set next to his, rather than at the foot of the table where she belonged? Come to think on it, she'd sat in the same place during the preceding two meals they'd shared in this room. It was not at all the thing. How the deuce had this happened? Surely even Allegra would not be so brazen as to request such a thing! But if not Allegra, then who? Mrs. Helmsley seemed not to care for Allegra, and had not a romantical bone in her meager body. And Manners—surely not prudent, proper Manners!

The devil of it was that Nigel would probably never know. He could not very well interrogate his staff, nor could he request a change without raising eyebrows. He might be dissatisfied with his marriage, but he had no desire to advertise that fact to his staff.

And so he sat next to his wife, trying to maintain his distance as she engaged him in small talk, trying not to inhale the light, lingering scent of wildflowers that always emanated from her, trying not to gaze into the warm brown eyes that met his so searchingly, nor to let his wayward eyes contemplate the brevity of her rose silk gown. And he vowed that once again, tonight, he would keep himself from her bed.

Katie had long since departed. Allegra had brushed and rebrushed her hair. She thought that Kingston had departed Nigel's chamber as well. And still Nigel didn't come.

She watched the candle at her bedside gutter in its socket. He would not come. There was no use pretending otherwise. And tonight she could not put it down to travel fatigue. He had avoided her all day and was still doing so. He wanted her—she could see it in his eyes. But he would not come.

She missed him, missed his warmth, missed the extraordinary sensations his touch brought to her body. But more than anything, she missed the closeness she'd felt with him those few times they'd made love.

He had felt that closeness, too; she was certain of it. And that was why he was staying away. She did not understand it, but every ounce of her intuition told her it was so. And yet, she needed that closeness with him if she was ever to breach the walls he'd erected around himself.

She debated the wisdom of going to his chamber. He'd made his thoughts on that subject very clear. Yet last time, he had not turned her away. He'd taken her to bed and it had been wonderful. . . .

Yes, a little voice at the back of her head reminded her, and then he'd disappeared the next morning for four days! True, she answered the voice, but he cannot very well do that again, can he? No, she thought, even he would have to own that a second trip would look most odd. Besides, they were engaged for Lady Wickens's dinner party.

He would not leave, she assured herself. At worst, he would chide her for the impropriety of coming to his chamber, and send her back to bed, alone. She told herself she would not be unduly overset if he turned her away. She had, at the least, to try.

She did not trouble with a wrapper this time, merely crossed to the connecting door and tapped softly. She heard the sound of rustling bedclothes and then his footsteps. He swung the door open and stared down at her, his jaw set, eyes narrowed.

"Yes, Allegra?" he said crisply. "Is something wrong?"

Yes, she wanted to say. Everything is wrong. He stood erect, his dressing gown hastily donned and loosely tied. She wanted him to enfold her in his large embrace. Instead he filled the doorway, implacably blocking her way.

"M—may I come in?" she stammered. It was harder this time than the last.

He stepped aside, but she could sense the tension in his body as she passed into his chamber. He did not want her here. A taper flickered at the bedside table. The pillows were propped up at the massive headboard, and an open book lay on the comforter. Perhaps he could not sleep. She took heart from that.

"Yes?" he inquired, his jaw barely moving.

She looked up at him; his green eyes were frosty. Oh, Nigel, she thought, why are you making this so hard for me? She moved as close as she dared, without touching him. He smelled of brandy and masculine soap and . . . and Nigel. She wanted to put her hands to his broad shoulders, perhaps to run her finger over the strong planes of his face. She balled her hands into fists and kept them at her sides.

Nigel had not moved a muscle, but she was certain his

body had tensed even more. This was not like the last time. It was as if he'd wrapped himself in bands of steel to keep himself from touching her.

Well then, it was up to her. Nigel was still awaiting her reply. She sashayed past him, allowing her body to brush his ever so lightly, and moved round the bed to the chairs flanking the chimneypiece. Between the chairs stood a small round table containing a brandy decanter and a snifter.

"I could not sleep," she said softly, standing next to one of the chairs, "and I thought we might—ah—share a drink."

He took three steps toward her, then stopped. "There is only one glass, Allegra," he said repressively.

She looked down at the table and back up at him, her eyes widening in surprise. "Oh! So there is. Still—"

"Perhaps you had ought to read a book if you've trouble sleeping, Allegra. Now if you'll excuse me—"

"Is it helping you, Nigel?" she queried.

He blinked. "That is neither here nor there, Allegra. Now, if there is naught else, I shall say good night."

She sidled back round the bed and came to stand before him once more. This was not going at all as she'd imagined and time was running out. She took a deep breath and did what she was longing to do. She raised her hands and put them to his chest. She could feel the heat of him through the folds of his dressing gown. His eyes flashed with fury and something else. Desire, perhaps; at the least they were no longer frosty.

"Nigel, I—"

"Dammit, Allegra, I said *good night!*" he snapped, and thrust her hands away. He turned from her, toward the door, indicating with the thrust of his chin that he expected her to leave.

You *must* leave, the inner voice told her. You've tried

214

and failed. But she could not go yet. He wanted her. She was certain of it.

His back was to her. She came up behind him and leaned forward so that the tips of her breasts just grazed his back. She kept her hands to her sides. "I do not mean to disturb you, Nigel," she murmured. " 'Tis only that I — I missed you, when — when you were gone."

He whirled round, his face suddenly twisted with rage. "Get out!" he spat. "You've played the harlot once before, Allegra, and I'll not have it! You disgust me with this unseemly display! Now, leave my chamber!" His hand shot out to point at the door. "I shall inform you when next I require your services," he sneered.

Allegra flinched as if he'd struck her. She could not breathe for the huge lump that had formed in her throat. Slowly she backed away from him, shaking her head slightly in disbelief. That he could speak that way, that he could reduce what had passed between them in bed to "her services." She blinked the gathering moisture from her eyes. She *would* not let him see her cry.

Somehow she got through the connecting door, her eyes riveted to his. She closed it behind her, slowly, carefully, and with finality. She would never pass through there again.

And then she turned and ran to her bed. She buried her face in the pillows and only then did she let go with shuddering, wracking sobs.

Why? Why was he doing this? Why did he hate her so? She had not done anything *so* terrible to him, had she?

Why could he not see that she only wanted to love him? Love him! She choked on a sob and held her breath for a moment. No, she did not love him. She could not love a man who hated her, could she?

Her body convulsed again, more violently this time,

the tears pouring out, hot and scalding, drenching the pillow as she tried to muffle the sounds so her husband would not hear.

Nigel paced from the window to the bed and then to the empty grate. He poured himself another snifter of brandy and downed it in one stinging gulp. Dear God, why did she not stop crying? She was going to make herself sick. Surely she must stop soon. Such violent, gut-wrenching sobs. He couldn't bear it.

He had done this to her. He'd been odiously, inexcusably cruel to her. But by then he'd hardly known what he was doing. She'd been tormenting, torturing him with her soft words, with her sweet-smelling body so close to his.

Her night rail had been laced modestly up to the throat, but of so fine a lawn as to be almost sheer. Every time she moved the candlelight had illumined those lush curves that his hands already knew so well. He could not bear it. He *had* to get her to leave. He would not be seduced, entangled in her web.

And so she'd gone. And he would never forget the look on her face, the haunted, ravaged look as her eyes brimmed and she backed out of the room. And now these wracking cries . . .

What had he done?

Damnation! He'd done what he had to do. She'd had no right to come here at first stop. He'd told her that.

He ran a jagged hand through his hair. She was going to be ill. He had not meant to make her ill. It sounded as though her cries were muffled by the bedclothes, but still he heard them clearly. And every one tore at him.

He realized that desire and anger had long since deserted him. In their place were remorse and some other emotion he did not care to explore. He only knew that had anyone else reduced her to this, he would have been ready to do murder.

The bedside taper guttered low and still her sobs did not abate. And Nigel lost a battle with himself. He could no longer keep himself from going to her. Logic told him it was absurd—he was the last person from whom she'd want comfort—and foolhardy. Hadn't all this come about from his need to keep away from her?

But logic had nothing to do with it. He crossed the room in several swift strides and gently pushed the door open without knocking.

She was curled upon the bed on her side, her face buried in the pillows, one hand balled into a fist. Her curly brown hair was damp, her small, delicate body shaking as she wept. He climbed onto the bed; she did not seem to notice. He turned her toward him and gathered her close. She seemed beyond words, but he said them nonetheless.

"I'm sorry, Allegra. I'm sorry. I did not mean it," he crooned softly. "Don't cry anymore, please. Don't cry."

He hardly knew what he was saying, only that he had to keep talking. He pulled her tightly against him. Miraculously, she came to him, and clung. More words tumbled from his mouth, endless murmurings of comfort.

She did not stop sobbing, but she clasped her small hand to his neck and burrowed her face in his shoulder. And he held on to her for dear life, feeling like the worst kind of bounder. He had hurt her, cut her to the quick, and yet she'd turned to him, with utter trust, for comfort. Never had he felt so humble. And never, he realized, had he felt so protective of anyone. He might not want her for his wife, but he did not want to hurt her, nor would he ever allow anyone else to.

No, she was not the wife he wanted. But she was his

. . . and she would never be anyone else's.

It was a very long time before her tears were spent and her body quieted itself to sleep. But for Nigel it was even longer. The first rosy fingers of dawn crept àcross the sky before he, too, was able to sink into sleep. But even as he drifted off, still holding his wife close, he reminded himself that he needs must be gone before she awoke. In truth, it was the only way.

Chapter Eleven

"You took the moon at full, but now she's changed.
Yet still she is the moon."

Love's Labour Lost
William Shakespeare

Nigel slept fitfully, which was just as well, for he was able to wake before Allegra and betake himself to his dressing room. He did not know what he would say to Allegra when she did arise. Would she recall all that had transpired? Had she even been fully aware of his presence in her bed? Would she remember his words of apology? He had meant them then, but he did not wish to repeat them. He was sorry he'd been so cruel, but not that he'd sent her away.

She would be angry this morning, hurt, perhaps embarrassed. As for him, he hardly understood his own behavior. What could they possibly say to one another?

In the event, it didn't signify, at the least in the morning, for Allegra did not emerge from her rooms. In response to his query, Nigel was informed that her ladyship had the headache and was resting.

Nigel wondered for a moment whether she was indeed unwell or merely avoiding him. He decided on the former. It was not in Allegra's nature to hide from anything and besides, such terrible weeping would of a certain bring on the headache. Had he not feared that very thing?

That much determined, he considered going into see her, but quickly scotched the notion. He was the cause of her indisposition; she would not want to see him. She would want to nurse her headache and inevitable red eyes in private.

And so he left her alone but was distracted soon thereafter by a most odd conversation with Jamie.

The day was overcast and a breeze was up. Nigel stared out the window of his study, certain rain was imminent and wondering if he'd be able to ride out to the eastern tract of the home farm later as he'd planned.

That was when Jamie knocked at the door and entered, looking deuced uncomfortable, as if he did not like what he was about to say. Nigel motioned him to the tufted leather chairs flanking the empty grate.

" 'Tis aboot my uncle, ye ken," Jamie began without preamble, but his blue eyes never met Nigel's. "He's come doon from the Hielands, my lord, to Londontoon. And he's in the way o' needin' my help. 'Tis verra strange, the land o' the Sassenach, when a mon first come."

Uncle? What uncle? Jamie never spoke of family, in fact, gave the impression that what little family he'd had had been lost in the infamous Clearances.

"I was not aware that you had any family left in the Highlands," Nigel said carefully.

"Well, there's only Uncle Angus, and a cousin or two, ye ken." Jamie finally raised his eyes. They looked haunted, almost desperate. Surely he would not have such feelings about an uncle he'd never mentioned, nor seen for years. No, it was something more. He sensed

220

Jamie was in some kind of difficulty. Nigel was surprised. Jamie's circle of acquaintances in London had been havey-cavey at best, but he'd put that life behind him. Nigel would swear he had. Nigel weighed his next words carefully. Jamie was entitled to privacy, and yet . . .

"Jamie, of course if you needs must go to London, then go. But if there is some kind of difficulty, if there is any way in which I may be of help, you have only to ask."

Jamie's blue gaze became intense, piercing. He stroked his red beard. "Aye, my lord, I'll remember that," he said at length.

Nigel nodded, and they spoke now of practicalities. Jamie hoped to be gone only a se'ennight, would leave in about two days' time. In the meantime he would instruct one of the grooms in the matter of the horses, Wiggins on estate matters, Manners—the list went on. It amazed Nigel, as it always did when he thought on it, how much Jamie really did for him. This despite Nigel's man-of-affairs in London, the stewards at each of his holdings, and the entire staff at Deben. By his own choice, Jamie almost never had taken a holiday. He was certainly entitled to time off, but he would be sorely missed. Nigel vowed to give him a hefty raise upon his return.

"Well, I'll be off then, laddie. I've much to do afore I leave." Jamie rose, averting his eyes again, and all of Nigel's uneasiness returned. Jamie was entitled to a holiday, but this did not sound anything like a holiday. What the deuce was the fellow up to?

It had been easier than he'd expected, but still Jamie was uneasy. The earl had not believed the faradiddle about an Uncle Angus. No, not for a minute. Because there was no Uncle Angus. Only an old Hieland friend by that name. Jamie had written to him at his favorite haunt, the Burning Sow Pub, which stood in a most unsavory part of London. Many's the night they'd sat there and shared a bottle of what passed for whisky in this Sassenach land. Jamie hadn't heard from Angus in nigh onto two years, but he'd need help in his quest and so reckoned it was worth a try.

At all events, there was no doubt his lordship might fash himself over the matter, but he would not stop Jamie from leaving. And now there was work to be done. All that he'd told the earl, and more. For Jamie had got to speak to Katie once more. It was time to formulate a plan.

She was a bit less timid this time. They sat once more in the laundry garden, and slowly, Jamie elicited the information he needed. "Emerald's" room was a tiny chamber on the second floor at the back of the house. Together he and Katie counted rooms and windows so that he would know her window from the outside. Jamie knew from experience that getting into *Le Petite Maison* from the front was nigh onto impossible, leastways for the likes of him. He would have to try to scale the back wall and have a peek through Emerald's window. Then, if she was indeed Flora, he would see what needs must be done.

He also talked to Katie about the guards. Hurley, the man from the inn yard, was one, more was the pity. He'd seen Jamie once and might well recognize him. But Katie confirmed what Jamie had guessed—that early morning, just after dawn, was the safest time to approach the house. The customers had gone home, the girls were asleep, and even the guards and servants slept then. For in *Le Petite Maison,* everyone worked until the wee hours.

Jamie had one final question. He needed to know what the back of the house looked like, whether there were trellises or vines or trees he might climb.

"I do not know, Jamie," she answered softly. "I was never allowed outside, nor into the garden, in all the time I was there."

Jamie's gut clenched. He could not wait to get there.

The rain began sometime about midday, the gloomy air matching Allegra's blue-deviled spirits. Her head was pounding, her eyes puffy, though somewhat less red than when she'd awoken hours ago. For that she blessed Katie and her camomile poultices.

She knew she had got to make an appearance below-stairs soon. There was work to be done, tradesmen with whom to confer. Applegreave, the carpenter, seemed to have a question every hour. And besides all that, she would not wish Nigel to think her cowardly.

Indeed, she was nothing of the kind. She would face him, would be all smiles and politeness itself. She would be all that was proper in a countess. She would be an impeccable mistress for this and all his houses.

But never again would she offer herself to him, nor speak from her heart. Never again would she give him the opportunity to hurt her so deeply.

She remembered last night in painful clarity. Her entrance into his chamber, their conversation, his hateful words of dismissal. He thought her a harlot; he would inform her when next he required her "services." Dear God, wasn't that the word Katie used when describing men who requested her? Is that really what Nigel considered their times together in bed to have been? An act of harlotry?

No! She would not believe it! It had not been some cold, callous, commercial transaction. What had passed between them in those times had been deeply felt by both of them. It had been . . . the beginning of love, she thought now.

A love that would never be. A might-have-been love. It would never be because Nigel did not want it, and because she did not think she could endure the pain of trying to win him.

That realization, and the resignation accompanying it, calmed her somewhat. But one thing baffled her. She could not ignore it, pretend it did not happen, but she did not at all understand it.

Nigel had come to her last night. Nigel, who seemed to hate her, who'd called her that odious name, had come to her and held her while she wept. She had been too far gone to protest the irony of it. She had hardly known what she was doing. He had offered comfort and she had taken it. She remembered him murmuring words she did not comprehend, soft words, soothing words.

Why had he come? Remorse? Guilt? Was he one of those men who could not bear to see a woman cry?

She did not know, but it did not signify. Whatever emotion had prompted his uncharacteristic behavior in the dark of night, he would deny it by the light of day. In essence, he had already denied it, for he'd been gone from her side long before she awoke. And he had not come to see how she went on this morning.

The night just passed had not changed Nigel Hayves. But it had changed Allegra, irrevocably, she thought.

Allegra made an appearance just after nuncheon. Nigel espied her conferring with Applegreave, the very earnest carpenter, who was gesticulating in the air, shaping his hands into what looked like door handles and wood carvings. When they'd finished, Nigel sauntered over to Allegra. She was standing before the open door of her new sitting room. Nigel peeked in over her shoulder. Someone, the linen draper he supposed, was measuring one of the chairs, and bolts of fabric were draped across the sofa.

"Good afternoon, Allegra," he said pleasantly. "Are you feeling more the thing? Mrs. Helmsley said you had the headache." He searched her face for clues as to what she was feeling, but she appeared extremely composed. They needed to talk, and now was as good a time as any. They could move to his study . . .

"I am well, thank you, Nigel," she said in a disconcertingly formal tone. Her brown gaze was level, giving away nothing. It was not like her. Her composure had an artificial quality to it that he did not like.

Her eyes were swollen, though not red. He felt an urge to stroke her brow, but wisely did not heed it. "How is the work coming?" he asked, wanting to keep her talking.

"Quite well. I am sorry for the disruption. I expect it will all be done within the se'ennight. Now if you'll excuse—"

"Allegra, why do you not come along to my study? We can be private there and talk."

Her eyes flickered with some unnamed emotion. Surprise? Anger? But a moment later she had herself under control. "Thank you Nigel, but I have a great deal to do just now. I expect I shall see you at dinner." She gave him a polite smile that did not reach her puffy eyes, and then she was gone, leaving Nigel cursing inwardly after her. And what, he demanded of himself, had he expected?

She proved evasive all afternoon but had time, he noted in some irritation, to talk to Jamie. Feeling restless, Nigel had dashed through the rain out to the stables to confer with Jamie when he overheard them. And what

225

the deuce was she doing out here? It was raining rather steadily; she could not mean to ride. Had she come out here looking for Jamie?

He could not see them, but as soon as he heard the voices he stood stock-still. It occurred to him that he ought not to eavesdrop, but he dismissed the notion. He would make his presence known momentarily.

"London! How exciting, Jamie!" she was saying. " 'Tis all the talk belowstairs, you must know." Now, how the deuce did she know that?

"Is't so, lass?" Jamie's tone sounded bemused.

"Oh, yes. Tell me, Jamie, is London as crowded and bustling and *wonderful* as I've always imagined?"

"I reckon some would say so, lass. For m'self, I prefer the green grass and the blue skies."

"I suppose I do as well. But still, I should like to see London. Once at least." Her voice drifted off wistfully. Nigel was painfully reminded of how young she was, how little she'd seen and done in her life. He'd have to see about taking her to Town, perhaps for the Little Season.

"Why, of course, ye will, lass. Ye'll be going doon fer the Season, I make no doobt," Jamie said bracingly.

"Oh, I do not think so, Jamie," Allegra responded guilelessly. Lord, what sort of cad did she think he was? Did she imagine he meant to bury her in the country all year? "But that doesn't signify. Ah, Jamie, this trip of yours. 'Tis rather sudden, is it not?"

"Aye."

"Is—is everything all right, Jamie?" It was the degree of concern in her voice that disconcerted Nigel.

"Why, of course, my lady. And why should you be thinkin' any different?"

"I don't know, Jamie. But they say 'tis most unlike you. Jamie, you—you have not landed yourself in any trouble, have you?" Clever girl, Nigel thought, and wondered if

226

Jamie would be any more forthcoming with her than with him.

Jamie took his time about answering, and then he only mumbled a negative. He was lying. Nigel was certain of it.

"Well, as long as you remember that we are friends, Jamie." Nigel frowned. Just when did they become "friends"? "And if there is aught that I can help you with, you have only to ask."

He heard Jamie move. Closer to her, perhaps? "Aye, lass, I ken that. I—I will call on ye if need be." Nigel did not like this at all. Why, she'd got more of a response from Jamie than *he* had!

From there the conversation drifted to horseflesh, Nigel's horseflesh, and Allegra asked about her horse. *Her* horse?! Jamie's reply indicated that he'd allowed Allegra to ride Windstar. Blast the man! What made him think he could take such liberties? And why, Nigel demanded of himself, had *he* not seen to it himself that his wife have a mount? And, now he thought on it, did Allegra not have a mare at Caulfield of whom she was fond? Why did he not have it sent here?

Nigel quickly retraced his steps and made a great deal of noise about reentering the stable. "Jamie, are you there?" he called.

Jamie stepped round within his sight, Allegra just behind him. "Ah, there you are," Nigel began, then blinked in surprise. "Allegra! What brings you out here in the rain?"

She stepped out from behind Jamie. Her eyes were a bit less swollen now but there was a dullness to them that had not been there yesterday. She carried a woolen cloak, yet her thin turquoise muslin dress looked damp and clinging anyway. He tried not to frown. "I came to talk to Jamie . . . about Windstar," she said neutrally. Not precisely a clanker but not the truth either. He waited for her to say more. Jamie looked from Nigel to Allegra and then, with a pointed glance at Nigel, moved back into the shadows. At length Allegra spoke again, "Windstar is a beauty. Jamie said I might ride him. You do not mind, do you?" She spoke so formally. She might have been a guest speaking to the host at some tedious house party.

"No, I do not mind, Allegra," he said softly.

She smiled that polite smile again. "Very well then. Thank you. If you'll excuse me, I'll be getting back to—"

"Ah, Allegra. You may ride Windstar if you like, but it has occurred to me that perhaps you'd like your own horse. The one from Caulfield."

"Leda?" For a moment her eyes lit with the sparkle he'd become accustomed to, but she extinguished the light immediately and, he thought, quite deliberately.

"Yes, Leda," he responded, smiling. "Shall I send for her?"

"Yes, thank you, Nigel. I should appreciate that very much," she said with practiced civility, the kind one learned from one's governess. And what had he expected? That she'd throw her arms about him and sing her gratitude? "Well, I shall be on my way. Good afternoon, Nigel," she added, then called a somewhat less formal farewell to Jamie. And then, evading Nigel's attempts to help her with her shawl, she darted away.

Nigel wanted to kick something. Jamie reappeared but Nigel had forgotten what he'd wanted to speak with him about. Abruptly he turned and left, telling himself he did not hear any chuckling coming from the depths of his stables.

Allegra contrived to evade Nigel for the remainder of

the day, and maintained a formal demeanor throughout dinner. She was not accustomed to this kind of detachment, this polite reserve, but she told herself she would get used to it. She really had no choice. Curiously enough, Nigel seemed perturbed by her remoteness. She would not have expected it. Had he not wanted her to keep her distance? Had he not, now that she thought on it, treated her with just this sort of icy civility for most of the days of their brief, ill-fated marriage?

She had not intended it this way, but now *he* seemed to be the one trying to break through the walls of reserve. He exerted himself to make conversation all through dinner, and she, taking a leaf from his book, favored him with unemotional, meaningless rejoinders.

She declined coffee in the drawing room and excused herself early, pleading fatigue.

Nigel did not come to her chamber. She did not know what she would have done if he had.

By Wednesday morning the polite, formal demeanor, rather than wearing thin for Allegra, seemed to have settled upon her like an impenetrable security blanket.

Nigel did not like it one whit.

And yet, was this not what he wanted? a niggling voice reminded him. A proper, polite wife who would run his household, fulfill her role as Countess of Debenham efficiently, compliantly, with dignity and without emotion. He watched her with Mrs. Helmsley, with Applegreave, with the elderly Pettigrew sisters, who paid a short, pleasant visit to introduce themselves and welcome Allegra to the neighborhood. He watched her and knew she was fulfilling her role just as he had wished.

But she wasn't being Allegra, damn her eyes!

She was too busy for more than a brief chat with her

husband, but she had time for the housekeeper, the carpenter, Jamie, and even for two of the maids, to whom she was apparently giving reading lessons. Reading lessons to the servants! In the schoolroom, in the middle of the day! Good God! But at the least, he reminded himself, that was the Allegra he knew.

He hoped to have her to himself at luncheon, but she outmaneuvered him, taking lunch in her sitting room as she supposedly worked on her correspondence.

He did not like it one whit.

The rain had dwindled to a mere drizzle. A ride on horseback was not possible but a carriage ride was. Nigel decided it was as good a time as any to accompany Allegra to return her bride visits of the week before. At the least they might talk in the carriage.

But all Allegra spoke of on the way to the vicarage was Katie's progress. Katie seemed more comfortable. Katie seemed less timid. Katie seemed less and less afraid that the blackguard Hurley was going to catch up with her.

Blast it all! Nigel was simply not all that interested in Katie. A word or two would have sufficed. He must have made his boredom obvious because Allegra shifted subjects. She began to speak of Jamie and his imminent trip to London. Hellfire! Nigel liked this topic even less. Why the devil was his wife so preoccupied with his head groom? Jamie was a dashed sight more than a head groom, he reminded himself, and then decided that *that* was precisely the problem.

Aldous Bailey, the placid-faced, balding vicar, and his blue-haired wife were all that was kind. Their welcome to Allegra was genuine and she responded to their offer of friendship. She seemed more relaxed than she had since that night . . .

The vicar was congratulating Nigel on his charming bride and asking about his turnip crop while Mrs. Bailey prattled away to Allegra about life in Debenham. Nigel listened with half an ear.

"And perhaps you would be interested in helping with the annual church fete, Lady Debenham. 'Tis held at the end of November, you must know. But, of course, we'll all understand if you are too busy—"

"Oh, no, Mrs. Bailey, I should love to help!" Allegra exclaimed. "I've always adored the fete at Caulfield. Tell me, do you have a fortune-teller's booth?"

"Well, no, dear, I don't believe we do."

"Oh, goodness me! You simply must. I run the booth every year at Caulfield. I shall do it here if you like." Allegra had clapped her hands together in her enthusiasm. Bailey had stopped talking about turnips and turned to listen to Allegra. Nigel watched his wife change facial expressions, lifting her brow and sucking in her cheeks. "I am Madame Potrushka," she drawled in a guttural voice with an absurd Slavic accent. "I vill tell your fortune eef you cross my palm with gold."

Mrs. Bailey squealed with delight. The vicar looked enchanted. Nigel chuckled inwardly. How like Allegra, he mused. She would probably don some hideous scarf and tawdry earrings and not care a hang that her dignity had gone a-begging. This was something, he instinctively knew, that Meg would never do. Just as Meg would never have taken on Katie. Meg would never have come to his chamber so brazenly . . .

Meg would be proper and polite and dignified at all times. Just as Allegra had been all day today and yesterday. Nigel frowned inwardly, not at all liking the direction of his thoughts.

And then Mrs. Bailey spoke and moments later Nigel was frowning outwardly, "Splendid, simply splendid, Lady Debenham! Of course we shall have a fortune-telling booth. The ladies of the committee will be so pleased at your offer to join us. A *most* pleasant surprise, my dear."

"Surprise? Why, did you not think I would wish to help?" Allegra asked with genuine curiosity.

For the first time Mrs. Bailey looked uncomfortable. "Oh, well, I only meant that, what with all of your duties at the Court, you mightn't have time and—well—the last countess never cared for the fete you see, and—"

"The last countess? Do you mean Lucinda?" Allegra asked. The vicar's wife nodded. "Whyever not?" Allegra was genuinely puzzled. Nigel ground his teeth.

Poor Mrs. Bailey looked very flustered. "Well, I do not rightly know. I daresay she was quite occupied with Deben Court. She always had many guests, you must know."

Allegra did not look convinced. She cocked her head, as if she meant to make further inquiry, but she caught Nigel's forbidding glance and said nothing.

It was the vicar who filled the ensuing, uneasy silence. "Perfectly right, my dear," he said genially. "The late countess was a most gracious hostess. Not everyone has a talent for church fetes, you must know."

Mrs. Bailey murmured some assent and Allegra nodded obligingly. Nigel met the vicar's eyes. Bailey's words had been innocent enough, but both men knew very well the kind of guests Lucinda liked best, and just what talents she displayed with them. They exchanged a look of complete understanding. Neither of the ladies knew any such thing and it was best kept that way.

Nigel shook the vicar's hand warmly as they departed.

Allegra retreated behind her wall of reserve as soon as the vicarage door closed behind them. It was a mark of her determination to stay there that she did not ask the questions he knew she must be burning to ask. Questions about Lucinda. Questions he did not want to answer.

Allegra's reserve resolved itself into tension as they neared their next destination. And it was no wonder; the requisite half hour spent with Phillipa Wickens was decidedly unpleasant.

"How nice that you are back in residence, my lord," Lady Wickens cooed as she served elegant pastries from an ornate silver tray. "I own it must have been a matter of great urgency that took you away from your bride." She smiled sweetly but her gray eyes were cold.

Phillipa Wickens was, Nigel guessed, in her early forties, a stout, formidable woman who could never have been called pretty. It was quite obvious to Nigel that she was a woman who did not like men, in or out of the bedchamber. Her husband, Sir Randolph, was a handsome man who liked women very well indeed, especially *in* the bedchamber.

"It was, as you say, a matter of some urgency, Phillipa," Nigel said at length. "Else, of course, I should not have left Allegra at such an inopportune time." Nigel decided he was not precisely lying; he had, after all, felt a great urgency to leave. Phillipa raised a skeptical brow. Nigel reached over to grasp Allegra's hand and run his thumb along her palm.

He felt a slight jolt in her at his touch. Was it merely surprise or something else? And then she smiled up at him, a dazzling smile that made him curse inwardly because he knew it was meant for Phillipa's sake.

They chatted about pleasantries, the unpleasant currents just barely below the surface. Allegra held her own, though Nigel felt the tension emanating from her as she sat near him on the sofa. And then Phillipa mentioned her dinner party, promising an "interesting mixture" of people. That was very much what Nigel feared.

He was very grateful when their half hour was over.

"Thank you for accompanying me, Nigel," Allegra said when they were once more settled in the carriage. The rain had begun to fall in earnest now. "I should not want to find myself alone with that woman. There is something about her. . "

"Yes, my dear, I know," Nigel said soothingly, "but you did quite well." Her eyes widened at that and he thought she would respond but instead she busied herself with her clothes. Nigel watched her arrange herself as she sat across from him. The skirts of her ice blue gown were muddy and her chip straw bonnet was askew and drooping, for they had tried to outrun the rain. Damp curls were clinging to her face. She was trying to make herself look more presentable but he thought she looked adorable.

"You look quite fetching as you are, Allegra. No need to fuss," he heard himself say.

Allegra's mouth dropped open for one indecorous second. Then she closed it and turned just a wee bit pink. Nigel was pleased; perhaps he was making progress.

A moment later she stopped fussing. "Why doesn't Lady Wickens like me, Nigel?" she asked with that endearing candor of hers.

"Because you are everything she is not," Nigel answered without thinking, and then wondered what the devil he'd meant by that. Allegra looked most baffled, but wisely refrained from saying a word.

And there was another reason Lady Wickens did not like Allegra, Nigel thought—because Phillipa Wickens and Barbara Lacey were very good friends. He wisely refrained from saying so.

He did, however, remind himself that it would be the better part of valor to pay Barbara a visit before tomorrow night's little dinner party. Lord only knew what Phillipa had up her ample sleeve. Nigel did not want any unfinished business floating about.

It was obvious he could not go today. The rain was beginning to fall in sheets and the day was lengthening at all events. Tomorrow, then. He would go on the morrow.

He focused his attention back to Allegra, but she had shifted back behind her wall of politeness. Hellfire! How had she gotten so good at that in so short a time?

The first real breach in that wall came that very night at dinner. Allegra was quite deliberately uncommunicative and quite unwittingly tantalizing in a deep violet gown cut rather low across the bosom. Nigel marveled at the fact that she instinctively knew that deep, vibrant colors became her. Most young girls wore insipid pastels and endless yards of white fabric. Thank God his wife had more sense. Of course, her wardrobe was somewhat out-of-date and not as sophisticated as befit the Countess of Debenham. Nigel looked forward to remedying that situation when he took her to London.

London? What was he thinking? He had no intention of taking his wife shopping, if indeed he *did* take her to London!

Allegra could not credit it. For the second night in a row, her husband was actually trying to draw her out in conversation! He was exerting himself to be charming! She had never seen him like this, except perhaps when he first met Meg. She did not understand this new Nigel, nor did she trust him. He did not want her, had made it very clear what he thought of her. Then why in the world was he suddenly so attentive?

He was making it very difficult for her to maintain her resolve to keep her distance. Did he know that? Was that what this was all about? Had she become a challenge or some such fustian?

She did not want to be a challenge. She wanted to be a wife. *His* wife, in every sense of the word. But if she tried again, she would be hurt again. She was certain of it.

Nigel sat at the head of the table, to her right. He wore a dark brown coat of superfine that fit him to perfection. Its clean, dark lines somehow emphasized the strong planes of his face. She stole a glance at him whenever he was not looking at her. He really was a very handsome man. Had she ever really noticed that before? His green eyes were warm now. She did not want to react to his warmth. He smelled of—of Nigel, a masculine, outdoor scent that made her want to lean closer to him. She would not allow herself to do any such thing!

She kept her back ramrod straight, her elbows off the table and her chin as high as possible when one was eating one's dinner. And so she would have remained had dinner not turned out to be rather unusual.

The meal began with *le potage a la Monglés*. Allegra recalled discussing it with Mrs. Helmsley. It was a creamy brown soup, flavored with Madeira and made with *foie gras*, truffles and mushrooms. It was quite delicious and Nigel complimented the cook as well as Allegra for her choice of soups. She tried not to be too pleased by the praise.

The soup was removed with a dish which was conveyed to the table in an ornate silver tureen. This proved to be *la garburé aux choux*, a country-style vegetable broth full of shredded cabbage. Nigel looked at her in surprise as the footman served them both, but he said nothing about the fact that they were to consume soup once again. Allegra could not recall discussing this with Mrs. Helmsley, but of course she must have done.

The next remove made its appearance in a large rounded server of very fine gilt-edged bone china. It was, however, another soup, this time a bland pink puree of pearl barley and carrots. It, too, was delicious, but . . .

"Ah, Allegra," Nigel ventured as she delicately spooned her soup and tried to pretend nothing was amiss, "are you aware that this is our *third* bowl of soup?"

She decided to brazen it out. "Why, yes, Nigel. Do you like it? Do you not think it could use a dash more salt? And my goodness me, do you know I cannot remember what it is called! Do you—"

"Yes, Allegra, I do remember what it is called and no, I do not think it needs more salt. And that is neither here nor there. My dear, we are to dine on naught but soup tonight?"

Allegra put her spoon down. Something was wrong and there was no sense shilly-shallying. "Well, I don't precisely know, Nigel. I cannot imagine—"

She stopped as the footman returned to clear away *this* remove and serve the next. It was, unfortunately, another soup. Nigel asked the footman the name of this particular delicacy and was told, in a dreadful attempt at French, that it was *le potage de poisson a la russe,* which meant of course, a Russian-style fish soup.

When the footman departed, Allegra put her hand to her spoon, still hoping, she supposed, to maintain a semblance of normalcy. Nigel stopped her with a hand on her wrist. She tried to ignore the sudden warmth she felt.

"Allegra," Nigel began blandly, "I am beginning to think my teeth will atrophy. Could it be that Monsieur Andre wishes to show off his entire repertoire of soups tonight, or did you have something to do with this?"

"I?" Allegra's hand went to her bosom in disbelief. "What could I poss—ah—" She stopped abruptly as a decidedly unpleasant thought came to her.

"Yes, Allegra?" Nigel pressed.

Allegra's hands slipped down to her lap. She twisted them nervously. She tilted her head and gazed at Nigel with her lips downturned. "Well—oh, dear, Nigel. You must know that I did warn you that—ah—the day-to-day running of things is not my forte. And I'm afraid I—well, there's no wrapping it up in clean linen, is there?"

"No, Allegra," he agreed gravely.

"Well, I do recall doing the menus with Mrs. Helmsley on Monday morning, you see. Your mother used to do them on Mondays and so I thought it would make it easier for all concerned if I did the same."

"Oh, indubitably." He nodded solemnly. He was not helping at all and so she went on.

"We worked on them for some time until we were interrupted by Applegreave. He's the carpenter, you must know. The rather thin man with—"

"Yes, my dear, I know who Applegreave is. Pray go on."

"Yes, well, he needed to speak with me about the cupboard in my dressing room and one of the stairwell railings. The third floor, east wing, I believe it was. He said it was crumbling and what with all of his questions I thought it best that I go to see everything for myself. And so I—I am afraid I finished the menus rather hurriedly. It all looked fine to me—we were almost finished at all events. I am persuaded that I must have mixed up the page with Wednesday's meals with—ah—a list of soups I wanted Monsieur Andre to try over the—ah—next fortnight." Her voice had dwindled by the end and she peered at Nigel out of half-closed eyes. He was going to explode; it was only a matter of seconds.

Nigel stared at his wife, openmouthed. Of all the muttonheaded things to do! He ought to deliver a good stern lecture on her responsibilities as—oh, hellfire! She looked so adorable in her chagrin. His lips began to twitch. Allegra had been most remiss. A fortnight's worth of soups—

Suddenly he could contain himself no longer. His lips gave way and a most undignified burst of laughter poured forth. Now it was Allegra's turn to stare open-mouthed. It took only a minute before her eyes crinkled in merriment and she, too, gave way to laughter.

"Good God," he gasped, his body still shaking. "Four soups. I wonder what's next. Dare I hope—dessert?"

"A fruit soup," Allegra blurted between giggles.

And when the footman arrived not long after with a chilled tureen of plum and berry soup, Allegra and Nigel went off into a paroxysm of laughter that had tears streaming down their faces. The poor footman retreated in great confusion. Nigel tried to take a sip of wine to calm himself but his hand was shaking too much. He finally grabbed Allegra's hand in an effort to steady them both.

When they had finally calmed, he said, "I haven't laughed like that in years." Her face became more serious suddenly, a soft smile suffusing it. She looked down at their clasped hands. He waited a moment before withdrawing his, and then they each picked up a clean spoon. He ought to have noticed before that the table had been laid with an inordinate amount of spoons, but he hadn't.

"We'd better give this a try at the least, lest we deeply offend Monsieur Andre," Nigel remarked.

Allegra grinned and dipped into her soup. It was excellent, Nigel thought, even after what he thought was a surfeit of soups. It was sweet and tangy all at once and quite refreshing for a warm, albeit rainy, summer evening.

They adjourned soon after to the drawing room for coffee, but somehow the change in setting caused Allegra to retreat behind her wall of reserve. Even a teasing request by him that they begin dinner with anything other than soup for the next few days failed to elicit any more reaction than a dutiful, "Of course, Nigel."

He gave up soon after and gently suggested that Allegra go on up to bed. He watched her go, debating with himself. Minutes later, he too rose.

Katie lit the bedside taper and quietly departed. Allegra climbed into bed with a book she knew she would not read.

It was very difficult, this business of keeping her distance from Nigel. Why did he find it so easy to do to her and why was he not doing it now?

She had slipped up for a time tonight. But what could she do? The whole matter *was* very funny! Never had she laughed so much. And never had they laughed together. It felt so good.

Oh, Nigel, she thought, whatever do you want of me? And how long could she keep up this role she'd set for herself? And whatever would she do when next he crossed the threshold into this chamber? He had never said a word about what happened the other night. Did he think she could simply pretend it hadn't happened?

The knock came in the next moment, as if she'd conjured him. He hardly awaited her reply before stepping through the dressing room and on into her bedchamber, closing the door behind him. She did not at all like the sound of that door closing—it was as if he knew he would not be leaving soon.

"Good evening, Nigel," she said in her best drawing-room tone. "Did you want something?"

He chuckled deep in his throat and moved slowly toward the bed, one hand in the pocket of his dressing gown. "Yes, I did, my dear. And that is a very foolish question." He sat down beside her and slid the book from her hands. "You are my wife, are you not?"

Allegra was determined to ignore the special scent of him that wafted toward her as he sat so close. She was determined not to look at his well-muscled chest, bare where the dressing gown draped open, nor to remember the feel of his hands . . .

She *had* to speak; the words must be said. "Yes, I am your wife. But—but you said I was a—"

He put a finger to her lips. "Pray do not repeat what I said, Allegra. I spoke in anger. I am here now, and I am your husband. Can we not put it behind us?"

It was, she knew, as close to an apology as he was like to come. True, she reminded herself, he might have apologized that dreadful night, while he held her, but she did not know of a certain. His words had been unintelligible to her then. What she longed for now was for him to gather her in his arms and tell her how sorry he was, that he'd never meant such an odious thing, that—that she could come to him anytime she wished.

But, of course, Nigel Hayves would not say any such thing. He lowered his hand and she looked into his eyes. There was something implacable in them, despite the softness of his tone, and suddenly the message was clear. "I am here now, and I am your husband." Oh, yes, he was sorry for what he'd said the other night, but not necessarily for his anger. He did not want her venturing into his room. There were conditions to this marriage.

Damn him! She did not want a marriage with conditions.

Nigel watched her lift her little pointed chin determinedly. "I see, Nigel," she said with a spark of challenge in her eyes. "When *you* come to *me* I am a wife, but when *I* go to *you* I am . . . something else entirely."

"No, dammit! That's not it at all, Allegra," he snapped, then gentled his tone. "You are always my wife. But a

241

wife must obey her husband . . . in all things."

She met his gaze levelly and searched his eyes for a long time. "Yes, Nigel, I understand," she said flatly.

Damnation! He hadn't wanted to hurt her again. But he wasn't capable of total capitulation. He never would be. She was staring ahead stonily, her eyes suspiciously wet. He took her face in his hands and told her the only truth he could. "Allegra," he rasped, "I . . . want you."

She tried to steel herself against the plea in his eyes, his voice, but could not. His voice spoke of want, but his eyes bespoke need. He had hurt her, would go on hurting her, but something told her he was hurting, too. Nigel Hayves was not a man to plead lightly. He was her husband. She could not turn him away and yet, she knew she must hold something back. She could no longer trust that if she gave everything, she would remain whole.

She covered one of his hands with hers and closed her eyes.

With a groan, Nigel pressed her back against the pillows. He kissed her eyes, her cheeks, and finally lowered his lips to hers. It had been so long. That was all he could think of as he drank in her sweetness. Why in God's name had he denied himself, denied them both, for so long?

Allegra lay very still, pliant but determined not to respond to the feel of Nigel's mouth on hers, of his large, gentle hands, now sliding from her throat to begin unfastening the buttons at the front of her nightgown. The kiss deepened; he lifted the gown from her body. She moved to accommodate him, but willed her body not to match his growing urgency.

It took only minutes for Nigel to realize something was wrong. She was soft and sensual and . . . and submissive. Damn her! He did not want her this way.

He lifted his head, propping himself on his elbows. "Don't do this, Allegra," he whispered.

"What, Nigel?" Her expression was bland, too bland, her voice calm when it should have been breathless.

"You know what." He took her by the shoulders. "Yield to me, Allegra," he demanded urgently. "Give me what I want."

"You do not know what you want, Nigel."

"Here, in this bed, I know what I want," he whispered fiercely, and did not wait, even permit a reply, but took her mouth with his even as his hands claimed her body with intimate familiarity.

No! Allegra cried inwardly. She would not let this happen! It was not enough. She would—she—oh . . . How could such strong hands be so soft? How did he know exactly where . . . Oh! She felt fire when she wanted only cold. She was moving, twisting, arching, when she wanted to be still. And then her mind ceased functioning, and her body, with a will of its own, turned to Nigel and clung.

The storm, when it came, seemed more turbulent, more frantic than before. And in the calm aftermath, as Nigel pulled her into the curve of his arm, she wondered if perhaps something was, indeed, changing. He needed her, and tonight they had reaffirmed that special bond between them.

Allegra awoke to the sound of the lark. She was alone. There was a visible impression in the pillow next to hers, but it was cold. He'd been gone a long time.

Nothing had changed, after all.

Chapter Twelve

"These late eclipses in the sun and moon portend no good to us."

King Lear
William Shakespeare

Nigel wondered if last night had been a victory won at too high a price, for Allegra seemed more remote now than ever, immersing herself in a fervor of domestic activity. All to the good, he decided, for did he not wish to maintain some distance from her as well?

Jamie was meant to have left this morning, but it was raining in virtual sheets and so he postponed his journey one day more. Nigel was still unsuccessful in eliciting from Jamie any further information about the journey. Nor was Jamie any more inclined to accept an offer of help. Frustrated with the lack of response from wife or friend, Nigel betook himself to his study.

Allegra hid her wretchedness behind a calm facade of domestic industry. She began with the menus, which she carefully reviewed, and to good purpose. They were to dine at Lady Wickens's tonight, but Allegra found to her chagrin that Friday night's dinner consisted of six kinds of sweet!

By midmorning she had completed her essential tasks and was feeling decidedly blue-deviled, the rain, which seemed endless, not helping a jot.

And so she greatly welcomed the commotion as an over-sized wagon clattered up the front drive, apparently heedless of the rain. A glance out of the morning room window revealed a large, misshapen piece of cargo buried beneath a firmly tied length of burlap. Most curious, Allegra ventured down the great stairwell toward the front door.

She could not hear all of what the wagon driver said as he stood beneath the front portico, shaking rainwater from his hat. It was something to the effect of a delivery meant for Deben Court.

Two maids joined Allegra in the entry lobby, their ears tuned to Manners's reply. "Well, that's as may be, my good man, but 'tis the servants' entrance you'll be wanting. You can't be meaning to convey that — that — whatever 'tis through the *front door!*"

"Well, and that be exactly what I *am* meanin' to do, yer Nibs, and to pinch a few footmen fer the job, too," replied the wagoner in a voice loud enough to be heard over the din of the rain. "The long and short of it is, see, this plaguey contraption ain't never fit through no servant's door I ever seen. And can't one person carry it neither. Deuced thing's got arms and legs, it does, what fly about makin' the most God awful racket. Why anyone would want — well, makes no never mind to me, 'ceptin' I'd be much obliged for those footmen, so's I can get this plaguey thing outa this here rain and be on me way."

Manners, Allegra realized, was staring openmouthed at the wet and garrulous wagon driver. She had, by this time, a fairly good idea of what lay hidden beneath the burlap and thought it prudent to intervene.

"Why, Manners," she said cheerfully, stepping forward through the small crowd that had gathered in the lobby, "I do believe the new chimney-sweeping machine has come. Am I not right, good sir?"

The wagoner avowed that indeed it was so, and Manners, quickly recovering his composure, dispatched the requisite footmen out into the pouring rain.

It was some thirty minutes before the large machine had been conveyed, at no small effort on the part of the footmen, and with exclamations of trepidation and wonder on the part of the maids, to the Yellow Salon on the first floor. Manners dispatched the wagoner to the kitchens to partake of a bowl of soup before venturing out into the rain, there being, Allegra imagined, plenty of soup left over from last night's dinner. And then Allegra found the eyes of half the household staff trained upon her as she stood before Mr. Smart's machine, which stood upon the lemon yellow carpet before the hearth in the Yellow Salon.

She gazed at the odd-looking machine with its cranks and cogs and various appendages, trying to recall just how the thing worked. There was silence in the room. Manners finally cleared his throat.

"I'm persuaded I'll remember in a moment how it works, Manners. 'Tis merely a matter of which crank to turn first," she said brightly, and then inspiration struck. There had ought to be a page of instructions, she informed the butler, whereupon a footman, his head still sprinkled with raindrops, remembered just such a page fluttering out of the wagon onto the wet pavement. He proceeded to draw the sodden paper from his pocket, with much apology, and Manners set to drying it with his handkerchief.

Half the lettering, unfortunately, had been smeared beyond recognition by the rain. Still, Allegra peered diligently at the paper, Manners at her shoulder.

"Well, do let me see now," she began, thinking aloud, "I recall that it took three people to run the machine. One to turn the main crank"—she pointed to a long black appendage that obviously turned one of the cogs—"one to maneuver this long shaft"—she pointed to a stick with a rounded top which governed the direction of the sweeping arm—

"and one to prod the sweeping arm up the chimney."

Manners positioned three footmen for the tasks as the maids all hung back with a look of terror on their faces. Allegra smiled fleetingly, remembering a similar scene at Caulfield all those months ago. Marcus had been there, too, more frightened than all the rest. But once he'd watched the machine in action, he'd become fascinated with it and made it a point to learn all of its intricacies. If he were here now, he'd have it working in a trice. Allegra sighed, inwardly, realizing how very much she missed the little boy.

"I think we're ready now, your ladyship," Manners interrupted her reverie.

It was then that she recalled the need for dust covers on the carpet and nearby furniture. Much of the soot would fall into the grate, but the machine had been known to send forth quite a black cloud. The machine did come with a bag to be attached to the sweeping arm but, as she explained to Manners, that was the one part of the machine Mr. Smart had yet to perfect. The bag probably caught less than half the chimney residue.

Nonetheless, Manners secured the bag while several reluctant maidservants laid the dust cloths. Finally, the three footmen once more in place, a hush fell over the small crowd. Allegra instructed one footman, Peter, to turn the large crank. The mechanism was stiff, and all waited with baited breath as it turned ever so slowly clockwise.

Then suddenly it lurched, and a large metal cylinder clanged into place, and Mr. Smart's machine began to rumble and vibrate and give off small clouds of dust. The sweeping arm clattered from side to side and fell out of its bracket, causing Jake, the footman assigned to it, to jump back in terror. One maidservant shrieked, another began to pray. Only then did Allegra recall that there was, somewhere, a release mechanism for the long shaft.

"My lady," Manners said in some agitation, as the rumbling grew louder, "I do not think it safe for you to be here. This machine appears to be very unstable and—"

"What in the name of all—oh!" Mrs. Helmsley bellowed, stalking into the room with her hand to her bosom.

Right at her heels, heaven be praised, came Jamie. His blue eyes took in the scene at a glance. He winked at Allegra and strode forward, taking the instruction sheet she proffered.

While Manners attempted to placate the housekeeper, Jamie located the release mechanism. He pulled it and quite suddenly the rumbling became a hum. The third footman was able to maneuver the shaft to the right and the sweeping arm reacted immediately. Everyone stood agog as Jake, with Jamie's instruction, guided the sweeping arm up into the chimney. Jake held on for dear life, but Allegra knew his task was not all that difficult, as the shaft did much of the work. Even Peter seemed to be turning the crank with little difficulty now.

Strange muffled noises came from within the chimney, along with a cloud of soot which half blackened Jake and the dust cloth surrounding the hearth. After a few minutes, when the chimney seemed to emit no more dust, Jamie, again consulting the instruction page, guided the footmen in disengaging the machine.

When it was over, everyone, excepting Mrs. Helmsley, clapped, and two more footmen volunteered to do the next chimney. Even one of the maids said she would be happy to have a go at the shaft or the crank, but she didn't know about the sweeping arm.

Allegra grinned and thanked Jamie profusely.

Nigel threw down his quill, no longer able to maintain even the pretense of working. What in God's name was all that racket? He strode into the corridor and on to the direction of the noise. Aha! So, it was the Yellow Salon.

"What the devil is going on here?" he demanded as he stormed across the threshold. No one seemed to have heard him in all the din, but instead of repeating himself he stopped to survey the room. At the center of the riot and rumpus stood a large, awkward-looking machine with appendages shaking about as dust clouds billowed in the air. Allegra's chimney-sweeping machine, he realized in a flash, and stood with arms folded to watch Jamie and the footmen guide the beastly contraption into a position of repose.

That done, there was a great deal of chatter until Manners and Mrs. Helmsley espied Nigel and came rushing toward him. They were full of explanations, Manners in a tone of apology, Mrs. Helmsley of umbrage, but Nigel paid them little heed. Nor did he heed the maidservants who scurried from the room, nor the footmen who maneuvered the misshapen machine across the carpet. Instead, his eyes focused on Allegra and Jamie.

They stood close together, engaged in conversation. His eyes twinkled down at her; she smiled up at him, that same smile Nigel had seen her flash several times before. Always for Jamie, never for her husband. It was all very innocent; the room was full of people. But Nigel did not like it one whit.

Allegra dressed with the greatest care for dinner at Wickens Manor. It was not, she told herself, that she was dressing to please Nigel, but that she needed all possible armor to face the ordeal ahead. She wore her newest evening dress—a round dress composed of silver net over a pink coral satin slip. The bottom of the skirt was trimmed with flounces of lace festooned with silk roses and bluebells. The corsage was tight, the bodice short, the sleeves little puffs of net and satin.

The dress had been her one extravagance in the past

year. She'd had a local modiste in Caulfield copy it for her from a picture in *La Belle Assemblee*. She'd thought to wear it perhaps when visiting Meg and her "new husband" in London. But now Meg's "new husband" was *her* husband, and she did not know when she would ever get to London.

Her hair, caught up with mother-of-pearl combs at each side, fell where it willed in soft curls about her face. She spared but a moment's final glance in the looking glass. She would never be a great beauty, she decided, but she would do quite well enough.

Nigel awaited her in the entry lobby, looking exceedingly handsome in a deep green coat, gold waistcoat, and buff satin breeches. She marveled at the breadth of his shoulders. Some men needed padding, but not he.

She had reached the bottom step and realized with chagrin that she'd been staring at him, but then, it seemed that he'd been staring as well.

"You look beautiful, Allegra," he uttered softly, a look in his eyes she'd never seen before.

Her mouth felt suddenly dry. "So do you," she heard herself reply hoarsely, and wondered whatever happened to her resolve to remain remote.

He took her light cloak from her hands and enveloped her in it as they stepped out into the dim, misty night. There was no moon visible, but at the least the rain had dwindled to a drizzle. The air was warm, heavy with moisture. Nigel lifted her hood and fastened it at her throat. The brush of his fingers made her shiver.

Nigel handed his wife into the carriage and sat across from her, trying not to stare, trying to think of anything but how delectable she looked tonight, nor to remember the way she'd said that he, too, looked beautiful.

The silence was oppressive and he felt compelled to break it. At first Allegra kept behind her wall of reserve, but Nigel began talking about his childhood, and Allegra began asking questions. He spoke of Charles and Roger and Cliff House but deftly shifted the subject when she asked about Charles and Lucinda.

Allegra and Nigel were greeted at Wickens Manor by a rather rotund butler who ushered them up the stairs and into the drawing room. They were, it seemed, the last to arrive. Lady Wickens took them round to make introductions with what Allegra could only describe as a sly smile. She did not know the cause of it, only knew that everyone in the room had gone unnaturally still at their entrance. A glance at Nigel told her that he, too, was still, but more, he was rigid with anger.

She turned back to the company, trying to fathom the undercurrents. Nigel, of course, knew everyone. There were Lady Wickens and her husband, Sir Randolph, a portly man who held her hand a moment longer than necessary and looked at her far too appraisingly. The Reverend and Mrs. Bailey greeted her in a most kindly manner, although both looked as if they had rather be elsewhere. The elderly, pink-faced Pettigrew sisters, whom Allegra had met previously, seemed like harmless prattleboxes. An equally elderly Major Beardsley and his gangling young son Walter exchanged warm greetings with Nigel and shyly offered their welcomes and felicitations to Allegra.

And then Lady Wickens guided them to the far corner of the room where sat a stunning woman of perhaps some thirty summers. She had sleek blond hair and wore a Clarence blue dress that revealed a generous bosom. Her name was Mrs. Barbara Lacey.

Her greeting to Allegra was languid. To Nigel she extended a hand and spoke in warm, husky tones.

"We have all missed you, Nigel. How lovely to have you back again! And my felicitations on your nuptials. Such a sweet-looking little bride you contrived to find, and so suddenly, too."

"Good evening, Barbara," Nigel replied tautly. "I thank you for your good wishes."

251

Allegra did not think Mrs. Lacey meant to convey good wishes, and she thought Nigel knew it. Confused, she turned to greet the tall, lean, fashionably dressed man standing to the right of the sofa upon which Mrs. Lacey reposed. He was a Mr. Hugo Lattimer, cousin and frequent visitor of the lady. Mr. Lattimer looked Allegra up and down in a manner bordering on insolent. He took her hand and Nigel moved several inches closer to Allegra. Mr. Lattimer looked vastly amused.

Allegra was relieved when dinner was announced but the relief was short-lived, for Hugo Lattimer was to be her dinner partner. He had a mocking, superior air that she could not like. Nor did she care for the fact that Lady Wickens had paired Nigel and Mrs. Lacey. She could not say why—perhaps it was the way Mrs. Lacey took Nigel's arm with such a proprietary air, perhaps something about the way she looked at him. Nigel, Allegra noted, held himself stiffly erect. It was all most bewildering; she could not wait for the evening to end.

Allegra was seated between her host, Sir Randolph, and Mr. Lattimer. Sir Randolph engaged her attention for the first part of the meal, pausing in his conversation for frequent dips into his claret. He grumbled about the tedium of rustication and of women's penchant for gossip and cat-and-mouse games. His increasingly reddened eyes were on his wife as he spoke, and Allegra realized he must already be deep in his cups. Still she wondered to what cat-and-mouse games he referred. Twice she'd seen Lady Wickens cast a shrewd and smug eye about the table, coming to rest, a moment too long, on Allegra. Why did Allegra begin to feel like the mouse?

When the footmen served the soup, *le potage de poissons a la russe*, Allegra realized with a bubble of merriment that they'd had the very same for their third remove last night at Deben. She raised her eyes to Nigel, who sat diagonally across the table from her, to share her amusement. But

Nigel was engrossed in conversation with Mrs. Lacey. The merriment died in Allegra's throat.

Mr. Lattimer engaged her attention next, paying her Spanish coin, and making observations about her gown and person that were most inappropriate. He was leaning so close to her as to make her distinctly uncomfortable, but when she tried to shift to her left, her elbow nearly sank into a platter of poached turbot with lobster sauce. She bandied his comments as best she might, determined not to make a scene by being impolite. But her pique was all the greater for sensing that Mr. Lattimer was well aware of her discomfort.

And what in heaven's name were Nigel and Mrs. Lacey conversing about with such intensity? Such . . . such intimacy. That was the word. There was a curious intimacy about them, almost as if they—but no, it could not be. Mrs. Lacey was a respectable woman, a lady. She could not once have been Nigel's . . . mistress. Allegra had overheard all about mistresses from the stable boys at Caulfield. Mistresses were bits of muslin, high flyers, no better than they should be. This woman—

Allegra's thoughts stopped and her eyes widened before she had the good sense to lower them and reach for her wineglass. She could not believe what she had seen. For just a moment, Mrs. Lacey had put her hand atop Nigel's. And Allegra had watched, across the table, in the gap between the candles and flowers and gilt-edged platters, Nigel very subtly turn his hand to clasp hers, give it a brief squeeze, and then release it.

It had all happened so quickly, but Allegra knew she had not been imagining it. A wave of nausea assailed her; she did not know how she would eat another morsel this night. Just what was this Barbara Lacey to Nigel? Did she not have a husband?

She heard a soft, sardonic chuckle from Mr. Lattimer. As if he'd read her mind, he whispered, "A delectable creature, my cousin. A widow, you must know."

A widow, Allegra thought, disheartened, and then felt mortified that she'd been so transparent. She murmured some piffle about Mrs. Lacey looking lovely in Clarence blue.

"Yes, what little there is of it, Lady Debenham," Mr. Lattimer replied in a low, intimate voice. He looked pointedly, unabashedly down at Allegra's bodice. "I am persuaded that you, too, would look most — er — charming in a dress of . . . Clarence blue."

Allegra wanted to slap him for the impertinent rake he obviously was, but a glance across the table at her husband and Mrs. Lacey caused her to hit upon another notion. She clasped her ivory fan tightly in her right hand and let forth a peal of laughter.

"Oh, sir, you do quite put me to the blush," she trilled, and gave his arm a flick of her fan. "You are altogether too provoking, you must know, and I shan't allow it. Now tell me why you choose to rusticate here instead of taking yourself off to Brighton or some such."

Hugo Lattimer leaned even closer and laughed deep in his throat. "Why then I should not have met *you*, Lady Debenham, should I?" he countered, then lowered his voice. "You'll do very well in London, I'll wager. Very well, indeed. I look forward to renewing your acquaintance, perhaps in the Little Season?"

Allegra very much hoped *not* to renew his acquaintance, but felt perversely pleased that her first and only attempt at the art of flirtation had succeeded. She looked across the table. Nigel was clenching his jaw. Yes, she had succeeded, but whatever was to come of all this?

She was greatly relieved when Sir Randolph addressed a remark to her, however slurred his speech by now. And then Miss Eleanor Pettigrew, to Sir Randolph's right, joined the conversation, which left Hugo Lattimer to turn to Mrs. Bailey on *his* right. Allegra sincerely hoped the vicar's wife could keep Mr. Lattimer occupied for a time.

Allegra's head was buzzing. Would the evening never end?

Nigel had had about all he could take of this infernal dinner. Lady Wickens, damn her eyes, was conversing most eloquently with the Reverend Bailey and Walter Beardsley about the need for new pews for the parish church. Of a certain she cared not a jot for any pews, but she had effectively left Nigel, on her right, with none but Barbara Lacey with whom to converse.

On Barbara's right sat Major Beardsley and Miss Clarissa Pettigrew, carrying on the same tentative, blushing discourse they'd had for all the years Nigel could recall.

And so Barbara had turned to Nigel, enjoying every minute of his discomfiture. She was nearly sitting in his lap, so close was she, but short of outright rudeness he did not know how to disengage her. He did not know whatever had possessed him to squeeze her hand. He'd meant to placate her after he'd refused a rather blatant invitation, but all he'd done was egg her on, for she had inched even closer.

Blast! He'd hoped Allegra hadn't noticed any of it. And then he'd seen her flirting so outrageously with Hugo Lattimer, and he'd wanted to murder the pair of them. But first he'd got to set Barbara straight about a few things. He began, when the truffled roast chickens, round of veal and steamed carp forcemeat were served, by apologizing for not having come to see her since his return. And he mentally cursed himself for not doing so, for such a conversation hardly belonged at a dinner party. But there had been the rain, and his concern for Allegra, and Jamie's imminent departure, and now there was no hope for it.

And perhaps it was for the best. She could not very well

make a scene at Lady Wickens's dinner table. And, indeed, why should she? She'd known he was to wed one day, although not that it precluded a liaison between them. And so he explained that, now he was wed, they simply could not go on as they had before, delightful though it had been.

Barbara raised one finely arched brow and favored him with a mocking glance. "Well, well. So, she's turned you into a dutiful husband already."

"Nonsense. I am no such thing," Nigel bristled. "But she *is* a dutiful wife, and I owe her the courtesy of discretion. This—for us to resume our—well, it would not be discreet. Not now. Perhaps sometime in the future, when Allegra is more accustomed to married life and the—ah—ways of society . . . She has not been about very much, you must know."

Barbara cast a shrewd glance across the table at Allegra. Nigel had never seen her blue eyes look quite so hard. "Perhaps I underestimated the charms of the schoolroom," she drawled. "I shall not do so again."

"Stay away from her, Barbara," Nigel said sharply.

Barbara delicately brushed a lock of blond hair from her brow. "Is that a threat, Nigel?"

Nigel did not at all care for the train of this conversation. He'd never known Barbara to be this way. He had got to diffuse her simmering anger straightaway. "No, Barbara. It is a request. For the sake of all we shared in the past. And what we might share in the future." He could see some of the harshness retreat from Barbara's eyes, but even as he said the last words he knew, suddenly, that they were not true.

They would never again share any intimacy. Not, of course, that he meant to become a pattern card of the faithful husband. It was simply that he would take his mistresses from among those who would not, could not, hurt Allegra. A French high flyer, an opera dancer, a woman who knew her place. He'd seen the look of . . . malevolence on Barbara Lacey's face as she'd gazed at his wife. Given half a chance, Lord only knew what she would say, or attempt to do, to Allegra. He would not give her the chance. A clean break now was the better part of valor. He smiled down at her to take the sting out of his words, and she returned a smile he did not quite trust.

Nigel was exceedingly grateful when the Reverend Bailey addressed him from across the table, asking how Coke of Norfolk was doing with his sheep. All the more was Nigel's gratitude for knowing that the only sheep the good reverend cared about were in his parish flock.

Talking with Mr. Bailey was not enough to distract himself from the sight of Allegra, however. She was talking to Lattimer again, actually flirting with him! He'd seen his wife flick her fan at him before—where the devil had she learned such a thing? And why was she allowing that rake to lean so close to her? Was his own seat not comfortable enough? Oh, blast! What had the reverend just said to him?

Nigel would have been most happy, when the meal and requisite after rituals were finally concluded, to take his wife and leave, but Phillipa Wickens had other ideas. To whit, a game of whist, which she announced in such a way as to make it a virtual command, not a suggestion. They were in the drawing room now, Nigel unfortunately two seats away from Allegra, Hugo Lattimer having appropriated the rest of the sofa on which she sat.

"Oh, dear. I'm afraid I do not play whist," Allegra said.

Nigel saw his chance and seized it. "Alas, 'tis true, Lady Wickens, and I really think we—"

"Oh, well, 'tis quite all right, dear Lady Debenham," Lady Wickens interrupted. "No need to apologize. Why, Lord Debenham can partner Barbara," she said as if the

257

idea had just occurred to her. "You've done that before, have you not my lord?" she added sweetly.

Nigel's jaw clenched and his eyes pierced hers, but his hostess's expression was bland. Barbara said not a word, merely walked dutifully to the game table. Nigel was trapped. He could not, with any semblance of politeness, demur. He turned to Allegra, hoping that he could convey in a glance that he was sorry. But she was standing by this time, Lattimer at her side, her body stiff, her eyes unreadable. He could not fathom her expression, but he knew it was not pleasant. He sighed inwardly. If he tried to approach her now, to soothe her, it would surely raise eyebrows. No couple behaved so in public. And then Phillipa Wickens bustled about, assigning everyone to their amusements, and the moment was lost.

Nigel could only keep half a mind on his cards. The other half was on his wife. She was playing chess with Major Beardsley, and apparently, from what he could hear, losing badly but charming the damn pants off the normally reticent older man. He heard a peal of warm, intimate laughter and turned to see her patting his arm. Blast her! Had she no sense of propriety? But of course she hadn't. Had she not behaved with the most shameful impropriety with Nigel at Caulfield, thereby trapping him into marriage? At the least Lattimer had taken himself off to puff a cloud. He was unscrupulous with women, and Nigel did not want his wife near the man.

Allegra watched Nigel from the corner of her eye. She could hardly bear it, but she could scarcely tear her eyes away. Oh, Nigel, she thought, why could you not have suggested that you would partner *me* and teach me the game? She'd thought he'd been about to suggest they go home, but apparently not, for he'd not offered any objection to Lady Wickens's plan.

The intimacy between Nigel and that woman was making Allegra's stomach turn. And then she saw something that made her eyes nearly pop from her head. Under the green baize game table, Mrs. Lacey had removed her slipper, and her foot was creeping up Nigel's calf! The audacity of the woman! He's *my* husband, she wanted to shriek. But, of course, she did not, and forced her eyes back into her head lest someone follow her gaze and see what she'd seen.

The major trounced her, as was to be expected, for she'd been paying no heed. And when Hugo Lattimer suggested she take a stroll in the garden with him, she tossed her head defiantly and gave him her arm.

That was it, Nigel decided. The last straw. She'd actually gone to the garden with him! The game was not half over, not five points having been played, but he didn't give a damn. He threw his cards down. "You must excuse me," he said to the others, "but I fear my wife is not well. She has gone to the garden to take some air and I must see to her." He ignored Lady Wickens's open mouth and Barbara's flashing eyes, and strode across the room and out the French doors.

The rain had dwindled to a fine mist, and he found them easily under the protective arch of a clinging vine. They were standing very close, facing each other. Lattimer lifted his hand as if to touch her face but then they must have heard him for they abruptly stepped apart.

With effort, Nigel leashed his temper and moved forward. "There you are, Allegra, my dear. I hope you are feeling more the thing. Thank you, Lattimer, for seeing to Lady Debenham's health. You may wish to rejoin the others. I shall see to her now."

Lattimer inclined his head. "The pleasure was all mine, Debenham," he drawled and then bowed to Allegra. "Your servant, dear lady."

Nigel kept a firm grip on Allegra's elbow all through the leave-taking, and a firm grip on his tongue and his temper all through the carriage ride home. Nor did he allow Allegra to say aught. He said not a word, in fact, until Kingston and Katie had finished their ministrations. Then he stormed into his wife's bedchamber and gave full vent to his fury.

"How dare you!" he railed. "How dare you behave in such a reprehensible manner!"

"I?" she demanded imperiously, brown eyes flashing in the candlelight. She stood at the window, one hand on the brocade draperies.

"You were flirting shamelessly with Lattimer and Major Beardsley and—"

"Major Beardsley? What utter fustian! Why—"

"And to go off into the garden with that rake Lattimer!" Nigel advanced on her, stopping just a foot away. "Have you no sense of propriety, no care for your reputation?" He was shouting now, his hands clenched at his sides.

She faced him boldly. "Have *I* no sense? What about *you*, Nigel? You and—"

"Damnation, Allegra!" He grasped her shoulders. "Do you not know there is only one thing a man wants from a woman in a darkened garden?" He shook her as he spoke, his whole body seething with anger. Her head was tilted up to his, her eyes distressed and fearful and angry all at once. But her lips—God help him—her lips looked full and warm and inviting . . . No!

He dropped his arms and stepped back from her. "Or is that what you wanted, Allegra?" he asked in a low, menacing voice. "Did you deliberately lure him—"

"No! Stop it, Nigel! Your accusations are odious in the extreme! Mr. Lattimer invited me to walk with him and I went. That is all. Surely there is naught exceptionable in that. I *am*, after all, a married woman now, not a green girl who—"

"You must think *me* very green indeed to believe that was a mere walk—"

"Ooh! Damn you, Nigel Hayves!" Allegra stamped her

260

foot and threw her hands to her hips. "How dare you berate *me*, when *you* sat in Mrs. Lacey's pocket all evening, the pair of you cooing and billing like—"

"That's enough, Allegra," he warned.

"Is it? I do not think so, Nigel. What is that woman to you?"

Nigel stiffened. "Mrs. Lacey and I are old friends. Not that—"

"Was she your mistress?" she asked bluntly.

Nigel felt his eyes blaze. His hands jerked as if to grab her again; with great effort he forced them down. "You will remember that you are a lady," he said between gritted teeth, "and ladies never ask such questions. Nor do gentlemen answer them."

"How convenient for the gentlemen," she muttered. He wanted to strangle her.

"I have known Mrs. Lacey since she came to Debenham after the death of her husband. I have many friends here, including Mrs. Lacey, as well as Major Beardsley, the Reverend and Mrs. Bailey—"

"I see," Allegra said all too genially. She slid away from the window, away from him, and went to stand by the bedside. He did not like the look in her eye. "And does your friend, Mrs. Bailey, also rub her little foot up and down your calf?"

Nigel coughed. He almost choked. Good God! How the devil had she seen that? He strode to her, careful not to touch her. "That was not my doing, Allegra," he said tautly.

She arched her brow, "I did not precisely see you recoil, Nigel."

"Did you wish me to create a scene, Allegra, to announce to all and sundry what she was doing?" he asked mockingly and thought she blanched. "But all that has nothing to say to the matter," he went on, "which is that you are my wife and I will not tolerate such a want of conduct as you displayed this night." He kept his voice stern but his wife was not cowed.

She raised her chin a notch. He found himself staring again at her lips, at the upper one with no indentation, the lower with its sensual pout. He wanted to trace them with his fingers, and then to let his hand drop, to glide lower, to caress her rounded breasts through the fabric of her ridiculously virginal nightdress. He could feel his breathing alter as his body reacted to his thoughts. But he did not move; he would drive home his point first. "Allegra, did you hear—"

"Look to your own conduct, Nigel!" she snapped, and then so did he.

He grabbed her and pulled her close. "Damnation, Allegra! I'll not have you behaving like a trollop! This is just how Lucinda started, with walks in the garden that she claimed were innocent. But even *she* waited until she and Charles were wed a year. You've not the scruples to do even that!" Dimly he was aware that his grip was too strong, but he could not release her. "I'll not have it, Allegra! You'll not do to me what she did to Charles!" he raged, and then lowered his mouth in a fierce, bruising kiss.

She fought him, and he crushed her more tightly to him, his lips and teeth digging brutally into her mouth. Only when she went completely still did he come to his senses. He released her so abruptly that she stumbled and fell back onto the bed.

He turned away, trying to catch his breath. Dear God, what had he done? He'd hurt her, assaulted her. His wife. He'd never meant . . . Reluctantly he looked back at her. She was sprawled back against the pillows, the back of her hand against her mouth. Slowly, he raised his eyes to hers, dreading the look of hate and fear he would see in them.

But he saw neither of those things. What he saw were tears glistening in deep brown pools, and in them a look of utter bafflement and—and compassion, he thought. Was that possible? He swallowed hard. He deserved her contempt, not her compassion. Nor, he assured himself, did he want it.

Allegra blinked back her tears and ignored the burning of her ravaged lips. She sensed that she was at some turning point in her marriage. She had tried withdrawing from him, but that hadn't worked. Besides, she simply could not keep up that pose for long. Now, she had got to go forward in the only way she knew how. "Tell me about Lucinda," she asked hoarsely from behind her hand.

He shook head and paced to the window, staring out at the misty moonless night. A tense silence fell between them.

Gingerly Allegra removed her hand from her bruised mouth. "I have a right to know, Nigel. I have a right to know what she did, of precisely what I am accused. I have a right to know why everyone at Debenham silently compares me to her."

At that his head whipped round, his eyes piercing hers questioningly. But she said not a word, merely met his gaze and held her breath. She did not know what she would do if he refused to answer, refused, once again to allow her past one of his barriers.

Rights, he thought. Did she have any rights? She was his wife. He was not obliged to tell her aught. And yet, perhaps the story itself would be a warning to her. And perhaps . . . perhaps the telling of it would be a way of apologizing for his inexcusable savagery . . . Damn and blast it all! He hadn't meant to hurt her. She was his wife. He only wanted to make her see— Hellfire! He did not know *why* he'd behaved so. Never had he felt so out of control. She was correct. She did have a right to know. And perhaps it was time he spoke of it; he'd been silent too long.

He heard his own voice as if from far away. His brow

was against the windowpane, its coolness a relief from the heat in his body. "It is not a pretty story," he began. "Lucinda, however, was beautiful, dark and sultry. Taller than you, but similar in coloring. Charles was besotted with her, adored her. Lucinda . . . Lucinda adored only herself. She collected men as other women collect hats." He said this with disdain, but it was pain that he felt. He ran a hand over his face, remembering. He heard Allegra move but didn't turn to face her. Now that he'd begun, he wanted to finish, and he could only do it staring out at the bleak, black night.

"She put the horns on Charles when they were wed little more than a year. When he found out he went into a rage and started drinking. But she would not cease her behavior, no matter what Charles did. Once he threatened to cut off her allowance. She laughed in his face and said there were plenty of men willing to pay for her dresses and jewels." He heard Allegra gasp but she said nothing. His voice grew louder in the telling. "One night, very late, she came into the library where I was reading and set out to . . . seduce me. When I turned her down, she became furious. She fumed at me and vowed vengeance, which she took . . . in spades."

Nigel grew restless. He had to keep talking but felt the need to move. Slowly he walked to the fireplace and put his hands on the mantel, his feet on the cold hearth. "She and Charles were having dreadful rows by now and he had long since quit her bed. And then . . . And then she fell with child. It could not possibly have been his and so she—she told him it was . . . mine."

"No!" Allegra said in a strangled whisper.

He forced himself to go on. "Charles was so crazed by then, hardly ever sober, and he believed her. The worst was that my father did as well. I do not know if he ever quite forgave me for what happened next, even though years later I persuaded him it was not true."

264

He felt her hand on his shoulder. He felt so cold and she was so warm. Slowly he turned to face her; he did not touch her. "It was raining that night. Charles was in a towering rage, foxed, beside himself. He dragged Lucinda into his new phaeton. I—I tried to stop him but he drove away in a frenzy. By the time I found them, hours later, the carriage was a—a splintered, bloody wreck at the bottom of a ravine." His voice shook as he finished. Allegra was crying. He stumbled forward. Dimly he realized that she caught him in her arms.

"Come to bed, Nigel. I'm so sorry. Come to bed," she urged softly.

No, he told himself. He must go to his own bed. But he needed her warmth. All his fury and heat and desire were gone; he was so cold. She led him to the bed and he shrugged out of his dressing gown and climbed in beside her, pulling her into the curve of his body.

Allegra listened, crying silent tears, as her husband's ragged breathing evened into sleep. She grieved for him, and yet felt a great relief that part of the puzzle of Nigel had fallen into place. He had allowed her to breach the wall, or part of it.

She understood his suspicions now, his fury at her going off with Hugo Lattimer, even, in part, his need to keep some distance from her. But she knew she had yet to find all the pieces to the puzzle. She did not know if she ever would.

Nigel threw an arm about her waist and drew her closer in his sleep. Never before had he come to her for other than desire. It had been a terrible night, but for all that, she felt hope, more than she'd ever felt before. She snuggled back against Nigel's chest and promptly fell asleep.

Chapter Thirteen

"You would lift the moon out of her sphere."

The Tempest
William Shakespeare

Nigel was piqued at himself and even more furious with Allegra. Why had he stayed with her, slept with her without even the excuse of physical need? It had been comfort he'd sought, warmth to ease the coldness of grief. That was not what he wanted of a wife! He would not let it happen again.

But he was even more overset to realize, as he dressed for his early-morning ride, that nothing had been resolved last night. She had admitted no wrongdoing, had not said she would behave more circumspectly. All she had done was get him to speak of something he'd never had any intention of speaking about, and then, luring him into bed!

Damnation! Would he never be free of the machinations of women?

He was gone, of course, by the time Allegra awoke. But he had talked to her, really talked to her, for the first time. Something, at last, had changed.

The sun had not deigned to make its appearance, but as there was no rain, Allegra presumed that Jamie would leave today. She went out to the stables before breakfast to say good-bye to him. They were in conversation but a few minutes before they heard hoofbeats outside. A moment later Nigel stepped into the stable. He looked from Allegra to Jamie and frowned, his prodigious brows arching into "V's." Allegra narrowed her eyes in bafflement. What was Nigel so displeased about? Was he still piqued at her over last night, or was there more? She heard the rather brusque manner in which he addressed Jamie, saw the way he looked from her to his friend and realized that he didn't want her here, with Jamie. But why?

Jamie had stiffened at Nigel's tone. Allegra did not want to be the cause of a strained leave-taking between them. She wished Jamie Godspeed, flashed him a smile, and exited the stables with a brief word to Nigel.

She pondered that brief interlude all through breakfast. She thought she understood her husband a little better after last night. But surely Nigel's disapproval this morning could not mean he thought that there was anything untoward between — no! It was a nonsensical notion. Jamie was his friend, a servant — of sorts — and she'd merely been bidding him farewell.

Nigel was not going to become het up every time she talked to another man, was he? She recalled that he'd even accused her of flirting with dear old Major Beardsley! Oh, goodness! This could become excessively unpleasant, for Allegra *liked* talking to men, although of a certain she did not *flirt* with them. Why, the only time she'd ever flirted deliberately had been last night with Mr. Lattimer, and that was only because Nigel and Mrs. Lacey were sitting in each other's pocket!

Allegra took a slow sip of her coffee. Why had the sight of Nigel and that woman overset her so? She had been furious, even . . . possessive! He was her husband. No other woman had the right—Good Heavens! She set her cup down abruptly. Was that how Nigel felt when he'd seen her with—no. It was not at all the same thing. She'd merely been talking with the major and Jamie, even with Hugo Lattimer. None of them had had a foot slithering up her calf! Besides, if Nigel had felt possessive it must only have been out of some masculine need to stake his territorial rights, claim his property, as it were. It wasn't the possessiveness that came out of jealousy. Jealousy was what Charles had felt over Lucinda, whom he had loved beyond all reason. Nigel did not love Allegra. Why, he did not even like her!

As for Allegra, she, too, had felt possessive. Had she been jealous? She paused in the act of raising a forkful of scrambled eggs to her mouth. Perhaps she had been jealous, but—but she did not love Nigel, did she?

Allegra put the fork down. How could she love a man who did not want her in his life, who could hurt her so easily? His tender passion in bed, his concern for his dependents, his integrity, his intelligence—surely all of these were not enough to make her love him.

But he was her husband. And last night he had confided in her, and held her closely in sleep. Allegra sighed. It was going to be very difficult not to fall in love with her husband.

Nigel was decidedly piqued. She'd smiled at Jamie again. Nigel liked it less each time.

He worked Wiggins, his steward, to near exhaustion going over estate accounts all morning, and himself to near exhaustion visiting four tenant farms in the afternoon. It was best this way; he needed the distraction.

But it was not enough distraction, not that day nor the days following. He did not go to Allegra at night. He wanted her too much, almost . . . needed her, and that was dangerous. He would not allow himself that need. He would cure himself of it. He wondered fleetingly if bedding another woman would help but dismissed the notion. There was no one in the vicinity with whom he cared to dally. Barbara was out of the question. And while he might once, in his salad days, have assuaged his physical hunger with a local barmaid, the thought now fairly turned his stomach.

And so he tossed and turned at night and sought the solace of work during the day. But somehow, one way or another, Allegra was always there. Either he met her in the corridors, or heard her voice, or heard one of the servants saying, "Her ladyship says," or "Her ladyship wishes," or "Ask her ladyship." Blast them all! What did they do before "her ladyship" arrived?

Her very presence pervaded the house, and thoughts of her pervaded his mind. He did not know how much longer he could go on like this.

Week's end had come and gone. Life settled into a routine of sorts for Allegra. That is, she got through her days, but with a heaviness of spirit to which she was unaccustomed. Nigel avoided her by day, and no longer came to her at night.

Jamie had been gone nearly a se'ennight, and Allegra was running out of distractions. Applegreave had finished his work, the painters were down to the last few touchups, the upholsterers had come and gone. The blue-green sitting room was almost ready.

Even the chimney-sweeping machine had ceased to be a nine-days' wonder. The footmen had become adept at using it. In fact, she had it on good authority that one of the upstairs maids had been so taken with the way Jake the footman handled it, that she finally agreed to walk out with him at night.

Twice, when Allegra had paced the moonlit garden, too restless to sleep, she'd seen them, walking hand in hand. She'd had to stifle a stab of envy, and she'd gone back to her lonely bed and ached for Nigel. Ached not only for the delicious sensations his touch unleashed within her, but also for that special, ineffable bond she felt with him whenever he held her.

And so she had vowed to be patient, to give herself freely to him whenever he came to her. She would reinforce that bond whenever she could, hoping that someday, it would grow into more. But Nigel had not come to her in over a se'ennight. It was difficult not to become discouraged, not to feel helpless to change anything.

She did not, however, make the mistake of going to his chamber again, as she had that dreadful night, Wednesday last. Nor did she try to seduce him as she had at Caulfield. All of her instincts told her that the next move was Nigel's. And she reminded herself of the night of Lady Wickens's dinner party, when he'd finally confided in her, and turned to her for comfort in bed. She refused to lose hope. Something would break the impasse of her marriage.

Dinner was the one time when Nigel could not avoid his wife. He couldn't very well request a tray in his study every night. Besides, one had to keep up appearances before the staff. As it was, he was slowly coming to feel like an unwelcomed person in his own house. It was all very subtle, but unmistakable. It was there in the slight brusqueness with which the servants, from Manners on down, addressed him of late. It was there in the way his bed was made with the sheets just a trifle askew, in the way his eggs were always slightly overcooked. All this in marked contrast to the solicitousness with which they treated "her ladyship."

270

The staff seemed to have decided that "her ladyship" was unhappy and that the earl was the cause. How they had deduced that bit of moonshine he did not know, but there it was.

Nor did he know how his wife had contrived to wind the entire staff around her little finger, but she had. All except Mrs. Helmsley. He did not know if the housekeeper would ever forgive Allegra for the chimney-sweeping machine.

At all events, he thought it prudent to dine nightly with his wife. It was, however, a slow form of torture. She was always seated next to him. (That, he'd discovered, was Manners's doing. Who would have thought the old chap had it in him?) She always smelled of wildflowers. And her gowns, no matter how woefully out of fashion or how modestly cut, always tantalized him. All he could think about was taking them off her.

Nigel Hayves was slowly going out of his mind.

He was staring out his study window, watching Allegra below, her gamin face turned up to the sun, her bare feet—bare feet!—wriggling in the grass.

He had got to get away from Deben Court! He and Allegra were too isolated here; there was too little distraction. The best place for distraction was London.

He poured himself a snifter of brandy and sat down in his leather desk chair. London. Why not? He certainly had matters enough to see to there. He was suspicious of Creeve, concerned about Jamie, desirous of checking with the Revenue Office about their progress in Dorset.

True, London would still be very hot, and rather thin of company, it being the end of August. But within a few weeks enough of the ton would have trickled back for the Little Season to start. There would be diversion enough. And there would be White's. A quiet dinner at his club with an old friend or two would be most welcome. But exactly what was he to do with Allegra while he went off to Town? He could not very well leave her here. There would

271

be unpleasant talk in the village, and his own servants were like to murder him in his bed. Besides, Barbara and Lattimer were still in residence. He could not leave Allegra to the tender mercies of either.

Lattimer, he reflected, had already stayed longer than usual in Debenham. He and Barbara had been raised together and acted more like brother and sister than cousins, confiding in each other and squabbling in turn. They had never been lovers, but Lattimer never lacked for female companionship and had few scruples where the fair sex was concerned.

No, clearly Nigel could not leave Allegra here. Nor could he exile her to another of his estates. He had no just cause and besides, he did not care to end up with another houseful of servants treating him as a pariah.

There was only one solution. He would have to take her with him. The notion seemed preposterous, he knew, since he was going at first stop to get away from her. But the truth was that in Town, what with all the diversion and people about, one could contrive not to see one's spouse for days at a time if one wished. Why, he knew several couples who'd been living that way for years!

Allegra would be kept quite busy, even before the Little Season began, refurbishing her wardrobe and meeting members of the Polite World as they filtered back to Town. She had, after all, never had a come out and it would all be very new to her.

It occurred to him in an uncomfortable flash of insight that she might not be the only one whose hopes were dashed by their forced marriage. Might Allegra not have dreamed of cutting a dash at her come out, of young bucks paying her court? Yet she'd never complained, never made reference to any shattered dreams.

Abruptly he remembered her one foray into society here in Debenham. If she thought she could make up for lost opportunities by setting up her flirts now that she was a married woman, she could think again! Nigel would introduce her to the ton, would teach her how to navigate among the more dangerous shoals of Society, and would make sure she comported herself with the utmost propriety.

And then he would see about his own diversions.

It had taken Jamie two full days to reach London, for the rain had left the roads in a bad way. And then he'd spent yesterday searching for his friend Angus, finally finding him in some stinking rat hole that Jamie shuddered to think he'd once felt at home in. Angus had been very glad to see him and more than happy to help a fellow Hielander and not ask too many questions at that.

And now here they were, at dawn, staring up at the garden wall of this terrible place, *Le Petite Maison*. They glanced at each other for a moment and then silently, simultaneously, vaulted the wall.

It was eerily quiet in the garden as they moved toward the back of the house, which was, Jamie noted, crisscrossed with vines. He had not known what to expect, had hoped mayhap to find a tree which he might climb. The vines might be better, if they would hold his weight. He gave one of them a shake. It was strong, but then Jamie was no wee lad. Angus shrugged, and Jamie began counting, up and over, until he located the window Katie had indicated.

Angus gave him a leg up, and he grabbed the nearest vine and began climbing. The vine held him, although just barely. He used the lower window ledges to boost himself as he went up, and then, finally, his hands were on the ledge of the window that might be Flora's. Slowly, hardly drawing breath, he hauled himself up and peered through the window. It was open a bit. The curtains were partially drawn, and he had to shift over to see inside the room.

The light was dim, but he could make out a wee form on the bed. Blast! Her face was turned away from him. Turn aboot, he silently willed her, so I can see ye. Endless moments went by. Somehow Jamie kept his grip on the wooden ledge, his feet anchored in twisted bits of vine.

And then she turned. And he saw the face, so pale and lined with strain and looking ever so different from the lass he recalled. It could be Flora, he reckoned, but he could not be certain, not with her eyes closed and her hair covered with a mobcap. And then she stirred again, this time twisting beneath the blanket, just enough to dislodge the torn lace cap. And there it was. He could not believe it! Flaming, curly red hair, matted down, lifeless, but still that same hair, the hair that haunted his dreams. He began to shake. Could it be, or was there another woman here with such hair? Open yer eyes, lass, he willed the figure on the bed. I'll ken when I see yer eyes.

But she did not open her eyes. Instead she called out, called to a maidservant for water. And then he knew. He could not mistake the voice, soft and lilting, even in illness. Flora's voice. Flora! He felt tears pouring down his face. His Flora was here; she was alive! He wanted to call to her, to push the window completely open and vault through, to catch her in his arms and carry her away. But he could not do that. Not today. He needs must plan their escape carefully.

Jamie waited for his eyes to clear before descending to Angus. And he waited until they were a safe several blocks away before speaking at all. That was when he told Angus, for the first time, just who it was in the room beyond the window.

He supposed, he thought aloud, that now was the time to write to the earl and beg his aid. But Angus, guiding him into some dark cellar that passed for a pub, pointed out how much time it would take. The letter, he said, and the journey, and then the magistrates, for surely his nibs would want to do it right and proper. No! Jamie thought. It would be a sordid business; he could not involve his lordship in such a scandal broth. Especially when Angus was right here offering to meet him tomorrow morn with a blanket and rope ladder and a file for the garden gate.

And so it was that on the very next morning, before the sun rose, they returned to *Le Petite Maison*. This time they broke the lock on the garden gate, for there would be no vaulting the wall with their precious burden on the way out. Again they moved silently forward, and Jamie climbed the vine, this time with nails and a hammer, to secure the rope ladder, and a blanket and the ladder itself. For it was certain he could not climb down that vine with Flora. He wrapped the hammer in a cloth and slammed it into one nail and the next. But the sound was not muffled enough. He knew it even before he heard the cry raised. Cursing inwardly, he slithered back down the vine, blanket and ladder draped on his shoulders, and he and Angus darted into the bushes.

Jamie's heart was pounding at the sound of the guards circling the house and calling to each other. He prayed they would not come round the back and find the broken lock, and, miraculously, they did not. But Jamie caught a glimpse of one of them in the torchlight. God's teeth! It was Hurley, the man from the inn yard, the man Katie had escaped.

Jamie felt his disappointment as a physical pang as they eventually crept out of the garden, knowing they would have to wait yet another day. She was so close! It was almost more than he could bear! But, in truth, what choice had he?

That night Jamie resolutely shaved his beard, much as it pained him to part with it, lest Hurley recognize him. He hardly slept at all, his thoughts all of Flora.

Once more, just before the sun came up, he and Angus returned to that terrible house. They slipped through the garden gate and Jamie climbed the vine and secured the ladder. The window creaked as he pushed it open, further and further. He held his breath, waiting for the cry of a guard, but there was none. He poked his head in. She was there, asleep in the bed, her breathing labored, her beautiful hair covered by the torn mobcap.

Quickly, silently, Jamie climbed through the window. And then he stood before her, gazing down with tears in his eyes. He wanted to wake her, tell her who he was and what he was about, but, of course, he could not take such a chance. Instead he wrapped the sleeping form of his poor wee wife in the blanket and carried her to the window. Angus, standing guard below, gave him a sign that all was clear. And so, very gently, Jamie hoisted Flora onto his shoulder, praying she would not wake.

It was not without difficulty that he wriggled back out of the window and set his foot down on the first rung of the ladder. He kept one hand at Flora's back, the other in a tight grip on the window ledge, as he tested the ladder to make certain it would hold them. And then, heart pounding, he began the slow descent. They were almost there! Almost! Dinna wake, Flora lass, he told her silently, dinna wake yet, lass.

She did not stir, and finally he felt the ground beneath one foot, and then the other. Angus's hands steadied him as he shifted Flora and settled her more securely on his shoulder. And then he and Angus turned and ran for all they were worth.

They had left a hackney waiting round the corner. Angus threw open the door, and it was just as Jamie was bundling Flora inside that the cry was raised. Angus cursed fluently; he and Jamie jumped into the hackney and slammed the door. The coach lurched forward even as Hurley and one other guard rounded the corner. Jamie felt the blood pound in his temples. He held Flora on his lap, unwrapping the blanket from her head and face and then turning and craning his neck, alongside Angus, to see out the back window.

Angus had a pistol at the ready; Jamie could see that Hurley, still giving chase, had one as well. God's blood! No! Jamie thought. Not now! He could not lose her now! Angus banged on the roof of the hackney; the driver sprung the horses. The guards were on foot; surely they could not possibly keep up. Hurley raised his pistol. Jamie gulped. But the distance must already have been too great, for the shot echoed harmlessly in the early-morning air.

Still, Angus lunged for the door, pistol cocked, but Jamie stayed him with his hand. Hurley looked murderous, but his figure was receding. The guards could not possibly catch them now; there was no sense buying further trouble with gunshots.

Even so, they had the driver take them on a most circuitous route, to be certain they were not followed. All the while Angus kept his eyes trained on the back window, and Jamie stared down at Flora. He pulled off the torn cap and gently brushed the matted hair from her face. Her breathing was frightfully raspy and she coughed several times. But she did not wake, and he wondered if she were drugged. The thought infuriated him, but perhaps, for now, it was just as well.

Once they were certain they'd lost the guards, they directed the driver to Deben House. It was full dawn by now. Angus refused to accompany Jamie inside the gates, saying that even the stables of such a house would be too grand for him. And he refused the money Jamie pressed into his hand, all but enough for a dram or two. Jamie had to content himself with saying to Angus what the Earl of Debenham had once said to him: that if ever Angus wished a position, or found himself in trouble, he was to come to Jamie MacIntyre. To this Angus agreed, and Jamie alighted from the hackney, paying the driver well for his silence. Then he made his way quickly, with his wee precious burden, to the rear of the house and his rooms above the stables.

Gently he laid her on his bed and loosened her clothing and tucked her up. And then, belatedly, he began to shake, and tears fell from his eyes once more. She was here now. His Flora. Somehow, she was here in his bed, asleep. He could hardly credit it, after all these years. But he knew he could not have done this years ago. He'd not known exactly where she was, had thought she wanted to be there. And he supposed he'd never been quite sober enough to think through a rescue at all events. But he must not dwell on the past. She was here and he must make her well.

Her every breath was so labored that he feared it would be her last. He sent one of the stable lads, without telling him aught, to fetch an old sawbones to see her. The man examined her cursorily and left some potion which Jamie had little faith in. But he was afraid to call a real doctor. Somehow the abbess of that evil house might get wind of it.

He sat by the bedside and held her hand. Her eyes opened several times but there was not a flicker of recognition in them. Each time he gave her water and then she drifted back to sleep. He had got to get her to Debenham, he thought, to the country air and the privacy of his cottage. It was too hot and stuffy in Town. But he reckoned she was too sick to move. As the day wore on she mumbled in her sleep; she seemed delirious. Still she had not recognized him, for all he'd been sitting at her bedside for hours. He bowed his head and began to pray.

At length, she stirred, and he lifted his head. Her green eyes fluttered open, and his throat swelled with unshed tears as she looked at him and seemed to know him. Flora! Her face was lined beyond her years, her beautiful red hair matted and lifeless and tangled, but she was here. He'd never thought to see her again, until Lady Debenham had rescued Katie in the inn yard.

Flora's thin hand touched his sleeve. "J—Jamie?" she rasped. "Is it ye, Jamie?"

"Aye, lass," he said in a chocked voice.

"Have I died, then, at long last? So long I wanted . . . to die."

"N—na, Flora, yer no dead, lass," Jamie managed in a thick voice. "But ye're verra ill, and I'm meanin' to make ye well again."

"Na, Jamie. I dinna want . . . to be well. Have to be—be workin' again . . ."

"No! Och, no, Flora! Do ye no ken? I've taken ye oot o' that place. Ye dinna have to—to go there, ever again." Gently he stroked her hair, and soothed her, and told her not to be tiring herself with more talk, and that no one would hurt her anymore.

And she looked at him out of pained, bewildered eyes, and he knew she didn't quite believe she wasn't dead. Finally, she drifted to sleep, and Jamie wiped the dampness from her brow, and his. He understood now her long illness. 'Twas an inflammation of the lungs, as Katie had guessed, as the sawbones had said. She'd not gotten better because she'd not wanted to. He had got to make her want to live again! He would care for her, and mayhap in a se'ennight's time he could think about conveying her to Debenham, if she showed signs of improvement. If not . . . if not, he would write to the earl. He would do whatever needs must be to keep Flora alive.

"London!" Allegra clasped her hands together, her face lighting in a smile. "You're taking *me* to *London?*"

He could not help smiling in return. Her enthusiasm was infectious, and that smile of hers . . . so open and childlike and thoroughly engaging. But he did not want to be engaged by her, he reminded himself. That was why

279

they were going to Town at first stop.

And then he thought about her tone of voice and realized she was truly incredulous. She could not believe he was taking her with him. She had expected him to leave her home. Such expectation did not, he knew, redound to his credit as a husband. But that did not signify in the least!

He did not, of course, tell her his true reasons for the journey. Instead he merely said, " 'Tis a bit early yet, I know, and London will be rather thin of company, at first, but the Little Season will start within a few weeks and—"

"And in the meantime there are all the sights to see, Nigel! The Tower and the Museum—I should love to see it all! Oh, but you mustn't think I will drag you about to see everything, for I own you have already done so and—"

"Allegra," he interrupted, putting up a hand to stem the rush of words, "of course you may see some of the sights, but I had thought you might wish to use the extra time to refurbish your wardrobe."

Her reaction was not at all what he'd expected. He remembered the way Gina's eyes had lit with a calculating excitement when he'd presented her with a bauble, or taken her to buy her a new gown, and how she'd always wheedled one more from him. Allegra's eyes, however, dimmed considerably. "Of course, Nigel," she said dutifully. "I realize that my gowns are sadly out of fashion. I would not wish to be a disgrace to you."

Nigel blinked. He'd hurt her, somehow. He'd not meant— "Allegra! Surely you must know I meant no such thing. 'Tis merely—well, every woman I know makes a veritable occupation out of renewing her wardrobe."

"Oh! Do they?" She looked genuinely surprised. Could she be? "Why, I—thank you, Nigel!"

Allegra's thoughts were in a whirl. He'd been avoiding her for days and now—she cocked her head, debating with herself. She'd meant to broach this later, but perhaps now was a better time. Nigel appeared to be in a good humor for spending money. And besides, would it not be best to have the work done whilst they were away, in London?

They were to leave in a few days' time, Nigel said, and before they parted Allegra screwed her courage to the sticking place and began. "Nigel, indeed, I am most eager to accompany you, and I should like a few new gowns. But they can be frightfully costly and I own I do not need so very many. I was—ah—wondering if some of that money might not be spent for—for something else."

Jewels, Nigel thought in disgust. She was just like Gina, fluttering her eyes and tilting her little head just so. She was not excessively interested in clothes, it seemed. She was going to ask for jewels.

"What is it?" he asked tautly. He stood a few feet from her, his hands at his sides.

She wandered from the side of a wing chair to the back of the sofa, fingering the new fabric. Then she turned to face him. "Manners has informed me that as far as he can tell, there are but three chimneys here at Deben which the new sweeping machine cannot clean. They are too narrow up top, you see. Two are in the north wing and one is—ah—here, in my sitting room. And I wondered if, as long as we are to be away and might avoid the noise and the mess, well, if we might not commission to have them rebuilt."

She twisted her hands nervously and Nigel stared at her, thunderstruck. She wanted to use her wardrobe money to rebuild *chimneys?* She wanted *chimneys,* not *jewels?* He'd never in his life met a woman like her. He wanted to laugh, to grab her and— He stopped himself before he'd taken a step, recalling why they were going to London.

He schooled his face to a grave expression to match hers. She was quite in earnest. She stood before him in a girlish dress of primrose muslin, two years out of fashion at the least, calmly telling him she wanted chimneys instead of new dresses. He glanced about the room, her new sitting room, done up in vibrant shades of blue and green with his grandmama's mahogany desk beneath the window. The room looked charming, and suited her well. Come the autumn, she would need a fire, and then the chimney would need to be cleaned. And Allegra could not bear to have a climbing boy do it.

"Allegra," he began gravely, "I cannot, in good conscience, allow you to use wardrobe monies for household repairs. You will find your clothing needs quite different in Town, my dear, than in the country. But I believe I have told you that I am not pressed for funds. I shall instruct Wiggins to send for the stonemasons while we are away."

"Oh, thank you, Nigel!" she cried with almost childlike pleasure, skipping toward him as if she meant to fly into his arms.

But she stopped just before him and caught herself, and clasped her hands demurely at her waist. "I thank you, Nigel. That is very kind of you," she said in proper, ladylike tones.

He told himself that such a decorous manner was exactly what he wanted in a wife. And yet he missed that childlike cry of joy.

Before taking his leave of her, he informed her that she was to have a quarterly allowance, and named a sum that would have had Gina in raptures. Allegra merely blinked at him in confusion.

"I am to have an allowance?" she whispered incredulously.

Good Lord, did she think him a nip-farthing?

"Yes, of course," he assured her.

Whereupon she thanked him again, her brown eyes warm, and added, "But truly it is not necessary. Why, I cannot imagine spending so much money!"

He tried not to let his mouth gape open before he told

her that, nonetheless, she was to have it, and that, indeed, such befitted the Countess of Debenham.

And Allegra was left to wonder, as he took his leave, how he could be so generous with his money, and so very *un*generous with himself.

They left three days later, Allegra riding alone in one carriage, Nigel on his mount, and Kingston and a very nervous Katie following in the luggage coach. Katie had been terrified at the idea of going to London again, but she seemed to fear being away from Allegra more. Stiff, proper Kingston had surprised everyone by telling Katie, in a most kindly, paternalistic manner, that he would see no harm came to her during the journey. And Allegra had assured her she needn't leave the house in London if she did not wish to.

And so they had set off, and Allegra had found herself almost wishing it would rain, so that Nigel would come into the carriage with her. She got her wish near to dusk, but the rain came suddenly and in such buckets that they were obliged to stop for the night at the first available inn.

Quite a few other travelers had the same idea, however, and the little inn with the weathered shutters and gabled roof was filled to capacity. The innkeeper informed them, after much bowing and scraping and countless "your lordships" and "your ladyships" that he had, indeed, only one room to offer the earl and countess. A large room, and commodious, offering an excellent view of the pasture out back, but a single room nonetheless.

Allegra watched as Nigel impassively informed the innkeeper that one room would be fine. They ate a passable dinner in the only private parlor available, but the conversation was desultory. There was a decided tension between them, and Allegra wondered if Nigel felt it as well. There was one question uppermost in Allegra's mind. It had been so long since Nigel had come to her at night. Tonight they must share a room with only one bed. What would happen this night?

Nigel knew exactly what was going to happen this night. He had stayed away from Allegra these many days quite deliberately. It had been difficult enough when she was merely in the next room. Sharing the same room—the same bed—it would be impossible not to touch her. He had no intention of trying. And, indeed, perhaps it would be best this way—to visit his wife periodically, enough to assuage his hunger but not enough to fall under her spell. Besides, in London there would be other distractions, but here . . .

He sent Allegra up to their chamber and waited enough time for Katie to tend to her. And then he went to join her.

Moonlight poured into the room. Allegra watched as her husband came toward her, shedding his coat and cravat as he moved. She had never seen him undress before; it was a heady feeling. Her heart beat erratically as she gave him a tentative smile.

And Nigel marveled, as he took his wife into his arms, that she could be so warm and welcoming, whenever he chose to touch her. No matter what had gone on before, Allegra's mouth would answer his, her body sway to his.

Nigel's last rational thought, before he carried his clinging wife to the bed, was that this was undoubtedly more than he deserved.

Nigel awoke to the sound of the lark and the feel of his wife curled against his side, her head pillowed on his shoulder. He had got to get up; he wanted to be gone before she woke. But her eyes fluttered open as soon as he stirred. They widened in surprise for a moment, and then she blinked and gave him a radiant smile.

He smiled back at her and ran a finger through her short, feathery curls. "Good morning."

"Good morning, Nigel," she said sleepily.

He kissed her brow, telling himself that in a minute he would get up. But it was so very comfortable to lie here like this, Allegra's smooth, silky body intertwined with his. He did not want to move. And then her hand found its way to his chest, and her foot began meandering up his calf. His body reacted instantly, but he rigidly banked the rising heat. He would not be seduced. Resolutely he rose and went behind the screen to dress.

They arrived late the next day and found the household ready for them. Deben House on Grosvenor Square was, Allegra decided, not so large as Deben Court, but even more grand, the marble entry with its gilt moldings and huge crystal chandelier conjuring for Allegra a picture of exquisitely clad ladies and gentlemen dressed for an elegant ball.

Thorpe, the portly butler, was even more proper than Manners, his dark hair slicked down, his white shirt points as high as she imagined those of any dandy. But he smiled when introduced to her, and so did the equally rotund housekeeper, his wife. Allegra breathed an inward sigh of relief. So far, everything was all right.

All except Nigel. He was distant again and she could no longer deny the fact that the closer they became at night, the more remote he became by day. Last night had been . . . wonderful, and for the first time he'd been there when she awoke in the morning. But he'd ridden his mount all day and left her alone in the carriage once again.

And now they were here. They spent the next hour settling in, and Nigel went in search of Jamie. Jamie, Allegra thought, looked different somehow, and did not look over-joyed to see them. He seemed decidedly uncomfortable, and hurried back to the stables at first opportunity. It was only when he'd gone that Allegra realized what made him look different. "Why, Nigel, Jamie's shaved his beard," she commented as they stood together outside the library.

"So he has," Nigel concurred, frowning slightly.

"I wonder why he did it," she mused, "though I own he looks rather handsome, and years younger."

Nigel's frown became prodigious, his brows arching into those "V's." She wondered what had got his dander up, but could not draw him out, and a moment later he disappeared into the library.

It was near dusk when Allegra finally sank down onto the satin coverlet of the canopied bed in the countess's room—her room, she reminded herself. And it was then that she allowed herself to think of Meg. Today was the day she would wed John Dalton. Allegra felt a wave of homesickness, let it wash over her, and then replaced it with a feeling of satisfaction. She'd had some small part in bringing this about, and for that she could only be glad. And she sincerely hoped—she sighed as the thought came to her—that Meg would find the happiness that still eluded Allegra.

Nigel did not come to her that night; she was not surprised. But the next day he did surprise her. She told him of her desire to take a drive about town to see some of the sights. She would have a groom drive the carriage, of course. Nigel, however, said that was not at all the thing, that he would take her himself, in his phaeton. He took her to Westminster, the Tower, and Hyde Park. Allegra enjoyed herself hugely, and though Nigel was his usual reserved self at first, by midafternoon even *he* was smiling with enjoyment.

He had not meant to enjoy himself, Nigel thought as he drew the phaeton up at Deben House. Why, he had not meant to convey her anywhere. But he could not have let her go alone, with only a groom for company. As he handed her down from the phaeton, he heard himself informing her that on the morrow they would pay a visit to the modiste to see about refurbishing her wardrobe.

Allegra blinked in surprise. "Why, thank you, Nigel. But, indeed, you need not trouble yourself. It was most kind of you to take me about today. I enjoyed myself excessively and shall not cavil if you wish to repeat the experience. But shopping!" Her eyes danced. "Nigel, I am persuaded you *cannot* truly wish to accompany me. It has always been my impression that gentlemen considered shopping for ladies' fripperies to be the greatest form of torture. Why—"

"Allegra," he interrupted, resisting the urge to grasp her chin ever so lightly between his thumb and forefinger, "I do not consider it torture and I insist on accompanying you."

Nigel watched the smile leave her eyes and her body stiffen. She lowered her head. "Very well, Nigel."

He knew instantly what she was thinking. This time he did touch her chin gently, forcing her to look at him. "Allegra, it is not that I do not trust your judgment in the matter of your clothes, merely that I suspect that, if left to your own devices, you will not order nearly enough. I do not think you have any notion of what constitutes a full London wardrobe, my dear."

"But—"

"Besides, you cannot go about alone, and if I do not mistake the matter, Katie will be loathe to venture forth, even with you."

"I am persuaded I can find someone—"

"That will not be necessary, Allegra," he interjected, having no doubt she *would* find someone. Last time when he wasn't about, it was Jamie. He was having none of that. "We shall go to Celeste on the morrow. She is the best modiste in London." Allegra cocked her head, looking curious and piqued all at once. "You needn't get your dander up, Allegra. I am not in the habit of conveying ladies there. But every gentleman in town knows she is the best, just as every lady knows Weston knows no equal for gentlemen's attire."

"Oh," she uttered, her expression lightening.

His lips twitched. "Indeed, I have never taken a lady there before." Her look of relief was so obvious as to be almost comical. He could not help adding, "I have always sent my mistresses to other establishments, you must know."

She gasped in outrage, but a moment later she was grinning. "Oh, Nigel, I own you are hoaxing me! I had a truly lovely day and I shan't allow you to put a damper on it."

She turned to ascend the front steps of the house, but swiveled back, rose up on tiptoe and kissed him lightly on the cheek. "Thank you," she said, and ran up the stairs.

Nigel stared after her in amazement. She had kissed him! In broad daylight! Well, he supposed the carriage, still standing here, had hid them from prying eyes on the Square, but still . . .

It had been a kiss of affection, not of passion. Such had never passed between them before. He was smiling as he ascended the stairs in her wake. Thorpe, as he opened the door, was smiling as well, all too knowingly. Blast the man! And blast Allegra for such a public display!

He was scowling by the time he reached the library and his pile of correspondence. Why had Allegra taken such liberties? He did not want her affection. He wanted her obedience and respect. And what, now he thought on it, had come over him, responding to her enthusiasm as he had today, twice reading her mind?

He did not want that kind of communication with her, did not wish to respond to her in that way. It was bad enough that they communicated, responded to each other

288

so well at night . . . This was somehow worse.

Hellfire! Women, no matter how engaging or disarming or ingenuous they seemed, were not to be trusted. And wives, or wives to be, were the worst of the lot. He would *not* let his wife seduce him, not by day *or* by night!

Nigel left her to her own devices for the remainder of the day, and Allegra went about in a haze of happiness. It seemed they were at another turning point in their marriage. They had spent the day together, a most delightful day. That bond she'd first felt in the bedchamber was slowly growing. An evening spent together here, a day there. Slowly the barriers Nigel had erected about himself were crumbling. And Allegra was learning to muster a patience she never knew she possessed.

At dusk she wandered out to the gardens, and past the stables. And that was when she heard the strange whining sound coming from above the stables. It could have been the wind, but there wasn't any. It could have been a cat, but she could almost make out words. It could have been a child, but the sound was too low and husky. Besides, what would a child be doing above the stables?

She turned toward the sound, knowing that curiosity would eat at her did she not investigate. Impulsively, she set off for the stables. She did not know, however, that though she was indeed at a turning point in her marriage, it was not the beginning of some fairy tale ending. It was simply the beginning of the end.

Chapter Fourteen

"To follow still the changes of the moon with fresh suspicions."

Othello .
William Shakespeare

As Allegra climbed the outside stairs to the rooms above the stables, the strange rasping sound continued. She thought she heard the word "water," but she could not be certain. She did not even know who occupied those rooms. Was it Jamie? The stable boys?

She knocked on the door of the abovestairs apartment. In answer she thought she heard the voice call Jamie's name. No one came to the door, however, and after knocking one more time, Allegra slowly turned the door handle. The outer room was dim, the curtains of the single window partially drawn against the lengthening shadows of dusk. The voice called out again, asking, she was certain, for water.

Allegra made her way to the inner room; the door was partially ajar. The lighting was a trifle better, there being two windows, both open to admit what little breeze there was. The room was furnished with several sturdy oak pieces, but Allegra's eyes went immediately to the four-poster bed against the south wall. A woman, clad in what looked to be a white nightshirt, lay back against the pillows, her hair untidily braided and her eyes closed.

"Jamie, is't ye?" she rasped. She sounded Scottish, Allegra realized in surprise.

"No," Allegra whispered. " 'Tis I, Lady Debenham. Would you like some water?"

The woman's eyes fluttered open. "Yer ladyship! I—och! Ye maun no—that is—no one maun—"

"Hush, now. 'Tis all right," Allegra said soothingly and moved to the bedside table to pour a glass of water from the pitcher.

The woman tried to lift herself but seemed too weak. Allegra propped her up and put the glass to her lips. The woman drank thirstily, then sank back against the pillows.

"Ye are verra kind," the woman whispered. "But ye maun no bide here. No with the likes o' me."

Allegra frowned. Who was she? What did she have to do with Jamie? There were beads of sweat on the woman's brow; the air, even at this hour, was very warm. Allegra wiped her face with a cool, wet cloth. It was a face that undoubtedly had once been pretty but had been ravaged by illness, and something else perhaps. There was in her eyes a look of despair and resignation, the look of one made old before her time.

Allegra was full of questions, but there was one thing she suddenly understood. Jamie had not come to London to help an "Uncle Angus." It was for this woman, whoever she was, wherever she'd come from. She put a lid on her curiosity, however, and asked the only question that seemed relevant. "Can I get you anything else?"

They both heard the footsteps before the woman had a chance to muster a reply.

"My lady!" Jamie appeared in the doorway, his eyes flitting from Allegra to the woman on the bed and back to Allegra. Then he sighed deeply, almost as if in pain, and sagged against the door frame. Allegra was acutely aware that she had inadvertently intruded where she was not wanted.

"I heard her call for water," she explained, and started to move from the bedside. "I'm sorry if I—"

"No, my lady, I—I thank ye." He went to the other side of the bed and took the woman's thin hand in his. "May I—May I present my wife, Flora MacIntyre."

Allegra's eyes flew to Jamie's in shock. Her mouth fell open; she resolutely closed it and fought for composure. "I am pleased to meet you, Flora," she said softly.

Flora gave her a wan smile. "So kind, my lady," she whispered and her eyes fluttered closed.

Jamie whispered that he would join her in a moment in the sitting room, and she went to wait for him. Her curiosity would allow her to do naught else.

Fifteen minutes later, as she descended the outer stairs to the stable yard, Allegra was completely shaken. Jamie had told an incredible tale, and she was certain it had been greatly abridged. A tale of six long years, of thinking Flora was lost to him, of the hope that Katie's story had kindled within him. And now Flora was here and in need of constant nursing. It was obvious that Jamie could not do it all himself. But he cavilled at Allegra's offer of help. It wasn't proper, he could not ask it of her, it was not necessary. As soon as she was well enough Jamie meant to convey her to Debenham, where he could get some farmer's wife to look after her. Meanwhile—

Meanwhile, Allegra had pointed out, he needed help with her. He did not want to ask any of the staff at Deben House; word would spread belowstairs with the speed of dandelion seeds. Jamie had looked beseechingly at Allegra. He did not want anyone to know about Flora.

And then Allegra asked him why he had not told Nigel. The earl, she pointed out, could have helped in the rescue, could provide the best physician, would be only too happy to—

292

"Aye, my lady," Jamie had interrupted, his blue eyes filled with anguish.

And then he went on to explain. Flora had already shown signs of improvement. Before, she had wanted to die, but now she was beginning to want to live again. Jamie would see to it that she recovered. He would involve the earl only if it were absolutely necessary. He meant to introduce her to the earl when she was on the mend, when her bonny hair was shining again and she could sit up in bed wearing a new pink bed jacket.

" 'Tis no that I am ashamed of Flora, my lady, but—but 'tis mysel' I am ashamed of, ye ken. I—I left her there . . . 'tis fer me to care fer her noo. I canna speak yet. The earl would understand. He, too, has his pride. He has never spoken of Gina, and I never spoke of Flora."

"Gina? Who was Gina?"

Jamie looked chagrinned, realizing a moment too late that he'd spoken out of turn. He tried to gammon her with some vague Banbury tale, but Allegra pinned him with her eyes.

"I need to know, Jamie," she said firmly.

And so an unspoken bargain was struck. Allegra would say naught about Flora, would allow Jamie to tell the earl in his own time, and in return, Jamie would tell her what little he knew of Gina. He would also accept Allegra's help with the nursing, as well as Katie's if the girl could finally be convinced to leave the confines of the house.

Allegra thought about poor Flora all the way back to her rooms. And Jamie, and all they had suffered. And then her mind switched to Gina. Here was another piece of the puzzle that was Nigel, though Allegra still did not know what it meant. Nigel had met Gina in Italy, they had been betrothed, and someone had cried off. That was not very much information, but its significance, Allegra mused, lay in Nigel's silence on the matter.

When Katie came to help her dress for dinner, Allegra

decided to wait a few days before asking her help with Flora. Katie would be loathe to refuse, and yet she was still afraid that Hurley would reach out and snatch her did she so much as set foot in the garden. Allegra would give her time, and in the interim would be discreet about her own visits to the rooms above the stables.

Jamie had been strangely elusive since their arrival, Nigel mused. He'd been trying to run the fellow to ground since his return with Allegra this afternoon. First he'd been told that Jamie had gone on some unnamed errand, later that he was in his rooms, then belowstairs. Nigel did not want to summon his friend peremptorily, as, of course, he could do. He suspected that for some reason Jamie needed a bit of privacy just now, something to do with his reason for hightailing it to London at first stop. Nigel would wait; still, he found it deuced frustrating.

The corner window of the library was long and thin. It overlooked the side garden, and the stables. The shadows were lengthening, and so at first Nigel did not think he'd seen correctly. Surely it could not be! He blinked, and stared again, and knew he could not mistake his own wife. And there she was, descending the stairs from . . . from Jamie's rooms!

What the devil was she doing there? Had she no sense of propriety? He felt a vein throb at his temple and his hands clenched into fists. He whirled round, striding for the door, but stopped before he'd gone two yards.

It was *not* merely a matter of propriety. A sick feeling settled in his stomach, almost obliterating his anger. Why would Allegra be coming from Jamie's rooms? Why had she gone?

Why does any woman go to a man's rooms, an inner voice mocked him?

No! It was not possible. The thought was unworthy of

him, and of Allegra. But he remembered the special smiles that had passed between his wife and his friend. And the way she'd called him handsome and said he looked younger without his beard. And then suddenly remembered Lucinda's mocking smiles, every time Charles had accused her—

No! Allegra was too young, too innocent, her passion too genuine . . . Or was it? Was *she?*

Blast it all! What had he done by bringing her here?

Nigel was taciturn, even cold, all through dinner, much as he'd been in the first days of their marriage. The anger that had gradually been dissipating seemed back, just below the surface. Try as she might, Allegra could not draw him out. She found it excessively frustrating, first of all because they ought to have got beyond this long since and secondly . . .

She sighed inwardly. The second reason was not at all ladylike, but the truth of it was that she found her husband deuced attractive. He wore a beautifully cut claret-colored coat, his britches stretched tautly across his thighs. She had a most improper urge to run her hand along his shoulder, or chest. He sat so close to her, and yet she could not reach him, not with words nor with the touch of her hand. He had once more retreated behind all his walls. She had made a tentative move to rest her hand atop his strong forearm just moments ago, but he had neatly forestalled her by reaching for the plate of curried asparagus.

And so she bided her time, watching his silent anger build, wondering what it would take to set it off. Anything would be better than this icy demeanor and simmering rage.

He waited until they had adjourned to the drawing room after dinner. He allowed her to pour the coffee and then he set his cup down and rose abruptly. He paced to the empty grate and back to tower over her as she sat on the blue damask sofa.

She expected an explosion. Instead, the controlled calm of his voice chilled her, and his question shocked her into momentary silence. "Why did you go up to Jamie's rooms earlier this evening, Allegra?"

Her eyes flew to his face. How had he known? What could she say? She could not lie, and yet there was her unspoken word to Jamie. It was not Allegra's place to tell Nigel about Flora. And whyever was Nigel so very het up about it at first stop? Propriety, she supposed, and said the first thing that came into her head.

"But Nigel, I did not know they were Jamie's rooms!" That, at the least, was the truth. He frowned, his bushy brows arched into "V's," and took a step back, regarding her piercingly. She jumped up to face him squarely. "Truly, Nigel, I—"

"Then *why*, pray tell, did you go there?" he demanded.

She blinked at his tone. It reminded her of the night of Lady Wickens's dinner, when he'd railed at her for going off into the garden and accused her of acting like Lucinda. Good Heavens! Did he actually think she'd gone to Jamie to—No! He *could* not think that of her, or of Jamie!

Still, he was in a dreadful taking, even if he had not exploded yet. She had got to diffuse him, but she needs must choose her words carefully. She did not wish to tell an outright lie. Nigel folded his arms across his chest in a gesture of impatience.

Allegra prudently resisted the urge to smooth her fingers down his perfectly creased lapels. Instead she took a deep breath and did not let her gaze waver from his. " 'Tis very simple, Nigel. I was walking in the garden, you see, and I heard a strange, whining sound coming from above the stables. I had no notion what was there but I *could* not ignore so plaintive a cry. Surely you can see that?"

"Oh, but of course," he drawled.

She ignored his sarcasm. "Well," she clasped her hands at her waist, "I knew it must be some poor wounded creature in need of help. Why, what else could it be?" She threw her hands up in question.

Nigel planted *his* hands behind his back. "What else, indeed?" he fairly growled.

Oh, dear. He was making this exceedingly difficult. In a Nora Tillington novel the heroine would at this point hurl her person against the hero's chest and beg him to cease frowning at her so frightfully. Somehow, real life always deviated from romantical novels at the most critical parts. She could not imagine doing such a thing now!

Nigel would merely push her away and regard her with an icy disdain and she would have accomplished naught.

"You were at the part about a wounded creature," Nigel prompted skeptically, and she squared her shoulders.

"Yes, well, and so it was," she said firmly, "and quite desperately in need of water." Flora *was,* Allegra assured herself, a poor wounded creature. And she *had,* after all, needed water. If Nigel jumped to the conclusion that the "creature" was other than human, well, she had not said so, had she? Nevertheless, she held her breath, awaiting his reply.

Nigel stared at his wife. Blast her! What she said was just plausible enough, and knowing Allegra, with her penchant for rescuing wounded children and unfortunate young girls—well, why not this creature as well? Her brown gaze was wide and innocent, and yet . . .

Damnation! Those were Jamie's rooms! It was the outside of enough to think that *he* was collecting wounded kittens or some such! True, the fellow had a way with animals, but this was coming it much too brown!

"And I suppose you'll have me believe Jamie wasn't even there!" he snapped, knowing full well that Jamie had, indeed, gone back to his rooms just then.

Allegra narrowed her eyes, obviously cogitating furiously. She slid past him and sauntered to the chimney-piece, then turned to face him. He told himself that he was not affected by the impudent swivel of her hips beneath the thin silk of her deep blue gown. Nor had he been the least moved, as he'd towered over her moments ago, by the whiteness of her throat and the soft swell of her breasts. He had more important matters to think about!

"The truth, Nigel, whether you will it or not, is that Jamie was *not* there when I arrived." Aha! He'd caught her out. He strode to her, feeling the vein at his temple throb. If she was lying about one thing . . .

"He did, however, arrive before I left, and I — ah — stayed a few moments to chat with him."

Nigel stopped just short of the hearth. Devil take her! Just what was going on in that devious female head of hers? It was just possible, all of it, and yet it had a havey-cavey ring to it.

He moved closer to her, ignoring the way the candlelight played on the dark brown curls of her hair, ignoring the scent of wildflowers that he knew would forever remind him of— No! He drew himself up.

"And just what does Jamie intend to do with this benighted creature?" he asked silkily.

"Why, care for her, of course," she replied without hesitation, and he ground his teeth.

So, the creature was a "her," a kitten, perhaps, or puppy, or even a cat almost ready to drop a litter of kittens. But why in Jamie's chambers?

"I should think the stables would be a more appropriate place—"

"No! Jamie would not agree with you," she interrupted in a voice he could only describe as odd.

As the whole thing was deuced odd. He suspected truth and falsehood were somehow cleverly woven together, as only a female could do. But at this point there was little he could do about it. With no evidence to the contrary, he had got to believe her, at least for now. He could not very well insult his friend with his suspicions, nor would he lower himself to ask to see that feline, or whatever it was.

And just what *were* his suspicions? He did not know anymore, knew only that at best Allegra was guilty of a breach in propriety, and that she was fast developing a rapport with his majordomo that he did not like. Just what, he wondered, had they "chatted" about? It was, he decided, beneath him to ask.

And at worst—he did not want to think about the worst possibilities. But he knew he would do well to keep a close eye on his wife in future.

"Allegra," he finally said in his sternest tone, "you will kindly conduct yourself in future with appropriate propriety and discretion, wounded kittens notwithstanding."

Allegra murmured her assent—she would indeed be discreet—and breathed an inward sigh of relief. He was not going to question her further! She would not be forced to betray Jamie's confidence. And if a niggling prick of conscience told her she'd not been entirely truthful with her husband, she stilled it by reminding herself that she'd done nothing wrong. Besides, Flora needed care. Eventually Jamie would tell the earl and all would be well.

But still she did not like the fact that he'd been so suspicious at first stop. Of what sort of perfidy did he think her capable?

Wounded kittens, he mused as the drawing-room door closed behind his wife. He had sent her up to bed. He wanted to think. *Were* there wounded kittens? *Was* his wife as sweet and innocent as she'd looked moments ago, standing so close to him, her tempting lips parted ever so slightly, her dark eyes warm and compelling?

Hellfire! The long and short of it was that he could not be sure of her innocence, and he would not allow himself to taste of her sweetness. Not this night.

On Monday morning, Nigel, despite their little contretemps of the night before, took Allegra to Madame Celeste's select dressmaking establishment. And, indeed, he had been right; she *had* needed him there. It was not that she could not make her own decisions; in truth, he allowed her to do so. Rather, it was that she could not, *would* not have done on her own exactly what Nigel had said — purchase the quantity and variety of dresses he apparently deemed necessary for his lady wife. His manner was reserved; he did not smile. And yet when he approved her choice of color or fabric she could not help but flush with pleasure.

First there were pattern books to peruse, bolts of muslin, satin, sarcenet, kerseymere, brocades, silk, all to be draped across her person, then fittings to be endured. Madame Celeste stood in the midst of it all, paper and quill in hand, directing her various minions and complimenting the earl and countess, time and again, on their exquisite taste in choosing this trim to go with that gown, that Bishop's blue for the underskirt of that walking dress, that zephyr cloak to complement this evening gown.

And when it was done, orders had been placed for carriage dresses, dinner dresses, evening gowns, morning gowns, ball gowns — the list went on and on. She was quite dizzy by the time they were ready to leave with the promise of delivery of at least the first few dresses the very next day.

"Oh, but Madame," Allegra demurred just as Nigel was ushering her out, "I own the seamstresses will have to work like veritable demons to finish anything that soon. Please, I would not want them to do so on my account. A few more days can hardly signify."

Madame's eyes widened in shock. She turned to Nigel as if to say, "whatever does her ladyship mean?"

300

Nigel's lips twitched despite himself as he took Allegra by the elbow. "Wednesday, two days hence, will be fine, Madame," he told the gaping modiste, and led Allegra away with undue haste.

"Thank you, Nigel," she said softly as they reached the pavement.

Nigel tried not to smile. Allegra was making it increasingly difficult to remember his vexation of the night before. "You are welcome, Allegra. Poor Madame will wonder for a week about the ways of the Quality. Only the size of our order, and of my purse, kept her from shrieking that she knew her business and did not have to be told it. But then, of course," he added, "she does not know you." He heard the softening of his voice and wondered what the deuce was wrong with him.

For a moment Allegra thought he might reach a hand up, to brush her face, perhaps. For a moment she thought there might have been affection in his tone. But then the smile was gone and he led her firmly to the waiting carriage and she knew she must be imagining it. And, indeed, as he conveyed her now to the Burlington Arcade and various shops along Oxford Street and Mayfair, there was none of the camaraderie of yesterday's outing.

Nigel was, in fact, all business. A footman accompanied them now collecting parcels as Allegra chose fans and shawls and parasols and ribbons and gloves and she hardly knew what else. She kept protesting that all of this was not necessary, but Nigel merely pointed with his walking stick to the next shop.

They were just emerging from the milliner's when a voice called, "Debenham? Is that you?"

Nigel's face lit in a smile as a large, black-haired man and a red-headed lady, much Allegra's height, came toward them. "Penderleigh!" Nigel exclaimed, grasping the man's outstretched hand. "How good to see you! And this must be your wife."

The man put his arm about the smiling lady and drew her forward. "May I present Penelope, Marchioness of Penderleigh. Pen, this is Nigel Hayves, the Earl of Debenham and one of my oldest friends."

The marchioness extended her hand and they exchanged greetings, Nigel felicitating them on their marriage last spring. And then he turned to Allegra, introducing her to Damon Southerly, Marquis of Penderleigh, and his wife.

"How do you do," Allegra said to both of them as the marquis took her hand.

"My pleasure, Lady Debenham, and what a delightful surprise! I had no idea, Nigel, that you had wed. May I assume this is rather recent?" Lord Penderleigh asked genially.

"Yes, 'tis some three weeks now," Nigel replied. Allegra wondered if the marquis and his lady could sense the tautness in his tone. The marquis's arm still rested comfortably about his wife's waist. Nigel stood apart from Allegra by several inches, inches that seemed a very great distance.

"Oh! You are newly wed, then. How very exciting! And not a single ondit about it to be heard in Town!" Lady Penderleigh exclaimed in a rush, then cocked her head in a gesture that sent a cluster of red curls dancing about her face. "I wonder"—her green eyes twinkled—"do I scent a mystery here?"

"Pen!" the marquis groaned.

Allegra sensed her husband stiffen beside her, but he said nothing and so after an awkward moment she stepped into the breach. "Oh no, Lady Penderleigh. Indeed, there is no mystery. 'Twas rather sudden, is all. You see, my lord came to Devon and—"

"And quite swept Allegra off her feet," Nigel interjected, then actually drew her arm through his. Allegra glanced up at him, trying not to look stunned. "I gave her no chance to refuse me, and here we are. We've only just arrived and I've not even had a chance to send an announcement to the *Gazette*."

"Oh, I knew it!" The marchioness clapped her hands together. "I do *so* love a romance! And you must call me 'Pen,' dear Lady Debenham! Near everyone does. May I call you Allegra?" Allegra nodded and Pen went on. "And how clever you are to persuade your husband to bring you to Town straightaway to refurbish your wardrobe. Damon has kept me tucked away in Lancashire ever since we wed last spring, and only now does he bring me to Town. But now is hardly the time for me to buy a new wardrobe, when I own most of it will not fit me by—"

"Pen!" The Marquis groaned even louder this time.

Pen blushed and her hand flew to her mouth. "Oh, dear. My rather loose tongue does land me in a bumble-broth rather too often for Damon's piece of mind. I own I am a great trial to him." She sighed but looked not the least perturbed.

The marquis was gazing fondly at his wife, who seemed to be repressing a giggle. Allegra tried not to let her amazement show. Never had she heard such an exchange between husband and wife.

"May we assume, then, that congratulations are in order?" Nigel put in, disengaging his arm from Allegra's to shake his friend's hand once more.

Lord Penderleigh grinned. "You certainly may. Which reminds me. Have you heard from Charles Ainsley?" Nigel shook his head. "His lady presented him with an heir not a fortnight ago."

"Splendid news!" Nigel rejoined. "I take it mother and child go on well?"

The marquis nodded and the two men lapsed into conversation about mutual acquaintances, while Pen asked Allegra all about her morning's purchases. And then the marquis invited them to join him and his wife two nights hence at his box at the Drury Lane. Edmund Kean, it seemed, was playing King Lear.

"Oh, may we go, Nigel?" Allegra asked, looking up at her husband. "I have never seen Shakespeare performed before. Indeed"—she turned to Pen and the marquis and laughed softly—"I have never seen any play at all, except for amateur theatricals at home."

Nigel blinked in surprise. "Of course, we may go, Allegra," Nigel said, and actually smiled at her. She wished he would take her arm again, but of course he did not.

And so the plan was made, and they parted in high spirits. Allegra and Nigel stood on the pavement, several inches apart, watching the Marquis of Penderleigh lead his wife away, his arm about her waist.

Allegra stifled a sigh. "I like your friends very well, Nigel."

As did he, Nigel thought, though he had been very surprised at the degree of devotion Damon obviously felt for his wife. Damon had always had a healthy distrust of the fair sex . . .

"I am glad that you like them, Allegra," he replied at length. "But now you had best pray that Madame Celeste finishes one of those evening gowns early, after all."

"Oh, but it cannot signify, Nigel, what I wear. I have no wish to cut a dash and besides, I own everyone will be intent on the stage, not on the audience."

Nigel stared at his wife in amazement: He had never known a woman so—so very delectable to look upon, and yet so indifferent to her looks.

The Marquis of Penderleigh handed his wife up into their waiting carriage. He sat down next to her on the plush leather tufted seat and pulled her close, drawing the curtains closed at the same time.

Pen snuggled into his shoulder, her hand on his lapel. He smiled down at her, then bent his head and took her lips in a deep and tender kiss.

"Mmmm," Pen murmured dreamily when they parted. "Delicious. It's been hours since the last one."

Damon chuckled. "So it has. 'Tis time to go home, is it not? Time for your . . . rest?" he asked devilishly.

"Most definitely," Pen replied with a gleam in her eye. She yawned delicately.

"Pen, you are all right, are you not? Did you overtax yourself today?"

"Of course not, silly man. I am not an invalid, you must know. Just a lady in need of her . . . rest."

Damon grinned. "Ah, the side benefits of your very delicate condition, and not a servant may bat an eye. For, indeed, a husband must be most . . . solicitous at such a time."

"And you claim I have no sense of propriety! For shame, my lord marquis!" Pen quizzed him, then sighed contentedly.

Moments later she was frowning. "Damon, something is not right between the earl and countess, is it?"

Damon sighed. Sometimes he wished his wife were not quite so astute. "I fear not, love. There is undoubtedly some mystery there, as you so impetuously pointed out."

"Allegra is not happy. I can tell. Perhaps if I befriend her and—"

"By all means befriend her, Pen. You are of an age, after all. But I'll not have you interfering in any way. Matchmaking is one thing, but coming between a man and his wife is quite another."

"I know that, Damon, 'tis only—oh, I don't know. There was a wistful look about her eyes. As if—as if she saw something between *us* that she knew was missing in her own marriage. And Lord Debenham seemed—well, not quite comfortable with her somehow."

"I know, love. But this is not one of your romantical novels. They must work it out for themselves."

"I suppose," she said doubtfully.

"Pen!" he warned.

"Oh, very well, Damon," she said dutifully. "They must work it out for themselves."

Damon breathed an inward sigh of relief. He had always thought Pen needed a keeper. He thanked God every day that it was he.

Nigel closeted himself with his secretary after luncheon, and left later in the afternoon to see, he said, to certain business matters.

It was only then that Allegra, quietly and discreetly, made her way to the rooms above the stables.

She was certain no one was the wiser, and Flora was pitifully grateful for the company. As for Jamie, he looked exhausted. He had told Nigel that "Uncle Angus" had disappeared and that he was searching for him. He spent every waking moment either with Flora or attending to the stables and the affairs of Deben House, and Allegra imagined he was up most of each night as well. He could not long go on this way.

Nigel returned from his afternoon's inquiries in a pensive mood. He'd gone first to the newly rebuilt Custom House off Lower Thames Street. The Revenue officers had not been able to tell him much about the situation in Dorset. There had not, according to reports from the Preventative men there, been a run of goods in well over a fortnight. Or at the least, there had not been a run that the Revenue was aware of.

Cliff House was only one of several suspected locations in Muddleford parish for the base of operations of this particular gang. There were several other possibilities farther up the coast, and even Creeve Hall was not being totally discounted. There was as of yet no hint as to the identity of the venturer. Whoever the leader was, he was undoubtedly a local man, for he had the loyalty of all the inhabitants in Muddleford.

In other words, Nigel thought as the officers answered his questions, they knew next to naught. They did, however, know that Creeve was in London. Apparently, he came to the Custom House at least twice weekly, demanding the apprehension of the venturer and his cohorts.

Why was Creeve here and not in Dorset? And who *was* the leader of this band of "gentlemen?" The questions nagged at Nigel, and as he made his way to White's, he realized that he would have to pay a visit to Cliff House in the near future. But he could not go now, when he had just brought Allegra to London.

He would not leave her, and of a certain he could not take her. Where there were smugglers and preventative men, there was danger. And knowing Allegra, she'd somehow get herself mixed up in it. Probably "rescue" one of the "gentlemen of the night" and try to reform him.

At White's he learned that Creeve had been in Town for about a fortnight, that he was never away for long, and that no one was quite certain where he spent most of his evenings. Creeve was very discreet and not, as Nigel was well aware, particularly well-liked.

And now he had come home, expecting to take tea with his wife, but was informed that she was somewhere in the gardens, having taken a book from the library.

But he did not find her in any of the gardens, did not find her for a good half hour. She was making her way toward the rear of the house, coming from the direction of the stables. He looked pointedly up at Jamie's apartment and back at his wife. No, it was not possible! He looked down at the book in her hand.

"You've been reading?" he asked.

"Yes, Homer's *Odyssey.*" She turned the book so he could see the cover. He glanced back up at her. Her brown eyes were wide, innocent. Yet in their depths lurked . . . He did not know. She was telling the truth and yet he was certain she was lying, hiding something. He nodded in dismissal and watched her walk back to the house, watched the swivel of her softly rounded hips through the thin blue muslin of her dress. Watched and clenched his jaw.

He went to find Jamie for the purpose, he told himself, of asking about his Uncle Angus. Jamie was in the tack room and looked, once again, uncomfortable to see Nigel. Uncle Angus, it seemed, could not be found and Jamie was looking for him. What he was not doing was looking Nigel in the eye. And he was not telling the truth, Nigel was certain.

The sick feeling that he'd sensed in his belly yesterday, when he saw Allegra coming from Jamie's rooms, intensified. He banked it down. Perhaps his vague, ugly suspicions were unfounded. That very possibility made it impossible to ask. He would have to wait. And watch. And wonder.

Chapter Fifteen

"Oh, swear not by the moon, the inconstant moon."
Romeo and Juliet
William Shakespeare

Madame Celeste had, indeed, produced two gowns by Wednesday morning. One was an exquisite evening gown of deep rose satin with a very tiny corsage and even tinier sleeves, all trimmed with ecru Brussels lace and silk rosettes. Madame had fashioned a matching ribbon of rosettes for her hair, and Allegra thought the gown would be perfect for the theatre. The deep rose color brought out the creaminess in her skin, Madame had said, and Nigel had seemed to agree.

Nigel. Allegra sighed as Katie helped her into her gown. He had been brooding of late, treating Allegra to icy civility, pensive stares, and lonely nights. When she asked him what was wrong he merely regarded her in stony silence.

She could not reach him. Perhaps tonight, being with his friends would lighten his mood.

Nigel's mouth fell open as his wife came down the stairs.

As it had once before, Allegra's beauty took him by surprise. Meg was the beautiful one, not Allegra. Hadn't Allegra herself told him that?

But tonight Allegra was beautiful. There was no other word for it. Her curly hair was wreathed with rosettes and her face glowed in the candlelight. She wore one of her new gowns, a vibrant rose color in a satin so soft and shimmering that it fairly molded to her body as she moved slowly, sensuously down the stairs. His mouth went dry. He wanted her. By God, he wanted her. Here, now, and the Drury Lane be hanged.

No! She did not have that kind of power over him! She stood before him now and he saw that her gown was outrageously low cut in the bosom. Why had he not noticed when the patterns were discussed? What could Celeste have been thinking? He frowned and took the gauzy shawl she carried and draped it across her shoulders and throat. It was better than nothing.

Allegra stifled a pang of disappointment. She had seen the admiration—no, more than that—the hunger in his eyes as she'd descended the stairs. But now he was frowning. Was there no pleasing him? She could not ask; she would not fish for a compliment. But neither did she refrain from telling him how handsome he looked in his bottle-green coat and creme-colored britches. He seemed taken aback, but did not comment. It was not, she thought, an auspicious beginning.

She was dazzled by the Drury Lane, by the myriad candles glimmering in the chandeliers, by the magnificently carved ceiling, the plush red velvet curtains, the boxes and galleries and above all, the people. She had never seen, only imagined, such a gathering of resplendent ladies and gentlemen, the richness of their clothing fairly sparkling in the candlelight. She was dressed far more simply than most, yet she did not feel the least inadequate. Her gown was lovely, and it suited her. Nigel thought so, too, despite his puckered brow.

If Allegra felt a pang at all, it was that the array of priceless jewels displayed tonight reminded her that all she possessed, besides her gold wedding band, were the pearl earrings she wore tonight and a pearl necklace that had been her mother's. Not that she had ever craved jewels. She hadn't and still did not. It was only that a gift of jewelry, from her husband, no matter how small a token, would have meant so much.

She banished the thought as they reached the Penderleighs' box. She would not let anything mar the magic of this night.

Lord Penderleigh was a gracious host, seating them and responding to Allegra's formal greeting by asking Nigel if they mightn't all be on Christian-name terms. "My wife will end up doing it at all events, Nigel, so we might just as well forestall her," he said with a ready good humor that easily erased Nigel's frown.

And Pen, quite oblivious to how ravishing she looked in a good of teal blue silk, was bubbling with what Allegra took to be her customary high spirits. Allegra liked her very well, and felt she had found a friend.

And then the lights dimmed, the curtains rose, and Kent and Gloucester came on stage. Allegra was enchanted immediately, never having seen such a production. But moments later she was startled as Lear made his entrance and the audience erupted in thunderous applause. This was Edmund Kean, the already legendary Kean. He was a small man, rather homely looking. And then he began to speak and Allegra knew whereof came the legend. It was his resonant voice, his commanding stage presence. He *was* Lear, and Allegra was mesmerized. She forgot her surroundings, gripping the arms of her chair as the action unfolded.

She could not stop the tears from welling up as Lear disowned his one true daughter, Cordelia. Oh, could he not see that her motives were true? She swiped surreptitiously at her moist eyes, telling herself she was *not* thinking of her father and herself. It was Lear and Cordelia . . .

Nigel surprised her moments later by wordlessly handing her his handkerchief. She was embarrassed and pleased all at once. She hadn't thought Nigel had paid her any notice all evening.

And then the curtain came down and the lights went on. It was intermission. Allegra felt jarred. She did not want to leave the action, did not want the lights, did not want to see all these people who were already getting up to stroll, to see and be seen. But there was no hope for it. Their box seemed besieged by people, all of whom wished an introduction to the new Countess of Debenham, for the announcement of their marriage had that morning appeared in the *Gazette*. Allegra met so many people that she was dizzy.

Most, Nigel was quite pleased to present. There was one, a Lord Creeve, whom Nigel was obviously reluctant to introduce. He kept her close as he did so, and Allegra noted that Damon had put a protective hand to his wife's nape. Allegra could understand why. There was something about the way Lord Creeve looked at her and Pen that made her very skin crawl. Nigel's later warning that he was a man to avoid met with complete agreement from Allegra.

When there was a lull of activity in the box, Nigel and Damon left to procure refreshment, leaving Allegra and Pen to a comfortable cose. It was just as the men returned that Allegra noted a very beautiful woman, her voluptuous charms quite blatantly displayed in a filmy violet gown, staring across the way into their box. With her was a tall, lean, striking gentleman with chestnut hair and a strong, hawklike nose.

"Who is that woman, Nigel?" Allegra asked.

"Who?" He handed her a glass of Madeira.

"Why, the one in the violet gown with the large feather in her hair. Nigel, I do believe she is signaling you. Do you know her?"

Damon choked on his claret. Pen murmured "Good Heavens!" Nigel took a gulp of his wine.

"She's—ah—with a very old friend of mine," Nigel began. "Adam Damerest, Duke of Marchmaine. He looks good, Damon, don't you think?"

"Oh, indeed," Damon concurred.

The duke saluted their box but Allegra thought he looked uncomfortable doing so. And no one had answered her question. "But Nigel, the lady—who is she?"

Nigel looked at Damon, who shrugged. Allegra was certain he was suppressing a grin. She turned to Pen, who did not bother suppressing her smile.

"I do believe that she is *not* a lady, Allegra, which accounts for our husbands' sudden tongue-tied state."

"Not a lady? But—"

"She is a . . . Cyprian," Pen informed her. Damon looked thunderous.

"A Cyprian?" The word meant nothing to Allegra.

"Yes," Pen leaned forward conspiratorially, a gleam in her eye. She ignored a warning from her husband. "You know. One of the fashionable impures. A gentlemen's bit of—"

"Oh! Bit of muslin!" Allegra exclaimed, enlightenment dawning. "You mean a high flyer! I—"

"Ladies, please," Nigel groaned.

Pen giggled, but Allegra was still confused. "But, Nigel, why is she so interested in *you?*" She glanced back at the woman and then at her husband. "Nigel, was she another

313

one of your mistresses?"

This time Nigel choked. Damon appeared to find the bottom of his wineglass very interesting. It was left to Pen to say, "The significant word is *was*, Allegra. All gentlemen are entitled to their salad days. *Before* marriage." She smiled complacently at her husband, who grinned and drew her hand through his arm, just as the lights dimmed once more.

Allegra's last thought, before the action resumed, was that Nigel had never answered her, had not reassured her of the *was* in her question.

But then the play captivated her once more. It was so sad, so tragic, the action building inexorably to a dreadful end. They were going to die, Cordelia, Lear, all of them. Forgiveness and understanding had come too late. Allegra clutched at Nigel's arm, hardly knowing what she was doing. Tears fell unheeded. It was all confused in her mind—Lear, her father—she did not know for whom she cried. Dimly she felt Nigel's hand enclose hers. With his other he dabbed his handkerchief to her wet cheeks.

Nigel had been exceedingly grateful when the curtain had gone up once more. He'd had no intention of discussing his erstwhile mistress with Allegra, particularly not in the presence of Damon and Pen. Damon, blast him, had been no help at all, and his wife—his wife was incorrigible, a fact which seemed not to trouble Damon one whit. Nigel could not credit it.

He'd actually been pleased to see La Plume—so called by all her admirers because of the large feather she always wore—in company with Marchmaine. Nigel had given her her congé some two months ago and was happy that she'd found a good protector. As to Adam, it was unusual for him to have a woman in keeping. He was usually too restless, his personal demons driving him too hard for him to stay with any one woman for long. Perhaps this was a good sign.

We all have our demons, Nigel mused, only half concentrating on the action on stage. He knew well enough what his own were, and Damon—Damon, too, had had his dark side, but somehow, he seemed changed since his marriage. He seemed . . . at peace with himself. Nigel did not understand it, for Pen, as charming as she undoubtedly was, did not seem at all a restful woman.

And then Allegra clutched at his arm, and Nigel's thoughts were diverted. She was entranced by the drama, with the pure delight of a child. He could not help enjoying the play of expression on her face at least as much as the play on stage. But just now he saw that it was not delight she was feeling, but the full weight of the tragedy. And Nigel found, somewhat to his chagrin, that he could not bear to see his wife cry, even be it over a stage play. He wiped her tears and clasped her hand tightly in his, and enjoyed the sensation far too well.

They were in the carriage. Allegra had hardly spoken since the curtain went down to a standing ovation. She had been subdued during the farewells to Damon and Pen, and Nigel had found himself keeping a protective arm around her as he'd shepherded her out of the theatre and into his carriage. She was so young, so vulnerable, felt things so very deeply. And her naivete was genuine. She turned her wide, moist brown eyes up to him now and he wondered how he could ever have thought her capable of deceiving him with another man.

He moved closer to her on the leather seat. She smelled of wildflowers and he had the urge to nuzzle into her neck and inhale her. Her shawl had fallen back, revealing her

315

creamy skin. He wanted to touch her . . . Instead he brushed a tear from her cheek.

" 'Tis over now, Allegra," he whispered.

She shook her head slightly and suddenly he understood that it was not merely Shakespeare's characters for whom she cried. "Nigel, do you—do you think my father will ever forgive me?"

He thought for a moment and gave her the only answer he could. "Yes. In time he will."

She smiled tremulously and parted her lips and he knew she was about to ask another question, one for which he had no answer. He did not know if *he* could forgive her. She was not the wife he wanted.

"Nigel, do you—" she began, and he gave her the only answer he could.

He brought his mouth down onto hers. Her lips were warm, willing, yielding, her body, arching to his in silent invitation. Dear God, it had been days, and he'd missed this so!

His frenzied hands were caressing her through the fabric of her gown. She moaned into his mouth and only then did he realize that she would not stop him. She was as caught up as he, and she would let him take her right here, as the carriage clattered through the night. She would not deny him; she never had.

But she was his wife, not some Covent Garden lightskirt! He could not—Resolutely he lifted himself from her. She whimpered in protest.

"Soon," he murmured soothingly, and pulled her into the curve of his arm, where he held her tightly and tried to still his raging heartbeat.

Finally they were home. He swung Allegra into his arms, unwilling, unable to let her go as he strode up the stairs and through the front door. He ignored Thorpe's gaping mouth, ignored the whispers in the shadows, and at length reached Allegra's chamber. He cursed inwardly to find Katie still there.

"Oh! My lady, what is wrong? My lord, what—"

"Nothing is wrong, Katie. Go to bed," he growled. Allegra kept her face firmly turned into his shoulder.

Katie looked most perturbed. "But—"

"Good night, Katie!" he fairly shouted, and suddenly the girl turned crimson, gasped, and fled.

Nigel kicked the door shut and very gently laid his wife on the bed. He followed, shedding his coat and boots as he lowered himself to her. And then he grasped the bottom of her skirt and slowly drew it up.

And in the moments that followed, as they set each other on fire, as she met his frenzied need with equal need of her own, he knew that he had never, ever, wanted a woman as much as he wanted his wife.

Allegra drifted up from a deep and languid sleep to find herself wrapped in Nigel's arms. Moonlight streamed in through the open window, and she could see their tangled clothing strewn over the bed and floor. She did not feel the least embarrassed. She remembered every delicious moment of what had happened and thought she would like to do it all over again. There was such a rightness about being here with Nigel, making love with him. She snuggled closer to him and his arm pulled her tighter in his sleep. She sighed contentedly. When he held her like this, nothing else signified. It was only here, in bed, that Nigel ever let his guard down with her, and it was only here that she could show him—

Show him what? She inhaled his scent and let her hand graze his hard, well-muscled chest. The answer came to her slowly, peacefully, as she lay with her head on his shoulder, listening to his steady heartbeat. She had been afraid this would happen, but now that she realized it had, she was not afraid. A bubble of joy welled up in her chest. She wanted to jump up and shout it from the rooftop.

She loved him! She had fallen in love with her husband! Despite his anger, his remoteness, she loved him. For she had also seen the other side, that which she was certain was the true side of Nigel Hayves—his tenderness, his passion, his kindness, his integrity, his dedication to his work. But the list did not signify. One could not explain these things. She simply knew that she loved him and always would. And had probably done so a long time since.

She must not tell him. She knew, without his ever saying so, that he would not want to hear it. For he did not love her. And even if he was coming to care for her, he would not admit it. Not yet.

Allegra would not give up hope. But now she knew it was not merely a companionable marriage that she wished for, worked for. She wanted her husband's love. Somehow, some way, she would have it.

She lay quietly, savoring the closeness with him, savoring the feel of his shoulder beneath her head, his legs intertwined with hers. There was one more thing she would not tell Nigel yet. Her monthly flux was late. Ten days late. It was never late.

But that did not necessarily mean—why, it was much too early to tell! There had been a great deal of upheaval in her life of late. Perhaps that accounted for it. And at all events, was not one supposed to have symptoms—queasiness, excessive tiredness? That much she had learned from the servant girls at Caulfield. Allegra had no symptoms.

She must bide her time. She would not say aught to Nigel until she was certain. Suddenly, she longed to have his child. And she longed to be able to tell him, to see his face light up with joy. Patience, she cautioned herself . . .

Nigel shifted and mumbled something in his sleep. She

turned and pressed a kiss to his shoulder, whispering his name. His eye quirked open. "Allegra, why aren't you sleeping? Is it dawn?"

Her hand drifted down his chest. "No, 'tis full night. I'm merely enjoying lying here with you. I . . . like when you hold me, Nigel."

He groaned her name, and in one fluid motion rolled atop her, his hands cradling her head. Then he lowered his mouth.

It was different this time, slow and languid and infinitely sweet. Instead of being consumed by frenzied flames, she felt hot molten liquid undulating, pouring through her body. The tension rose in her, slowly but inexorably, and she felt an answering tension in him. And the explosion, when it came, was no less intense for its languorous beginnings.

They lay back, sated, panting, Nigel pulling her close. He kissed her brow. "By God, woman, whatever do you do to me?" he rasped, stroking her head.

And the words, aching to be said, came to her tongue so easily, so naturally. She could not hold them back, for all she knew she must not say them.

"I love you, Nigel."

His hand stopped its stroking. She held her breath. Seconds went by. She could feel the sudden tautness in him.

"No," he whispered, and then more firmly, "No!" He moved aside, lifting himself partly so he could look at her. "You must not say that, Allegra. You do not love me. You may wish to believe it or wish *me* to believe it, but—"

"Nigel, I—"

"No, Allegra!" Nigel pivoted away from her and swung his feet to the floor, searching with his hands for his dressing gown. Blast! It was not there, of course. He'd been in such a damned hurry to—

Quickly he drew on his drawers and breeches, then

319

stalked away from the bed to the window. He turned back to face Allegra. She was sitting up in bed, her eyes wide, the sheet drawn to her throat. "Love has no place in marriage, Allegra. You are old enough to put aside such foolish, romantical notions."

He watched her slither from the bed, taking the sheet with her and wrapping it around herself. He would not let the sight of her affect him in any way.

She came to him, stopping just a foot away. "I know you do not love me, Nigel. I suppose I should not have told you but I — I could not help myself. You do not have to do anything about it. I just . . . needed to tell you."

He looked down into her eyes and then away. He did not want to see the warmth, the intensity in them. Perhaps she believed her own words, but he did not. He had been cured of such notions a long time ago. He stared out at the moonlit night. "I do not want your love, Allegra, or whatever it is you think is love."

She inhaled sharply and he turned back to her; he could not help himself. A shadow of pain crossed her eyes; her lip quivered and she bit it. Nigel cursed himself for a bounder. He had hurt her again, but he knew it was best this way. Certainly for him, and even for her. It would do her no good to indulge in romantical fantasies.

"Good night, Allegra. I shall retire now to—"

"Why, Nigel?"

"Why what?"

"Why do you not want my love? Why is the whole idea of love so . . . odious to you?"

His eyes widened in amazement. How could she ask such a question? Had she no pride? No sense of when a dignified retreat was in order? And yet, she did look oddly dignified, standing before him clutching the bed sheet, her chin raised, her eyes pleading but determined. She had not wrapped herself in her pride and stormed off, as surely any other woman would have done. Instead, she faced him, with . . . with courage. Yes, she was a courageous woman, if misguided, and perhaps she deserved an answer. At the least, his answer would serve to quell whatever romantical notions were whirling about in that overactive mind of hers. He would discuss this once, briefly, and never again. He stepped closer to her, towering over her, not touching her.

"Once before, a woman told me she loved me. I was young and foolish and I made the mistake of believing her. I do not make the same mistake twice."

He saw Allegra swallow hard. She put her free hand to his arm. "Tell me about her," she whispered.

He pulled away. "Good night, Allegra," he said with finality, turning toward the door.

"Tell me about Gina," her soft voice sounded from behind him.

He froze, then whirled around. "What do you know about Gina?"

She shrugged. "Very little. Only that you were betrothed and someone cried off."

He was furious that she knew even that much, and was about to ask who had told her, but then he knew. It could only have been Jamie, in one of their little tête-à-têtes.

Damnation! Nigel felt his jaw clench. He clasped her upper arms none too gently. "You want to know about Gina, do you?" he growled. " 'Tis very simple. I met her in Italy. She was warm and passionate. Like you, Allegra. She declared her love for me, swore eternal devotion, until the day my father said he'd disown me if I wed her." He paused, his mouth turning into an ugly sneer. "She was gone in the blink of an eye!"

He was squeezing her arms hard enough to bruise her, but she knew he hardly noticed. He was in his own private world of remembered anguish. She could see it in his eyes.

She could also hear what he had not said. He had loved Gina, and she had made a mockery of his love.

"I'm sorry, Nigel," she whispered. Her voice seemed to recall him to himself. He dropped his hands and stepped back. "I'm sorry, but Nigel, *I am not Gina.*"

He looked at her with that icy disdain with which she was all too familiar. "No, you are not Gina. She tried to manipulate me into marriage out of greed," he said bitterly. "You had other reasons. The main difference between you is that *you* succeeded. Do not talk to me of love, Allegra. I am not that gullible."

He strode from the room without a backward glance.

The announcement in the *Gazette* and their appearance at the theatre were enough to start what seemed to Allegra a deluge of invitations to various entertainments. If this was London still thin of company, Allegra shuddered to think what the spring Season was like. For now, with the Little Season barely underway, there began a whirlwind of soirees, breakfasts, musicales and invitations to two balls. The first would be given in a few days and Allegra eagerly awaited the arrival of her ball gowns from Madame Celeste.

She knew exactly which gown she would wear to the first ball, given by Lady Embers, Pen's godmama. It was a filmy creation of sea green chiffon and silver net that made Allegra feel almost other-worldly. She would need all the other-worldly charm she possessed to captivate her husband, who was avoiding her once more, by day and by night. Oh, he escorted her to the various entertainments, but he spoke little to her and left her soon after their arrival with Pen or any one of her growing number of acquaintances. And while she found the people she met and the entertainments she attended pleasant enough, yet she was not enjoying herself. For Nigel spent each evening across the room or in some card room, or in the host's library with other gentlemen.

Oddly, despite his inattentiveness, Allegra often had the sensation that he was watching her, warily, with barely concealed pique. Was he waiting for her to commit some solecism? Or was it that he disliked seeing her in the company of other men? He seemed to be frowning at her whenever she spoke to a gentleman acquaintance. This she put down to some perverse possessiveness, for she knew he had not sufficient feeling for her to be jealous, and she determined to ignore him. She was not very successful in this nor in persuading herself that husbands and wives rarely stayed in others' pockets all evening. True as that might be, she could not help watching Damon and Pen, and the closeness they shared, and knowing she wanted no less for herself and Nigel.

Such a thing seemed further away than ever. The night of the theatre party, when Nigel had said he did not want her love, was never far from Allegra's mind. Even now, nearly a se'enight later, she remembered every painful word. She remembered how desolate, how hurt she'd felt when he'd stalked out of her chamber. And she'd known it would be awhile before he returned. He still had not.

She'd also known that he'd given her a vital piece of the puzzle of himself. Lucinda had betrayed his trust in women. Gina had betrayed his love. Allegra told herself that at the least now she knew that which she had got to counter. And she was more determined than ever to do so. She loved Nigel, and somehow she was going to convince him of that.

She needed something to break the impasse between them. Perhaps Lady Embers's ball would be just the thing. Surely her husband would dance with her at a ball . . .

In the meantime, Allegra smiled and laughed and flirted

at soirees and concerts—sometimes two in a night—and filled her days as best she could. Mrs. Thorpe, the housekeeper, was a gregarious, motherly woman who immediately took a liking to Allegra and helped her establish her routine as mistress of the house. And so she attended to menus and inventories and her correspondence, which grew in volume as her acquaintance grew.

A letter came from Meg just two days before the ball. She and John had just returned from a short wedding trip on the Devon seaside, and her words bespoke deep happiness and joy in her marriage. Allegra stilled a pang of envy. Someday . . .

It was while she was penning a reply to Meg on Thursday, sometime before luncheon, that she felt a sudden, overwhelming wave of nausea. She put her head on the desk and clutched at her stomach, waiting for the feeling to pass and wondering all the while what she had eaten at breakfast to cause such discomfort. The queasiness, however, did not pass but rather intensified. Suddenly she jumped up, bolted for the basin on the washstand, and was wretchedly sick.

When she was done she bathed her face in cool water, and sat down on the bed for a few moments to catch her breath. Feeling markedly better, she resumed her work and surprised herself an hour later by actually being hungry for luncheon. After luncheon she went to her rooms to select a gown for the musicale that evening. She would decide quickly and then, if Nigel was still closeted with his secretary, she meant to spend some time with Flora.

But pulling gowns out of the wardrobe seemed a great deal of effort. Suddenly she was inexplicably tired, and lay down on the bed to rest for a few minutes.

She was awakened by the sound of Katie closing the curtains against the late afternoon sun.

"Katie! Oh, my goodness! I hadn't meant to sleep so

long. I *never* sleep in the afternoons. What time is it?"

" 'Tis going onto five of the clock, my lady."

"Oh, dear. I had so wanted to go to stay with—ah"

"With Flora, my lady?" Katie asked softly, and Allegra's eyes widened. Katie smiled. "I went out to the garden this morning. To take the air, you see. Jamie found me there and he told me. I've just now come from her."

"How is she?"

"Better than the last time I saw her in that . . . dreadful place. But still needin' care."

"I'll go now to sit with her awhile. Do you know where Lord Debenham is?"

"He's gone to his club, I believe. But do you not want to dress now, my lady?"

"I shan't stay out above half an hour, Katie. And you needn't fuss overmuch with my hair tonight," Allegra replied, and made her way to the apartment above the stables.

She found Flora alone, trying to eat some of the broth that sat at the bedside table. But she was still weak, albeit getting better, and her hand was none too steady. Allegra helped her spoon the soup and when she was done Flora smiled softly.

"Ye've a good heart, my lady. What ye've done fer me, and fer that bonnie wee Katie . . . well, the Heavens will smile upon ye, I make no doobt."

Allegra clasped Flora's hand, forcing back tears. In truth, she had done little enough. She was glad that Flora and Katie had been freed from that place, and she tried not to think of the others, still there . . .

Nigel had been to the Custom House again and to Brooke's this time. He was trying to ferret out information about Creeve. The viscount surfaced only every few

nights; the rest of the time his whereabouts were unknown. Each time Nigel had seen him and tried to talk to
him about the Dorset smugglers, about possible leads as to
the venturer, Creeve had been surprisingly evasive. Nigel
did not like it.

A Muddleford neighbor of theirs, an elderly squire who
frequented Brooke's, was in Town, and Nigel had gone to
see him. But all the squire could tell Nigel was that
Creeve's vendetta against the smugglers seemed odd to
most of the Dorset gentry, had even infuriated some who
rather enjoyed their run brandy and bolts of French lace.
Further, though many of the fisherfolk were undoubtedly
involved in the smuggling operation, they were all resolutely closemouthed about the name of the venturer.

The squire, although not close to Nigel's family, had
known Nigel since his childhood. Today he'd peered at Nigel over his newspaper in a cozy corner of Brooke's and
said, " 'Tis not as if the folk are keeping mum because
they're afraid of the venturer, you must know. I think they
want to protect him."

He'd said no more, and Nigel had taken his leave, feeling none too reassured. Roger had grown up on the Dorset coast. He had many friends there . . . Blast! Nigel did
not like the sound of it at all.

As the carriage clattered up the front drive, he thought
of Allegra and wondered how the deuce he was ever going
to get to Dorset. He was surprised to see Katie in the
abovestairs corridor. It was late and he'd assumed she'd be
helping Allegra dress. When he questioned the maid she
became very flustered and stammered something to the effect that her mistress was in the garden and would return
shortly. Nigel felt that pain in his stomach again. Katie
avoided his eyes; he thought she was lying. And yet, she
was always reticent around Nigel.

Hellfire! He didn't know. And he could not, would not,

326

go storming up to Jamie's rooms. What if his friend were simply up there alone, changing his shirt? What could he possibly say? It was not as if Nigel made it a habit to visit Jamie's rooms, after all. But where was Allegra? This was an odd time for her to be lounging about the garden.

The sick feeling deep in his gut grew worse.

On Friday morning Allegra woke early and felt that wave of queasiness again. She made it to the basin just in time, and had barely recovered when Katie came in. Instead of expressing consternation at Allegra's illness, Katie smiled broadly.

"I must be ill, Katie. That's the second time in two days that I've been sick in the basin."

"Yes, my lady." Katie did not seem the least overset. "And yesterday you had a nice long nap, didn't you? I'm persuaded you'll want to be taking a good many naps in future."

"I will? Katie, what are you talking about?"

Katie wiped her face with a damp cloth. "You do not look ill to me, my lady. Your color's fine. Not but what you are a bit pale, but you'll be right as rain in a few minutes. And you don't have a fever."

"No, I don't. What—oh! oh, my goodness me." Allegra stared at Katie. Her voice came out in a whisper. "Do you really think . . ."

Katie smiled again and Allegra went on, thinking aloud. "I *am* late, and have never been before. How silly of me! I didn't even connect—oh, Katie!" Allegra grinned. "A child! An heir for Nigel! Oh, but I must not tell him just yet. I must be absolutely certain, and then I must pick just the right time."

"Of course, my lady, but 'tis fair certain I am. I—I've seen the symptoms often enough, you see . . ." Katie's voice trailed off and a pained look crossed her face. Allegra knew she was thinking of that terrible place and squeezed her hand in comfort. A moment later Katie brightened.

"But for you it will be wonderful, my lady. His lordship will be so happy!"

Would he? Allegra wondered as she made her way belowstairs a short time later. He was not pleased about his wife. Would he be pleased about her child? Of course, she answered herself. He wanted an heir. He'd told her that the first day they were wed. Perhaps, if they danced together at the ball, he might soften a bit. And perhaps, later that night, she might tell him . . .

That night they attended a musicale at the home of Lady Gresham. Nigel had just led Allegra to a seat in the overcrowded drawing room when Hugo Lattimer came in and sat on her other side. Allegra was most surprised; she hadn't known he was in town. Apparently neither had Nigel, and he looked none too pleased to see him. The greetings were strained and when Allegra smiled a welcome to Mr. Lattimer, Nigel gave her a fulminating look. What was she supposed to do, for pity sakes, ignore the man?

A moment later, the lights were dimmed and the chamber music began, and under cover of the sound of violins, she leaned toward Nigel and whispered, "I was only being polite, Nigel. *I* did not ask him to sit here, you must know."

Nigel spoke in a low growl. "I am aware of that, Allegra, but you are encouraging him. You cannot be so naive as not to know that, and I tell you I will not have it!"

He was seething, and Allegra found that she was, too. How dare he accuse her of such a thing! And where, she wondered, was Mrs. Lacey? What kind of welcome would Nigel give *her?*

Allegra held herself stiffly in the uncomfortable chair,

careful not to lean too close to either man. But one violin was scratchy and she did not care for the selections played. She found her eyelids growing heavy and tried desperately to keep herself awake.

And then Lady Gresham's two unmarried daughters, Priscilla and Eloise, got up to sing. Priscilla's voice was passable but dull, Eloise sang off key, and Allegra finally gave herself up to sleep.

"Wake up, Allegra," Nigel whispered. " 'Tis over now and time to go home."

Allegra came slowly awake and realized that her head was pillowed on his shoulder. Lattimer was gone; indeed, half the room was empty. She lifted her head and looked up at Nigel in confusion.

"The music did not—er—improve, and I was loathe to wake you," he explained, almost defensively.

She blinked. Was this man, who had allowed her, *in public,* to rest her head on his shoulder—was he the same man who had berated her just a short while before? Would she ever understand the puzzle of Nigel?

"I . . . thank you. I do not know what came over me." She yawned delicately. "I was sleeping so soundly," she murmured, trying to clear the cobwebs from her head. "I even dreamt . . ." She let her voice trail off. She'd been dreaming of Nigel, and of herself big with his child. But she could not tell him the former, and would not tell him the latter. Not yet. She wanted to be more certain. After the ball, perhaps . . .

Nigel looked at her curiously, but she said no more. However, the secret smile on her face was eloquent. He clenched his jaw. He did not trust that smile, nor the dreams which begot it. For he did not know of whom she'd dreamt, nor for whom she smiled. And she did not mean to tell him. That could only signify—

Dammit! Why had he let her head remain where it fell on his shoulder, her feathery curls grazing his throat? Why had he let himself be beguiled by the sweet angelic expression she wore in sleep? Did he never learn?

Chapter Sixteen

"And anon he casts his eye against the moon."

Henry VIII

William Shakespeare

" 'Tis like a fairy princess you look, my lady," Katie breathed in awe as Allegra regarded herself in the looking glass. Indeed, she could not disagree. Her new seagreen satin ball gown, with its wispy overlay of silver net, was all that she had hoped it would be. The gown molded to her figure and glimmered when she walked, the sway of the skirt enhanced by its deep flounce of fine green and silver lace, intermingled with rows of satin cockleshells. The waist was very high and the corsage lowcut, which Madame Celeste had insisted was all the crack. She hoped that Nigel would not get into a pelter over it.

It seemed to her that she filled the corsage out more now than she would have two weeks ago. She adjusted the small bodice, raising it up gingerly, for her breasts were sore. That, and the fact that she had been sick in the basin again this morning and had fallen asleep again this afternoon, served to erase any lingering doubts Allegra had about her condition. She *was* increasing! Tonight, much later, she would tell Nigel.

Katie brushed her curls into a gentle tumble about her face and wound a silver net ribbon through her hair. And then Allegra gathered up her fan, reticule and shimmering lace shawl, and made her way belowstairs.

Nigel stood with his back toward her in the entry lobby at the base of the stairs. He turned when Allegra was perhaps halfway down and her pulse accelerated. He looked achingly handsome and . . . and powerful in his black evening coat, olive green waistcoat and buff satin knee britches. How she wanted to be gathered against his broad chest and enfolded in his arms! As she reached the bottom step he surprised her by extending his hand. She felt a jolt of heat between them. His eyes met hers and she knew he felt it as well.

He dropped her hand as soon as she reached the lobby floor. His eyes swept over her, twice. She saw the admiring gleam in their green depths and waited for him to comment on her gown. But his comment was not what she'd expected, or rather, what she'd hoped for. She should have expected it.

"You seem to be developing a penchant for shocking necklines, Allegra. I do not like it," he said tautly.

She looked at him in dismay, not troubling to hide the sudden moisture in her eyes. She had so wanted to please him. What did he want of her?

Nigel saw the stricken look overtake her, saw the tears threatening to spill out, and cursed himself silently. He did not trust her, did not want to get too close to her, and yet he could not bear to see her cry. But he seemed to bring her to that point far too often.

He watched her force back the tears and rally herself. "I own you are most unreasonable, Nigel! *You,* after all, helped me select this dress, and Madame said it was all the crack. Is that not what you wish?"

His lips twitched. "Hoist on my own petard, am I? It *is*

332

a beautiful gown, Allegra. I simply wish there were more of it."

And with that, Allegra thought, she would have to be content.

The reception line seemed interminably long, the crush of people quite overwhelming to Allegra, especially when everyone kept insisting that the Little Season was not quite underway yet. Finally, they were announced and were greeted by their host and hostess. Lady Embers, Penelope's godmama, was a lovely woman of middle years with a dithering air and soft silver blond hair. She wore clouds of yellow chiffon and welcomed everyone effusively. Her husband, the Baron Embers, seemed rather bored with the proceedings, but regarded his wife with a fond and indulgent eye.

As soon as they cleared the reception line, Penelope swept toward them, Damon in tow. Pen, looking dashing in a gown of turquoise and gold, expressed her delight in seeing them. Allegra saw Damon and Nigel exchange masculine looks of bemused tolerance as Pen and Allegra prattled on about the delights awaiting them this night. Their tête-à-tête was interrupted by Hugo Lattimer, who bespoke of Allegra the first set of country dances. Allegra sensed Nigel's displeasure, but knowing no gracious way to refuse, she nodded in acquiescence. Damon signed her dance card as well. Nigel signed Penelope's and then Damon and Pen were hailed by another friend of theirs.

As they drifted off, Nigel turned to Allegra. "You will save the first waltz for me, as well as the supper dance," he said, his eyes impassive. It was a command, neither a request nor a question. She wanted very much to waltz with him and to have supper with him. But his manner and tone took all the pleasure from it. That same command, issued in tones of warmth, would not have come amiss. But even that, he could not give her.

"Yes, Nigel," she said obediently, and reminded him that she'd not yet been granted permission to waltz.

He rectified that straightaway, presenting her to one of the patronesses of Almack's and procuring her a voucher to that hallowed institution at the same time.

They moved off into the ever thickening crowd, Allegra marveling at the splendor of the ballroom and the elegant costume of all the ladies and gentlemen. She found, as she and Nigel stopped to chat with various groups, that she knew quite a few people and her dance card rapidly filled up. The orchestra began tuning up for the first dance, and Allegra was surprised that Nigel was still by her side. Moments later, she was profoundly grateful.

The Viscount Creeve made his way to them and, after letting his cold, blue eyes roam over Allegra in a manner that made her want to hide behind her husband, bespoke a waltz.

"I'm afraid all of my wife's waltz's are spoken for, Creeve," Nigel said affably.

Lord Creeve did not look pleased, but contented himself with a quadrille.

"Thank you, Nigel," Allegra uttered finally when the viscount had gone.

Nigel looked at her and almost smiled. "You are welcome, Allegra. How many waltzes have you free?"

"Only one."

"I shall have that one as well, then," he responded, but the smile never materialized. She wondered what the waltzes would be like.

And then the orchestra struck up the first dance, a cotillion, and her partner came to claim her. Allegra loved to dance, and resolved to enjoy the evening, come what might.

The cotillion was followed by a set of country dances, which she had promised to Mr. Lattimer. He made her giggle with his acerbic comments about some of the more outlandish costumes to be seen this night. There was Lady Gresham's foot-high toque with the three ostrich plumes all waving in different directions, the dandy whose coat was so tight that he danced like a wooden soldier, and the lady swathed in layers of gold silk that looked more like harem pants than any English garment. When the set ended she was breathless and laughing. Out of the corner of her eye she saw Nigel, watching her from across the floor, his brows arched into "V's." She turned away, determined to ignore him. She had done nothing wrong. One was supposed to dance at a ball, after all, and it was not at all the thing to sit in one's husband's pocket all evening.

Apparently Mr. Lattimer had followed her gaze for he laughed intimately into her ear. "You are getting very good at this game, my dear. Very soon you will be ready."

"Ready? Ready for what, Mr. Lattimer?"

He grinned. "I always did like young matrons the best." He took her chin in his hand. "They are ripe and juicy, you see, ready to be—"

"Mr. Lattimer," she interrupted, "I am not a piece of fruit! Now if you'll excuse me . . ."

She twisted away from him and blended into the crowd. She wanted to find Nigel, to ask him how to politely refuse to dance with a gentleman whose company she did not wish.

But she did not see Nigel, and her next partner came to claim her for a Roger de Coverly. And then it was Creeve's turn. She tried to smile at him but found it difficult. There was something about him that made her decidedly uncomfortable. He took her hand for the first steps of the quadrille and she willed herself not to cringe. His hands were long and thin, clammy and as cold as his eyes. She was glad that the steps of the dance kept them apart much of the time, and excessively relieved when it finally ended. Creeve brought her to the side and she thanked him perfunctorily, darting away toward the terrace. She nearly collided with Nigel just before the French doors.

He steadied her at the elbows and looked beyond her shoulders, his face suddenly going rigid. She turned to see Creeve coming up behind her. Her eyes flew back to Nigel. His brows were arched, the planes of his face taut with fury. No! He could not imagine she'd been making for the terrace with . . . with the Viscount Creeve! She turned back to Creeve.

"Oh, Lord Creeve. I did not realize you were behind me. I merely needed a breath of air . . ."

The viscount's pale blue eyes narrowed, but he made her an elegant leg, nodded to Nigel, and withdrew. Nigel half dragged her out to the terrace and over to a darkened corner. She clung to him but he set her away from him, his face still stern.

"Thank heavens you were here, Nigel! I did not like dancing with Lord Creeve, you must know. I do not like his touch, nor the odious way he looks at me. I needed some air, but I had no notion he'd come after me."

Nigel gazed down at his wife. She seemed genuinely distressed, and he wanted to believe her. And could, when it came to Creeve. There was something about him that made even Nigel shudder.

But that didn't explain the others. He'd been watching her dance and flirt all evening. He kept his hands clasped resolutely behind his back, ignoring the appealing picture she made. Her brown eyes were luminous, her hair a trifle tousled from the dancing. And that dress—by all that was holy, that dress ought to be outlawed! True, he'd helped her pick it out, but he had had no idea it would look like that! It was beautiful and shimmering and made her look like an unobtainable goddess and a sensual courtesan all at once. The tops of her breasts swelled from the bodice, looking full and rounded and creamy white. He wanted to put his hands on her, to lower his mouth and—hellfire! Just the thought was pumping fire into his blood.

He took a deep breath and stepped back. What he wanted was to cover her, so that no one else, no other man, could see . . . Instead he forced himself back to the matter at hand. Creeve, and her other dance partners. "That's as may be, Allegra. I am pleased that you have sense enough not to go to a darkened terrace with Creeve. But that does not explain your flirting with Lattimer, or batting your eyelashes with that captain of the Guards who stood up with you for the Roger de Coverly."

Allegra sighed. If she did not know better, she would think him jealous. "Nigel, I do assure you the movements of my eyelashes are quite unexceptionable. Why, I do it all the time, no matter who is about! As to Mr. Lattimer, he can be quite amusing and I did laugh at his pithy observations, but then, at the end, he spoke to me in a way that I could not like. I do wish, Nigel, that you would instruct me in how to refuse a dance with a gentleman with whom I do not care to stand up. For I vow I do not know how!"

He could almost believe her. He wanted to. But he forced himself to recall that she was a seductress and undoubtedly a consummate actress. She was bamming him, playing the innocent to deflect his suspicions.

She was saved his seething reply by the entrance onto the terrace of his friend Adam, Duke of Marchmaine. Adam begged of Nigel an introduction to his bride. Nigel obliged and they all chatted for a time, while Nigel fumed inwardly. He saw the admiring gleam in Adam's eye for his wife and knew she was doing it again—flirting, sending out her lures. It was not Adam's doing. Rake though he might be, he had scruples about his friends' wives. Allegra, it seemed, had no scruples.

And then the first strains of a waltz drifted toward them, and they parted, Nigel leading his wife inside. He wanted to throttle her, to banish her to the country, to tear her clothes off and possess her here and now. And he wanted . . . to dance with her. Blast her! He wanted to hold her in his arms and dance with her.

Allegra looked uncertainly at her husband as he led her onto the dance floor and turned to take her in his arms. He confused her, his quicksilver moods so very unpredictable. He'd been excessively vexed with her moments ago, yet he still wanted to dance with her. She would have thought he'd suggest that they sit the dance out. Instead, he put his right hand to her waist, clasped her hand, and spun her into the dance. The only time Allegra had ever before danced the waltz was in practice sessions with Meg. But dancing in one's own drawing room was nothing at all like dancing in a glittering ballroom with resplendent couples whirling about one and the rich melodious sounds of the music enveloping one. And dancing with Meg was nothing at all like dancing with Nigel.

Dancing with Nigel was a heady experience. His steps were strong and sure, like everything he did, and the small of her back tingled where he held her. They were dancing a proper distance apart, but she noted that some couples were not. She smiled up at her husband, and leaned as close to him as she dared, silently willing him to pull her closer. And in the next moment he did, and rather fiercely, until her entire body was pressed against the hard length of his.

She reveled in the feel of him, in his strength, his fluid movements, his masculine scent. It had been so long since Nigel had held her.

"Mmm," she murmured, hardly aware that she spoke aloud, "I vow I could stay like this forever."

338

She quite unnerved him with statements like that, Nigel mused, as if her nearness were not robbing him of what little sanity he had left. He should never have bespoken a waltz, should never have gone through with it, should never have pulled her close. But he had not been proof against the not so subtle invitation of her body.

Dear God, she felt so good, so natural, so right in his arms. Her body was a perfect fit to his, and the feel and sight and scent of her were making his blood pound, his loins tighten, his head spin.

But somewhere in the back of his mind he recalled that she was a temptress, that the fit was false, the rightness an illusion. He would deal with all of that later. For now he would give himself up to the sensual delights of his first waltz with Allegra.

They circled and swirled and dipped and swayed. She smiled at him and he found himself smiling back and wishing he could lower his head to kiss those soft and yielding lips. Instead he heard himself say, "You look enchanting tonight," and wondered what was wrong with him. She was merely a temptress . . .

The dance ended, and with it the enchantment. A handsome young cavalry officer came to claim Allegra's hand for the next dance, and she went willingly enough.

Nigel took himself off to the card room.

Allegra had only one dance unbespoken for, and she was most grateful for the opportunity to sit it out and rest awhile. But her pleasure in watching the dancing from the sidelines, indeed, her pleasure in the evening, was abruptly curtailed. For there, across the ballroom dancing with a tall man in regimentals, was Barbara Lacey! Allegra's heart sank. Had Nigel seen her? What would he do when he did?

Nigel was at this moment making his way about the card room, trying not to appear as if he were deliberately tracking his quarry. Creeve was engaged in a high stakes game of faro. He was drinking and losing heavily, and seemed patently unconcerned about his losses. Nigel wondered at his source of funds; he did not think the Creeve fortune all that great.

For one wild moment he speculated as to whether Creeve might be the mastermind of the Muddleford smuggling ring, whether his vendetta mightn't be just so much posturing. But he dismissed that notion presently. Creeve had, by all reports, been deeply humiliated by the smuggling having been traced to his land. Besides, instinct told Nigel that smuggling was far too rugged and risky a business for Creeve. Creeve would be attracted to something more elegant, and far more villainous.

Nigel waited until Creeve rose before sauntering over to him. He exchanged desultory remarks with the viscount and then steered the conversation to the Dorset smugglers. As before, Creeve was evasive. This time, Nigel determined to push him a bit.

"I was thinking of doing some investigating of my own," Nigel said nonchalantly. "Perhaps, I shall pay a visit to Cliff House."

Nigel saw a flash of something unpleasant in Creeve's eyes before he masked it with a bland expression. "I do not know that that would be such a good idea just now, old chap," Creeve said with studied casualness. He leaned negligently against a paneled wall and twirled his half-full brandy snifter in his hand. "The Revenue has gone to some length to set their investigations in motion. Your sudden presence might arouse suspicions in certain corners, do you not agree?" Creeve drained his glass. "Then again, 'tis your house to do with as you please, is it not?"

"Perhaps you are in the right of it, Creeve," Nigel responded. He thought the viscount's face relaxed almost imperceptibly and he was glad he'd put him off guard. That would give Nigel time to plan his next move carefully. For he was more determined than ever to go to Dorset, when the time was right.

Allegra's second waltz was promised to Nigel's friend, the Duke of Marchmaine. He was, she noted as he led her out, very tall, taller even than Nigel, and very lean. He was a very attractive man, though not as handsome as Nigel, of course, with a strong hawklike nose and piercing tawny eyes. He was an excellent dancer and held her at a respectable distance. Once or twice, however, the spin of the dance caused her body to brush against his. Strange, she mused, that she felt none of the heat that Nigel's touch engendered.

She smiled at the duke, who was recounting various escapades he and Nigel had got up to while at school. She liked the duke, who was putting himself out to amuse her without being the least flirtatious.

And then her smile faded as her eyes focused on a couple across the floor. Her husband and Barbara Lacey!

Adam Damerest, Duke of Marchmaine, watched the play of expression on Lady Debenham's face and followed her gaze. So, he thought, she knows about Mrs. Lacey. Her little elfin face was turned into a picture of abject misery, which she seemed not to have the guile to hide. And what the deuce was wrong with Nigel to flaunt his former mistress before his innocent young wife?

It was obvious to Adam that she loved her husband. He wondered if Nigel was aware of it, or if he realized how rare it was for a woman to look at her husband the way the countess was looking now at him. Nigel laughed at something Mrs. Lacey said and Lady Debenham smiled determinedly at Adam and asked about his ancestral home in Yorkshire.

341

Nigel Hayves, Adam mused, was ten times a fool.

It was time for the supper dance. Allegra was not certain whether to be pleased or not as Nigel came toward her.

"Did you enjoy your dance with Mrs. Lacey?" she could not help asking.

"No more than you enjoyed dancing with Marchmaine," Nigel snapped, and then the steps of the dance separated them. Which, Allegra decided, was just as well. Whatever was Nigel so wrought up about? Did he not wish her to be gracious to his friends? It was she who should be vexed. Surely it was indiscreet of him to dance with Mrs. Lacey, if she had been what Allegra thought she'd been to Nigel. But she did not wish to chide him. She wished only to ask him a question. Recalling Penelope's words about men and their salad days, she wanted only to know if Mrs. Lacey was, indeed, part of Nigel's past and not the present. But the lively country dance did not afford much opportunity for conversation, certainly not any discussion of import. And when it was over Allegra found herself in a crush of people, being ushered by Nigel to a table in the crowded supper room.

They shared a table with Damon and Pen, and with the Duke of Marchmaine and a pretty, raven-haired heiress with whom he seemed excessively bored. They were joined by another old friend of Nigel's, Reginald Ayres, Duke of Milburne and his bride, whom the duke introduced as Susanna but called "Scotty" all the while. The duchess was beautiful, with auburn hair and creamy skin and dancing midnight blue eyes. It was plain as pikestaff that the duke was besotted with her, and she hardly took her eyes from her husband, except to glance now and again at a table across the way.

A very lovely blond girl, younger than Allegra, sat there with a young man who looked not much older than she. "Who is that, your grace?" Allegra could not help asking as Nigel engaged Milburne in some other discourse.

The duchess, insisting that she was delighted to have a new friend and that Allegra must call her "Susanna," explained. "That's Reggie's sister, Phoebe, ye ken. We're even now bringing her out, for the Little Season, and she's bonny and sweet, but very young, as ye can see. I promised Reggie's mama I'd have a care for her."

Allegra thought that a great charge for a new bride, especially since Phoebe had the look of a charming, somewhat addlepated little flirt. But Susanna seemed not to mind at all. She spoke of her husband's family with great affection. It made Allegra think of her own family, so distant from her now, in more ways than one, and of Nigel's, gone forever.

Well, we'll make a new family, Allegra told herself staunchly, surreptitiously patting her still flat belly. But as the spirited conversation went on around her, she wondered if that would ever be, if they would ever have the loving family for which she longed. Yes, Nigel did serve her dutifully from the buffet, just as Damon and Milburne served their wives, but somehow he showed no more interest in Allegra than the Duke of Marchmaine showed in the vapid heiress whose name Allegra could not recall. While Milburne brushed Susanna's hand, or nape, every chance he got, and Damon whispered in Pen's ear to make her giggle, Nigel was formal and distant with Allegra.

And then several things happened to distract her thoughts. The young man across from Phoebe took the girl's hand, Milburne half rose, a murderous look on his face, and Susanna patted his forearm and spoke very quietly to him. The duke subsided, and moments later Phoebe's young man removed his hand and Phoebe, blushing painfully, pulled her hands out of reach. A scene had been avoided.

Susanna's eyes twinkled up at her husband as if to say, "I told you so," and the duke's answering grin was rueful. It was a scene, Allegra decided, that had undoubtedly been played before. And the intimacy of it, the ease of communication between Susanna and her "Reggie," reminded Allegra anew of what life could be. If Nigel was likewise reminded, he gave no notice, but turned his attention to his food, which he appeared to find quite pleasing.

Allegra, however, found that little of the food appealed to her. The lobster patties, which she'd always liked excessively well, turned her stomach, as did the glazed meats. She settled on some buttered muffins and fruit tarts, and wondered whether it was her disquieting thoughts or the new life she carried that had caused her stomach to behave so oddly. She hoped no one noticed her picking at her food; of a certain Nigel did not appear to. She had wanted to tell him later tonight about the babe. Now she did not know; he seemed as distant as ever.

She also hoped no one else noticed that distance. It did not appear that anyone did, all, that is, except Marchmaine. Those piercing tawny eyes of his regarded her pensively, and Allegra was afraid he saw too much. But then his eyes met hers and she saw . . . understanding in them and she could not help but draw some small comfort from that. Marchmaine, she thought, would one day make some woman very happy. But he did not stir Allegra's blood. Only one man did that.

After supper Allegra made her way to an anteroom that had been set aside for the ladies' withdrawing room. A chamberpot had been discreetly placed behind a chinoiserie screen, and when Allegra was finished with it she rose and adjusted her skirts. But before she could take a step she heard the door open and two ladies, in the midst of conversation, stepped inside. And Allegra knew immediately that she had got to stay perfectly still, concealing her presence until they'd gone. She could not see them but imagined them standing before the gilt-edged mirror, adjusting their gowns, a feather here, a flower there.

"Well, Winifred dear, what do you think?" a vaguely familiar voice with a hint of sharpness was saying.

"About Debenham?" Winifred, whoever she was, answered.

"No, dear, about his little bride, of course. Straight out of the schoolroom, I daresay, and such a provincial! When I think he could have had Eloise!"

Eloise? Just who *was* this?

"Now, Augusta, you'll simply have to look elsewhere for Eloise. As for Lady Debenham, I think perhaps you do her an injustice. She's rather engaging, you must know, and Debenham hasn't taken his eyes from her all evening." Thank you, Winifred, whoever you are, Allegra said silently.

"That is only because he wants to make sure she does not make a cake of herself," the lady called Augusta replied, laughing unpleasantly. "I doubt she's been out in society much. And I make no doubt he'll return to Barbara Lacey soon enough."

"Barbara Lacey?"

"Oh, hadn't you heard? She's the dashing widow he was waltzing with before supper. They were *very* good friends before his marriage, you must know. At the least up there in Suffolk. Here, of course, he had La Plume in keeping. But Marchmaine has her now and I think Mrs. Lacey is making her play for Debenham. Actually —" Augusta paused as the door opened and what Allegra took to be two more ladies came in. Oh dear, it was becoming crowded in here. Augusta greeted the newcomers without using their names and went right on.

"Actually, Winifred, I overheard Mrs. Lacey." She lowered her voice conspiratorially but as Allegra could hear every wretched word, she knew the others would as well. "She was saying to that handsome Mr. Lattimer that Debenham said he would not see her for a while, to give his bride a chance to—well, you know—adjust to the realities of married life. But Mrs. Lacey, I am persuaded, has no intention of waiting."

"Augusta, truly, it amazes me, how you always seem to know such things," Winifred put in.

Could she really admire this viper of a woman?

"Oh, my dear, one can learn so much if one simply listens at all the right times," Augusta replied smugly, and then one of the new ladies spoke for the first time.

"My dear Lady Gresham," the voice of a younger woman began. Lady Gresham! That's who it was. She had given the musicale, and Eloise had a voice that could shatter glass. Lady Gresham, Allegra had learned tonight, was sometimes referred to as the Dragon Lady. Now Allegra knew why. "I could not help overhearing, and I am persuaded you are right," the voice went on, and then, of course, Allegra realized who it was. The timbre, the intonations, were already familiar to her. "One does learn a great deal about people from listening, and watching. That is why, while you might be quite right about Mrs. Lacey, I own you are far off the mark with Debenham. You see, I am persuaded he has a tendre for his wife." Oh, Pen, Allegra thought, thank you for the kind words, but you are fair and far off.

"There, you see, Augusta," Winifred said. "I knew—"

"Fustian, Winifred! Dear Lady Penderleigh is simply given to romantical notions, aren't you, dear? Pray do not confuse Debenham with Penderleigh, who, I will own, is

346

obviously besotted with *you*. Of course, *I* do not hold with such things, but I am certain it is none of my concern."

How odd, thought Allegra piquedly. Everything else seemed to be her concern.

"And that is not, I do assure you, what I want for my Eloise," the Dragon Lady said haughtily. "We must find another eligible, Winifred. I had thought of Marchmaine, but he is too intense, too . . ."

"Strong?" Winifred ventured, and Allegra silently applauded.

"Indeed," Lady Gresham replied, sounding a bit put out. "Someone who will be sensible of the great honor my Lord Gresham and I are bestowing on him along with my daughter's hand. After all, she is quite an heiress and the family line an ancient one."

Allegra felt sick, and it had naught to do with her condition. She heartily wished she knew of a fortune hunter who might pay court to Eloise.

And then the fourth woman spoke for the first time. "If I might be so bold, Lady Gresham, I ken a man who might do very well for yer daughter." Susanna! Allegra did not know whether to be grateful or mortified that it was her friends and not strangers, who were privy to this distasteful conversation. She *was* grateful that she was no longer the topic of discussion. But she did wish they would all leave. Her limbs were stiff from standing so rigidly, and she longed to take a few deep breaths.

"Oh?" Lady Gresham responded imperiously, but she did not reject Susanna's suggestion out of hand.

"Aye, he is a handsome man, from a very old family in Devon. Son of the Baron Hastings of Beverwil Manor, ye ken."

"I see, your grace. And what is his name?"

"Oswald Hastings. And I ken he is looking about for a wife, but, well, no, perhaps ye'll not be interested."

347

"Why do you not allow me to be the judge of that, my dear?" the Dragon Lady said ever so sweetly. "Now, what were you about to say?"

"Well, only that although the Hastings have been in Devon for centuries, Oswald is a younger son, and I do not think Beverwil will go to him. And, in truth, I do not think he is always plump in the pocket."

"Hanging out for a fortune, is what he is, Augusta. And a good thing, too, for I daresay he'll never gainsay you," Winifred put in.

"Hmmm," Lady Gresham murmured. "Of a certain money — such a vulgar subject, do you ladies not agree? — money is not nearly so important as impeccable lineage. I do think this bears looking into, Winifred. I thank you for the suggestion, your grace."

And with that, the Dragon Lady and her friend Winifred departed.

"Ohh!" Pen erupted. "What a perfectly odious woman! How could you have put her onto this Oswald Hastings? Eloise is as bad as her mother!"

"Aye, and Oswald Hastings is worse than that, I assure ye!" Susanna retorted and they both laughed. Allegra had to stifle a chuckle herself. "Oswald tried to turn Phoebe's head this summer past, ye ken, and I thought Reggie would have the apoplexy. Phoebe is over him, but still I'd like to see him elsewhere occupied," Susanna went on, then asked Pen to help her pin a rose back onto her dress. Shortly thereafter she took her leave.

Only Penelope remained, softly humming to herself. Dear heavens, would she never leave?

"You can come out now, Allegra."

What?

"Come now, that *is* you, is it not? They've all gone. 'Tis quite safe."

Slowly, stiffly, Allegra moved out from behind the

348

screen. "How did you know? she asked hoarsely.

"Why, I saw you headed this way earlier, and then I heard someone breathing behind the screen. Well, and anyone else would have had no reason to stay there, would they? Of course, you did the only thing you could. And don't pay any heed to that dreadful woman. She never means anyone any good."

"I know but—"

"And besides, Allegra, I meant what I said, even if I spoke out of turn. I *do* believe your husband has a tendre for you."

Allegra shook her head sadly. Pen turned to peer into the mirror, patting several wayward red curls into place. "Believe me," the marchioness went on, "I have some experience in these matters. It took Damon forever to admit he had a care for me. Instead he spent all his time ringing a peal over me! Lord Debenham may not know it yet, but he has met his match."

Penelope grinned into the mirror and Allegra found herself grinning back. Nigel might, indeed, *not* have a tendre for her yet, but it did not mean he wouldn't develop one. And as to Barbara Lacey, she had neither Allegra's youth, nor Nigel's wedding ring. Nor was she carrying Nigel's baby. Allegra had no intention of giving up this fight!

Pen hugged her in encouragement, and they left the anteroom arm-in-arm. Damon met them several doors down and took Penelope away. Moments later Hugo Lattimer appeared and without so much as a by your leave took Allegra's arm and strolled with her toward the ballroom. Allegra tried to disengage her arm but Lattimer would not relinquish it. She could not make a scene for there were other people about, but she did not enjoy having Lattimer so close.

And then, just as they neared the ballroom, Nigel emerged from between its massive doors. He stared at them, at their linked arms, and said nothing. Lattimer let go her arm, nodded to Nigel with his customary smirk, and took himself off.

"Where were you?" Nigel said icily.

"In the ladies withdrawing room." She raised her chin a notch. "With Pen." Oh, dear, why did she feel the need to defend herself? She had done nothing wrong.

And then she heard the strains of the next waltz. Without a word Nigel led her into the ballroom and onto the dance floor. But this waltz was nothing like their first. Nigel refused all attempts at conversation. His jaw was rigid, his stance no less so. He held her at more than respectable distance, and no wriggling on Allegra's part would change that.

And suddenly she was overwhelmingly tired. Tired because of the babe, perhaps, tired from the effort of fathoming Nigel's moods, tired from the lateness of the hour. She could barely move one foot in front of the other and when the dance ended she asked Nigel if they mightn't go home, as she was exhausted.

He frowned down at her. "I was under the impression that you were enjoying the dancing, Allegra. The ball is far from over. I daresay there are three dances at the least remaining, and your card is signed for all of them."

"I know that, Nigel. Can we not make my excuses? I really am quite puckered out, you must know."

"Very well," he said, with tight lips. It was almost as if he were suspicious of her motives. But why?

He ushered her from the dance floor and made their farewells and excuses efficiently and quickly, and within a quarter of an hour handed her into their carriage. But not once had there been a smile for her, a soothing hand at her nape, a supportive arm at her waist. Not once had he evinced concern for her sudden tiredness. He simply did what she asked and she supposed she had oughtn't to fret about it. He treated her, after all, with all due respect in public. But it was not enough. Not nearly enough.

He sat on the seat opposite her, and was disinclined to converse, which was just as well. For her lids grew heavy and she began to drift to sleep as soon as the carriage started moving. Her head banged against the side of the carriage. Nigel's shoulder was not there to cushion it. Nor did he move, as her head banged again and again. Finally, Allegra slept.

Nigel watched her. Watched her and wanted her, as he had all evening. And hated himself for his weakness. He knew what she was. He had only to watch her with Lattimer or Marchmaine or any one of her admirers, or to recall her behavior in the garden at Caulfield, to know the truth. And he had only to recall Lucinda to know that he would never be the pathetic, besotted fool his brother had been.

Nigel roused her as they neared the house and Allegra woke with difficulty. She had actually been deeply asleep. She must have stumbled, for Nigel put a hand to her elbow to steady her. But as soon as they reached the front portico he dropped her arm. Thorpe opened the door.

"Good night, Allegra," Nigel said.

She tilted her head in confusion. "Are you not coming in?"

"No. I am going to my club," he said in clipped tones.

She stared at him, trying to fathom his expression. He had never done this before. What did it mean? She could not ask, could not remonstrate with him. Not in front of Thorpe.

"Good night, Allegra," he repeated, and stepped back.

And then suddenly she knew, understood all too well. He was going to Barbara Lacey. She was certain of it. But he was gone before she could say a word.

Heartsick, Allegra straightened her shoulders and made

her way abovestairs. Katie was waiting for her in her dressing room, but suddenly Allegra was too restless to contemplate sleep. Her tiredness had gone, perhaps because she'd slept in the carriage, perhaps because her mind was suddenly whirling with images she did not care to think on. Images of Nigel and another woman. She needed to ride, she decided on impulse.

Katie tried to dissuade her when Allegra eschewed her night rail in favor of a riding habit, but Allegra overrode her. Telling Katie not to wait up for her, she hurried down to the stables. She hoped no one was about; she had rather not explain anything. Somehow, she would saddle her horse herself.

But Jamie greeted her from the depths of the stables. He came forward, carrying a lantern. "My lady! And what might ye be doin' oot here this time o' the night?"

"I want to ride, Jamie. Would you saddle Windstar for me?"

Jamie regarded her out of piercing blue eyes. "Beggin' yer pardon, my lady, but the earl—"

"The earl is not here, Jamie. He brought me home and he—he's gone out again." She swallowed a lump in her throat and blinked back the tears that pricked the back of her eyelids. She wondered if Jamie knew where Nigel was really going.

"I see," he said, frowning. "But 'tis verra dark oot there, I'm thinkin'. I dinna imagine he'll be thankin' me for lettin' ye go."

She sighed heavily. "In truth, I do not think he would care, Jamie, and he'll be . . . otherwise occupied for some time now, I am certain."

"Lassie? What is it troubles ye?"

She ought not to say anything. He was Nigel's friend, and servant, after all. But he was her friend as well. She badly needed a friend just now.

"Jamie, have you—have you ever heard of . . . Barbara Lacey?"

"Barbara Lacey?" he echoed in disbelief, and raised the lantern higher. And that was when she realized for the first time that his eyes looked red-rimmed. Why, he'd been crying! Suddenly her own problems could wait.

"Never mind, Jamie. 'Tis of—of no moment. What of you? What are *you* doing out here? Is Flora all right?"

"Aye, my lady." Now it was his turn to sigh. "She goes on better everra day, praised be. But she—she's overset, and I dinna ken what to do wi' her."

"What is oversetting her, Jamie? Perhaps I can help."

"Och, nay, my lady. 'Tis only—" he paused and took a deep breath. Allegra thought he was wrestling with some deep emotion. "She—she's sayin' as how she'll be leavin' once she's right and mended." His voice broke. "She doesna want to bring me disgrace by bidin' with me, ye ken, and I canna convince her . . ."

"I'll go to her, Jamie," Allegra ventured.

He shook his head. " 'Tis late, my lady. Perhaps on the morrow—"

"Is she awake?"

"Aye. But—"

"I want to go, Jamie. I—I'm too restless to sleep." She tried to smile at him.

"Och, verra well, then. 'Tis better, I warrant, than havin' yer husband hand me my head fer lettin' ye ride at such an ungodly hour." He smiled gently down at her. "And he *would* care, lassie, I am certain of it." Allegra shook her head, patted his arm, and left him.

She found Flora propped up in bed, a vacant look in her eyes. Allegra thought her color was good, although her breathing was still labored.

"My lady! What are ye doin' here so late? Should ye no be abed?" Flora's voice was stronger, albeit still hoarse.

353

Allegra shrugged. "The earl is out and I wanted to talk to you." Flora looked curiously at her. Allegra went to sit in the bedside chair. "Do you know how desperately Jamie wanted to find you, Flora?" A spasm of pain crossed Flora's face and she shut her eyes.

"Please, my lady, I canna—"

"Flora. He loves you. He's never stopped loving you. Do you not know that?"

Flora slowly opened her eyes. "Aye. I ken that. And I— God help me—but I love him. But after where I've been, the things I've done—"

"The things you were forced to do," Allegra corrected.

Flora shook her head. "It doesna signify, my lady. The disgrace is the same."

"I think it will kill him if you leave again. Do you wish that?" Allegra asked softly.

Flora closed her eyes again and two tears trickled from their corners. "Nay, but I—" she paused, her voice a threadbare whisper, "I dinna ken if I . . . can ever be a wife again."

Allegra took her hand and squeezed gently, suddenly understanding. It was not the disgrace after all. She was afraid, and who could blame her?

"Flora, Jamie is a kind, patient man, I am persuaded. He will give you all the time you need. The love that he feels for you, the way that he takes care of you—well, it is a very rare thing. You must not throw that away!" Allegra had not meant to speak so fiercely, but she did, and Flora opened her eyes and smiled faintly.

"Ye are too young to have such wisdom, my lady."

Allegra sighed. "Sometimes we are forced by life to grow up rather fast, are we not?"

"Aye, my lady," Flora concurred, and then, as if the two points were related, asked, "And where is yer fine husband this night?"

354

"He's—he's at his club." So he says, Allegra thought, but did not say. Flora was regarding her with a knowing eye. "Life is never simple, is it?" This time, it was Flora who squeezed *her* hand.

Minutes later she heard Jamie come into the outer room, but Flora still clutched her hand, although her eyes had begun to flutter closed. A glance through the doorway told Allegra Jamie had sat down on the sofa, and so she stayed where she was, waiting for Flora to fall asleep.

The next thing she knew, Jamie was shaking her shoulder. Her head was bent over Flora's bed. "My lady. 'Tis near dawn. We both fell asleep. I think ye'd best go back to the house noo."

Near dawn! Dear God! How had this happened? She sprang up and dashed for the stairs. And it was then, as she hurried down, that her eyes locked with Nigel's. He had just alighted from the carriage.

"Nigel!" she screeched, stopping short, two steps before the bottom.

The look in his eyes, clearly visible in the light of the carriage lantern, was murderous. The best defense, she decided, was a good offense. "Where have you been?" she inquired, forcing herself to take those last steps down.

He looked her up and down with a contemptuous sneer that chilled her. "There's no need to ask where *you've* been, is there, Allegra?" he drawled, his voice full of innuendo. Whatever was he implying?

"Nigel, what—whatever are you implying? I fell asleep and—"

"You whore!" he growled, and lunged for her.

Shocked, she jumped out of his reach and ran for the house. She would lock herself in her room until he calmed down. She ran for all she was worth, but he was on her in seconds, and half dragged her up the stairs to her bed chamber. He shoved her inside and followed, slamming the

355

door behind him.

"Nigel," she said unsteadily, "I do not know what you are thinking, but I—"

"How long, Allegra?" he shouted, grabbing her fore-arms. "How long have you been whoring with Jamie?"

"Oh, my God!" She felt sick, violently so. "No, Nigel, you are wrong! 'Tis nothing like that!"

"Do you deny that you were in Jamie's rooms?" he de-manded, shaking her.

She swallowed hard. "No, but it is not what you think. There is someone else—"

"Someone else! Damn you to hell, Allegra! How many lovers do you have?"

"No, Nigel! I have no lovers! I—"

"Don't lie to me, goddamn you!"

"I'm not—" She stopped midsentence, for suddenly the bile had risen in her and she knew she was going to be sick.

Somehow she wrenched from his grasp and darted for the basin. She fell to the ground, wretching, violently sick.

She heard Nigel come up behind her. He handed her a wet cloth but did not speak until she had stopped heaving and had wiped her face.

"What is it, Allegra? Are you ill?" His voice was gruff. She could not decide if it held concern or not.

He was crouched down behind her. She pushed the ba-sin away and peered at him over her shoulder. She might just as well tell him now. There was not going to be any special time, any right time. She did not know if things would ever be right again. And of a certain they could not get worse.

"No, Nigel," she said in a flat, emotionless tone. "I am not ill. I am with child."

"With child!" he echoed, looking stunned. He nearly fell back, but steadied himself and stood up. She did the

356

same, and watched the stunned look on his face change. His green eyes became shuttered, his jaw rigid.

"Well, madam," he snarled derisively, "you'd better pray it's a girl, for I'll claim no man's bastard as my heir!"

Chapter Seventeen

"My soul is in the sky; Tongue, lose they light;
Moon, take they flight."

> *A Midsummer Night's Dream*
> William Shakespeare

Nigel watched Allegra back away from him, a look of horror on her face. "No, Nigel," she rasped. "You cannot mean that. I have never played you false. The child is yours."

She was so beautiful. That little elfin face of hers looked so vulnerable, so distraught. But her eyes were still fuzzy from sleep. Sleep in another man's bed. He'd known women with a talent for looking just so, for professing love where there was none, for wringing a man's heartstrings. And all they really were were consummate actresses.

Well, he was having none of it. Nor did he want to hear her pitiful attempts to gammon him. "You'd do well to pack your bags, Allegra. We leave after breakfast for Caulfield, where you shall remain until your confinement, without, I assure you, my erstwhile head groom, Jamie MacIntyre. I shall dispatch him in an entirely different manner."

"No!" she exclaimed. "Nigel, you cannot mean to call

him out! Please, he's done nothing! He—"

"Call him out?" He laughed mirthlessly. "I do not think so, Allegra. Your honor is not worth defending. And I have no desire to leave a trail of corpses behind me—especially when half would be my so-called friends!" he ranted with contempt.

She took a step toward him; then another. She extended her hand and touched his forearm. "Nigel, listen to me," she said quietly. He did not want to hear the softness in her voice. "You do not know what—"

"What I know," he cut in brutally, flinging her arm from his, "is that my *wife* just emerged from the rooms of another man, her eyes still soft from sleep. I have suspected for a long time, Allegra, but until now I had no proof. As to the others, I will *never* know, will I, who else had you. Lattimer, Marchmaine—"

"No, Nigel!" she screamed, rushing toward him and flinging herself at him. " 'Tis not true! None of it is! Yes, I was sleeping in Jamie's rooms, but *not with him!*" She was sobbing now, her body convulsing against his, her head on his chest. He steeled himself against the feel of her, the scent of her, the hot, bitter tears. "Ask him, Nigel. I was helping him with—"

"No!" he exploded, shoving her away from him with a force that sent her spinning across the floor. She fell against the bed. "I am not my brother Charles to be taken in by a whoring, deceitful siren!" His voice crackled with rage. His body shook with it. He wanted to shake *her*, to beat her mercilessly. She lay in a crumpled heap before the bed, weeping softly now, her face averted. Damn her to hell! He wanted to reach for her, hold her, kiss her, one last time. No! No more!

He took a deep breath. "Pack your things, madam," he said through gritted teeth. "We will not discuss this further. I will convey you to Debenham. After that we will not see

359

each other until your child is born. If you are fortunate enough to birth a girl, I will permit you to raise her. If it is a boy I will decide then what is to be done with him."

Allegra did not move. She did not lift her head. She did not say a word. She did not look like a siren now, but like a lost little girl. He hardened himself against the picture of vulnerability she made. That was all it was—a picture, a pretense. And he brushed aside the niggling reminder that her child might well be his. He would never know, never be sure, and the doubt would kill him.

"I . . . love you, Nigel," she whispered brokenly. "I have been a good wife to you."

She still did not look at him. He stared down at her in disgust. "Spare me, Allegra, do not humiliate yourself further. I am not the young fool I once was, and I am not my brother Charles to be taken in by your wiles."

He strode to the connecting door. He heard her voice, no more than a threadbare whisper just before he slammed the door behind him. "I am not Gina. I am not Lucinda."

Yes, you are, he thought, right down to the child in your belly. But Nigel was *not* Charles. He had no intention of driving himself off a cliff. Thank God he'd had the sense, the fortitude, to keep himself from coming to care for her.

Why then, he asked himself, did he feel so terribly cold, so devastatingly empty inside?

Allegra did not move. She felt bruised and battered. Her arms hurt where he'd gripped her, her knees where she'd fallen on the floor, and her cheek throbbed where she'd banged it on the wooden side of the bed. But most of all, her heart was broken, torn into little pieces that she knew would never again form a whole.

It was over. Sometime during the last minutes she had

realized that. When he'd said she'd better pray it was a girl? When he'd viciously shoved her, child and all, across the room? She did not know. It didn't signify. She knew now, at long last, that there was no hope for this marriage. It was not only that he'd just proved, brutally, that he did not love her, did not have even a care for her. It was because he did not trust her, and never would. Oh, yes, she could try, tomorrow when he was perhaps calmer, to explain about Jamie. She could beseech Jamie to tell him the truth and set all to right.

But it would not set all to rights. He would still believe she'd cuckolded him, if not with Jamie then with someone else. She was, to him, Lucinda all over again. It would always be this way. Every time she smiled at a man, Nigel would be wondering. She could not live with the doubt, the mistrust, the anger.

And most of all, she could not live with a man who wanted to repudiate his child, *their* child. If it was a girl, he would barely tolerate her. And if it was a boy — she shuddered to think what he meant to do in that case.

Suddenly she could not bear to be here any longer, in Nigel's house, in his life, where she was not wanted. And she would not allow him to make some sort of prisoner of her at Debenham. She *could* not go back there in such humiliating circumstances. She forced herself to rise, trying to ignore her aches and bruises. She must leave. Straightaway. Suddenly it all became crystal clear. She had tried to make a success of her marriage. She had tried to win her husband. She had failed. She had tried to be a good wife, but obviously that was not enough. Her love was not enough. He did not want it.

So be it. She would not let him destroy her, and she would not let him destroy the child she knew she carried. And so she must leave.

Dawn was just breaking. She had a short while before

361

the servants arose. She must—oh, dear God, Jamie! What was Nigel going to do to Jamie? She started to run toward the door, but got only as far as the bench at the foot of the bed. Her knees ached dreadfully and she was dizzy. She sank down onto the tufted bench and forced herself to think rationally. Jamie was not in danger. Nigel had said he would not call him out, that Allegra was not worth it. Nor would he murder Jamie in his bed, for he'd said he'd not leave a "trail of corpses" behind him. Besides, despite his repudiation of her and their child, Nigel was not a murderer. And at all events, his rage had been for her, not Jamie. He considered Jamie only one of several for whom he felt contempt, not the kind of passionate fury that led one to do bodily harm.

She got up carefully and padded to the dressing room to listen for sounds coming from Nigel's chambers. She heard the clink of glass on glass. Was he pouring himself a drink? A soft thud, and then another. His boots, perhaps? She hoped so—then he would not be going out again. He would wait until later to confront Jamie. And then he would coldly, with deadly, contemptuous calm, order his friend of four years out of his house and out of his life.

Allegra hoped Jamie would have better luck defending himself than she'd had. She didn't want Jamie to lose his home, could not bear to think she would be the cause of a rift between Nigel and Jamie. But none of it signified in terms of her relationship with her husband. If Jamie was exonerated in Nigel's mind, there was a long list of candidates to take his place.

And at all events she would never know what happened. She would be long gone by the time Nigel went to Jamie. She would be sorry to go without saying good-bye to Jamie and Flora, but there was no help for it. She could only hope that Jamie would understand, and took comfort from the fact that she had done what she could for Jamie and

Flora. Perhaps they would achieve some measure of happiness.

It was almost worth her own unhappiness. Almost. She was not that selfless. Just as Meg's happiness was almost worth the wretchedness she had caused to bring it about. Why was it that both times she'd made Nigel so bitter and angry, when all she'd wanted was to help someone else?

She felt two large tears squeeze out of her eyes and roll down her cheeks. She brushed them away impatiently. She had not the luxury of such now. She listened again for sounds from Nigel's rooms. Silence. She hoped he'd fallen asleep.

At all events, the noise of packing ought not to raise any suspicions. He had *told* her to pack, after all. She rang for Katie, and now forced her mind to the question of where to go. Of a certain she could not go to Caulfield; Papa would hardly welcome her. And she could not turn up on Meg's doorstep. Meg was newly married and it would be cruel of Allegra to impose her unhappiness on her sister now. Besides, she would be a runaway wife, and her presence would force upon John Dalton a dreadful moral dilemma. Nor could she go to any friends or acquaintances. She would have to fend for herself. But where? And how?

She yanked a portmanteau from the wardrobe and began tossing in serviceable dresses and clean linen. In three years' time she would come into the inheritance her grandmother had left her. Not a great fortune, but enough for her to live in some degree of comfort with her child . . . and Katie, if she'd come. But three years was an exceedingly long time! Until then . . . until then, she reminded herself, there was her quarterly allowance. Nigel had just recently given it to her, and since he'd had all the bills for her wardrobe taken care of separately, she still had most of it left. She'd thought it a princely sum when he'd first named the amount, and now she realized that if she lived frugally she could probably get through the first year, the year her child would be born. After that she would see about finding some kind of work. She did not know what, but she would think of something.

She paused in her packing to consider the ethics of taking Nigel's money to run away from him. But after all, she told herself, she was not stealing it! He'd given it to her! Besides, it was because of the child that she would not be able to work this year, because of the child that she would need money for a doctor, extra food, clothes, because of *his* child! It was perfectly reasonable to take her allowance money!

Katie came into the dressing room hastily buttoning her dress. Her hair was tousled, her eyes still bleary from sleep. "My lady!" she exclaimed, and Allegra cautioned her to lower her voice lest she wake his lordship. Katie nodded and went on in a quieter voice, "I'm sorry I was not here, but you did tell me not to wait up for you. But here, I'll help you out of your gown."

Until that moment Allegra had completely forgotten that she still wore the beautiful sea-green ball gown. It had not, after all, lived up to its promise of enchantment. Katie had glanced at Allegra only briefly and was already extracting a night dress from the wardrobe. It was only then that she noticed the open portmanteau on the chaise lounge, and the clothing strewn about. She whirled round to Allegra. "My lady, what—my lady! Your face! What happened? You—"

"Katie," Allegra interrupted in an urgent whisper. "I must leave here. Now. I cannot stay any longer."

"Leave here? B-but what of his lordship? What—"

"His lordship does—does not want me. Or the child."

"No, my lady! 'Tis not possible. I have seen the way he looks at you. And every gentleman wants an heir. Why—"

"He—he does not believe the child is his, Katie,"

Allegra said quietly.

Katie's face crumpled "Oh. Oh, my lady, I am so sorry." There was a wealth of weary knowledge in Katie's voice, as if so much of what she knew of men had been confirmed. She was disappointed, near tears herself, but not surprised. "Let me get some cold meat for your face, my lady, before it swells up."

Katie did not, Allegra realized, ask how she had come by the bruise. She merely assumed the worst. For some odd reason Allegra felt called upon to defend Nigel. "There is no time, Katie. And truly 'tis not so bad. I fell against the bed, you see."

Katie said nothing. Allegra shifted the subject. "You must decide quickly what you wish to do, Katie. Of course, I should like you to come with me, but I shall understand if you wish to stay. I know you still fear going abroad and here you will be safe."

"Wish to stay? I beg your pardon, my lady, but how could you think I would allow you to go off by yourself? And in your condition, too! You know what you saved me from, my lady. And all these weeks, even though I've been seeing to your clothes and all, 'tis you who's been taking care of me. Now I shall take care of you!"

She had begun folding dresses as she spoke, but now she paused. "My lady, are you sure you will not reconsider? Perhaps in time—"

"No, Katie," Allegra said firmly, pulling more dresses out of the wardrobe.

"I expect you'll want to leave before first light," Katie ventured, her hands working faster. Allegra nodded. "My lady, do you know where we will go? Do you have any funds? If you travel without the protection of your husband's name, you might fall prey to—"

"I do have funds, Katie, at least for a time. We shall find a hackney several blocks from here, and then take the

365

stage." Allegra was thinking as she spoke. "I shall travel under an assumed name, for I do not wish to be pursued. Perhaps I shall masquerade as a—a widow! Yes, that will answer, especially considering the child. I shall be a recent widow. But as to where we will go, I . . . it will not be easy, Katie. I cannot go to my family. Perhaps we can find a small house to rent, somewhere in the country."

"It does not matter, my lady, as long as we have a roof over our heads. We can make even the most dilapidated cottage habitable, I am persuaded."

The most dilapidated cottage, Allegra thought. And then suddenly she had it! She knew exactly where they would go! She hugged Katie gratefully, asked her help in changing into a traveling gown, and then bade her finish packing while Allegra did the most difficult thing of all.

She sat down to write a farewell letter to Nigel.

Nigel came awake slowly, aware of a wretched fuzziness, a vile pain in his head, and the fact that every muscle he owned ached, and then some. He was further aware that he was not sprawled comfortably upon his bed under his down comforter. He was rather twisted quite *un*comfortably in his wing chair, still wearing his evening clothes, an empty decanter of brandy at his elbow.

And then, memory came flooding back to him and he immediately wished it hadn't. Allegra. His beautiful, whoring, deceitful wife. His beautiful, whoring, *pregnant* wife! He finally had the proof of what he'd long suspected, and he was almost sorry. Now he would never hold her again, never make love to her again—and a good thing too, dammit! He'd come frightfully close to being taken in by her.

Even last night, at the ball, he'd wanted her so much his body had ached with need. He'd wanted her, but he'd been furious with the way she'd been making eyes at every man in her path. And so he'd left her here and gone to White's, not trusting himself to stay out of her bed if he followed her into the house.

Instead she'd gone straight to Jamie's bed, harlot that she was! He hoped they'd both rot in hell!

He glanced at the ormolu clock on the mantel. Five past seven. He would ring for Kingston, dress and break his fast. And then he would have it all out with Jamie. He rose to go to the bellpull, but his head rattled so much that he sank back into his chair. The rattling stopped, but not the memories. Allegra in the stable yard, fresh from Jamie's bed. Her mendacious, tearful denials of what was so painfully true, her shocking announcement of her condition, her small form, huddled against the bedside as he'd left her.

He'd slammed out of her bedchamber, through the dressing room and into his own room, desperately needing a drink. And then he'd meant to confront Jamie straightaway. Not to call him out—as he'd told Allegra, her honor was not worth defending, and one did not call one's servant out on a field of honor, after all. As to Jamie's being his friend, well that was no more true than his wife's fidelity had been. No, not to call him, but to beat him within an inch of his life before ordering him to leave. Forever.

But as Nigel had closed the door to his own room, the rage he'd felt moments before, and which he would have welcomed, seemed to dissipate. Had he spent it all on Allegra?—She with her elfin face and secret wiles, she who could lure the most stalwart of men . . .

He'd sunk down onto his bed, head in his hands. And instead of fiery rage, it had been vast and icy emptiness that engulfed him. Allegra *was* Lucinda, much as she denied it, *and* Gina, and all beautiful, passionate, perfidious women, and her betrayal left a deep hole inside him.

Finally, he'd risen and taken his drink, but he had not gone to Jamie. He'd suddenly felt inutterably tired, so . . . defeated. All that he'd suspected and feared had come to pass. He had banished his wife; he would wait a few hours to banish his erstwhile friend. He sank down in his wing chair and drank enough to make him forget. Temporarily.

Now it was morning and he could no longer forget. Nor did he want to. He rose, forcing his fuzzy head to remain as still as possible. He no longer felt defeated. Charles had been defeated. He was not. He did not feel the heated rage he'd felt when he'd realized where Allegra had been. He felt instead a very cold, very determined fury. And he knew exactly what he was going to do.

He rang for Kingston, and as his man saw to his toilette, Nigel downed the special brew that Kingston had not been obliged to make in quite some time. Nigel had no idea what was in it, but one half hour after drinking it, the fuzziness in his head had receded and he could stand the sound of his own voice.

Fully dressed in dark brown riding clothes, he pounded on Allegra's door and entered her dressing room without awaiting an answer. She was not there but he smiled grimly at the evidence that she'd obeyed him by packing. Drawers and cupboards were open, although it seemed she'd left quite a bit behind, including several portmanteaux. Why had she not taken more? Surely she knew her stay at Debenham would be lengthy. He peered into the wardrobe. All of her ball gowns and most of her evening gowns were still there. At the least she had the sense to know she would not have need of them in the country. Her life would no longer be a round of parties.

She was not in her bedchamber or sitting room, nor, he discovered, was she in the breakfast parlor. Annoyed at having to search for his wife, he summoned Katie. She did not come.

He summoned Thorpe and was told that her ladyship had not been seen belowstairs this morning. No, she did not go out riding, he said when Nigel questioned him further, and was affronted that his lordship should think he'd not been at his post and so missed the countess when she went out.

Mrs. Thorpe had not seen her either and assured his lordship, with a smile on her motherly face, that her ladyship must still be abed. "After all, my lord, 'tis a late night you had, and her ladyship needs her rest." The way she said it made Nigel wonder if she knew about Allegra's condition, but there was no time to speculate. "No, she is not abed, Mrs. Thorpe," he snapped, and then bellowed at the housekeeper to find the countess and her maid, straightaway.

She looked shocked at his tone and hastened away, but Nigel had no intention of waiting for her. With mounting fury he realized that there was probably only one person who knew the whereabouts of his wife.

He stormed out to the stables and threw open the doors of the nearest one. Jamie was sitting on a barrel, working with some tacking. Two stable boys were brushing down the horses.

Jamie rose at his entrance. "Good mornin' to ye, my l—"

"Where is she, Jamie?" Nigel demanded harshly.

Jamie narrowed his eyes and cocked his head. "What? Where is who, my lord?"

"My wife, damn you! Where is my wife?" Nigel's voice grew louder and the stable boys scampered out. Just as well, Nigel thought.

Jamie's eyes widened now. "The countess? Laddie, what can ye be meanin'? Is she no abed? 'Tis early yet, and—"

"Don't come the innocent with me, you blackguard!" Nigel shouted, advancing on him and, heedless of Jamie's

369

larger size, grabbing him by his shirt collar. "Where is she? Is she abovestairs in your bed, even now, waiting for you? And do you think to take her with you when I toss your worthless hide off my land? Well, I'll—"

"In my *bed??*" Jamie erupted, trying to pull free. "What's come over ye, laddie? Of course, she's no awaitin' me, nor ever has been. What—"

"Goddamn you, you miserable cur!" Nigel ranted. "I know she was with you last night!"

"Oh, my God!" Jamie rasped, paling visibly. "You dinna understand. She—"

"I understand well enough, you whoreson bastard!" Nigel could not stand the denials. He felt the blood pound at his temples. "Where is she?" he raged.

"I dinna ken, laddie," Jamie said with maddening calm, trying once more to disengage Nigel's grip.

That was when Nigel drew his arm back and sent his fist hurling through the air until it collided with Jamie's jaw. Jamie staggered back. "Now *where is she?*" he seethed, his eyes blazing.

"My lord," came a woman's voice from the doorway.

As one, he and Jamie turned to see Mrs. Thorpe enter hesitantly, her eyes darting from one to the other. "Did you find her?" he asked, knowing that she wouldn't have, knowing that Allegra was here, above the—

"No, my lord, but I—I found this." Tentatively she stepped forward and held out her hand. Nigel saw an envelope in the pale blue that Allegra favored. Slowly he took the envelope from the housekeeper. His name was on the front written in Allegra's careless scrawl. Nigel swallowed, a terrible sense of foreboding overtaking him. His eyes went from his housekeeper to his majordomo. Mrs. Thorpe's eyes regarded him with a strange mixture of curiosity and . . . sadness. Jamie was rubbing his jaw; his blue eyes were intense, piercing and reproachful.

Nigel looked back down at the envelope. It almost burned his hand; it seemed charged with emotion.

"Will that be all, my lord?" Mrs. Thorpe asked, and when he nodded, she tactfully withdrew.

There was a charged silence between Jamie and Nigel until, moments later, Jamie stormed out, slamming the door behind him. Nigel went to a window and tore open the envelope. His hands shook; he did not know why. And then he began to read;

Dear Nigel,

Writing this letter is, I think, the hardest thing I have ever had to do. I have loved you for weeks now, though it seems forever. Perhaps one day you will believe that.

But I know that I can no longer stay with you. For even if you speak to Jamie and learn the truth, there will always be another man who crosses my path, and you will always think the worst . . . Just as you have from the very beginning. Perhaps I could endure that for myself, but I cannot bring up a child in a place where he, or she, is not wanted and is denied his heritage. Better that he not know it at all, and at least have his mother's love.

I am sensible of the fact that much of the debacle of this marriage is my fault. I know that you did not want to wed me. Though you still may not believe it, it was not my intention to force your hand that night in the Caulfield gardens. Yet I *had* been meddling, and I realize now, much too late, how wrong that was. For much as I cannot regret Meg's happiness, I do regret the *un*happiness I have caused you.

I thought, mistakenly, naively, that my love for you would be enough to vanquish the demons of your past. But, of course, it wasn't. Perhaps it only made

371

it worse.

Yet there were times, when we came together in the deep of a moonlit night, that I felt the greatest happiness a woman can know. I felt connected, bonded to you in a way that went well beyond the physical. And I know that, however briefly, you felt it as well. But that, too, was not enough.

Please do not make any attempt to find me, Nigel. It is best this way. Perhaps as we have not been wed very long, you can obtain an annulment. If not, then I am persuaded my leaving will enable you to procure a bill of divorcement. The scandalbroth will be most unpleasant, I know, but when it is over, you will be free to marry a woman who meets all of your requirements and whose child you can embrace with no cloud of suspicion. As to Jamie, I fear I was meddling again, though as usual with the best of intentions. I hope that he will find some measure of happiness now, and that you will make your peace with him. It pains me greatly to think that I have come between you. I thank you, Nigel, for my moonlight memories, and for my child.

Godspeed.

Allegra Caulfield Hayves,
Countess of Debenham

His entire body, not just his hands, was shaking when he finished. He read it through again and by this time his eyes were wet and the words blurred. He did not really understand it all, certainly not the part about Jamie. He only knew that he felt as if someone had kicked him viciously in the gut, and all his insides were torn and bleeding.

She was gone. She had left him. He had wanted to send her away temporarily. He had not meant for her to leave.

He—he did not know *what* he had meant!

He stumbled out of the stable. The morning was gray, bleak. Only Jamie stood there. The others had fled. He blinked back the moisture in his eyes and stared at his friend. *If you speak to Jamie and learn the truth* . . . What truth?

"She—she's gone," Nigel uttered disbelievingly.

"Gone? What can ye mean, laddie? Gone where?"

"I don't know. I've got to find her!" Nigel heard the urgency in his own voice, yet he felt engulfed in a fog of confusion.

"B-but why, laddie?" There was no reproach in Jamie's eyes now, only concern. *Speak to Jamie* . . .

Nigel ran his hand jaggedly through his hair. "I saw her last night, coming from your rooms. It wasn't the first time and I—I . . . well, dammit, what *was* I to think? And I still don't know—Hellfire, Jamie! I considered you my closest friend. What was my *wife* doing in your rooms?"

Jamie looked horrified. "Oh, dear God! 'Tis all my fault." Nigel's jaw clenched. "God's teeth, laddie! What did ye say to her?" Nigel shook his head, that sense of foreboding he'd had before intensifying. "What did ye do to her, laddie?" Jamie asked more quietly.

Nigel stiffened. "She's *my* wife, Jamie. I ought to ask *you* that question." His eyes glanced meanfully up to Jamie's apartment.

"Come," his friend said gruffly, and after a moment Nigel followed.

As they entered the dimly lit sitting room a woman's voice called, "Jamie?" Was it Allegra? No, the voice was too weak, different. But perhaps, if she'd been asleep . . .

"Jamie, what the devil—"

"Please, my lord. Wait here a moment. There is someone I'm wantin' ye to meet."

Jamie went into the bedchamber and came back

promptly to usher Nigel inside. Nigel's eyes widened. The woman in the bed was not Allegra. She was older, her face sallow from illness, her hair dull and matted. But she had once been beautiful.

Nigel looked questioningly at Jamie, who stunned him by taking the woman's hand and saying, "My lord, this is Flora MacIntyre. My wife."

"Your *wife?*" Nigel's eyes flew to Jamie. "But when—I do not understand."

"Aye, 'tis a long story." Jamie sighed, and Nigel remembered his manners.

He greeted Flora belatedly. "You've been ill," he said. "Is there anything I can do for you? A doctor, medicines?"

Flora smiled wanly. "Ye're verra kind, my lord. But I vow I'm on the mend, much thanks to Jamie . . . and Lady Debenham."

Lady Debenham. Allegra. Oh my God, Nigel thought, unable to speak. For suddenly he understood everything. A "poor, wounded creature," Allegra had said. Flora MacIntyre, another one of her rescue missions. Why hadn't he guessed? Why hadn't—

"Why didn't Allegra tell me?" he finally rasped.

Jamie motioned him out of the bedchamber, closing the door behind them. "I—" Jamie ran his hand over his jaw, where a new beard was sprouting. "I am to blame, laddie. I—I didna want ye to ken."

"But why, Jamie?"

Jamie turned away. His voice came out in a mere whisper. "She was verra young when we wed and we were so poor. She ran away. I trailed her to . . . *Le Petite Maison.*" Nigel inhaled sharply and Jamie turned to him, eyes moist. "Aye, that evil place. They would no let me in and I—God help me—I thought she wanted to be there." Jamie put his fist to his mouth, obviously trying to control himself. His words were unsteady, his voice thick. "And I—I

374

left her there, laddie." He pounded the wall, his voice a cry. "For six years! I didna ken if she were alive or dead. I didna ken they held girls there by—by force."

"Until Katie," Nigel supplied softly, putting a comforting hand to his friend's shoulder.

"Aye. Until Katie."

"I would have helped you, Jamie. You must have known that."

"I couldna tell ye. I was so ashamed, laddie. There are certain things a man maun bear, and do, by himsel'. Surely ye ken that, laddie. Are there no things ye've ne'er spoken of?"

Nigel nodded, thinking of Gina, and dropped his hand. "I am ashamed now, Jamie, for what I said and thought. And I hit you. I'm—"

"What did ye do to yer wife, laddie?" Jamie asked quietly.

"I . . . banished her to Debenham, until the child is born."

"Child? She is to have a bairn?"

Nigel nodded bleakly. "Jamie, I told her I would not acknowledge the child, that it might be . . . anyone's."

"My lord, how could ye think such a thing of Lady Debenham?" Jamie's voice was gentle. "Do ye not ken how much she loves ye? I'm thinkin' ye confused her with Lord Charles's wife, or mayhap . . . Gina."

Nigel stared at his friend for an endless moment. Suddenly, it was as if some evil miasma that had been engulfing him were lifting. Like a disease it had invaded his mind and body until he had seen everything through the filter of Lucinda and Gina. He had never really seen Allegra for herself, for what she was. He had never given her a chance. And now he saw everything so clearly that he hated himself bitterly. All these weeks . . . he'd—he'd been so cold, and then last night . . .

"Dear God, Jamie! What have I done?" he cried raggedly.

He began to pace the room. "I've got to find her! It cannot be that difficult. She only has several hours' head start." He stopped abruptly. "Saddle my horse, while I go to Penderleigh House. Lady Penderleigh may know something. And then I'll go to Devon. Like as not she's gone to her sister."

"I'll go with ye."

"No! Flora needs you here."

"Then at the least let me check the postin' houses at the outskirts o' town. In case . . ."

"Yes," Nigel said heavily. "In case she's not gone to Devon."

He did not want to think of that possibility. But he knew he must face it. "Thank you, Jamie. Have my secretary make discreet inquiries as well."

"Aye, my lord. We'll find her. Dinna be losin' hope."

Nigel's eyes clouded over, and somehow, in the next moment, he and Jamie were clasping each other in a fierce bear hug.

And then he raced down the stairs and across the square. But Damon, having just come down to breakfast, had neither seen nor heard from Allegra. One look at Nigel's ravaged face had him sprinting abovestairs to wake his sleeping wife, but she knew nothing. Nigel asked his friends to send word if they heard anything and to put it about that he and Allegra had gone to the country for a while. And then, refusing all other offers of help, he rushed back home.

Kingston and Mrs. Thorpe between them had already packed his saddlebags. He bid a hasty farewell to Jamie and mounted his stallion. He would go alone. It was the fastest way, and as Jamie had said, there were some things a man must do by himself.

She was not at Meg's. Nigel could hardly credit it. He stared at John and Meg, fighting off panic as he assured them that Allegra would be fine. They'd merely had a little tiff and he'd have her home in a trice. They promised to send word if they heard anything, and Nigel set off immediately for Caulfield.

He doubted she'd be there. She could not have anticipated a warm reception from her father. But if not there, then . . .

Caulfield was furious. No, she was not here! No, he'd not heard a word! But when he did, he'd wring her damned neck! What did she think she was about, running away from her own husband? Hadn't she caused enough trouble?

"Caulfield, calm down," Nigel ordered softly, realizing that the baron's bluster masked his real concern for Allegra's safety. "She is not at fault. Allegra has been . . . has been all I could ask in a wife. The fault is mine, and I will find her."

Caulfield subsided, and looked at him a bit oddly, but he did not calm down until Mrs. Bridgebane entered his study. She poured both men a drink and sat down on the arm of Caulfield's chair. And that was when the baron announced his betrothal to Mrs. Bridgebane, his favorite chess partner.

Nigel smiled for the first time in two days. He partook of a light collation with them and took his leave shortly thereafter, for he did not want them to see his mounting despair.

Where had Allegra gone? Caulfield hadn't a clue, and at this point, neither had Nigel. And he wanted to go back to London straightaway to see if Jamie had had better luck. If not . . . if not he would comb the entire country if he had to! And meanwhile he would send a message to Deben Court. Surely she'd not gone there, but he must leave no stone unturned.

He had just turned into the lane leading out from the circular drive of Caulfield Manor when a youthful voice called his name. He pulled Mercutio to a halt and turned. Little Marcus, Allegra's climbing boy, was running toward him, and Nigel could see that the boy's face was streaked with tears.

"Where is she?" he cried. "Where is Miss Allegra? What's happened to her?"

Good God, Nigel thought. How had he found out so quickly? He vaulted off his stallion and, holding the reins, hunkered down near Marcus. "Nothing has happened to her, Marcus. She's gone off on holiday without me, you see, and I want to surprise her and find her before—before she comes home."

"Oh," Marcus sniffed back his tears. Nigel wondered if he was convinced.

"Would you take me with you? I could help you look!"

"Yes, I can see that you could, but you're rather big, you know, and I do not think Mercutio can carry both of us." Marcus looked crestfallen. "But Marcus, there is something you can do for me. Something important." The little boy's eyes widened. "If Allegra comes here, or if word comes that she's gone to Meg—er—Mrs. Dalton—at the vicarage—I want you to convey a message for me. Will you do that?"

Marcus nodded solemnly. "What shall I tell her, m'lord?"

"Tell her—" he paused, not having any idea of what he wanted to say. "Tell her that I . . . I love her . . . very much, and I want to come and take her home."

Marcus's eyes filled with tears again. "I'll tell her, m'lord," he said gravely. A minute later Nigel was back on his stallion, the little boy waving farewell. Perhaps, Nigel

378

mused, as he urged Mercutio to a canter, we'll send for Marcus when Allegra comes home. For, of course, she would. He would find her, no matter what it took.

Tell her I love her . . . He hadn't meant to say those words, had never, until the moment he'd uttered them, put words to his feelings, even in his mind. And now that he had, he whispered them into the air, and listened to them, and felt his heart fill with gladness. He loved her! He had fallen in love with his wife! Allegra, with her beautiful elfin face and her generous spirit and her innocent passion. She had been right about that special bond between them, but he had been afraid to see it. He was afraid no longer.

Oh, Allegra, he pleaded silently, come back to me so I can tell you, so I can make it up to you.

It had taken Nigel three days to make the journey to Devon and back. He had driven himself and his horse much too hard, but time was of the essence. With every day that passed, Allegra's trail grew colder.

And so he was bitterly disappointed to learn that Jamie had come up empty-handed. At none of the posting inns had anyone recalled two young women answering Allegra's and Katie's descriptions. Discreet inquiries about Town had revealed nothing. It was not possible! They could not have vanished into thin air!

It was very late, the night of Nigel's return. He and Jamie sat in the study of his London house, planning what to do next. Or rather, Jamie sat. Nigel paced. Tomorrow he would hire several Bow Street runners. One to make further inquiries here in Town, though he doubted she'd have stayed here, and the others to comb the countryside. Nigel, armed with a miniature the baron had given him, would do the same. Jamie would remain here, caring for

Flora and coordinating the search by receiving and dispatching messages.

It sounded like a most sensible plan, but Nigel was not feeling sensible just now. He was fighting down panic. And then a thought struck him, and his heart pounded in terror. What if they had stayed in London and had been . . . captured and dragged off to *Le Petite Maison,* or some equally vile place? He voiced his fear to Jamie, who gave him a drink and made him calm down. Katie knew the pitfalls of that place, he said, and would be on her guard. And those places preyed on poor, lone women, not well-dressed ladies with their maids.

And besides, Jamie did not think, any more than Nigel did, that they had stayed in London. Just in case though, Jamie would set one of the runners to finding out if Mrs. Graves had any new girls. Surely Bow Street had ways of ascertaining that, even if they had not the wherewithal to do aught about it.

With that Nigel had to be content.

It was well past midnight when Jamie retired to his apartment. They had talked further strategy and drunk brandy and then Jamie had told Nigel all about Flora. Nigel wished them happy. When all this was over he meant for them all to retire to Debenham for a long, quiet winter. Jamie would need a larger cottage, and Nigel and Allegra would refurbish the nursery.

When all this was over. When Allegra was home, where she belonged. He held her miniature in one hand and a half-full brandy snifter in the other. *Where are you, Allegra?* He would leave at first light, following a northerly course, but he had no notion if it would yield anything. He only knew he must try.

He'd gone to Allegra's rooms after his solitary dinner to search for any clues she may have left behind. He'd found none. He'd only learned that she'd taken a very practical wardrobe, her mother's pearls, and her quarterly allowance money. Thank God she'd taken that, and Katie. The thought of Allegra alone and without funds made him shudder with terror. But what protection, after all, was a girl younger than she? And what would happen when the funds ran out? Would she come home? Dear God, he hoped so. As it was, he had not slept in two nights and didn't expect he would tonight either.

She was out there somewhere. His wife and the child she carried. *His* child. He had driven her away, out of fear that she would leave him, betray him. The irony of it ate away at him.

He downed the brandy and refilled the snifter. He peered at the miniature of a slightly, younger Allegra with long hair, but the same deep brown eyes and pointed chin, the same gamin face, the same innocent sensuality. And for the first time since her disappearance, he allowed himself the luxury, and the pain, of remembering. The first time he'd seen her, rising in a dripping wet chemise from the pond at Caulfield . . . the kiss on the terrace in the rainstorm . . . making love in a moonlit chamber. Allegra, so warm and willing and passionate, always. Allegra, vehemently defending Katie, demanding that godawful sweeping machine, beseeching him to rebuild the chimneys.

And then other memories. The night when he'd accused her of tricking him into marriage . . . all those days when he'd barely spoken to her . . . the hateful accusations he'd hurled at her— He'd been cold, odious, brutal. What kind of bounder was he? How could he have treated her so? He slammed his glass down and buried his face in his hands. He knew how and he knew why. But the reasons did not exonerate him.

He lifted his head and picked up her miniature.

He remembered her first words to him, when he'd caught her out, swimming in that pond. Something like,

"Good heavens! No one *ever* comes here." And then a little later, when he accused her of inviting his kiss, "I was merely curious . . . for I do like men, you see. So different from my sex." The innocence and blatant sensuality had been a devastating combination, and that and her spirited conversation had made her irresistible.

And he remembered her last words to him. "I love you, Nigel. I have been a good wife to you." Spoken on a pitiful sob, until the last whispered, "I am not Gina. I am not Lucinda." She had lain huddled against the bed, vulnerable, defeated.

What had he done to her? What had happened to her spirit? Had he broken it completely? No, he told himself. She'd had enough spirit, enough courage, to leave. She was not broken.

He thought of all the weeks of their marriage. There had been so little banter, so little laughter between them. He had not allowed it. He had shown her anger, and she had responded with love. He had stomped on that love, broken it, abused it.

He remembered now something else she'd said that very first night. They'd been speaking of the ramshackle inn near Caulfield; she'd once run away and stayed there.

"And do you run away often?" he'd asked.

"No, my lord," she'd answered. "Only when necessary."

Only when necessary. He had made it necessary. And she had gone.

And what if—he paused, and took a healthy swig of his drink—what would happen if he found her, and she refused to come home? No! He would convince her of his love! They belonged together. They had made a child together. They would make a home together.

Tomorrow he would set off. Surely within a se'enight he would find her.

* * *

Nigel had been gone three weeks. It seemed as if he had traversed the length and breadth of England. And whatever parts he'd missed, the runners had covered. All to no avail. There was not a sign of Allegra and Katie. Oh, there had been leads, but they had been dead ends. Every trail was cold.

In desperation Nigel had gone to Debenham but, of course, Allegra had not been there. He had said naught to the staff beyond the fact that her ladyship was traveling and he thought she'd come to Debenham. Manners and Mrs. Helmsley drew their own conclusions, however, and they and the rest of the staff treated him to a cold civility for the short time of his stay. How had Allegra contrived to win them all over, even the formidable Mrs. Helmsley, in so short a time? By being herself, he thought, and he had been too blind to notice.

Despondent, he'd returned to London. He sent the runners back out again and told himself that he had got to attend to business matters. He could not neglect them. Allegra, he told himself, would be found, or would come home eventually. How could a woman fend for herself, especially in her condition? He tried to take hope from the one positive note, that his informants were certain Allegra and Katie had not, in fact, been apprehended by Mrs. Graves' cohorts and dragged off to *Le Petite Maison*. Still, he could not concentrate on business and he could not sleep at night. He found himself aimlessly walking the streets of London, staring into the faces of dark-haired women, hoping against hope that one would have dark eyes and a gamin face. But none did.

Damon came to visit and again offered his help, but of course, there was nothing he could do. Nigel canceled all social engagements, giving out that Allegra had gone to the country to rest and that he was merely attending to business. He made perfunctory visits to Custom House, but the problem of Roger and the Dorset smugglers seemed remote now.

Days turned into weeks. She'd been gone more than a month now. Nigel saw almost no one, not even going to his clubs. He and Jamie grew closer, and Flora was slowly regaining her health. He was happy for them, as he knew Allegra would have been.

Somehow, he got through the days, but the nights were sheer hell. If he slept at all, it was to dream of brown eyes and lips without any indentation in the top, and to reach out in a fever of desire, only to wake and find the place beside him empty and cold.

And he had only himself to blame.

Chapter Eighteen

"I am marble constant; now the fleeting moon
No planet is of mine."

Anthony and Cleopatra
William Shakespeare

Allegra had known from the time they set out where she meant to go. But she had no intention of being followed. And so she and Katie had donned oversized bonnets, hiding their hair, and had taken a most tiring, circuitous route. Katie had become Sarah, which was her middle name, and Allegra had, out of the blue, conjured the name Alicia Crane. The initials were the same as Allegra Caulfield. Most convenient since she still had her monogrammed handkerchiefs, and Alicia wasn't so far from Allegra as to be totally alien.

Mrs. Crane, poor bereaved widow of a soldier in His Majesty's cavalry, had engendered sympathy at every inn at which they stayed, and the fine quality of her wardrobe and the presence of her maid had engendered respect. The absence of mourning clothes was explained by her husband's dying wish that she not grieve overmuch for him, and the ready presence of tears quelled any doubts. The tears were not at all difficult to come by, for Allegra was, in truth, grieving, alive though her husband might be.

And all the ploys worked. They were not pursued, and after four exhaustive days of travel, they had reached their destination.

Cliff House. Nigel's summer home in Muddleford parish on the Dorset coast. He had only spoken of it briefly, had recounted some fond childhood memories and told her that the house was sadly neglected, with only an aging couple, the Crowleys, taking care of it. Allegra had manufactured an elaborate ruse to gain entrance to the house, but it proved completely unnecessary.

Mrs. Crowley, the housekeeper, was a small, bent, elderly lady with a kind smile. She took one look at Allegra, standing under the dilapidated portico in the late afternoon light, and clapped her gnarled hands together.

"Oh, my lady, you've finally come! Crowley and me, we been awaitin' you," she exclaimed in a rush. "And where might the earl be? Comin' in another carriage is he?" She ushered Allegra and a hovering Katie inside.

Allegra cast an alarmed glance at Katie. Katie's eyes widened in confusion and fright. Allegra cleared her throat. She would have to brazen it out. She hated to lie outright, but there really was no hope for it. "Ah, Mrs. Crowley, his lordship will not be coming. That is, you see, I am not—we . . ."

She paused as an elderly man shuffled into the entry lobby, his gait unsteady. "Crowley! Look who's come at last!" the housekeeper exclaimed, and her husband's face lit in a smile. He bowed so low that it was several moments before he was able to straighten up. He greeted "her ladyship" with slurred words and a puff of fumes that could only have come from a bottle of spirits, or several. As he came closer Allegra could see the bulbous redness of his nose, the red lines in his eyes. He was quite bosky, and she imagined it was not all that unusual.

"Fetch their bags, would you, Crowley, and see to the carriage," Mrs. Crowley went on, then turned to Allegra. "But where be the boys?"

"The boys?" Allegra echoed uncertainly.

"Oh, my little scamps! A-hidin' from Mrs. Crowley already, be they?" She giggled. "Well, I'll just let 'em get a whiff o' my gooseberry tart and they'll come round soon enough." What boys? Allegra wondered, exchanging a perplexed look with Katie. Crowley shuffled out in search of their portmanteaux and the nonexistent carriage, and his wife continued. "Roger keeps askin' 'bout Charlie and Nigel. He'll be glad to see 'em again. But come, my lady, 'tis plum fagged out you must be from your journey. A nice hot cup o' tea and a bath be what you'll be wantin,' just like allas."

Allegra's head was spinning when Mrs. Crowley finally paused for breath. Roger, Nigel, Charlie . . . She took a deep breath and grabbed Katie's hand to steady herself as realization slowly dawned. Charlie was Charles, Nigel's late brother. Roger was the friend he'd spoken of, the one with whom he and Charles used to play in the caves and the beach around Cliff House. Mrs. Crowley, poor dear, was assuming that Allegra was, indeed, Lady Debenham. But not Nigel's wife. Mrs. Crowley assumed she was Nigel's long dead *mother!* She allowed the housekeeper to lead her and Katie abovestairs, all the while debating what to say. It was quite convenient, actually, to be mistaken for the late countess, but Allegra's conscience would not allow her to contribute to Mrs. Crowley's delusions without at the least trying to correct her.

When Mrs. Crowley led them unerringly to the master suite, and "her ladyship's" lovely bedchamber, Allegra patiently explained that she was *not* her ladyship, but rather Alicia Crane, a cousin come to visit. But the housekeeper merely looked confused, even hurt, and a moment later was telling "her ladyship" to have a nice rest while Mrs. Crowley had some tea sent up. She welcomed the countess's new maid and seemed to accept the fact that the "boys" were not coming just yet. Mrs. Crowley was most disappointed but smiled and said she would just keep making her gooseberry tarts until the day her "scamps" came to eat them.

Allegra felt a lump in her throat. Moments later old Crowley came staggering into the master suite with their portmanteaux and bandboxes, and informed her "ladyship" that the carriage had been sent round to the stable yard, the horses seen to. Allegra did not trouble to tell him there *was* no carriage, that she and Katie had walked from where the stage had let them off. He would simply not have believed her. He bowed, asked whether she and his lordship would be entertaining and should he lay in a new stock of brandy.

Allegra shook her head and Crowley said, "Don't signify, your la'yship. Got a-plenty left since last time, I reckon. 'Tis port we're a-runnin' low on, but the gentlemen'll take care o' that, won't they, like they allas have. And there's gin aplenty, praise be. Allas favored gin, I did." He grinned, then blinked, recalling himself, and took off down the corridor, his legs wobbly and his mouth whistling an unrecognizable tune.

And so began Allegra's tenure at Cliff House. By the next day she knew that what she'd suspected was indeed true. Mrs. Crowley lived in her own world, some twenty years in the past, and her husband simply lived from gin bottle to gin bottle, paying heed to whatever his wife said. And yet they were rather devoted to each other, and even content in an odd sort of way. Allegra disliked intruding on them, hated deceiving them, yet soothed her conscience with the notion that the elderly couple was excessively pleased to have her there. And that she was, after all,

Lady Debenham. At least for now.

Mrs. Crowley spent hours in the ancient kitchens, began lifting holland covers from the public rooms, and prattled on about all the work her nonexistent staff was doing to ready the house for the arrival of the rest of the family. Old Crowley padded about the house with his workbox, making feeble attempts to repair broken door hinges, leaking ceilings and peeling wallpaper.

And Allegra, putting her guilt aside, realized that, the sadness and tragedy of it all notwithstanding, she could not have asked for a better circumstance. She and Katie had a roof over their heads, even if it did leak in more rooms than not. Their presence was accepted, not questioned, and there seemed to be plenty of food. The larder was kept very well stocked, for Mrs. Crowley always wanted to be ready for any unexpected family visits. From what Nigel had said, the last one was some years ago, but this seemed to trouble the housekeeper not one whit.

Apparently, Nigel sent Mrs. Crowley a regular allowance, which she used to lay in provisions. Allegra was concerned that the merchants that came would tumble to the fact that there was someone in residence, and start the neighborhood gossip mill turning. But Katie reported, when the butcher came, that he merely nodded understandingly as Mrs. Crowley prattled on about how her ladyship was in residence and his lordship and the boys were soon to come. Mrs. Crowley's order, more than enough for four people, did not faze the butcher in the least.

And so Allegra's presence at Cliff House went undetected in Muddleford parish. She and Katie kept to the house and the overgrown gardens, not even venturing down to the beach lest they be seen. Besides, the footpath to the beach looked steep and overgrown and Allegra, mindful of the child she carried, thought it prudent to stay away. The house was perched atop a cliff, and Allegra contented herself with the view from the house or garden parapet. She could see multicolored cliffs all around, gray and orange, like molten lava, fading into an exquisite shade of slate blue. Trees and shrubs grew riotously out of the cliffsides, and on the sandy beach just below the waves broke in a ceaseless rhythm.

Allegra knew that one day she might begin to feel confined, or bored, but for now, the peace and the solitude suited her admirably. She needed, more than anything, a time and place to heal, to come to terms with the end of her marriage. Thankfully, she had found that.

Days became weeks and she and Katie settled into a routine. In the mornings when Mrs. Crowley was occupied in the kitchen, they set themselves to cleaning various neglected rooms in the house. Allegra had never done such work before, but she needed something to do, and of a certain the house needed to be made more habitable. Each time a room was transformed from cobwebs and dust and mustiness to the smell of beeswax and the look of polished wood and gleaming chandeliers, Allegra felt a deep satisfaction. Mrs. Crowley was delighted, assuming that her "staff" had been busy, and Allegra and Katie were careful never to be caught at their task. For it would not do for a countess and a lady's maid to be dusting the furniture!

In the afternoon, Allegra preferred to be alone, sitting in the garden, even weeding some of the neglected flower beds, if the weather permitted, or tucked up next to a roaring fire in the library if it were raining or particularly chilly. She took a nap every day before tea, for she was still exceedingly tired, and she was still sick every morning in the basin, albeit not as violently so.

Outwardly, Allegra's life was calm, peaceful. Inwardly, she was fretful, her spirit churning as violently as the Dorset sea in a storm. Some days when the sea was choppy, she would stare at it from her bedchamber window, feeling at one with its incessant, restless churning.

She missed him so much, her husband, the father of the child he would never see. She missed him, grieved for him in her heart all day and ached for him with her body all night. She was losing weight, despite the babe, and there were hollows under her eyes attesting to all the sleepless nights. But she knew she had done what she had to do, and now she must wait for time and its natural healing process. She would never heal completely, never forget that glimpse of Heaven she had known so fleetingly with Nigel, perhaps never feel whole again. But at least she would have enough of herself and her spirit intact to continue her life.

She knew well that they could not stay here indefinitely, but it was perfect for now. Perhaps they could stay until the child was born. After that, she would see . . .

They had been at Cliff House for more than a month now. Allegra's dresses were growing tight on her; Katie had been letting out seams. There were subtle changes in her body, changes she had always imagined sharing with her husband. She brushed the thought, and accompanying tear, aside, as Katie selected a night rail for her to wear. It was a cold night; the sea was rough and she thought a storm was imminent.

She had always loved storms, but tonight she felt only restless, even agitated. Drawing on her wrapper and slippers, she made her way down to the kitchens for some warm milk. She found Katie there, also in her nightclothes. They fixed themselves glasses of milk and plates of gooseberry tart, of which there was an abundance, and settled down to a midnight repast.

And that was when they heard the noises. First a loud thud, and then a scraping sound, coming from belowstairs. And then what sounded like a man's voice, but which, Allegra decided, might well have been the wind. But there was no mistaking that thud, and now there was another. She and Katie exchanged looks.

"Crowley?" Allegra whispered, wondering if the old man were making a late-night foray into the wine cellar. But Katie reminded her that the wine cellar was far to the right of the noise. Still, it might well be Crowley, and since Allegra had never seen him sober, she worried that he might hurt himself stumbling about. She heard another sound, this time certain it was a man's voice. Was Crowley talking to himself, or was someone else there? And if not Crowley, then *who* was below this house?

She felt the first prickles of fear, and Katie's face mirrored her feelings. And she wondered just *what* was below the house. Katie told her that there was a stairwell in the back of the larger kitchen. Mrs. Crowley had said it led down to a storeroom of some kind. And somewhere beneath that must be the caves Nigel had played in as a child. The caves that had long since collapsed.

Allegra was concerned about Crowley, and she was most curious about what was going on. She would not be able to sleep at all until she found out. What if—what if there were strangers in the house? Nigel's house. She simply could not permit intruders. She must go down to investigate.

Katie was horrified at the notion, and did her best to dissuade her. "Why, you do not know *what* you will find, or who! You have no weapon and—and you are not even dressed, my lady!" she pointed out desperately.

Allegra had, in fact, overlooked the latter small point, and there was no time to change. "Fetch me my cloak, Katie. It will cover me enough for modesty's sake and keep me warm as well."

Katie looked most perturbed and still hesitated until Allegra assured her she would take a cast iron skillet for protection. Finally, seeing no choice, Katie went to do her bidding. She returned moments later, surprising Allegra by having brought *two* cloaks. "I'll not let you go down there alone, my lady," she said staunchly, and Allegra giggled conspiratorially as they fastened their cloaks and each took up a taper and skillet.

The door to the lower stairwell creaked and made them both jump. They left it open as they descended into the bowels of the house. The storeroom was dark and musty and curtained with cobwebs. It was a long, narrow, low-ceilinged room. Allegra heard a scurrying sound and swiftly moved her taper. Mice, she thought. There were definitely no men here. There were no thuds, no sound of voices. There were, however, innumerable cartons and kegs. They were unmarked, insofar as she could see. The kegs might hold brandy, but surely more than Cliff House would need were there parties every night! And what could be in the boxes?

Katie drew her attention to a partially opened carton. They nudged open one flap and Katie gasped. Even in the dim light they could see that it contained layers of fine French lace.

"My lady! What in the world can this mean?" Katie whispered.

Allegra was beginning to have a suspicion about just what it did mean, but it seemed too preposterous even to speak of. And then there came another thud and what sounded like a muffled curse. Katie jumped. Allegra realized that the voice was coming from directly below them. But as far as she knew, below them there were only rocks and water and the remnants of collapsed caves.

She must be wrong. There had to be a room below this. It was madness to try to find it, to investigate further. If the kegs and cartons here were any indication, she doubted it was Crowley down below. Still, how could she sleep not knowing who or what was under the house? Curiosity, Allegra knew, had always been one of her besetting sins. Now, as always, she gave in to it.

Slowly, a reluctant Katie several feet behind her, Allegra made her way to the rear of the storeroom, her eyes scanning the walls for a door that might lead them belowstairs. They wended their way between barrels and kegs and boxes, neither speaking as the noise from below grew louder.

And then everything happened at once. Allegra slipped, her right foot falling into what seemed like a deep hole in the floor. She screamed. Her taper fell, sputtering, and the skillet went flying as she tried to regain her balance. But there was nothing to grab on to. Katie hurried toward her, but she was too late. Allegra's left foot followed the right, and she tumbled down what seemed a dark bottomless pit.

Her back bumped painfully into something hard, but then the pain receded as sheer terror took its place. One large cold hand wrapped itself around her ankle and the other grabbed at her waist.

"What 'ave we 'ere, now? Looky 'ere, gov'nor, we got ourselves a wench!" shouted a harsh sinister voice as rough hands jostled her and pulled her down, down, down.

"Bates, what the devil are you—Good God!" exclaimed a second voice, smoother, more cultured.

The man called Bates finally let her go as her feet touched the ground. She could see him for the first time. He was large, unkempt, with a ruddy face and one front tooth missing. His expression was not pleasant.

Allegra backed away, drawing her cloak tighter around her. She realized that she had fallen through a trapdoor of sorts, banging her back against a wooden ladder. Hoping that Katie had enough sense to run back abovestairs, she ventured a glance at her surroundings. She knew straightaway that this must be one of the supposedly collapsed caves. The floor and walls were earthen and rocks protruded at odd intervals. Torches, propped on barrels and scattered about, burned brightly. Her scrutiny stopped as soon as she espied the other two occupants of the cave. The first one moved forward almost languidly.

"Well now, we had not been expecting company. Just *who* might you be, and more to the point, *how* did you get here?"

Allegra heard the steel beneath his mild voice, but she noted again the speech of a gentleman, saw the fine, chiseled features, pale blue eyes and blond hair. Though his clothes were as shabby looking as what the others wore, he hardly looked like a ruffian. She took courage from that and drew herself up. "I am Mrs. Alicia Crane, cousin of Lord Debenham. I am visiting at Cliff House. And now I might ask you the same. Who are *you* and what are *you* doing here? You are trespassing, you must know."

He grinned. It was a very engaging grin, which surprised her.

"Trespassing, am I? Well, Mrs. Alicia Crane, I—"

"Roger, there's another one!" broke in the third man from behind Roger.

Bates, the large man, started up the ladder.

"No! Don't hurt her!" Allegra blurted before she thought better of it.

"Easy, Bates," Roger commanded, and Allegra heard Bates telling Katie to come down or he'd drag her.

Moments later a shaking Katie stood beside Allegra. Bates leered at them and informed the others that the "wenches" wore only their nightclothes beneath their capes. Allegra could feel Katie shudder violently beside her. She put her arms about the younger girl and glared defiantly at Roger, who was regarding them pensively. The third man, called Alfie, was short and wiry and powerful looking. His hand hadn't moved away from the knife in his belt, and he looked decidedly piqued to have his business interrupted.

"Mayhap there be a third wench up there, gov'nor. One for each of us," Bates said, taking a step closer to Katie. Katie huddled against Allegra, terrified.

"They're not wenches, I'm afraid, Bates," Roger said easily. "They're ladies. Is that not so, Mrs. Alicia Crane?"

Allegra lifted her chin. "Yes. This is . . . Sarah, my maid. She is the daughter of a minister."

"Ah. Well, Bates, Alfie, I'm afraid there will be no sport tonight. Go on back to the others while I find out to what we owe the pleasure of this visit."

The others, Allegra thought. How many were there? Alfie grunted, finally taking his hand off the knife, and disappearing into the depths of the cave. Bates cast them both a malevolent look before he stormed off in Alfie's wake. Katie's shaking began to subside.

"Come now, Sarah, no one's going to hurt you," Roger said gently. Katie stood up straighter. "My name is Roger. Why don't you come and sit down?" Roger reached for Katie's hand. Katie flinched and jumped back.

Roger threw a questioning glance at Allegra, then stepped aside and indicated two barrels on which they could sit. When they had done so he dragged a third over, placing himself across from them.

"Now then," he began, "I am a patient man, but I'll tolerate no shilly-shallying. You know as well as I that this place is barely habitable. Lord Debenham hasn't set foot in it in years, neither have I, and there certainly have not been any visitors. According to village gossip, the Crowleys are in their dotage, and so I ask you again, Mrs. Alicia Crane, what are you doing here?" The way he said her name made Allegra wonder if he doubted it. He had not answered *her* questions, but she decided it would be the better part of valor to answer first. She heard the rumble of a number of voices in the depths of the cave and knew she had got to talk fast.

"I am aware of all that," she said, and launched into the story she had never gotten to tell Mrs. Crowley. "Lord Debenham had always said, years ago, that I was welcome to visit here at any time. And when I lost my husband so recently—he was a soldier, you must know—well, I came home from the Continent and had no place to stay. So I came here, just for a while, until I could decide where to go and—and what to do with my life." That latter, at the least, was true. Allegra decided that she did not care for all this dissembling at all, but what choice had she?

Roger's eyes flitted from her to Katie and back again. "And when you saw the state of things here, why did you not go on to Debenham? Surely you would have been welcomed there as well, and a good deal more comfortable."

Allegra had been prepared for such a question. "I do not want my—my cousin to know I am here. I know he would welcome me, but he is newly wed, and I—I do not wish to intrude."

Roger's blond eyebrows rose. "Nigel is wed?"

"Yes, he—oh! Why, you're *Roger!*"

He blinked, bemused. "Yes, I thought we'd established that."

"No! I mean, you are Nigel's Roger! Nigel—er—Lord Debenham—used to talk about you."

Roger tensed. "What did he say?"

Allegra reminded herself that she hadn't seen her "cousin" in some years. "Only that you were friends as children, you and he and Charles, and that he saw little of you in recent years."

Roger nodded, relaxing. "I've often regretted that, but—well—it could not be helped." He frowned. "You two present me with quite a problem, you know. I cannot sim-

397

ply allow you to go back abovestairs having seen what you have." Allegra heard Katie's sharp intake of breath and decided once again, that the best defense was a good offense.

"And you, sir, present a problem to me. You have not answered *my* questions, have you?"

Roger arched a brow, then nodded slightly. "Like you, I was issued a blanket invitation by Nigel to make use of Cliff House whenever I pleased."

"I hardly think he had this—er—part of the house in mind." Roger chuckled, and Allegra found it very difficult to be frightened of him, but instinct told her he would be ruthless when necessary. Nonetheless, she went on, deciding that conversation might in some way distract him. "At all events, I thought the caves had collapsed."

"Most had. Not all. Part of this was intact. The rest we dug out." He leaned forward. "You see, Mrs. Crane, this cave is very important to my work, and my work is very important to me. And you, and little Sarah here, have gotten in my way." Now Allegra heard the ruthlessness and scoured her mind for a denial, a way out of this predicament.

"Almost time, Boss," called Alfie, emerging from the shadows. "I reckon the lugger'll be here soon." He pointed his finger. "What's to do with them?"

Roger sighed and rose. "Tie them up for now. I'll decide when the run is completed."

Katie moaned and Allegra saw that she had gone completely white. "No! Wait!" Allegra heard herself say. "I—I have a better idea." She jumped up. Alfie glowered at her but Roger's attention was focused on Katie. He drew a flask from his hip pocket. "Drink this," he said gruffly, proffering it to Katie, who hesitated. "The finest French brandy, little Sarah. Come now, drink up." His voice was so soft, his expression so concerned, that when Katie glanced at Allegra, she nodded almost imperceptibly.

Katie coughed as the liquid went down, but at Roger's insistence took another swig, and her color began to return.

Roger turned his attention back to Allegra. "I do not wish to hurt you and I regret that I cannot let you go, but you must of a certain have divined my business by now."

Katie shook her head but Allegra knew it was useless to dissemble. Roger motioned to Alfie, who produced a length of rope.

"You are right, of course," Allegra said quickly. "I *have* guessed. And that is what gave me my idea. We — we could help you, Sarah and I. And then we would be unable to report you, as we too would be implicated. Can you not use extra hands, or — or a place within the house itself to hide some of the — the goods, or yourselves?"

Alfie cursed, admonishing Roger not to listen to her.

Roger and Katie both stared at her openmouthed. Finally Roger found his voice. "I am to believe, Mrs. Crane, that you, a bereaved widow and cousin to an earl, and your maid, daughter of a *minister*, want to join a smugglers' gang? Surely you jest."

"Not at all. After all, you, friend to an earl, seem to have no problem with it, and I suspect we share a common motive. You see, I find myself quite with pockets to let, and no ready way to remedy that situation. I don't fancy becoming some dowager's companion you must know, nor some gentleman's mistress. So you see," she concluded, warming to her own notion, "smuggling will suit me admirably!"

"My lad — Mrs. Crane!" exclaimed Katie, horrified.

Roger began to pace, while Alfie kept telling him he was daft to consider it. Bates returned to remind Roger that women were good for only one thing, and that when they'd finished with these two they ought to take them aboard the cutter and feed them to the sharks, and Katie reached once more for the brandy flask.

Alfie suggested he tie them up after all, and Bates reminded Alfie it was high time he crawled through the tunnel to the lookout, almost time for the signal from the lugger. The men were itching to take their places on the beach, and with a storm brewing and the preventative men so vigilant lately, time was of the essence.

Alfie grumbled something about it being high time they enlarged the lookout tunnel so someone else could crawl through it for a change, and that was when Katie shocked them all. She stood and spoke for the first time, her soft voice interrupting all the harsh masculine ones.

"I—I could crawl through the t-tunnel," she stammered.

The men fell silent, staring at her. She repeated her suggestion, adding that she had excellent vision and would follow directions precisely. And Allegra, after her initial shock at Katie's pronouncement wore off, ventured that she could sort merchandise or help them conceal it or load packhorses or whatever else was required. And she reminded Roger that he would be able to use the house itself when necessary, whether for storage or to sit in the drawing room claiming to be paying Mrs. Crane a visit should the Revenue come calling. For good measure she added that Mrs. Crowley would adore seeing him, even though the poor dear might mistake him for a very young "scamp," and that she made gooseberry tarts for him every day.

Allegra never knew if it was her offer of help, or the mention of Mrs. Crowley and her gooseberry tarts, or Katie's face, her eyes frightened but her chin held bravely, resolutely high, that did it. But Roger acquiesced and by the end of the night, Allegra and Katie had become part of the Muddleford smugglers' gang.

Alfie volunteered to take Katie through the tunnel and teach her how to receive and transmit the signal from the smuggling vessel. Katie stiffened, her face registering panic. Allegra reached for her hand, but it was Roger who soothed her.

He came to stand before her, his blond head just inches away from hers. "No harm will come to you, little Sarah. Alfie will see to that." He swiveled his head to Alfie. "Is that not right, Alfie?"

"Yeah, that's right, Boss. Now can we be goin'? 'Tis gettin' late," Alfie replied impatiently.

Sarah smiled tentatively at Roger and followed Alfie without a backward glance. And Allegra marveled at Katie's bravery, and felt a pang of guilt. Katie was doing this for her. She was here because of her. Whatever had she gotten them into?

Telling herself they'd had little choice, she turned her attention to the instructions Roger was now firing at her. She was put to sorting cargo so the men could load it onto packhorses that would make their way into the village, or onto wagons that would take the goods—brandy and tea and silks and spices—into the cave. From there the cargo gradually made its way to the storeroom and out a side door Allegra had not known existed.

The skies had let loose not long after the lugger had anchored and sent off her tugboats, and by the time they were done for the night they were all quite drenched. But Allegra did not mind. She and Katie had saved themselves from an unknown but surely most unpleasant fate, and they had found a way to earn money that they would need quite desperately later on.

She knew they could not do this for long, of a certain not once her condition became obvious, but for now she felt exhilarated. And though she knew there was danger inherent in this less than honorable profession, she had seen no evidence of it this night. And Roger, as the leader, or venturer, of the gang, obviously planned carefully and took no unnecessary chances. As to the dishonorable nature of the work, Allegra soothed her conscience with what she'd seen of the men on the beach. Most of them, with the notable exception of Bates, seemed to be solid working men who needed to feed their families. They were not hurting anyone, not defrauding anyone but the government. She supposed it was wrong, but found it hard to condemn them. And now she was one of them.

The next days passed swiftly, Allegra and Katie taking long naps so they might be awake for the night's work. There was something to do almost every night. If not a beach landing then sorting and moving the kegs and cartons of dry goods abovestairs, even into the house itself, until they could be spirited away to their final destinations. Of that part of the operation Allegra knew little and Roger refused to discuss it, claiming that the less she knew, the better. Allegra was inclined to agree with him.

If Allegra was rather pleased with herself for adapting so well to her new life, she was thoroughly amazed at Katie. Except for the few times when a woman or two joined them on the beach, they were almost exclusively in the company of men. And yet, with the exception of Bates, who would make any woman uneasy, Katie moved among them fairly comfortably. The reason was very simple: Roger. Though he frequently cast mooncalf eyes at Allegra, which made her most uneasy, he had set himself up as Katie's protector. He made clear to the others that both she and Katie were off limits, but he treated Katie with a gentleness usually reserved for skittish horses. He was careful, at first, not to touch her, even in the most casual ways. He called her "little Sarah" and more than once coaxed a smile out of her.

Several times, after the first few nights, Allegra saw Roger put a friendly hand to her shoulder, or pat her cheek in approval, and Katie did not flinch. Katie, whether she knew it or not, was becoming smitten. During the days she talked of "Roger this and Roger that." And at night her eyes followed him about the cave.

They often talked while they worked, Allegra, Katie and Roger, with Alfie sometimes joining in. Bates remained aloof. Allegra learned that Roger was quite successful at this smuggling business and had been doing it for years, although he used Cliff House only intermittently. A short while ago he'd been using the beach of a large manor house belonging to another peer. Alfie let slip one night that it was Creeve Hall, seat of the Viscount Creeve!

Allegra was astonished and wondered if Creeve was aware of the use to which his beach was put. Clearly Nigel was not aware that Roger was here at Cliff House. But when she questioned Roger about Creeve, careful not to mention having met him, he turned taciturn. She did learn, as the days went on, that he fully intended to return to Creeve Hall one day soon. He spoke of unfinished business there, and seemed quite driven about it, though he vouchsafed no details. Katie expressed her concern one night about the dangers inherent in his chosen occupation and asked if he ever thought of giving it up.

Allegra expected him to clam up as he often did when he wished to avoid a discussion. But instead he'd smiled and said cryptically, "Yes, I mean to stop when my business is finished. It will not be long now, I think."

With that Katie had to be content, but Allegra knew she was somewhat relieved.

There were several other subjects Roger avoided. One was where he lived and another was his parentage. Roger had long since taken to addressing her as "Alicia," Mrs. Crane being absurdly formal for their current situation. But he had always been simply Roger, and one night she asked him what his surname was. His face hardened. "Everyone simply calls me Roger," he said brusquely. "My father did not see fit to give me his name."

There was a wealth of bitterness in his tone. Allegra glanced at Katie and knew she had caught it, too. So, thought Allegra, this explained a great deal. Why a man who spoke and acted like a gentleman lived the clandestine life of a smuggler. Why Roger seemed to drift in and out of Nigel's life. He was undoubtedly the natural son of a highborn father and a common mother. She supposed such things happened all the time. Perhaps his mother had been a maid in a great house. Would that explain his affinity for Katie?

Then she thought about Katie. Katie and Roger. Roger, whose birth would make him forever an outcast in polite society, yet would ensure he never quite fit in with the lower orders. Katie, whose horrid experience had put her beyond the pale, yet who was not meant to spend her life as a lady's maid. Clearly Allegra had got to do something about those two. Roger had taken to acting like a big brother with Katie, and casting looks that were far too intense, far too full of masculine interest, at Allegra. Somehow she had got to convince Roger that his regard was misdirected.

A little voice at the back of her head told her that she was meddling again. But how could she not? she asked herself. Besides, this time Nigel was not here to be hurt by it.

Nigel. It had been more than six weeks since she'd seen him, more than a fortnight since she'd become involved in this smuggling business. Sometimes, especially at night when she was busy in the cave or on the beach, she was able to pass several hours without thinking of him. But during the lazy afternoons, and most especially in the early hours of dawn, his image haunted her and she knew the ache had not lessened with the passing weeks.

The child in her grew and she hoped it would be a boy

with green eyes and dark brown hair and brows that arched into "V's" when he was angry or laughing. At the least that way she would have a little bit of Nigel with her for all of her days.

And in the meantime she tried to occupy her thoughts with finding ways to bring Roger and Katie together. Her first opportunity came one night when they'd had a dreadful scare on the beach. Someone had thought he'd espied a riding officer on a nearby cliff, and they'd all run for cover in the shrubs and crags of the cliff. There had been no time to reach the cave. Unfortunately, Allegra had become separated from Katie, had instead ended up in a small aperture at the base of the cliff with . . . Roger. The lugger was already approaching shore; there was no way to warn the captain. They sat tensely, waiting for the thunder of hoofbeats that would bring the preventative men swooping down on them. Minutes went by; the only sounds she heard were their thumping heartbeats. More time. Probably one half hour. She felt Roger begin to relax.

"Probably a false alarm," he murmured, and Allegra sighed in relief.

She knew, however, that they had got to stay hidden awhile longer. That was when Roger leaned close to her and ran a finger lightly over her lips.

"Alicia," he whispered, "you must know how I admire you, your spirit, your courage, your beauty. I mean no disrespect. Please believe me." He put his hands to her shoulders and she knew he was about to kiss her.

"Roger, please, I—I do like you exceedingly well, and you are a most attractive man. But I gave my heart a long time ago, and I no longer have a whole heart to give."

"But he is gone!"

"I know. It . . . doesn't seem to make a difference." Slowly he slid his hands from her shoulders. She could feel his disappointment, although he said nothing. "Roger, you do not want a woman who dreams of another man." He turned away and she continued. "I am persuaded that one day you will find someone who will have a most tender regard for you, who will look upon you as her hero."

"Smugglers do not make good heros, I fear, my dear Alicia."

"I think you would be surprised," she replied.

And soon after that Roger decided that they had waited long enough. There was no riding officer and the operation proceeded as planned.

After that night Roger was more reticent with Allegra, although he still looked at her with eyes too intense to suit her. She tried to find ways to maneuver him and Katie together, but was not successful until several nights after the false alarm. She had claimed the need of an extra shawl and had gone abovestairs before Katie could volunteer to fetch it for her. When Allegra returned to the storeroom, she stood near the trapdoor and could overhear Katie and Roger just below. She eavesdropped shamelessly.

"But you *have* enough funds already, Roger. You have told me that. You have enough to buy a small place of your own, to make a life for yourself. Why do you continue flirting with such danger?" Katie pleaded.

"You do not understand such things, little Sarah. There are certain things a man must do in this life. Certain wrongs he must right. I am doing it the only way I know how." Allegra heard the hard edge to Roger's voice. Apparently Katie did as well.

"I hear the anger, even hatred, in your voice, Roger. You are on some kind of crusade, perhaps for vengeance. I do not know, but I know it is wrong to live with such hatred inside you."

"Sweet Sarah, you do not know the evil that there is in the world. You—"

"You think I do not know evil?" she cried. "Roger, I am

406

sixteen years old. I have seen more evil than most women see in a lifetime. But I have also seen goodness. Lad—ah—Mrs. Crane has shown it to me. It is all around, if one only knows where to look, or how to grab onto it when it appears. It does not make the evil go away, but reduces it so that it does not destroy one."

"Ah, little Sarah," Roger said regretfully, "you almost make me believe. Almost."

Perhaps, Allegra thought, there was hope for these two. Perhaps, in the end, whatever demons that drove Roger would not keep him from Katie, as Nigel's had kept him from her. "Almost," Roger had said. There was hope.

Seven weeks. Nigel stared at the calendar. It was the end of October. Allegra had been gone for seven weeks, and with her departure all the light had gone out of his life. How could he have been so blind, so stupid, so cruel? He poked mercilessly at the logs in the grate, venting his anger and self-hatred, knowing that he had got to stop berating himself every hour. He had got to stop living in some black limbo. He had got to face the fact that it was no longer a question of *when* Allegra returned, but *if* she returned. He had runners and agents combing the country. He'd even sent a man to Scotland and one to France. He would never give up. But he had got to forge ahead with his life.

He'd made an attempt to be sociable last week when the Duke of Marchmaine had come to call. Adam had explained that he'd heard the *ondits* about Allegra having gone to Debenham. But the timing of her journey, Nigel's continued absence from all social engagements, and Damon's obvious discomfort in speaking of it sparked his concern. Several times he'd called on Nigel and found him gone. And so here he was, finally having run him to ground in his library one gloomy afternoon.

Nigel had poured them each a brandy and they settled down in adjacent leather chairs before the fire. When Allegra had gone it hadn't been cold enough to warrant a fire. Now the air was crisp, even cold, the trees going bare. Just like his soul, he thought morosely, cold and bare.

Adam's voice snapped him out of his reverie. His friend was expressing his concern, careful not to pry. Adam was not stupid; he knew something was wrong. Nigel had been avoiding his friends. He looked like hell; he never went out. And suddenly Nigel longed to talk to someone, besides Jamie. Adam had been a friend since boyhood. They were of the same class, had gone to school together. Nigel had, of course, spoken to Damon several times, but he and Pen had since gone back to Lancashire.

Nigel stared at his friend, at the sharply defined cheekbones and intense tawny eyes. "She is not at Debenham," he said at length.

"Not at—but then where is she?"

Nigel sighed and put his glass down. He leaned forward, hands clasped between his knees. "The morning after the Embers's ball, she—she ran away. I have not seen her since."

"What? But surely—"

"I've been the length and breadth of Britain, Adam. Even now I have agents combing the countryside." He pounded the arm of his chair with his fist. "Dammit, Adam, 'tis like she's disappeared into thin air, and I cannot find her!"

"But I do not understand? Why would she—"

"Because I behaved like a first-class bounder," Nigel said bitterly. "I said things to her that—that are unforgivable. I was crazed with jealousy. Every time I saw her with Lattimer, even with you—"

"With *me!* How could you—"

"I told you I behaved like a prize idiot. And it—it got worse. Much worse. In truth, I do not blame her for leaving." He gulped his brandy. "Adam," he said desperately, "what will I do if I never find her? It's been some six weeks."

"Nigel, for whatever 'tis worth, I think she'll come home, eventually."

"What makes you think that?" Nigel's voice was gloomy.

"She loves you."

"Past tense, Adam. I—how do *you* know that?"

Adam shrugged. " 'Twas plain as pikestaff the night of that ball. I do not think I have ever seen a woman look at a man the way she looked at you. I wondered at the time if you knew how fortunate you were." Nigel arched a brow in question. Adam sighed. "She also looked most . . . overset. You were—er—dancing with Barbara Lacey at the time."

"Christ!" muttered Nigel, and took another drink. "There was nothing in that. I just—oh, hellfire! I've got to find her, Adam! She will not return on her own, made that clear in her letter. She even suggested I get a bill of divorcement, for God sakes, despite . . ."

"Despite?" Adam prompted.

Nigel turned ravaged eyes to his friend, "She is with child."

There was a shocked silence and then, "Dear God. But surely that is all the more reason for her to come home."

Nigel shook his head desolately. He could not tell Adam that that was precisely why she would *not* come home. He could never bring himself to repeat the terrible words he'd said to her that first night. Instead he drained his glass and shifted the subject, asking Adam about his family, and the great Elizabethan pile, Damerest Hall, that was his seat in Yorkshire.

"My mother is her usual, indomitable self. She's in

409

France now, intimidating the Parisians, I make no doubt." Nigel chuckled and Adam went on to speak of his "baby" sister, who was expecting *her* first baby soon.

"Now tell me about Damerest Hall, Adam," Nigel requested after he'd refilled their glasses. "Which wing are you rebuilding this year?"

Adam grinned. "Probably the south. I'll work on the plans over the winter."

"You know, Adam, one day you'll finish Damerest Hall and it will be time to turn your prodigious talents elsewhere." Adam started to shake his head. "You're a brilliant architect, Adam. You should be rebuilding half of London."

An odd expression crossed Adam's tawny eyes, reflecting pain, and anger, and something else. "Fustian, old chap," Adam said lightly, "I merely amuse myself with my little drawings."

Nigel looked at him quizzically, wondering why he belittled his talent, but he accepted Adam's subsequent shift of subject. Every man, he supposed, had his demons.

Nigel had enjoyed Adam's visit, but now, a se'ennight later, he was still not ready to go about in society, or even to make an appearance at his club. His bride had been gone seven weeks. How could he explain it? And how could he be charming and sociable when part of him was dying inside each day? No, he did not wish for society, and yet he would not take himself north to Debenham, for he could better coordinate the search efforts from Town.

He did, however, begin visiting Custom House more regularly, and one day learned that Creeve had gone to Dorset. Apparently word had filtered out that a major run of goods was due. Nigel knew he had ought to follow; it was high time he began doing some of his own investigating there. But somehow he could not bring himself to go just yet.

At loose ends, fighting despair by day and by night, he found himself spending increasingly more time with Jamie and Flora. Flora was able to walk about a bit now, and sometimes in the evenings she would join Jamie and Nigel in the setting room of Jamie's apartment. She never spoke of Mrs. Graves's infamous establishment, never spoke of the life she'd led. But one night they somehow began speaking of Allegra, and the way she'd rescued Katie. Suddenly Flora leaned forward and said, "My lord, 'tis a terrible place, *Le Petite Maison*, full of evil. The girls so young, little more than bairns—" She paused, her voice growing thick, and finished in an angry whisper. "Mrs. Graves should be made to swing at Tyburn! Isna there a way to stop her?"

Nigel knew it had taken a great deal of courage for Flora to speak so. He answered carefully. "In truth I should like nothing better, Flora. But there are others involved. Men who, I suspect, are highly placed in society. Their identity is a closely guarded secret, and unless we know who they are . . ."

He let his voice trail off and watched Flora's face. It darkened with emotion and her eyes clouded over. She seemed to retreat into a world of her own, a world of pain. When she spoke her voice was ragged. "I overheard many conversations, especially when I took ill, ye ken, and people stood at the bedside and thought I couldna hear. Mrs. Graves has a—a partner. I allas thought he was a customer, but 'tisna so. He—he was one of the worst. He liked the wee girls, the youngest, ye ken?" Her voice broke on a sob. She put her face in her hands and began to weep.

Jamie put his arms about her and drew her close and Nigel, feeling guilty for pressing her but knowing he had got to, asked, "What was his name, Flora?"

" 'Tis a peer o' the realm, my lord. Mayhap ye dinna

want to ken."

"I want to know, Flora. He must be stopped."

" 'Tis—'tis the Viscount Creeve, my lord. The devil incarnate hissel'!"

Chapter Nineteen

"Hast thou not dropp'd from heaven?
Out of the moon, I do assure thee."

> *The Tempest*
> William Shakespeare

Creeve, Nigel thought, pacing the floor of his study. He was shocked, sickened, and yet he was not shocked at all. He'd always known there was something not quite right about Creeve. That the blackguard should commit such heinous crimes was bad enough, but that he should remain unscathed, be admitted to the highest levels of society, was not to be born. Something had to be done.

This, at the least, explained why Creeve spent so much time in London while ostensibly searching for Dorset smugglers. Dorset! Nigel stopped short and sank down into his leather chair. Hadn't the Customs officials told him Creeve had recently gone to Dorset? That a large haul was expected? Had Creeve decided to make his move? And just what *was* it he meant to do?

What *was* at the root of his zealous pursuit of the smugglers of Muddleford parish in Dorset? Was he himself involved and wanting to deflect the blame? No. He didn't see Creeve as a "gentleman of the night" and besides, it seemed he had another, far more villainous source of income.

Creeve had been embarrassed and enraged at the use of his beach by the smuggling gang. But even that did not seem enough to justify a veritable personal crusade, or vendetta. And that thought brought Nigel round to Roger. *Was* he involved with the smuggling at Muddleford? Had he deliberately chosen Creeve Hall to embarrass the viscount? If there was a vendetta, whose was it? Nigel had never forgotten Roger's youthful vow of vengeance. Did Creeve know of it? Had the smuggling "war" simply become the battleground for their far more personal battle?

Nigel did not know. It was all conjecture. What he did know was that Creeve was evil, ruthless, without conscience. Roger had a conscience, and therefore he would be the one in danger. If Creeve saw him as a threat . . . Nigel must go to Dorset. If Roger was there he must warn him, protect him in some way. And when the matter of the smuggling was dispatched to Nigel's satisfaction, it would be time to convey Creeve to London, to face the magistrates and what would undoubtedly be a host of young accusers.

He strode abovestairs to his chambers and rang for Kingston, instructing his man that he wished to leave on the morrow, straightaway after breakfast. That would give him time to give Jamie instructions for—he paused abruptly in the act of removing his coat. He had forgotten for perhaps an hour his overriding preoccupation of finding Allegra. How could he leave—no, he told himself. He *must* go to Dorset. And, in truth, Jamie could coordinate search efforts in his stead. Nigel knew that Allegra would be in his heart every moment, but he had got to resume some semblance of his life. It was time.

And it was time for something else as well. He had avoided Cliff House for years now, telling himself he was too occupied with his other pursuits, his other holdings. But, in truth, he had not wanted to face the memories that he knew would assail him there. Memories of Charles and Roger and himself in happier, carefree days, before Charles's violent plunge into a ravine and Roger's plunge into the smugglers' murky netherworld.

It was time to return. It was time to remember and to put the memories to rest. He felt up to the task now. Was it because he had memories far more devastating, far more personal, tearing at his heartstrings now?

There was a mounting excitement in the cave beneath Cliff House. They hadn't had a haul in days, but Allegra knew there would be one soon. A very big one. Roger did not talk about his business directly, but from the bits and pieces he and the others let fall, Allegra and Katie had learned that he ran a fairly large and very successful operation. That did not, however, diminish the danger. If anything it increased it. The preventative men were watching this part of the coast carefully, had been ever since Creeve Hall. Allegra wondered at Roger's daring at having used the beach there, but Roger would not speak of it. It was from one of his men that she learned he meant to shift operations back to Creeve Hall sometime after leaving Cliff House.

He did reveal that once the large run was completed, they would all have enough money to lay low for a while. He had already paid Allegra and Katie a goodly sum for their part in the work and assured them they would be well rewarded for this next haul. But he made it clear that after this they were well out of it. Allegra wanted to protest, but knew it was best this way. Her pregnancy was still not visible to any but the sharpest eyes, and while she was still queasy at the oddest hours, she was no longer sick in the mornings. But she was increasingly more tired and she knew well that scrambling over sand dunes and pushing brandy kegs about was no proper pastime for a woman in her condition. If Nigel knew he'd— No! What Nigel thought, what he would do, did not signify. She had *got* to remember that!

So Allegra vouchsafed no protest, but Katie did, surprising everyone. Allegra realized, however, that it was not for love of the "gentlemen's" trade. It was, Allegra guessed, for love of one particular "gentleman." For days on end Allegra had watched Katie watching Roger, her heart in her eyes. And Roger, blind fool that he was, still treated Katie like a fragile little sister, still regarded Allegra with eyes far too warm. But Allegra took hope from the fact that twice he'd seen Katie try to lift a carton far too big for her and had rushed to grab it away from her. He'd scolded gently and the second time had brushed Katie's silky blond hair from her face. Katie had smiled tremulously and Roger had merely stood there, staring.

But tonight Katie was off somewhere and Roger had run Allegra to ground amid boxes of contraband tea. She tried to move away but he clamped a hand to her wrist and urged her to set down on one of the cartons. He did the same, keeping her hand in his. His hand was warm, but it did not warm her. Despite his nefarious profession, she thought him a good man, a man who would protect a woman to the death. She could never be that woman.

"Alicia," he began in a low voice, "the lugger is coming in tomorrow night. Our largest haul yet. There is a storm brewing, which is all to the good. But after this, we'll be leaving here. It will not be safe any longer. As it is—well, I suspect we are being watched. We've put the word out in the taverns that the run is two nights hence."

"And after this run, will you give it up, Roger?"

He looked away. "I cannot. Not yet. We will be going

somewhere else. I have to finish what I started. 'Tis an old score I must settle."

"Creeve Hall," Allegra said accusatorily. Roger's head whipped around.

"How did you—"

"The men talk." Roger looked fierce and Allegra shook her head. "It doesn't signify, Roger. I shan't breathe a word. And you know perfectly well Katie and I never venture forth into the village. But Roger—think! Creeve Hall! I have met—ah—people who know the viscount. They say he is not the most pleasant of men. He will not take kindly—"

"Alicia, it is better that you not know any more than you do. There is . . . old business between Creeve and me, and it is time to settle it. But promise me you will not tell Sarah aught of this. I—I do not want her to worry, or worse, to come looking for me. She seems to have taken to this free trade business a bit too well and—"

"Roger," Allegra interrupted, firmly pulling her hand from his, "do you not see? It is not smuggling that Ka— Sarah has taken to. It is one—"

"Alicia, will you wait for me here, in the house? When next I come, it will be through the front door."

Allegra sighed inwardly and said the only thing she could. "Sarah and I will wait for you, Roger." After all, she told herself, Katie would not want to leave, and she herself had nowhere else to go.

It had taken Nigel a day and a half to reach this particular fork in the road. For the last half hour he'd been able to see glimpses of the blue channel as he rode Mercutio closer and closer to Cliff House. And now he stood, mounted, at the fork. Muddleford Church was straight ahead. Cliff House, and the sea, lay to the right. To the

417

left lay whitewashed cottages, dappled woods, and the residence of the Chief Riding Officer of Muddleford. Almost of his own volition, Mercutio turned left. Perhaps he knew that his master was not quite ready to face a dilapidated house with its dotty housekeeper and myriad memories. Not just yet.

Chief Riding Officer J. R. Mulgrew had been at Muddleford for three years now. Nigel had never met him but knew him by reputation with the Custom Board in London to be typical of his ilk. That is, he was reasonably honest and unreasonably ambitious.

He was shown by a housekeeper into Mulgrew's study. His host was a man of medium height, middle years, salt and pepper hair and a weathered face. His smile was ready but his gray eyes were shrewd and calculating. He was deferential without being obsequious. A few minutes of conversation with the man convinced Nigel that personal ambition, and not duty was, in fact, the overriding concern of J. R. Mulgrew. But then he cautioned himself not to judge too harshly. Mulgrew's position was unenviable, his job thankless. If he did not show sufficient diligence in the pursuit of smugglers he was chastised, if not dismissed, by his superiors. And if he *did*, he was hated by his neighbors.

What Nigel could not understand, as they sipped glasses of noncontraband Madeira, was Mulgrew's obvious discomposure at finding the earl on his doorstep. The London office had sent word sometime ago that Lord Debenham meant to pay a visit to Dorset, so his appearance could not be a surprise. And he would have expected Mulgrew to be happily cogitating on ways to use the earl's obvious interest in his work to his advantage.

Instead J. R. Mulgrew was visibly squirming in his seat. When Nigel made it clear that he wanted to work with the Revenue men, Mulgrew finally steeled himself to speak.

"Fact of the matter is, m'lord, begging yer pardon, that you've come at a deuced awkward time." Nigel arched a brow. Mulgrew drained his glass and went doggedly on. "We've been on the trail of the Muddleford gang for months now. Well, I warrant you heard about the commotion up at Creeve Hall. And then with Lord Creeve kickin' up such a riot and a rumpus— Oh! Meanin' no disrespect, m'lord, but—"

"Never mind, Mulgrew. Go on."

"Well, 'course the gang lay low after that for more'n one fortnight, and when they started up again—well, 'tis very cagey they been. 'Tweren't easy figurin' their new base. But now I have and we're ready to move. They're expectin' a large haul tomorrow night, too large to risk leavin' on the beach if they think we're near, or to spirit off that damned beach afore we close in." Mulgrew leaned forward and his eyes bore into Nigel's. "Tomorrow night, while they take in their biggest haul yet, I'm goin' to score *my* biggest coup."

Nigel kept his face expressionless. "All well and good, Mulgrew. I still do not see why my presence creates any difficulty for you."

"Because, my lord, the Muddleford 'gentlemen' are availin' themselves of the Cliff House beach!"

"What?"

Mulgrew nodded, looking uncomfortable again. "I'm afeared there's no doubt of it. Though beats me all to hell and back how they're gettin' the stuff—"

"It simply doesn't make sense, Mulgrew. 'Tis a good beach, perhaps, but the cliffs would make transport of goods deucedly difficult."

"But there *are* paths up to the village. They use packhorses for that. And the rest . . . well . . ."

"Yes?" Nigel's voice was taut.

J. R. Mulgrew looked away. "We think somehow they're storin' the rest in the house or under it."

"In the house! That's impossible! I may not have been here for an age, but I've a reliable couple who've been here nearly all their lives. And beneath the house, why there's naught but rock and collapsed caves."

"M'lord, I do not know the house, or what's under it. I haven't sent a man there, not wishin' to let the venturer know we're on to him. But as to yer housekeeper and butler, well, beggin' yer lordship's pardon, but I'm afeared old Crowley's clean raddled by nine o'clock of a morn, and she—well, butcher tells me she's queer in her upper works, is what she is. Keeps tellin' him Lady Debenham's come to stay."

Nigel felt his heart stop. "Lady Debenham!" he nearly shouted.

Mulgrew nodded gravely. "I'm afeared so, an' I know yer dear mother went to her reward some years past. But old Mrs. Crowley keeps talkin' like she's there, and bakin' gooseberry tarts for the little boys, you and yer late brother, I reckon."

His mother. Nigel felt his heart begin to beat again. Of course, Mulgrew meant his mother. He probably did not even know Nigel *had* a wife. And hadn't Mrs. Crowley, in her letter, confirmed exactly what the riding officer said? She lived in her own world, more than twenty years in the past. Nigel's wife had no place in that world. But she had a place in Nigel's world. Where *was* she? She certainly couldn't be here; she'd hardly have gone to one of Nigel's own houses if she meant to disappear from his life. Besides, he doubted he'd ever mentioned Cliff House, and if so only in passing. He grimaced inwardly at then thought of how little he'd actually talked to Allegra during their time together. And now—damnation! Where *was* she?

No! He must not let his anguish over Allegra overwhelm him. He must devote himself now to the matter at hand. He thought about what Mulgrew had said. He had often offered Roger the use of Cliff House, but would his friend use it for storing contraband? No, he could not credit that. But below the house—was it possible Roger had excavated some of the caves? And then, of course, there *was* the storeroom. Suddenly, Nigel could not wait to get to Cliff House.

He rose. "Well then, Mulgrew, my appearance had ought to expedite things for you. 'Twill be a simple matter for me to check out the house and its environs once I am in residence."

J. R. Mulgrew sprang up from his seat, his face growing red with agitation. "But do you not see, m'lord, that yer appearance, suddenlike, just before their largest shipment is due, well it'll put the fear o' Gawd into 'em, like as not, and mayhap make 'em think we're on to 'em."

Nigel frowned prodigiously. "Certainly you are not suggesting that I turn my horse round and go back to Town!"

"No! No, o' course not, m'lord." Mulgrew twisted his hands nervously. And well he might! The audacity— "I'm merely suggestin'—er—askin' if you'd consider lyin' low, here in *my* house, till tomorrow night. That way no one'll tumble to the fact you've come."

Blast the man! He was making sense, and Nigel did not like it one whit. He wanted to have a look at Cliff House, and it was imperative he go down to the alehouses tucked in along the coast. He'd taken a cap and jacket of Jamie's for just the purpose of moving about unobtrusively. Still, he supposed he could venture forth late at night, once J. R. Mulgrew had taken to his bed. Absurd to contemplate, but then, he needed to allay Mulgrew's unease, and perhaps he could turn this to his advantage.

Eyeing the revenue man pensively, Nigel sat back down and accepted a refill of his Madeira. "I shall consider your offer of—er—hospitality, Mulgrew, but first, tell me, what does the Viscount Creeve have to do with all this?"

A look of irritation crossed Mulgrew's weathered face, but it was gone in a moment. "Well now, m'lord, I reckon his lordship has been all that is helpful—"

"Cut line, Mulgrew. Where is he going to be tomorrow night?"

Mulgrew sighed. "He insists on bein' with us, on the beach. And, well, as long as ye're askin', m'lord, I'll tell you there's somethin' not quite right about it all. I know he's all het up about them usin' Creeve Hall. But there's somethin' more. I can smell it. It's almost . . . personal."

So, the riding officer was perceptive. That was not necessarily a good thing. "Very well, Mulgrew. I will stay here under two conditions. One is that I, too, accompany your men onto the beach. And the other is that you assign someone to watch Creeve." Mulgrew's brows shot up. "You want the venturer alive, do you not? You want to testify at his trial, and to try to get him to name his cohorts, reveal his suppliers across the Channel?"

"Of course."

Nigel took a drink and then said slowly, "I do not think Creeve wants him alive."

J. R. Mulgrew's eyes pierced his for long, silent minutes. Nigel could almost see his mind working away. Perhaps he thought Creeve was actually involved in the smuggling and so wanted the venturer dead. All to the good. Finally, Mulgrew took a deep breath. "M'lord, do you know who the venturer is?"

"No, I don't," Nigel said firmly, for after all, conjecturing was not knowing. Mulgrew looked as if he wanted to press him further, but Nigel's face assumed a forbidding loftiness and Mulgrew subsided. Nigel neatly shifted the subject.

It was after dinner that the messenger came. When he

departed Mulgrew sought Nigel out to tell him that they had been mistaken. The run was tonight, not tomorrow, and they were to leave within the hour. Nigel cursed inwardly. There was no time to prepare, to search for Roger. So be it. The run was tonight, and Nigel meant to be there.

Allegra and Katie did not speak as they made their way down to the storeroom. It was near to midnight. The promised storm had not materialized, but the bright moonlight was a two-edged sword. It made their work easier, but if they were watched, they would be visible. They wore their usual costumes of dark dresses and black cloaks. But Allegra felt a tension within herself, and saw it in Katie's face, one that had not been there before. This was a large shipment. Roger was counting on it too much. Did the Revenue know that? As to Katie, her anxiety was not merely over the run itself, but over the fact that it was the last, and she did not know when she would see Roger again. She never spoke of her feelings for him, but her eyes spoke volumes. How, Allegra wondered, could Roger be so blind?

They received their instructions in the cave. Their jobs were the same as always; the run would operate on the same system. But tonight, they must work faster. Time, and utter silence, were of the essence.

Everyone seemed a bit fidgety and Bates kept mumbling about the "blasted revenue swine" and Alfie kept reminding him they thought the run was tomorrow. Katie kept close to Roger; he patted her cheeks and assured her that all would be well. This was, after all, a night like any night. A few more kegs of brandy, another tub boat full of lace.

And then it began. The signal relayed, received, reported. Everyone moving silently into place. The lugger dropping anchor, sending off its tub boats. Allegra drew her hood more tightly about her, telling herself it was the night air, not anything else, that chilled her. Roger was a consummate planner. There was no reason to presume that anything would go wrong merely because it was his last run at Cliff House, and his largest.

And indeed, it all went according to plan. The tub boats were beached, the cargoes emptied. It was like a great, silent dance, perfectly executed. The packhorses were loaded first, then led away toward the steep hidden path in the cliff. Then came the wagons. One was filled, then the next, everyone including Allegra doing his part. She began to relax. It was going to be all right.

And then suddenly, the sound of hoofbeats. No! That was not part of the plan! A shout from above. On the cliff? The explosion of a gun, an answering shot, and then pandemonium!

Everyone seemed to be running in different directions. She heard a scream. Katie? Herself? "Run to the cave," Roger had always said, "if ever they come. Use the dunes and jagged rocks in the sand for cover." Frantically, Allegra looked for Katie, but she thought Roger had her, up ahead, beyond the next dune. Run, Allegra, she told herself. Another gunshot. Oh dear God, she thought. I cannot die! I'm carrying Nigel's child. I must not die. Oh, Nigel, what have I done?

Nigel followed in Mulgrew's wake as they descended the cliff, Mulgrew's men all around him. He craned his neck for a glimpse of Roger as chaos broke loose down on the beach. He kept one eye on Creeve, riding to Mulgrew's right. The blackguard had his pistol at the ready. They were almost on the beach now. The tub boats were barely visible as they made their frantic way back to the lugger. And the men on the beach were scampering away like frightened rabbits into holes which the very human Revenue forces might not be able to find.

One of the smugglers, a very large man, turned and fired a shot at one of Mulgrew's men. The officer fired back, felling the smuggler, who let out a ghastly cry as he went down. The man next to him screamed and turned toward the cliff. He seemed to be wearing a hood, which fell back. Blond hair! Roger! But no—what the devil! He had long hair! Good God! A woman! Only now, as she began to run, did Nigel notice the skirts.

"There he is, Mulgrew! The venturer!" Creeve shouted, pointing down at the beach. Nigel followed the direction of his finger and then he saw him. Roger! His short hair gleaned golden in the moonlight. He ran to the woman, pulling her toward the rocky part of the beach, where sand dunes and outcroppings of rock could provide cover as he made for the cliff. Creeve raised his pistol.

"Don't shoot, dammit, Creeve, there's a woman down there!" Nigel yelled.

"He's right!" Mulgrew seconded, and gave the order to charge.

Creeve, looking furious, urged his mount forward with the rest, but kept his pistol cocked. They were on the beach in seconds. Roger and the woman had not yet reached the cliff. And even when they did, they could be trapped, for most of the apertures were but shallow hollows. Unless they knew of a cave or hidden path—

Mulgrew and his men dismounted, fanning out toward the cliff and further up the beach where several of the gang were still running. Shots rang out, up and down the beach, but Nigel, swinging off Mercutio, kept his eyes on Creeve, who was on foot now, in pursuit of Roger.

Nigel followed and realized that Mulgrew still flanked

him. He called to him for a pistol. Mulgrew looked at him sharply, then reached inside his coat and tossed him a gun. Nigel shifted his gaze to Roger, still pulling the woman after him. Another man ran up to them and—dear God! More skirts! Another woman, this one with short, dark hair. What can Roger have been thinking?

Nigel was gaining on the smugglers but Creeve had moved off to the right, in an attempt, no doubt, to head Roger off before the cliff. Dammit! Now Creeve's path was such that he could use the rocks and scrub for cover. He disappeared for a moment and Nigel pivoted to follow him. A shot sounded from Creeve's direction. A woman's scream. Nigel swung his eyes back to Roger and the two women.

The second one, with the short dark hair, jerked her head round and for one moment her face was illuminated by the moonlight. And suddenly Nigel's feet stopped moving, his heart stopped beating, his breath left his body. No! It could not be! His eyes were playing tricks! But the first time he'd ever set eyes on her had been a moonlit night, just as this. Just so had her gamin face appeared, inside a mop of cropped curly hair. But now her eyes were narrowed in horror. Dear God, what was she doing—

Another gunshot from down the beach brought him to his senses. She was next to Roger, and Creeve must be gaining on them. The devil of it was that Nigel could not see the viscount. More shots, some ricocheting off the cliff. Nigel could no longer tell who was firing at whom. From off to his left he heard one of the preventative men shout something about halting in His Majesty's name. Ignoring them and the men they were pursuing, Nigel bolted ahead, knowing only that he had got to reach Allegra before Creeve did.

He ran as he had never run before. It was like a nightmare, not quite real. All of them converging on the spot

426

where sandy beach met rocky cliff—himself, Mulgrew, another preventative, Creeve, Roger, Allegra, the blonde. Katie, he realized suddenly, and then the thought deserted him and instinct took over.

He was only a few yards from Allegra and Roger. Where was Creeve? He had got to be just as close . . . Nigel sprinted forward, caught the gleam of metal from the corner of his eye. "Allegra!" he shrieked.

She whirled in shock. He lunged for her, knocking her to the ground just as a gun exploded. Roger cursed. Nigel felt a sudden, searing pain in his left forearm. He raised his head just enough to yell, "Run, Roger!"

Roger ran with Katie. Creeve let forth a stream of expletives far more vile than Roger's, and gave chase. Nigel's arm throbbed and Allegra's squirming and flailing beneath him wasn't helping. "Be still, Allegra," he murmured. " 'Tis I, Nigel." He clutched her tightly with his uninjured arm.

It took a moment for the words to register. Nigel! Could it be? Where had he come from? She'd been shocked when she'd heard her name called, but he'd been on her in a minute, knocking her down. She hadn't seen his face. And now—

"No one is going to hurt you, love," he whispered soothingly. He had never used such a gentle tone with her, never called her "love." Why would he do so now? And yet, she would know his voice anywhere. And the feel of him atop her, pressing her down . . . Yes, she would know that anywhere, too.

And suddenly, despite the shouts and gunshots and chaos around them, despite the fact that for all intents and purposes she was about to be captured by the Revenue, Allegra felt her heart fill with gladness. He was here! Nigel had come for her! She did not know how, or even why. But he had come; he had saved her life. And in that moment she could not recall the reasons why she'd left him at first stop, could not feel the bruises on her knees caused by the fall, nor the scratch of sand against her cheek, could not hear the sounds of battle raging above them. She was aware only of the feel of Nigel, pressing her into the sand, his hand on her head, his body protecting her from harm.

Allegra's flailing had stopped, her small body quiet beneath Nigel's. But all about them he could hear the noise and chaos escalating. He ventured a look to his right and cursed inwardly. Roger had not got very far, for Creeve had cornered him and Katie near a large jutting rock. Creeve was in shadow, but Nigel caught the glint of his pistol as he lifted it. Damnation! Where were the preventatives? Nigel was afraid to move; Creeve was close enough to catch the movement with his eye. If he turned and shot— No, Nigel could not take the chance that Allegra might be hurt. He heard an angry exchange of words between Creeve and Roger but could not make them out. And then to Nigel's amazement, Katie suddenly sprang up and launched herself at Creeve. She caught him in the knees, knocking him back and sending his pistol flying. Roger retrieved the pistol in short order and pulled Katie to her feet before Creeve could grab her. Roger looked at Katie and grinned. Allegra's Katie! Who could credit it?

Mulgrew shouted something and came running with one of his officers. And then Nigel realized it was over. The sound of gunshots had ceased. The preventative officers began filtering back. Mulgrew approached Roger cautiously, gun drawn, but Roger handed over Creeve's pistol and allowed himself and Katie to be taken in hand by Mulgrew's man. Creeve rose to his feet, clutching his head with one hand and brushing the sand from his britches with the other. He seemed dazed.

Slowly, Nigel lifted himself from Allegra and then took her hand and drew her to her feet. She stared at him, his wife whom he'd despaired of ever seeing again, her dark eyes wide with shock and confusion and . . . perhaps some gladness as well. He could not be sure. "Nigel, how did you—" she began, then closed her eyes for a moment. "You saved my life."

He touched her face, brushed her hair from her brow. His eyes traveled the length of her, enveloped in the cloak. "Are you all right?" he whispered.

"I—"

A shout from Mulgrew silenced her. He was barking orders to his men, one of whom dashed over and grabbed Allegra's arm. She gasped; her face had gone ashen, as if she'd suddenly realized what a coil she'd gotten herself into. And Nigel wondered how the devil his wife had become a smuggler at first stop?

"I'll hold her," he said curtly to the revenue man, who released her with a mumbled, "yes, my lord."

Allegra could feel herself shaking. Nigel held her now, his hand warm and steady at her elbow. How had he gotten here just in time, known where to find her? And why—so many questions, but now was not the time. But *would* there be time? What was to become of her, and Katie? Oh, Dear God, why had she let her impulsiveness get the better of her? And to have dragged Katie into this . . . It had seemed a good idea at the time, at first to save themselves from the smugglers, then as a means to earn money. And there had been Roger, a friend to her, and to Katie . . . Just now Katie was huddled close to Roger, staring at Nigel in open amazement. Thankfully, she did not say a word. Allegra did not think it was at all the time.

Dimly she realized the Chief Preventative Officer was instructing some of his men to search the village for the rest of the smugglers. The others were to round up the cargo. Poor Roger, Allegra thought, her eyes welling up. He had been so counting on this. But had the others escaped? All, that is, except Bates, who had been shot down. None of Roger's men were left on the beach. She hoped they'd be all right. Surely the preventatives would never be able to find them in the village.

"Congratulations, Mulgrew. You've got your man." The smug voice jarred her. She knew that voice. She peered into the shadow of the cliff but could not make out the face of the man who had shot at them.

"Reckon I do," answered the Chief Riding Officer. "I thank yer lordships for yer help." He smiled briefly at Nigel, then turned with a frown to the other man. "If it's all the same to you, Lord Creeve, you can pick up yer pistol tomorrow mornin'." Lord Creeve! Allegra thought. What was *he* doing here? "Now, then, I'll just be takin' my prisoners—"

"I will do no such thing!" Creeve declared imperiously, thrusting out his hand.

Mulgrew looked at Nigel, who imperceptibly shook his head. Roger looked dagger points at Creeve and then locked eyes with Nigel. She could not fathom their expressions, nor did they speak to each other. Was there animosity between them or was it that they did not want to reveal their relationship?

Only two of Mulgrew's men remained, and he signaled them to take the prisoners. Nigel knew he had got to think fast. He ignored the burning pain in his left forearm. It was bleeding, but no one seemed to notice, which was just as well. He was certain the ball had merely grazed him; the injury could wait.

Creeve was furious. Roger's look was pleading and defiant all at once. Allegra and Katie were terrified. "Mulgrew, I do not think the matter is all that simple. I suggest we adjourn to the house where we may unravel the whole," Nigel said with a hint of imperiousness.

Mulgrew's brows shot up. "Whatever do—"

"What game are you playing, Debenham?" Creeve snarled, stepping out of the shadows, his pale blue eyes glittering with anger. He pointed at Roger. "This man is your venturer, Mulgrew. The man who—"

"No!" Katie's high-pitched shriek startled them all. Nigel could see her shudder. "Oh, my God, my lady, 'tis he!" She raised a shaky finger and pointed it at Creeve. But then she couldn't seem to speak further.

"What, Katie? What is it?" Allegra cried.

"He's the one from—from Mrs. Graves's house! I never knew his name. He's the one who—who . . ." She seemed to choke on her words, and then fell at Roger's feet in a dead faint.

They had, at Nigel's insistence, adjourned to the drawing room of Cliff House. Mulgrew was impatiently pacing the floor; one of his men stood sentinel at the door. Creeve stood at the hearth, his eyes cold, his jaw rigid.

Roger had brought Katie round on the beach, and had carried her up the path that led to the house. He sat in the chair next to hers now, alternately sneaking worried looks at her and sending withering glances toward Creeve.

A cheerful fire burned in the grate next to Creeve, but no one in the room appeared particularly cheerful. Nigel, however, was coming close. He had, after all, convinced Mulgrew to come inside. At least it bought him time. And Katie's horrid revelation, which unfortunately came as no surprise to Nigel, might be used to advantage.

And then there was Allegra. She'd been appalled, when they'd entered the house, to find that he was bleeding. And so, while Roger had ministered to Katie and Mulgrew had gnashed his teeth and Creeve had glowered, Allegra had bandaged Nigel's arm with the greatest solicitude, despite the fact that, as he'd guessed, the ball had merely grazed

431

him. They had not, however, had a moment's privacy to exchange a word.

Once Allegra had secured the bandage to her satisfaction, Nigel had insisted she sit next to him on the sofa. Now that he'd found her he was not about to let her stray from his side. He kept her hand firmly clasped in his, despite her obvious discomfort. That earned him a glare from Roger, which Nigel did not understand. Time to deal with that later.

"Well, this is all very cozy, isn't it, Debenham," Creeve drawled, "though I am at a loss as to why you wished to waste Mulgrew's time in such manner. Mulgrew, there"— he pointed directly at Roger—"is your culprit."

Dear Mrs. Crowley, looking much older than Nigel remembered, chose that minute to bustle into the room. She wore a flannel wrapper and an oversized mobcap and carried a plate of pastries. She'd heard all the commotion, she said, and so had brought some gooseberry tarts, certain everyone would be hungry. She handed out the pastry and when she came to Nigel he greeted her warmly. She stared at him for a long minute and then exclaimed to Lady Debenham that it was so lovely to have Nigel home again. Nigel wondered if perhaps he'd misread her letter when she turned to her ladyship and asked where Charlie was, and her husband the earl. And just before she departed, she admonished Nigel and Roger not to smear gooseberry tart on their britches.

"Oh, for God sakes!" Creeve said harshly the minute she'd gone. "Mulgrew, if you've had enough of this tea party I suggest you take your prisoners. Here is your venturer, though it looks as if you've lost the rest of them, more's the pity. As to the women—"

"It is not, as I said before, quite so simple," Nigel interjected. Mulgrew stopped pacing and watched him. "There *is* first of all, the very grave matter of Katie's accusation."

"Katie? Who the devil is Katie?" Roger blurted.

"Whatever it is she thinks I did, she has obviously mistaken me for someone else," Creeve responded coolly.

Nigel heard Katie moan and decided to leave that for a minute. "And there is also the matter, Mulgrew, of Creeve shooting at Roger, when I know orders were that the venturer be taken alive."

" 'Tis true, Lord Debenham," Mulgrew replied. "What have you to say to that, Lord Creeve?"

"He was trying to run away. And all this is fair and far off." Creeve glowered at Roger. "He is the mastermind of this whole operation, Mulgrew. He's been running contraband through Muddleford for years."

"And most of that time using Creeve Hall as a base. Now, you do not suppose, Mulgrew, that I contrived that without the full cooperation of the Viscount Creeve, do you?" Roger retorted.

Mulgrew regarded him pensively. So did Nigel. He wondered if implicating Creeve had not been part of Roger's plan from the beginning, though of a certain he hadn't meant to be caught himself. Nigel did some rapid ruminating, trying to decide what could be done to salvage a devilish tricky situation.

"That is absurd! Surely, Mulgrew, you would not take the word of a smuggler, a commoner, above that of a peer!" Creeve declared haughtily, stalking away from the hearth toward Mulgrew.

"Well now, beggin' yer pardon, Lord Creeve," Mulgrew began, "but there *is* somethin' havey-cavey about this whole business. Like the riot and rumpus you set up 'bout the smugglers usin' yer beach. And you *did* shoot at the fellow. Mayhap to keep him from talkin'?"

"That's preposterous," Creeve fumed. "Mulgrew, I insist —"

"Sit down, Creeve," Nigel ordered. "You are not in a position to insist on anything. Any man capable of what Katie, at great cost to herself, revealed, is certainly capable of collusion in smuggling."

Creeve's eyes bulged in fury; his face went livid. He stormed back to the hearth. Mulgrew looked uncertain.

"Nigel, why do you keep calling her 'Katie'? Alicia, what—"

"*Her* name is Allegra, Roger," Nigel cut in.

"What *are* you talking about?" Roger demanded. "She's your cousin. You had aught to know her name! And why are you holding her hand?"

Mulgrew cleared his throat. "If we can get back to the matter at hand. Er, Lord Debenham, beggin' yer pardon, I'm sure, but would you mind tellin' me how it is that your cousin has been caught smuggling on the beach of Cliff House?"

"She's *not* my cousin, Mulgrew," Nigel replied affably, and drew himself up. "She is the Countess of Debenham."

"Countess of—your wife??" Roger erupted.

"Well, well," Creeve murmured mockingly. "Lady Debenham. What an—interesting life you lead. I had not recognized you."

"No, you didn't, did you?" Allegra replied sweetly. "Just as you didn't recognize Katie."

Creeve's face darkened. Nigel inched closer to Allegra and formally introduced her to Chief Riding Officer Mulgrew. Mulgrew, increasingly more perplexed, bobbed his head in acknowledgment.

"Your wife?" Roger repeated. "Alicia, what the devil is he talking about?"

"Her name is *Allegra*," Nigel said firmly.

Sighing in vexation, Roger turned to Katie, who sat nervously in the chair next to his. "Sarah, would *you* kindly tell me—"

"And *her* name is Katie," Nigel ground out.

434

"Oh, for pity sakes!" Creeve exploded. "What bloody difference does it make *whose* name is *what?* They're all as guilty as sin, Mulgrew. Take them away."

"Roger," Allegra chimed in, "I do think it time you told Mr. Mulgrew the whole."

Roger narrowed his eyes. Nigel merely stared at his wife, waiting. Something was churning inside that mind of hers! He found himself quite eager to know what it was.

"Truly, Roger, it cannot signify now, when the whole matter is resolved," she went on, then turned to Mulgrew. "You see, Mr. Mulgrew, Roger has been working for the government these many months now, trying to ferret out the mastermind of the Muddleford operation."

Mulgrew's cheeks puffed out. "And why was *I* not informed?"

"Oh, dear. Nigel, I told you Mr. Mulgrew would not like this part." Allegra clasped her hands together and looked earnestly at Mulgrew. Nigel thought Roger was holding his breath, but he himself was having a hard time repressing a grin. "You see, Mr. Mulgrew, there were— er—leaks coming from Dorset. Rumors of collusion, you must know. *You*, of course, have been completely cleared of any suspicion, but—but there was not time to communicate with you. And although Roger was hoping for a bit more time to gather evidence against Lord Creeve, we believe we have enough to convict. And thanks to you, we already have him in custody."

"And your role in all this, Lady Debenham?" Mulgrew asked.

"Oh, well, I was sent here at the end, to work with Roger and function as a liaison with Lord Debenham, who communicated with the London Office. I assumed the role of his cousin because—er—I was afraid Roger might slip and refer to me by my title, and that would have been a giveaway to all his men."

435

"Indeed. And the other young lady?" Mulgrew was seated now, his hands rhythmically tapping the arm of his chair as he considered Allegra's words.

"Oh, why, Katie—Katie Sarah, you must know—is my maid. You would not expect me to go anywhere without my *maid,* would you?" Allegra asked incredulously, her brown eyes flashing wide.

"Er—no—of course not," Mulgrew said gruffly. He stared at her for an endless moment, then nodded slightly and rose to his feet. Nigel wanted to let out a whoop. He wanted to hug his wife. Mulgrew was going to buy it!

Even now he was walking purposefully toward Creeve. "Now see here, Mulgrew, I'll not stand for this!" Creeve railed. "You cannot possibly believe any of this rubbish. I am not without influence and I can see you ruined for this!"

"Of course," Nigel put in, rising and sauntering to where Creeve stood at the hearth, "there is an alternative—"

Mulgrew, standing to the side, narrowed his eyes. "What are you talking about?" Creeve asked belligerently.

"You can come with me to London where you will be handed up before the magistrate."

"On the charge of smuggling?" Creeve retorted derisively.

"No." Nigel's tone was disdainful. "The charge is the forcible ruination of young girls. *Very* young girls." Creeve paled and Nigel pressed on, taking a leaf from Allegra's book of invention. "Even now, as we speak, Mrs. Graves's brothel, of which you own a share, is being raided. Besides Katie here, there will be innumerable witnesses. Perhaps you remember Flora, also known as Emerald. She is even now in an apartment above my stables, convalescing. And then, of course, Mrs. Graves may decide to talk. Need I go on?" Creeve staggered back against the mantel. Everyone else in the room was silent, save for a soft sniffling

436

which he knew was coming from Katie. "If I were you, Creeve, I'd take the smuggling charge."

Creeve looked ill. "Let—let me leave the country," he rasped.

"Out of the question!" barked Mulgrew.

"Oh, I don't know, Mulgrew," Nigel mused, thinking furiously. "It would not be unheard of for a peer to be allowed to do such a thing. And, after all, Roger does not need the credit for finding the venturer and putting the Muddleford gang permanently out of business. Roger needs, in fact, to remain anonymous if he is ever to do this work again. I daresay *you* would get all the credit. I should imagine this might be enough to gain you a promotion to the London office."

Mulgrew cleared his throat, considering this. Nigel turned to Creeve. "You will be known as a smuggler but that is all. If you ever again set foot on English soil, however, I will come after you. You will this night sign a confession of your . . . activities in Mrs. Graves's house."

"I will not—"

"The confession," Nigel went on, ignoring Creeve's interruption, "will remain sealed in a vault, where it will remain as long as *you* remain outside of His Majesty's realm. Do we understand each other?"

Creeve reluctantly nodded, his cold eyes furious. Nigel turned to Mulgrew, but any exchange between them was interrupted by a commotion coming from the corridor. Mrs. Crowley announced the arrival of two men asking for Mr. Mulgrew. Mulgrew left the room to confer with them. His man still stood silent sentinel, but as he was across the room Nigel was certain only the group gathered at the hearth would hear what he next had to say. "There is one thing more, Creeve," he said in a low, insistent voice. Creeve bristled. "You will, this night, deed Creeve Hall to Roger, effective straightaway."

The viscount's hands balled into fists. "I'll do no—"

"And you will amend your will, naming Roger as your legitimate heir, allowing him to succeed to your title and dignities, and your fortune, such as it is."

"I have no reason to do such a thing!" Creeve growled.

Allegra watched Roger lurch to his feet. *"You have reason!"* he shouted, advancing on Creeve, fist raised. Nigel quickly moved between them, silently reminding Roger of the revenue man posted at the door. The man had come to attention, his eyes sharp.

"You have every reason and you damn well know you do!" Roger hissed, the cords in his neck bulging, his fists clenched at his sides as he faced Creeve, whose skin had suffused with angry color.

And that was when she saw it. She had not noticed it before. Perhaps the resemblance was so obvious now when they both wore similar furious expressions. But then she realized that their hair and eyes were the same color, although Roger's eyes were kindly and Creeve's were cold.

So, Allegra thought, justice would be done. She was glad she'd had a little part in it.

Mulgrew came back to report that although they found trails of blood indicating some wounded, the rest of the gang had eluded his men. The packhorses, and most of the cargo, had been recovered, however.

Nigel caught Mulgrew's eye and they exchanged a long, level look that said a great deal. Mulgrew and his men would receive a hefty bonus for the confiscated contraband, and Mulgrew would receive credit for a major coup. And if he thought there were a few havey-cavey loose ends, well, he was not about to cavil. One didn't argue with the Quality, after all.

The documents had been signed and witnessed. Creeve

had departed, flanked by Mulgrew and one of his men, to await a ship for France, in the morning. Nigel and Roger had indulged in a belated bear hug, Roger thanking him profusely for everything, and Nigel had poured drinks all round. He still sat with Allegra on the sofa, Roger and Katie on the two facing chairs.

"Alicia, why didn't you tell me the truth?" Roger asked softly.

"It's Allegra, Roger. Her name is *Allegra!*" Nigel exclaimed.

"Very well, *Allegra.* Why?"

Allegra glanced at Nigel and took a deep breath. Since Creeve and Mulgrew had gone she'd seemed a bit aloof, uncertain. Perhaps now that the shock of Nigel's arrival and the threat of imprisonment were gone, she was recalling all that had transpired between them in the past. She had not allowed him to take her hand. Now she twisted her hands in her lap. "I—I did not want him to find me," she uttered softly.

. Roger leaned forward. "Alicia—er—Allegra, you do not have to go back with him if you do not wish to. I'll take care of you."

"And my child?" Nigel drawled, suddenly wanting to plant his old friend a facer. He had the satisfaction of seeing Roger's eyes widen.

"Child? Hellfire, Allegra! Why did you not tell me? To think I let you crawl through caves, lug cartons!" Roger ran a hand through his hair.

Allegra darted a glance at Nigel. *"My* child" he'd said. Since when had he come to that conclusion? Later, she told herself, and turned back to Roger. "Do not worry, Roger. I am fine. But, as to the other, you are most gallant—"

"It isn't gallantry, Allegra. Nigel, may I have a private word with—"

"You most certainly may not!" Nigel snapped.

Roger went doggedly on. Katie, Nigel noted, looked bleak. "Allegra, gallantry has naught—"

"Roger, please. We—we are friends. 'Tis all we were meant to be. I—I tried to tell you that some time ago. You needn't worry about me. I shall be fine."

"But—"

"Roger." Allegra's tone was gentle. "Whom did you protect tonight? Whose hand did you grab when the shooting started? No, I am not in the least overset. It is as it should be." Roger's eyes widened and his gaze went to Katie.

"Katie," Nigel said into the charged silence. "You truly amazed me tonight with the way you went for Creeve, knocking him down."

"I—he was going to shoot Roger," she murmured. Her cheeks flamed red as she cast her eyes down.

Roger stared at her as if he'd never seen her before, a most arrested look in his eye. Allegra grinned knowingly. So, his wife had been meddling had she? First Meg, then Jamie, and now it seemed as if she might have a third happy ending to her credit. It was time for their own.

"Allegra," Nigel said softly, taking her hand.

She did not protest. Her eyes met his. There was so much to say, to ask. His manner was so different. Why? He had come all this way for her. Did it mean he cared, at the least a little? He had cared enough to save her from a bullet. But what of all that had come before?

"Nigel," she responded, and seeing that Katie and Roger seemed rather absorbed in each other, asked the first of the questions that were burning on her tongue. "How on earth did you find me?"

Nigel looked uncomfortable. "I—er—" She watched his gaze shift to Roger. Sensing it, Roger tore his eyes from Katie and looked at Nigel with bemused curiosity. Nigel sighed. "I did not know you were here, Allegra. I came after Roger, fearing that Creeve meant him harm."

No! Allegra thought. It couldn't be! She looked miserably at her husband. So he *hadn't* come for her after all. It had been merely coincidence. He didn't have a care for her. Nothing had changed.

"Allegra," he said, tightening his hold on her hand, "you must know that I—"

"No!" she cried, and shook her hand free. She bolted from the sofa and ran for the door. She did not know where she was going, only that she had to get away.

"Damnation!" Nigel exploded, jumping up and sprinting to the door. He turned to see Roger grinning at him. "There is nothing remotely funny about this!" he growled. "And when we return I'm going to rake you over the coals for turning my wife into a smuggler!" And with that, he bounded out in pursuit, once again, of Allegra.

Chapter Twenty

"Sweet Moon, I thank thee for they sunny beams;
I thank thee, Moon, for shining now so bright."

A Midsummer Night's Dream
William Shakespeare

He found her on the beach. The moonlight illuminated her clearly, just as it had that very first night at Caulfield. Had he fallen in love with her then, and been too blind to realize it? Had he, indeed, married her for love, and not for honor? Ah, yes, very likely.

He approached quietly, but she turned and saw him and dashed off down the beach. Muttering an expletive, he went after her. She was no match for him and he caught her some twenty yards ahead, grasping her arms and turning her to him.

Her face was wet with tears. He felt his gut wrench. She shivered, whether from the cool air penetrating her thin muslin dress or from . . . him, he did not know. "Allegra, you must listen to me!" he pleaded.

"No!" she cried. "There is nothing to talk about!"

She yanked free of his grasp and turned to bolt again, and this time he was taking no chances. He grabbed her and as gently as possible tumbled her to the ground, on her back, and lowered himself right on top of her. She was fighting him, and he forced himself to ignore, for now, what the feel of her beneath him was doing to his body.

"Stop squirming, dammit, and listen to me! I'm deuced tired of chasing you!"

She bit back a sob and shook her head. "You haven't chased me, Nigel! You didn't come after me! It was best that I leave and you know it!"

He put his hands to either side of her face, feeling its contours, wanting so much to kiss those lips. But he knew he'd got to wait. "Allegra, Allegra! I've chased the length and breath of the kingdom looking for you. I've been frantic for seven weeks, not knowing where you were. Even now, I have agents combing the countryside, and France and Scotland as well. When you left, when I read your letter, it was as if blinders had been stripped from my eyes, and I realized what a wretched bounder I'd been. I've hated myself every day since!"

"It doesn't signify, Nigel," she cried frantically. "I know I am not the wife you want. I am not obedient and proper like Meg. I am—"

"I would have been bored with Meg in a fortnight, as you well knew." He ran the pads of his thumbs beneath her eyes, smoothing away the dampness.

"I am always meddling—"

"Yes, love, you are, and always it seems, quite successful at it." He kissed her brow. She sniffled, and stopped squirming.

"I am always getting into scrapes, trying to rescue—"

"You are the most unselfish, giving person I have ever met."

She blinked. Was he getting through? Dear God, he hoped so, for more reasons than one. Her body had grown still beneath his, and he could feel every curve . . .

"I—I could never be complacent, Nigel, looking the

443

other way when you went to your m-mistresses."

"Ah, but you have ruined me for other women, Allegra." He kissed her eyelids, gently, and then the tip of her nose.

She wished he would not. The warmth of his lips and the feel of him atop her were making it impossible for her to think. His words flowed over her like thick, rich, honey. She wanted to believe him, but there was still so much unresolved between them.

"There has not been anyone else," he went on in a low, throaty voice, "since the night I first laid eyes on you, dripping wet, the most desirable creature I'd ever seen. Nor will there ever be another. If you do not come back to me, Allegra, you condemn me to the life of a monk!"

She almost giggled, especially since it was perfectly plain, with the way he was pressed so intimately to her, that he was nothing like a monk. But then she sobered, forcing herself to remember the rest. "You do not trust me, Nigel."

A spasm of pain crossed his green eyes. "Forgive me, Allegra," he pleaded quietly. "I—I was not in my right mind. I was crazed with jealousy, comparing you to—to others. And you . . . you returned anger and coldness with love. Always. And I realized, when it was too late, how very much I—I love you. I do not know how I will go on without you if you—" he paused, and swallowed hard. "Come home, Allegra. Have my child and build a life with me. Without you I—I have no life."

His voice was thick with emotion and his eyes watered. Tears ran unheeded down Allegra's cheeks. He loved her! Somehow, miraculously—

"Allegra, for God sakes, say something!" he cried in anguish and Allegra smiled through her tears. Something *had* changed. At long last, *everything* had changed.

"Nigel," she rasped, "I—I love you so much. I've never stopped loving you."

"Oh, God, Allegra!" he groaned, and ground his mouth down onto hers. She wrapped her arms about him, pulling him closer, opening her mouth and answering the urgency of his.

Moments later he lifted his head. She felt bereft of his warmth. "Do you forgive me, Allegra?" he asked in a deep and gentle voice.

"If you forgive me for running away. I—"

"No! There is naught to forgive. These have been the most hellish weeks of my life, but your leaving jarred me into sense. But dear God, Allegra, what if I *hadn't* found you?" He ran his hands up and down her sides, as if to assure himself that he had, indeed, found her. She was here, and she was *his*.

"But you *did* find me, Nigel, and I—I think I would have come home eventually."

"You would?" He cocked his head and smiled.

"Yes. A person can take just so much gooseberry tart, you must know."

Nigel threw back his head and let out a roar of laughter. She watched his brows arch into those "V's" she found so fascinating. Then his face grew serious as his hands slowly caressed the curve of her breasts, then her hips. "Make love with me, Allegra, my heart."

"What, here? Now?"

Nigel grinned. "Yes, here. Now. In the moonlight. Make love with me in the moonlight."

Allegra's head shifted as she looked about, her brown eyes gleaming. "But, Nigel, I think 'tis dawn. 'Tis the daylight streaking across the sky."

Nigel glanced up at the pearly gray sky awash with pink and orange light, and then looked back down at his wife, the woman he loved more than life itself. "Well, then, my heart, make love with me in the daylight."

Allegra swallowed a lump in her throat. From the begin-

445

ning she had been a bride of moonlight. It was time, now, to embrace the day.

The Earl of Debenham was unfastening the top buttons of his wife's gown. She felt her breathing quicken as his fingers stroked her, lower and lower, as his lips seared her throat. "Love me, Allegra," he murmured softly, urgently.

And Allegra, Countess of Debenham, looked up at her husband with the age-old smile of woman, and did just that.

Author's Note

There were innummerable brothels in London during the Regency, some specializing in very young girls. Many of these were destitute children lured by unscrupulous procuresses, but others were victims of abduction. The more refined the girl, the more money she commanded. The girls were often kept in a drink- or drug-induced state of slavelike dependency.

The white slavery problem grew much worse as the century advanced. Britain was one of the few countries which did not have laws protecting its girls, so the demand for British girls in Continental brothels increased. It was not until 1885 that the age of consent was raised from thirteen to sixteen years, and very late in the century before a concerted effort was made to prosecute the white slave traders.

It was common practice for chimney sweeps to employ little boys, sometimes as young as four years old, to clean chimneys. They were thrust and prodded with pins, arms upraised and often naked, into burning chimney passages. Their skin was scraped raw and they suffered burns, near asphyxiation, and often fatal cancerous growths.

In 1788, Parliament passed an act meant to protect these children from the worst abuses, but it was largely ignored. In 1805, Mr. Smart invented the first chimney-sweeping machine. It worked on all but the most narrow chimneys, invariably those of the great manor houses. In 1818 and again in 1819, a bill prohibiting the use of climbing boys passed the House of Commons but not the Lords. By midcentury there were still hundreds of climbing boys in England.

In the waning days of the Regency, sweeping social reform was still far in the future. Yet there were always those individuals who tried, in some way, to right societal ills when they found them. The author would like to think that Nigel and Allegra, Earl and Countess of Debenham, were among those individuals.